D0045673

CARNIVORE

Works by Gregory Mcdonald:

RUNNING SCARED
LOVE AMONG THE MASHED POTATOES (Dear M.E.)
SAFEKEEPING

FLETCH
(in nine novels)

FLYNN
(in three novels)

Time^{2}
(to be included:)

ENTRANCES AND EXITS
MERELY PLAYERS
WISE SAWS
A WORLD TOO WIDE

Non-fiction:
THE EDUCATION OF GREGORY MCDONALD

A WORLD TOO WIDE

A WORLD TOO WIDE

GREGORY MCDONALD

HILL & COMPANY, PUBLISHERS • BOSTON

Mcdonald, Gregory, 1937-
A world too wide.

I. Title.
S3563.A278W67 1987 813'.54 87-8548
ISBN 0-940595-07-9

Designed by Milton Glaser, Inc.
Printed in the United States of America

His youthful hose, well sav'd, a world too wide
For his shrunk shank. . . .

—*As You Like It*
William Shakespeare

Dedicated to the Dear Hearts and
Gentle People
of Giles County, Tennessee

A WORLD TOO WIDE

1

Ellie said, "David, you have called the world down upon us."

"Not to worry. They won't accept."

The night before, after she had returned from a New York City theater and shopping trip he had told her what he had done. He told her it had been an irresistible impulse. He apologized for not consulting her first.

"But what if they do accept, and all these people land on us? By now, their backgrounds are so wide we can't possibly accommodate them, not on this old farm, or anywhere else."

From where they sat having coffee on the east porch of the main house on Bass Clef Farm, Jameson, Tennessee, they could see the pastures within their white fences greening in the April morning sunlight the half mile down to the river.

"You mean they can't possibly accommodate each other."

"You never could. Accommodate each other, I mean."

"We're all older now."

"People become more themselves as they get older, I've noticed," Ellie said. "The fantasies of their futures have become overweighted by the facts of their pasts."

David put his empty cup and saucer on the wicker table. "It was just a gesture on my part," he said. "I doubt I even got the addresses right." Jester, the dog, was scurrying around the near pasture, sniffing for traces of the groundhog he never could catch. "Guess I'll go ride the tractor. You do want the rose beds mulched?"

"Isn't it too late?"

"Probably."

"And I shall weed and aerate the tulips. Is aerate the right word?"

David laughed. "Who cares?"

Mr. and Mrs. John Bart Nelson
93, Blvd. Cartier
Paris, France

Dear John and Ms. Tuesday,

I just read in USA Today *that Lucille is to marry Dan Prescott's son, Anthony, time and place not stated. My, my. How did your kid become an internationally famous model already? How did Dan Prescott's kid ever become a presidential speechwriter? How on earth did they ever meet? I'm full of questions about them, about all of us.*

In brief, I'm writing you and The Reverend Mr. and Mrs. Dan P. suggesting, offering, to give the younguns their wedding here on Bass Clef Farm in middle Tennessee, whenever you and they like. The last time we tried a wedding together, in Paris, a little more than a quarter of a century ago, it nearly destroyed most of us. Maybe we'd all like another chance to come together, as grownups, over nuptuals. Bass Clef is a working farm, but has its modest splendors. At least the air is guaranteed to be fresher here than it was in the Club Solo. Probably the younguns already have made their plans, but even just offering pleases me. Besides, offering to give the wedding is my way of asking to be invited to the wedding, wherever and whenever it is.

Looking forward to your reply, seeing you both and, an opportunity to know the offspring a little, I remain, as always,

Yours,

David MacFarlane

The Reverend and Mrs. Dan Prescott
c/o Post Office
Columbia Falls, Maine

Dear Dan and Mrs. P.,

(I apologize for not being sure of Mrs. Prescott's first name. That we have gotten so out of touch is partly what provokes this suggestion.)

I have just read in this morning's newspaper that your son, Anthony, is to marry the Nelsons' daughter, Lucille, and have just written the Nelsons at their last-known-to-me address in Paris the suggestion that Ellie and I be permitted to give the younguns their wedding here at Bass Clef Farm, whenever. Such would please me mightily. Of course, I don't know the youngsters at all, but the fact that you, Dan, and Ms. Tuesday, brought up next door to each other, never married each other, and your son and her daughter, brought up a world away from each other, now announce their intention to be married strikes me as such an oddity, such a completion, somehow, of fate, kismet, such a full circle, that I've got to witness it somehow, be a real part of it, if possible, if permitted. It's high time I got on the side of the angels.

Besides, it would be a nice excuse to see you again, Dan. (And to meet your wife and kid or kids.)

Guess I've stumbled around enough here. If this letter reaches you, and you're in touch with any of the principals, please communicate my offer.

Cordially,

David MacFarlane

"Lucy?"

"Are you coming up tonight?"

"I'll be on the seven o'clock shuttle."

"Okay, so you'll be on the East Side by eight-thirty, quarter to nine?"

"Earlier, maybe."

"At eight-thirty I'll still be at Bernstein's apartment on Park Avenue. Remember the number?"

"I remember the cross street."

"We'll be at 21 shortly after nine. Maybe you should meet us there."

"Depends on what time it is."

"Tony, I absolutely have to be at the Vogue bash by eleven. You'll have to help move me."

"Should I bring my truck?"

"They want me up all night, up all day."

"Must be tough, being gorgeous."

"The fashion seasons have gotten so long. Why doesn't anyone ever realize that for us it's not a pleasure, it's a business?"

"And computer operators are allowed to go home at night, to sleep. I've heard that speech. You get paid more than they do, honey."

"Tony? Will you sleep with me tonight?"

"You think I'm coming to New York just to escort you around while being shoved aside and ignored myself?"

"I don't ignore you, and I'm all that matters."

"Listen, Lord Godiva just called."

"Yes."

"Is this the David MacFarlane, the old jazz pianist?"

"Jazz pianist, composer. I don't know how old."

"Why did I think he's dead?"

"Hasn't been very active in five or ten years. That's what mother said."

"She called?"

"Yes. From Milan. She thinks it's a good idea. She's going to try to get through to you this afternoon."

"Do you know David MacFarlane?"

"Never laid eyes on him, not that I recall. I remember something about MacFarlane's putting Daddy's voices poem, you know, "Pentecost"? to music. We all had to drag over to the Royal Festival Hall in London to hear it. Full chorus. Terrible drag. The same lines, sung over and over again. It seemed to me to be all minor key, without major relief. Won some kind of an award. Recordings of it exist, if you care. I never listened to it again. I was about twelve, thirteen. Mother made me wear blue jeans. I was brought back to the hotel before the party after the concert began, so I don't think I saw him even then. Now, suddenly, mother is calling him 'Uncle David' on the phone."

"You wore blue jeans to Royal Festival Hall?"

"Mother thinks she popularized blue jeans in Europe singlehandedly."

"How would my father know David MacFarlane? He said he met him in a jazz bar in Boston a long time ago. Typical Godiva. Answered very specifically."

"Tony? My mother may have been married to him at one time."

"To MacFarlane?"

"Maybe she was, maybe she wasn't. It depends upon the set of the moon, or something. When she's trying to raise her stature, at a dinner party, or something, she'll drop his name, straighten her back and say, 'David and I were married once, you know.' I guess she thinks it makes her seem interesting, as if she had a past. Next morning, if I ask her, she'll say, 'I have never been married to anybody but your father. You know that.'"

"Lucy, if your mother had ever been married to one of the all-time jazz greats, one of the greatest American composers—"

"That's it, you see. He's permanent. He's in the American lexicon like Stonewall Jackson and Babe Ruth."

"—don't you think it's a piece of family history you ought to establish?"

"There's no doubt about who my father is, sonny. Just look at me."

"Don't you think you ought to find out about your mother's previous marriage?"

"I have the idea everyone from that generation was so stoned one way or the other when they were young they don't know what the facts are. That's the generation that put 'stoned' in the dictionary, remember, with all sorts of meanings, except that of having people throw rocks at you."

"Lucy, this is what worries me. I know my being a presidential speechwriter doesn't mean all that much in the circles you travel in—"

"I'm impressed."

"—but politics is my life. At least until I decide to make some money by becoming a used car salesman."

"So?"

"So. A wedding, with me as groom, given us by The Great Stoned Set, all those old scandals we don't even know about getting replayed in the press, together with pictures of us—"

"You're marrying a mulatto born in Paris."

"Lucy. The whole damned world loves you."

"No, they don't. The whole damned world uses me. Tony, I was born into something, put to work at it early, my face and body grew into it miraculously, I got good at it, and make oodles of money at it. But I never lie to myself."

"Why are you marrying me?"

"Because you're coming from nowhere, Tony, making yourself. I want to know you for a long, long time, and love you, watch you and help you. I'm not going to be a model forever, and you're not going to be in the White House forever—"

"Don't be so damned sure."

"That's it. I'm not sure. Of anything. Our future looks interesting, Tony, but because of you, not me. What I do isn't all that useful, Tony. You have the instincts of a useful person."

"What are we talking about?"

"About whether David MacFarlane's offer to give us a wedding is anything we're going to accept."

"Okay. I've given you my reason for not accepting. It's bad enough being Lord Godiva's son—"

"You ought to stop calling him that, Tony."

"He doesn't know we call him that."

"It would hurt him, terribly."

"I doubt it. However much he mutters about being a victim, I think the whole thing pleases something deep inside him."

"You have good things from your father, Tony. Very few feel as committed as you."

"Why should we expose ourselves to anything more than a quiet wedding in Maine? Isn't that the wisest thing to do?"

"Right now, we are more from whence we came than where we're going."

"In how many languages can you say that?"

"Several, thanks to my father."

"Can you tell me what it means, in English?"

"It means, I think it would be interesting."

"Lucy, World War Two I'm sure was *interesting.*"

"Here's an interesting man, David MacFarlane, enormously creative, accomplished, about as permanently famous as Bizet—"

"Who?"

"Mozart."

"And probably just as crazy."

"—who has made a real contribution to history, to music, to pleasure, I've never laid eyes on, I think, and suddenly, this morning, talking to me on the phone from Milan, my mother is referring to him as 'your Uncle David.' Aren't you curious?"

"Curiosity killed the politician."

"Tony, our families are so here, there, everywhere—it's been almost two years since I've seen my father—getting them together on some tumbled-down old farm in Tennessee . . . I don't know what I'm saying. It would be interesting. We could learn some things, establish some of those facts about ourselves you were just talking about. We could do it for them."

"I hear what you're saying."

"What am I saying?"

"You're saying you're much more sure your father would come to your wedding if David MacFarlane gives it."

"I am not. Am I? Tony, my father would never miss my wedding. If he didn't get to my wedding I know at least he'd die trying."

"Weddings being what they are these days . . ."

"Tony . . ."

"You want to get The Great Stoned Set together one more time because you know that would attract your father. John Bart Nelson has a great sense of history; maybe not so great a sense of weddings."

"You knew my mother knew your father. I think they were sort of close at one time."

"I can't conceive of what my father had to do with all this, all these people."

"Let's find out."

"Let's talk about it tonight."

"You will stay with me tonight?"

"Sure. But I have to be on the first shuttle back to Washington in the morning."

Ellie went through the pool area in the sunlight and through the open sliding glass doors into the studio carrying the mail cradled in her left arm. There was one letter in her right hand.

David was using the rowing machine.

"At least one of your letters didn't go astray. It's from Paris, in a feminine hand."

David stopped rowing and opened the letter Ellie handed down to him, his body still sliding a little back and forth on the steel runners.

"Oh, oh. Now I've done it."

He handed the flimsy back to Ellie.

Mr. David MacFarlane
Bass Clef Farm
Jameson, Tennessee

Dear David:

Would June 11th be all right?

Both Luce and Tony are delighted at your most generous offer to give them their wedding at your farm in Tennessee. The gift really is yours, although it must be clearly understood from the beginning that it is most important to John and me to bear all expenses incurred. In fact, your offer solves an enormous problem.

With John and me, especially John, traveling so much these past years we've never had a residence except the same old apartment here in Paris. The thought of dragging everyone here for the wedding has been too much to contemplate. (Also, I've been very unsure that being married in Paris would strike the right image in Tony's political career.) That has left me with the cold thought of either hiring a hotel in New York, or (shudder), dragging everyone up to Columbia Falls, Maine. What lovely, neutral ground would be a farm in Tennessee.

Strongly doubt John will be able to make the wedding, as he is padding about in long robes in Ethiopia or The Sudan or someplace, per usual; it takes literally weeks to get in touch with him, although I will try.

Unsure as to whether you are married at this point. I've read both that you are and you aren't. Crass question, but is there a wife or secretary or someone at this point with whom I can communicate regarding all the incredible details of throwing a wedding?

How you must miss Chump!

Too sweet of you, David. You always were one for the beau geste. *Remember the Mercedes?*

Yours,

J. Twombly

"'A wife or secretary or someone,'" Ellie quoted.

David said, "'*Beau geste.*' I guess so. She signed it 'J. Twombly.'"

"Mmm," Ellie said. "Business executive."

"Shall I rescind the offer?" David wiped sweat from his face with the towel around his neck. "I don't know what got into me."

"You can't. There are a couple of young people trying to get married involved here. They have accepted."

"I could get sick." David faked a cough. "I'm not sure I'm all that well."

Ellie smiled. "You're as fit as Santa Claus on Christmas Eve, damn it."

"Oh, boy. What have I done?"

Ellie put that letter with the other mail in her hand. "We'll see."

2

"*Der Tag.*" Barefooted in his bathrobe David was eating from the breakfast tray Clara Reagan had just given him on the brick patio behind the house. "Nice June day for people to be arriving. What's the matter?"

Ellie slid off the saddle on Byron and dropped the reins over the back of a wrought iron chair.

"David. Someone has shot Brummel."

"No!"

Fighting tears, Ellie sat in the chair, leaning her back against the reins.

"Where is he?"

"Near the front of Halburtons' house, but on our side of the fence, you know? Near their damned driveway. Jester found him."

"Is he dead?"

"Oh, yes."

"That son of a bitch. I'll kill him."

Appropriately enough, *Missa Solemnis* was pouring through the back windows of the house from the Bang and Olufsen in the common room.

Beau Brummel was a peacock, their "watch peacock," their wonder, their friend, their scourge and their nuisance. In June, both his tail feathers and his cry were at their proudest. A fowl of great character and responsibility, he had disciplined all the dogs, cats, children on the place to keep their distance and let him do his job. His duty was to warn them with his piercing cry of anything moving or making a noise; one cry for a car, two for a pickup truck, three for a noisy car, truck, tractor, five for a motorcycle. He never learned, got used to, accepted noises as did other animals; it was always the same cries for the same reasons. His response was so loud and instantaneous that when there was an unusual noise on the farm, he would drown out the initial, provocative noise so that David could not identify it. In the daylight Brummel would strut on the porches of the house, fanning his feathers, admiring himself in the windows. He would also be admired through the windows.

He slept on a branch in the big tree in front of the house, between the house and the road, to protect the house with his warnings all night. It was a sometimes-ritual for Ellie and David to go to the upper balcony at the front of the house and watch Brummel pick his way through the barnyard across the road, or from wherever he was, to his tree at dusk. After looking at his branch innumerable times, raising and lowering his head on his long neck, as if confronting a challenge, with a jump and a great fluttering of his wings, his tail feathers aerodynamically straightened behind and below him, he would ascend to his branch and settle in for the night. There were light-sensitive spotlights around the farm, set to go on automatically at dusk. There was never more than a minute's difference between Brummel's ascending to his sleeping place and the lights around the place going on.

"You're not going to kill Halburton, David. But what are you going to do?"

"Damn it."

Behind Ellie, Byron the walking horse slowly, subtly, was pulling his reins up between Ellie's shoulder blades and the back of her chair so he would have enough rein to nibble the grass at the edge of the brick patio.

"I'll talk to him. Then I'll kill him."

"The Halburtons aren't from here, David. They're from up north."

"So are we. Or from somewhere."

"But they don't want to be here, as we do. They're only here because of his job. He was sent here."

"True. They don't care to understand much."

Halburton, they understood, was an engineer from Illinois. When his company bought the Kleen Ride Windshield Manufacturing Company in Jameson, Halburton was sent down to manage it. He had bought the five-acre place next to Bass Clef Farm, a squat brick house in a dank, wooded area, really the only near neighbor to the farm, and did little with it other than cut some trees and leave the stumps and let a few goats roam at will. Ellie and David had tried to be friendly, had invited the family over one Sunday afternoon but found Halburton hard-eyed and abrasive, Edith Halburton cowed, their son, Rupert, sullen. First William Fesdon, who managed Bass Clef Farm, had to speak to Halburton about his goats wandering all over the place, and then David had spoken to him. Maybe the man and his son had tried to fix their fences, but not well and not quickly. David suspected only the son had tried.

"They're damnedyankees," Ellie said quietly.

David chuckled.

"It's not funny, David." Ellie sniffed. "They hate it here. The people here hate them, or, at least, him. They resent the way he was sent in from the north to run their factory."

After running with the horse, Jester lay with his stomach flat on the cool brick of the patio under the shade tree.

"That wasn't his fault. A job's a job. Isn't that why we tried to be nice to them, that once?"

"We offered them Southern hospitality and he shouted at his son in our house like a damnedyankee. In the living room."

"He asked me how long it takes for me to make a recording and how much money I can make from one and tried to suggest ways I can increase my output." David noticed his breakfast had grown cold. "All over two beers."

"And that good old boy way he talks," Ellie said.

Ellie and David had observed together that when non-Southerners tried to talk Southern they would say you-all even when talking just to one person. A Southerner never, never made that mistake. His language had improved English by providing a plural for *you*, as exists in other languages, and was proud of it and conscious of its use. Halburton never said *you* without saying *you-all.* Generally, his accent was exaggerated and inaccurate because it missed the three essential elements in middle Tennessee conversation: grace, courtesy, and wit.

"I should have bought that place," David said, "when it came for sale."

"I said so."

"Couldn't think what to do with it. Not a particularly good house, and lousy land."

"Protection."

"Snobbishness."

"Damnedyankees."

"You win."

"Get dressed and go see him."

David glanced at his watch. "Don't have time. Have to meet Ms. Tuesday at the airport at eleven-something."

"Better not go see him. Might shoot you, too. Better bring Jock with you. And William. David, Halburton has to be crazy."

"He shot Brummel! I can't believe it! Where does he think that sort of behavior leads?"

"Brummel's dead." David had known Ellie a long, long time, ever since he had first played Chicago when he was a kid, a lifetime before. He knew the raw anger behind such a simple statement. Ellie was still one of the most trim, attractive women in the world. Anyone who did not know her past would think her most severe anguish would have been over her manicure. That was not Ellie at all. The things Ellie had done, first to survive, then to prosper, would turn the souls of Jameson County, which loved her, into irretrievable turmoil.

For Halburton's sake, David realized he had better handle this situation himself. "I'll call him before he leaves for the factory. What's his first name?"

"Joe." Ellie pronounced the name like the ultimate curse.

"Good morning, Joe." Still barefooted, in his bathrobe, David stood on the brick floor of the kitchen talking on the wall phone. Clara Reagan was cleaning the refrigerator. Packages of unidentifiable lumps were condensing on the counters. "David MacFarlane."

"Yeah."

David had turned off the music system.

"Glad I caught you before you left for the factory. Ellie just came back from a ride. Ellie tells me our peacock, Brummel, has been shot dead, over near your place."

At the refrigerator, Clara straightened her back, turned around, and stared at David. The shock and hurt on her face were genuine.

"Yeah," Halburton said. "I shot him."

"Mind if I ask why?"

"He kept me awake at night."

"He spent nights in the tree right in front of our house, Joe."

"I still heard him."

"More than a quarter of a mile away?"

"You doubt my word?"

"I wouldn't doubt the word of a man who just admitted shooting a peacock."

"I sleep late on Sunday mornings. Or try to. He wakes me up."

"It was our peacock, Joe, and you shot him on our land."

"I'd shoot you, too, if you made so much noise."

"I make a lot of noise, Joe. You'd be surprised how much noise I can make."

"What are you gonna do, MacFarlane?"

"If you don't like country noises, Joe, why don't you move back to the city, listen to the sirens?"

"I don't care about you, MacFarlane, or your Bass Clef Farm. I'm tryin' to run a factory here, full of lazy dumb bastards, and I don't need any rich, retired music star pretendin' to be a farmer botherin' me with his toys. You got that?"

Ellie came into the kitchen with a whole different expression on her face. "There's a man and boy out here," she whispered. "Taking luggage out of their car."

Into the phone, David said, "I'll think about it, Joe."

When he hung up, Ellie had gone back outside.

David realized he had not known a car had arrived because Brummel had not cried.

He said, "I'm sorry, Clara."

"'Sorry'? I'd think you'd be right mad."

"I am right mad."

"That Mr. Halburton. He been here in Jameson County three, four months, and never was a man so hated."

"That so?"

"You know, the people in the factory won't work for him. He's a rough, foul-mouthed man if there ever was one. Dirty-talks women and bumps men around."

"'Bumps'? What do you mean?"

"He walks into 'em, bumps against 'em hard. That way they can't say he actually hit nobody. My niece works in that factory. She says it's real unpleasant since that Yankee trash took over."

"Sorry to hear it."

There was at least one member of Clara Reagan's wide family connected with every section of Jameson County life. She had the inside line on every situation.

"Mr. Halburton shot Brummel?" Clara's blue eyes glinted like a hot day sky.

"He just said so. Said Brummel woke him up Sunday mornings."

"Better not let Jock know. Jock's never sorry for nothin'."

Padding through the east room to the porch David sighed. He loved the irrestrainable masculinity and femininity of the South but sometimes he found it a little unpredictable. Indeed, Jock Reagan might do anything to Halburton, and indeed, Jock wouldn't regret it.

In the driveway was a beat-up old station wagon already turned around, as if it were leaving rather than arriving. Jock stood on one hip at the back of the car, its tailgate up, short among lumps of green canvas baggage. Next to him stood a tall, slim, blond boy. Chatting with Ellie was a tall, slim, graying man. Both the boy and the man wore white T-shirts, khaki shorts, white socks and sneakers. Except for the extra breadth of his shoulders and the different tone of his hair, the man and the boy could have been twins, brothers. Unmistakably, they were father and son.

Seeing them in the sunlight from the shade of the east porch, David suddenly felt fat and old, gross in his bathrobe and bare feet—something he had not felt in some time.

The man's brown eyes focused on David.

"Dave?"

"Is that Dan Prescott?" David yelled. "Well, I'll be a grasshopper's boot!"

They met mid-path and hugged.

To David, Dan's chest felt like a rock; his arms like steel; there appeared to be no stomach.

"Wow," Dan said.

They backed off and shook hands.

Dan needed a shave.

"We were expecting you tonight, or tomorrow," David said.

"We drove straight through."

"You drove straight through from Maine?"

"Saved money on motel rooms."

David surveyed the old station wagon. "You must be exhausted."

"Josh is sixteen. Has a brand new license. He drove while I slept. He's a good driver."

David extended his hand to the boy. Josh had brown eyes, skin, hair coloring identical to David's memory of young Dan's.

"Hug him," Dan said to David. "It's okay to hug people now, when you want to. Even boys."

Dan held the boy's slim body to him.

Into David's neck, Josh spluttered, "Child abuse!"

Standing around on the lawn, they all laughed.

David noticed Josh looking at Ellie's riding boots, her jeans, all the way up to her throat, her hair. He wondered if Ellie had hugged Josh.

"Is it all right that we arrived early?"

"Absolutely," David said. "I'm just about to ride into Nashville Airport to pick up Ms. Tuesday."

Dan frowned. "Janet."

"Want to come along?"

Ellie watched Dan stretch. "Think I've had enough of cars for right now."

"I should think so. Where are these men to be quartered?" David asked Ellie, as if they hadn't discussed such matters more than completely.

"Over the common room," Ellie answered. "Last room on the right. Thought I'd give parents of the bride and groom the benefits of the back of the house. Farm noises can be disturbing, if you're not used to them."

"I still live on a farm," Dan said.

"Really?"

"A small farm. Nothing as grand as this. My father was a minister. Pauline of him, but he believed a minister ought to at least attempt to make a living similar to his congregation, take part in their lives, rather than just be a minister living off them. So when I was growing up, he kept a small farm." Dan smiled. "He owned it. I worked it."

"How interesting," Ellie said.

David knew she really was interested.

Dan squinted at the sign down the driveway. "Bass Clef Farm."

"Pronounced *base,*" David said.

"I met a musician, once." Dan grinned. David marveled at the remaining elasticity, the life of Dan's skin. "In a bar in Boston."

"One of the few times you've been in a bar," David said.

"Not exactly. But about the full extent of my knowledge of music."

"Think of the left hand, on the piano." David spread his left hand, palm down, and rocked it. "Setting the rhythm. Bass Clef Farm sets the rhythm of our lives." He smiled at Ellie.

Jock had a green canvas duffel bag in each hand. A cigarette dangled from his lips.

"Have you met Jock?" David asked.

Josh said, "Yes."

"Jock Reagan," David said. "Retired rodeo star. In case you think he walks funny."

Jock laughed through the smoke. Every bone in his skinny body had been broken, over and over. Often David wondered how much pain Jock was in, continuously, occasionally, sharply. Jock's had been an uninsured life of seldom more than twenty-five dollars a night for riding wild horses and bulls, of frequent terrible injuries, seldom fixed correctly. He never complained, but occasionally would draw off safely into one of the sheds with packs of cigarettes and kitchen matches and a couple of bottles of bourbon and lick his wounds. He liked to be thought of as a retired, heroic athlete, and some did think of him that way.

"Godiva," Josh said to his father. "Don't you want to carry the wedding present?"

"Oh, yes." Dan started back to the car.

Ellie glanced at David.

Jock and Josh passed them carrying the three canvas duffel bags.

"You must be hungry, Josh." Ellie followed them into the house. "Clara? Frying pan still warm?"

Dan returned down the path with a large, gaily wrapped box.

"Good things come in small packages," he laughed. "Is the car all right there?"

"Are the keys in it?"

"Yes." Dan shifted the apparently light package to his other arm. "David, I am sorry about Chump."

"Thanks."

"How long has he been dead?"

"May be. That's right."

"How long has it been?"

"Three. Three and a half years."

"For you, it must be like losing half your brain, half your heart."

"He's always a great worry," David said.

"Sure."

In the barnyard across the road, David, dressed in khakis and boots, climbed into his best pickup truck and rolled down the window.

William appeared at the side window of the truck.

"Well, William," David said. "They're beginning to arrive."

David had told William all about the wedding, the number of guests who were coming and expressed the hope they wouldn't frighten the animals too much.

William grinned. "That's a right Tennessee car. Except it's a station wagon with state of Maine tags."

William missed nothing. He would drive into the valley onto the place every morning before dawn and if anything had moved or been moved six inches, if anything were different at all, about the barns, the animals, the pastures, the fences or the house and garage, William would notice it instantly. He was the smartest, hardest working, kindest talking and acting man David had ever known bar none.

"Well," David said. "Maine isn't too far from Tennessee, except in distance."

"Gotcha," William said.

"William, Halburton shot the peacock, I guess last night."

William said, "Ellie."

"Right," David said. William was wonderful at notifying David of what David hadn't thought yet. "Guess I'd better go bury it when I get back from the airport."

Hearing himself say that, he realized he already knew the peacock would be buried within a half-hour. He wouldn't even need to go look for it.

"Admitted it?"

"Yes. I called him. Tough guy."

William snorted. Behind the personal gentleness of the Southern male is an equal or greater personal toughness he believes no Yankee can match.

"Well," William said.

"Let's not do anything about it, okay? I want to think about it. Jock will find out soon enough." There are absolutely no secrets on a farm, in a farm community. Everyone observes everything and waits to speak of it, sometimes after irretrievable action has taken place. "You'd better tell him about it, before he notices." David knew William had already noticed the peacock was missing. That's why he appeared at the side of the truck. "Then hold his wrists." The instincts of the retired athlete would be to mark up the Halburtons' place pretty badly, or Halburton himself, immediately. His pride would depend upon it.

William nodded.

"When are the new calves arriving? Did you call?"

"Tonight, tomorrow. His missus don't know what time during the night Billy left from here." William grinned. "Guess they been married five, six years now."

David laughed. "See you." He started the engine.

David loved to hear the great cackling from the henhouse in the next shed when he started the truck's engine.

"What time you suppose you'll be back?" William handed David two one dollar bills through the truck's window.

"I won't forget." David stuck the money in his shirt pocket. Once,

David had brought home some Whitbread ale from a specialty store in Nashville. He had opened one to sip while he looked around the barns. He let hot, thirsty William finish the bottle. Consumption of such was frowned upon by William's Church of Christ, of course, but William's taste was the equal of his soul. He had no idea how much it cost. David would never tell him. Sometimes when William knew David was going to Nashville he would give David two dollars for a six pack of "that right good beer." He never asked for change. "I should be back two, or three. Might stop for lunch with this lady I'm picking up. Never can tell, with me."

Driving down the road slowly behind an Amish horse-drawn buggy, David had the eerie feeling William knew better than he, to the minute, what time David would be back. Eerie especially, seeing William could have little comprehension of what David did when he was away from the farm.

Probably it would seem odd, to anyone but David, that a Tennessee farmer had picked up on David's rhythms better than anyone had since Chump Hardy. To David, it did not seem a bit odd.

3

Dressed in a gray, pin-striped suit, white blouse, red ribbon at her throat, at Nashville Airport Janet Twombly Nelson was overseeing the loading of many pieces of matched luggage and six cases of champagne into the trunk of a limousine.

David stood quite close to her, peering through her makeup, trying to be absolutely sure it was she.

"Ms. Tuesday, I presume."

"David!" Purse on straps dangling from one arm, Janet straightened up from her luggage, threw back her arms, and fell against him. They hugged, but did not kiss. "You darling man! To do such a nice thing for us all!" Hands on his shoulders, she stood back and stared at him. "Let me look at you, darling man! You look only a teensy older. But then again," she said, dropping her arms, bracelets clanging against each other, "you always did look older than you actually were."

"You look very well."

"Exhausted, dear, from the flight. I had the bad luck of sitting next to someone interesting."

"Is this your limousine?"

"Why, yes, dear. Of course."

"I said I'd meet you."

"But I have all this luggage, dear."

"I have a truck."

"A truck! My God, you really are putting on the farmer McGregor bit, aren't you?"

"Ms. Tuesday, it's eighty miles to the farm."

"Why don't you put one of those cases of champagne in the back seat?" Ms. Tuesday said to the driver. "It would fit better. And my makeup kit."

"Ms. Tuesday, there's really no need for the limousine. Why don't you let the driver go?"

"All this luggage," Ms. Tuesday waved her arm at the limousine's trunk, "would get spotted in a truck." She was not put off by David's wry expression. "Besides, the champagne, dear. Champagne shouldn't get all shaken up in a truck."

"We've got truckloads of champagne ordered. Why did you bother bringing any from Paris?"

"This is special champagne, dear, for the toast."

"Will you at least ride with me in the truck? The limousine can follow us."

"Yes, dear. Of course. Where is it?"

Speaking to the driver, David pointed across the short-term parking lots to the main road leading out of the airport. "I'll meet you over there," he said. "It's a sort of yellow truck."

David and Janet began to walk across the parking lots. "Is that what's called a power suit?" David asked.

Janet looked down at herself. "My own design. It's more comfortable than it looks, for traveling."

"I have the idea you've done very well in business."

"I'll explain all that to you," she said.

"Have you heard from John?"

"Doubt he's even gotten my message yet. News travels in that part of Africa by runners, or something." She noticed the license plate on the truck. "'C-note.' Does that mean you paid one hundred dollars for this truck?"

"Pretty close."

Inside the truck, she said, "David, it's stifling. Is there air conditioning?"

"No. Roll down your window. We'll catch a breeze as we go along." David turned the ignition key.

"You still have the most incredibly powerful looking hands and forearms, David."

Since he began doing work around the farm David had discovered a lifetime of playing piano had given him uncommon manual strength.

Cranking down her window, she said, "Has it been just awful for you since Chump died?"

David put the truck in gear and rolled it forward.

"Chump Hardy and David MacFarlane," Janet said. "David MacFarlane and Chump Hardy. Gilbert and Sullivan. Lerner and Loew. One name doesn't sound right without the other."

Passing the limousine snuggled against the curb, David tooted his horn and waved. "Last time I saw you was in Cannes."

"Please don't remind me of all that. I was a very confused young lady." As her hair was blowing a little, she cranked the window up again. "You all wanted things from me, and I never knew what."

"All who?"

"You and Chump. John. Dan Prescott."

"I never knew John was in the picture."

"He was, David. Very much."

"Obviously."

"One didn't marry blacks in those days. One couldn't even write about such a thing, and hope to get published."

"In retrospect, it seems you wanted things from yourself, and didn't know what."

"I didn't want to be what you all wanted me to be."

"What was that?"

"The girl next door, David. Your cheerleader." She ran the back of her fingers across her forehead.

"I suppose you're right."

"Women do exist for something other than saying, 'Ra ra, boom de ay.'"

"You never had to cheer John on?"

"He didn't expect it. Being black in an all-white world, he was used to isolation, you see. He was used to living in his own mind, following his own instincts."

"Has it been lonely for you?"

"Have you heard from Dan Prescott?"

"He arrived."

"He arrived?" She cranked her window up, tightly, to hear. "At the farm? He's here?"

"Arrived just before I left, with his younger son. They drove straight through from Maine, to save money on motels."

"David, stop the truck."

"What?"

"Stop the truck! 'We'll catch a breeze as we go along,' indeed! There's no damned reason why I should ride in a hot, dirty, smelly farm truck when there's a perfectly good limousine right behind me. Air conditioned."

David was slowing the truck on the soft shoulder.

"The dust!" Janet said. "Stop the truck!"

He braked hard. Janet fell forward a little. Behind them, the limousine almost went against the truck's bumper.

"Sorry," David muttered. "Sorry I didn't bring Jester."

"Who's Chester?" She was brushing imaginary dust from her suit with her hand.

"A dog."

"That would have completed the picture." She opened the door to get out.

"At least he would have kept me company. Ms. Tuesday, it's eighty miles to the farm."

"All the more reason for riding in the limousine!" In her narrow suit skirt she stepped down into the dirt of the road's soft shoulder.

"Your driver will never find it!"

"He knows where it is. He says your farm is famous, David." She slammed the door.

"Fine," David muttered, alone in the cab. "Please ask him not to tour people by on Sundays."

He put the truck in gear and, ignoring the limousine, roared past the turn for Route 65 South.

4

"Ellie, I resign from airport shuttle duty."

"You just started. This is your first trip."

"I don't care. I resign."

"Where are you, David?"

"Savior Hospital."

"I see."

"Ms. Tuesday is heading down Route 65 in her own rented limousine, with more luggage than you've ever seen in any store, and, six wooden cases of French champagne, one of which is in the back seat with her."

"She didn't like the truck?" There was laughter barely suppressed in Ellie's throat.

"She didn't like the truck."

"David, why didn't you use the Town Car?"

"Well. Crank Jocko up. Tell him he's making the airport runs from now on."

"David, you know Jock hates cars. He's afraid of anything that doesn't have four legs and a vicious streak. And I need Clara here this week. She can't do the driving."

"Simpsons," David said. "Somebody. Hire a driver for this week."

"David, it sounds like you had a point to make, and you made it."

"What point?"

"Picking up the mother of the bride, off an airplane from Paris, in a farm truck."

"Her Daddy owned the hardware store, in Columbia Falls, Maine, for Christ's sake."

"That was a long time ago, David. You've been on the farm too long."

"I have not. Ms. Tuesday's been in Paris too long. You might try to hire her driver for the week when they arrive. They'll be there in about an hour. I quit."

"David, this wonderful celebration of yours hasn't even started yet, and I've got people sprawled on chairs asleep in the common room—"

"Who?"

"Prescott, *père et fils.* After we filled them with scrambled eggs and skim milk, they never made it to their room. You can't quit now, David."

"Well, I do. 'Bye."

PERSPECTIVE: *Estelle Manning*

"Good afternoon, Ms. Manning."

"Good afternoon, Mr. MacFarlane."

It has always been like that, very formal, correct between us. Good morning, good afternoon, good evening, whatever time of day or night Mr. MacFarlane chooses to come in. He has the run of the hospital, of course. Who would ever say he couldn't come in, even though he's been known to show up sometimes either side of dawn, nights he couldn't sleep, I guess, and there have been many more than a few of those. He always walks and sits, his big shoulders stooped over a little as if they were too heavy for him, leaning forward as if just about to raise his hands to a keyboard and strike those first chords, start a magically tripping melody that would make the thousands in any audience stand and cheer, then be silent, to listen. Of course, to finish that image, always after that first chord, those first notes there would be the sound of the saxophone coming around the sound of the piano somehow. I've known David MacFarlane three years going on four, *seeing him,* working with him, whatever the expression, being the main custodian of his grief. I've seen him sit for hours slumped in a chair looking for all the world like a big sack of laundry, sometimes silently, more often listening to the strange tape recordings he brings his friend. I've seen this much of him for this long but it's always been *Ms. Manning,* never Estelle, even when speaking to me with eyes red with tears, throat choked. I believe he has kept me at a formal distance for good reason.

I am the nurse here, intimate with the facts, daily and nightly witness to the waste, the grief, the despair. And Mr. MacFarlane wants me never to say what probably he can read in my eyes and never would say, what he might think about my doing but what I would never do.

I play the tapes, too, whatever tapes Mr. MacFarlane leaves me, hours of them, softly, propping the tape player on the pillow above one or the other of Chump's shoulders.

"I am convinced he can hear, Ms. Manning," Mr. MacFarlane has said, over and over. "Chump could always hear things no one else could hear. He heard so much so well that whatever he was hearing would distract him from everything else, even the little simple things of living, and convince other people he was an idiot. He'd hear the obvious, what everyone else would hear, but then shades and tones within the obvious, all sorts of background sounds, and sounds from the next block, maybe the next world, even I don't know all that he could hear. Chump was never more than a couple of ears, a human sound receiver, that needed a body to hang from and walk them around. His real suffering now would be in the silence, the sound of his own breathing, hospital noises, *drip-drip,* your soft-soled shoes going along the polished, hard corridor floor, things you can't hear or don't notice, nothing progressive, with a beginning, a middle, an end, a sense, created as a sound to be heard. Our only mercy now is to give him something to which he can listen, to reward him, return to him just a little of the pleasure he has given so many millions of people."

Mr. MacFarlane and I play these tape recordings for Chump Hardy that Mr. MacFarlane brings in. The tapes are apt to be of anything. Some of the tapes are of their own music, of course, the music Chump Hardy and David MacFarlane made and played together. Some are the music of other jazz and rock performers sometimes I recognize, people like Erroll Garner, Sidney Bechet, Louis Armstrong, Paul McCartney, Eric Clapton, Ginger Baker, Peter Townsend, plus a lot of music I don't recognize. We play classical music for Chump, too, Beethoven and Mozart, Hayden and Bach, especially Bach, and some other classical music I don't recognize, some of which frankly I don't like very much. Then we play tapes of another sort altogether, very strange tapes. Street noises. Mr. MacFarlane must make these tapes himself. He must walk around the streets of Nashville and New York, wherever else he goes, with a tape machine in his hands recording all the noises, people walking, snatches of conversation as they pass by, car engines accelerating and slowing down, odd shouts, sirens. Other tapes when I play them appear to be blank at first. Mr. MacFarlane must make them at his farm. At first you hear nothing, then the sounds of birds chattering, after a while a screen door slamming, a bull bawling, at a distance a tractor starting, a peacock screeching, a dog barking.

I play the tapes for Chump Hardy, when I can, as much as I can, but really for David MacFarlane, as he is so eloquent, so loving of his partner. But I suspect that what I think is in my eyes.

It was a little more than three and a half years ago that I got a call from Dr. MacBride at about nine-thirty at night.

"Estelle? Are you going to be around? I mean, at the hospital?"

"I go off duty at midnight, Doctor."

"That's what I mean. Can you stand by?"

"Stand by?"

"Yes. I'll be checking someone into the hospital sometime in the early morning, real early, maybe shortly after midnight. I sure would appreciate it if you'd be around."

"I see." By the time patients got to the coma unit usually everything was known about them except the setting of their internal clock. Seldom was there a reason for examinations, diagnoses, at that point, especially after midnight. "Yes, I'll stay. I'll be here." I figured if the Doctor knew he was going to come in at that hour this had to be an important, or at least a different, sort of case. And the sad truth is that however difficult it sounds, I doubt there's any profession more boring than nursing in a coma unit.

"If anything happens to cancel or postpone, I'll call you."

"I'll be here."

Well, he didn't call. I woke up at three-thirty in the morning in the stand-by room and figured I might as well put on my shoes and wander over to the unit to see if any message had come for me from Dr. MacBride and just not gotten through. No message.

While I was standing there wondering what to do there was a great commotion at reception. The three elevator doors opened almost simultaneously. When the gurney was wheeled off the elevator it was surrounded immediately by a crowd of people, some of them talking official, if you know what I mean, a couple of them even dressed in uniforms, from Customs, or Immigration, whatever, having a four- or five-way conversation with someone who was clearly a lawyer, from the way he was dressed, and talked, kept talking the others down. Dr. MacBride was there, a part of the crowd. He followed the big-shouldered, hollow-eyed man to the reception desk where the man seemed to run out of steam. His mouth just opened and closed. Dr. MacBride said to Frannie, at reception, "Everything ready? What room? Is Nurse Manning here?" He looked over at me and smiled.

I thought I recognized the big-shouldered, tired-looking man.

I went through the crowd to get to the patient. Unconscious, he was a fairly heavyset man with dank blond, badly cut hair, remarkably wide facial features. I remember noticing there wasn't a wrinkle on his face. There was something strangely babyish about him, as if no one had ever mentioned work to him, if you know what I mean. He looked like he was napping.

He looked familiar to me, the man on the gurney did, as well.

There wasn't too much to piece together, from what Dr. MacBride said while we were doing the initial examination, which didn't take all that long, once we got started, from what I overheard the men in the corridor saying, from what Mr. MacFarlane told me a few days later, when he began to recognize me as someone taking care of his friend with some continuity, and as someone who cared. At some time during the night it dawned on me that this was Chump Hardy, this was David MacFarlane the incredibly famous jazz duo. The comatose patient was Chump Hardy.

Apparently some official, or doctor, in Puerto Venejo, Mexico, or wherever, somewhere in Mexico anyway, had called Mr. Farber, in New York, reporting that Chump Hardy had been admitted to a hospital down there unconscious and had remained unconscious for thirty-six hours. Mr. Farber is the manager of both Hardy and MacFarlane, a very old gentleman now, crippled, in a wheelchair; he's come to the hospital several times all the way from New York to see Chump, a real weeper, I can tell you; so old and frail sometimes I've worried he wouldn't survive the visit. Anyway, he telephoned Mr. MacFarlane, who has a farm south of here, down in Jameson County. Instantly, Mr. MacFarlane called Dr. MacBride. They flew together from Nashville in a chartered jet. Apparently, from all the noise there was in the hospital corridor that night from the officials, more of which showed up later, Mr. MacFarlane and Dr. MacBride took Chump out of the hospital down there and flew him to us at the Savior Hospital in Brentwood in a rather high-handed manner. I hadn't realized Dr. MacBride was in Mexico when he telephoned me.

Also, after I had time to think about it, I realized there were no press in the corridor that night. When you have government officials involved in any matter, especially in the middle of the night, doesn't at least one of them manage to tip off the press? They so love to see their own names in the newspaper. News of this has been in the press, telling where Chump Hardy is, but somehow it got to be old news before it ever was news, if you know what I mean; it was and is all handled so discreetly, just a paragraph now and again acknowledging that Chump Hardy is in a Nashville hospital, resting comfortably.

So after Dr. MacBride and I got done with our prelim we followed the gurney into the private room arranged for Chump Hardy.

David MacFarlane sat in a corner of the dark room, slouched like that laundry sack I mentioned to you, a position I was to see him in many, many times, long hours at a time.

Dr. MacBride waited until after the orderlies and I had moved Chump onto the bed, organized the intravenous, and the orderlies had left before speaking.

"Not good, David."

In his chair, head down anyway, Mr. MacFarlane nodded.

"Preliminary diagnosis, of course. It will be hours before we get the results of blood tests, urinalysis—"

Mr. MacFarlane said: "Get to it."

"Drug-induced coma. Heavy."

"Permanent?"

Dr. MacBride shrugged. "Who knows? Brain damage might already have taken place, of course."

Duly, Mr. MacFarlane said: "'Brain damage.'"

"Almost total paralysis."

Mr. MacFarlane looked up, terrible grief in his red-rimmed eyes. "How total?"

"He can breathe. I don't know how permanent the paralysis may be, either. If there is ever any recovery, it may be total or partial."

"What do you think?"

"I think you'd better prepare yourself for the worst, David."

"Which is?"

"That this situation could continue for a long time. The coma. The paralysis. Your friend, Chump, is a reasonably young man, early middle-aged. He's built like a farm worker. To my regret, I've seen other cases like this. Do you have any idea of Chump's habits?"

Mr. MacFarlane shook his head in apparent confusion. "He has a little apartment here in Nashville, a small hotel suite, really, but he's been spending more and more time in New York the last year or so. There's this young woman. This very young woman. He telephoned me from New York about three weeks ago, saying he was going with her to Mexico for a vacation. 'Vacation from what?' I asked. Hanging around the New York clubs."

"I wonder where she is now."

"I don't care. Someone must have taken him to the hospital in Mexico. Left him there."

"Did you know he took drugs?"

"He would always say he didn't. And I'd sort of believe him, more or less, even when I caught him with the stuff. I don't think Chump was aware of taking drugs. He'd sort of do it if people were doing it. Then he'd seem to forget about it. Chump wasn't really aware of anything, except his saxophone. Sound. I've never been able to explain Chump, exactly."

"Was he always that way?"

"Yes. I guess so."

"It adds up."

"I guess."

"Do you know what drugs he favored?"

"That's just it," Mr. MacFarlane said. "I have the idea he'd take whatever was available, without even knowing what it was, carelessly. If he'd had some sense . . ."

"I suspect chemicals, David," Dr. MacBride said. "Artificial, chemical drugs. What are called beguilingly 'designer drugs'."

"Chemicals," David snorted. "It's a marvelous technology we have, isn't it?"

"Yes. David, under the circumstances, as your physician, I have to ask you. I admit to having been curious, anyway. Are you, or have you been a drug user at any time in your life? I really ought to know."

"Aspirin," Mr. MacFarlane said. "Scotch whiskey."

"Sure enough?"

"I've been in the music business since I was a kid, performing in places you wouldn't take your wife. Never were drugs news to me. I saw what they did to people instantly I saw the temptation."

"You never even experimented?"

"No." Very softly, Mr. MacFarlane said, "I knew I'd like them." He raised his head and stared at the totally inert human on the bed. "Chump and I aren't the same sort of people. Not the same sort at all. He lived for only one thing, his music. That's why maybe he's probably a better, or a more natural, musician than I am. He always seemed ready to risk everything, kill himself, for one more exciting line of music no one had ever thought of or tried before. I'm more educated. I contrive my risks. I always stayed within the possible. Chump would run right at the impossible, over it, through it. He didn't care about anything else, even life."

"You can't make music if you're dead."

"I tried that argument on him. Again and again and again. He was really only addicted to music. Not even music, sound . . ."

Tiredly, glancing reluctantly at the inert form on the bed, Mr. MacFarlane stood and buttoned his coat.

"Where are you going now? David—want to come home with me? Sunny will make a nice breakfast."

"I don't know. My car's at the airport. Guess I'll go to the hotel. Stay in Chump's suite. Come back here later. What time do you think those reports will be ready?"

As with so many people I see here in the coma unit, Mr. MacFarlane visited every day for a while, sitting like a sack full of laundry. Sometimes he would talk to Chump, convinced he was listening. Then he thought of the music tapes, or sound tapes, for Chump, and started bringing those and playing them. He got me playing the tapes, too, whenever I was on duty. After a while, Mr. MacFarlane was visiting never less than three times a week, making especially long visits before and after he had to make a trip. Sometimes, when he's been in New York or something, he's telephoned me: "How's Chump?"

"No change." Believe me, the phrase a nurse in the coma unit, this nurse, hates the most in the English language is: *no change*.

Anyway, this particular afternoon Mr. MacFarlane came in, dressed in his khakis looking every bit the gentleman farmer. A small smile played around his lips. I'm always glad to see him looking a little happy. After all, there has been no change in Chump Hardy's condition in all these three and a half years.

After the *Good afternoon, Ms. Manning. Good afternoon, Mr. MacFarlane* bit, he said, "You'd ride in a farm truck, wouldn't you?"

"Is that an invitation?"

"Not for right now."

"I've seldom ridden in anything else. At least with any male I care about 'round here."

Standing over Chump's bed, looking at the nasal breathing tubes in the now gaunt, sallow face, at the bulge of the catheter under the sheet, Mr. MacFarlane said, "I just got an idea." He rubbed his hands together. "Yes. I think I'll do that."

He turned from the bed and started to leave.

"Not staying very long today," I said.

"No," he said. "I've got an idea."

He was too amused when he said it.

I knew the idea he must have had wasn't the idea he must have read in my eyes, all this long time.

5

Janet Twombly Nelson said softly, "Living next door to him, growing up, I never knew he was beautiful." In the common room at Bass Clef Farm, she and Ellie stood over Dan Prescott asleep in a chair, legs sprawled over an ottoman. "I thought every girl had a Dan Prescott living next door to her."

Janet gestured toward the boy sleeping on his back on the divan. "Is that Dan's son? He must be."

"That's Josh."

Janet stood over the boy. She touched the back of her fingers to his bare arm. "What girl in her right mind wouldn't love him?"

Josh's hand went to where his arm had been touched, and rested there.

"Are cucumber sandwiches all right?" Ellie asked. "I thought we might lunch on the porch."

"Just let me wash," Janet said.

"Of course, I suppose he's useless." Hair freshly brushed, Janet came onto the east porch. She had removed her suit coat.

A plate of quartered sandwiches, a pitcher of iced tea and two glasses were on the small wicker table.

"Who?" Ellie asked.

Janet sat. "Dan."

"I have no idea," Ellie said. "I believe he's an ordained minister."

"Not defrocked? He must have been."

"Perhaps. He has the two sons."

"But I take it no Mrs. Prescott arrived with him."

"No. None such has been mentioned in the wedding arrangements." Ellie poured Janet some iced tea. "And, of course, he is famous, in a way."

"He's famous for being famous." Janet bit into a sandwich.

"He's famous the same way your daughter is famous, isn't he? The bride? The internationally famous model Cille?"

"Luce has worked damned hard at the business," Janet said, "since she was a child. Yes, she models. She also designs clothes, with me, develops fabrics and patterns, helps administer the business, both in New York and Paris, and is the best salesperson we have."

"I see."

"Luce is a very successful *and* hard-working business woman."

"And Dan just stands around being handsome, is that it?"

"I doubt he owns anything. And now Luce is marrying into a political career."

"Dan means quite a lot to David. Even though they haven't seen each other in years."

Jester arrived on the porch with muddy paws.

Janet said, "The first time I saw photographs of the statue, the sculpture, in a French magazine, I looked at it with wonder. I said, 'How absolutely beautiful!' Then I said, 'Why, that could be Dan!'"

"You didn't know it was Dan?"

"How could I believe it? Dan was an ordained minister, last I'd heard. I was sure he was pocketed away in some small parish in Maine. How could this photograph of an elegant male nude in a French magazine be my Dan Prescott?"

"His name wasn't published?"

"No, no. If you remember, not at first. Just the title of the sculpture. *American Male.*"

"*Twentieth-Century American—Male,*" Ellie said. "With a hyphen."

Janet said, "The word 'male' in the title is clearly unnecessary." Worried about her skirt, Janet held a bit of sandwich out to the dog.

"We don't want him to beg," Ellie said.

"Right. Sorry. Too used to the lap rats in Paris they call dogs. Is this Chester?"

"Jester."

"What a beautiful dog. A Weimaraner, isn't he?"

"Yes."

"Well-mannered, too. Better-mannered than I, I guess. Anyway." Janet took another sandwich quarter for herself. "However much it may astound you, I never saw Dan naked, growing up, absolutely naked, I mean, standing so free and proud. How standards have changed. I knew it was wrong at the time, of course, but we were taught not to be so giving, that there was something precious about ourselves we always were to withhold from each other."

Ellie smiled.

"I didn't believe it, of course, but Dan did. And here he is now, famous as a nude! When I first spotted that handsome book of photographs of him in a bookstore window, I almost fell over. *Why, that is Dan!*"

"Did you buy a copy?"

"Several. I gave them away by the dozens. Chauvinistic of me. *Twentieth-Century American—Male.* You see, Ellie, the last time I had seen Dan he was wearing a black suit and collar." Janet was frowning.

"Yes," Ellie said. "How people move from one position in life to another is intriguing."

"Tell me about yourself," Janet said. "How long have you known David?"

"Forever."

"That's not possible."

"Since we were teenagers, in Chicago. We met while he was playing piano in a not very nice bar."

"Before Chump Hardy?"

Ellie looked off at the more distant pastures. "I was present the night they met; the night David literally scraped Chump off the concrete of an alley in Chicago. I was present the morning they first tried to play together."

Janet stared at Ellie. "And was it the magical moment so often described?"

Ellie laughed. "It was magical, yes. A rough sort of magic."

Janet said, "I knew David well, a quarter of a century ago."

"Oh, I know."

"Forgive me, but I don't ever remember his mentioning you."

"Well, you were in Europe . . ."

"Did you know of me?"

"Oh, yes."

"How?"

"When David would come to New York. I was having a career there. We'd meet. We were always friends."

"He would tell you about me?"

"Oh, yes. You, and Dan Prescott, and John Bart Nelson."

"Should I be embarrassed?"

"No. What's the expression? We were all working our way toward salvation with fear and trembling. More tea?" Ellie refilled their glasses.

"You worked in New York?"

"Yes. Before I packed it in I was under contract to several corporations to provide entertainment for their clients."

"You mean, arrange dinners, theater tickets, sports events, that sort of thing?"

"That sort of thing."

"But when did you and David, I mean—"

"About eight years ago. We saw we were getting older. David saw it was taking him longer and longer to get his energies back after a concert tour, or making a record, and he was never any good at vacations."

"I know. David was a compulsive."

"Yes," Ellie said. "Compulsive. Good thing he never took drugs. He knew he had to cut back somehow. He had the idea he could base himself in Nashville, spend some time in his maturity bringing younger musicians along. He always liked this area. Together we had enough energy left to take on this place—" Ellie waved her arm at the small garden next to the porch, "Bass Clef Farm."

"David never knew anything about farming."

"He still doesn't. Neither do I. Shocking the things we don't know. I had learned to ride in Central Park."

"Does David ride?"

"No. The rhythm is not certain enough for him. All this was difficult on Chump, of course: David's developing a rich, separate life."

"Did Chump kill himself?"

Ellie studied Janet's eyes, then said, "In a manner of speaking."

Janet put her empty glass on the table. "All this amazes me. I didn't think David knew anybody respectable in those days. Partly that was what attracted me to him. I was very naive. I couldn't stand discovering how respectable he really was."

"Yes, well," Ellie said. "You can't accomplish all that David has accomplished without formidable self-discipline." The dog was behaving toward Ellie as if it were time for Ellie to do something with him. "You must be exhausted, Janet, after your trip. Wouldn't you like to nap?"

Looking out at what she could see of the farm, Janet said, "It's so peaceful."

"Not all that peaceful," said Ellie. "Someone shot our peacock last night."

"How awful!"

"Yes, it is awful. A new neighbor, who doesn't belong here. I'm not sure he belongs on this earth. Come on, I'll show you your room. Upstairs, at the back of the house."

6

PERSPECTIVE: *Lank Kraft*

"Hey, bartender!"

Only two, three minutes before I had refilled his vodka-tonic. I could see his glass on the bar, half full. Yes, he had been looking around the dark joint. Sunlight streaming in through the dirty windows from the glorious June day outside and some people, not many, but this businessman on a trip from somewhere north still drinking his lunch at three-thirty in the afternoon, alone, wanted to be in this dark, smelly bar, The Spider Web, listening to three ugly girls on the little stage pickin' an electric, an acoustic, a banjo, praise the Lord, music they must have written 'cause I had never heard it before and I never wanted to hear it again. I myself would rather be outside on this beautiful June afternoon working on the engine of that old 'vette I just bought.

And yes, he had spotted him.

I let him wait awhile but I had to go to him.

He leaned over the bar at me as if what he had to say was so confidential. "That guy over there."

"What guy?"

"Over in that alcove."

I pretended to strain my eyes through the atmosphere.

"That guy?"

"Yeah. That guy."

"What about him?"

"If I'm not mistaken, that's David MacFarlane. You know? The jazz pianist."

"Naw," I said.

"I think he is. Saw him in concert, once, in Washington, D.C."

"I know he isn't."

"Think of a guy like that, drinking his life away in a dive like this." The drinking businessman smiled. "What a comedown." He could hardly wait to get home to tell people. "Maybe if I buy him a drink, he'll play "Sorry" for me."

"He's only drinkin' beer."

"So? I'll give him five bucks. Ten bucks. He can drink whatever he wants. I remember the name of the guy who used to play with him. What's his name? Chump Hardy. I'll ask him whatever happened to Chump Hardy." The man chuckled. "Drink and drugs."

The businessman stood up and took his drink from the bar and turned to go be a nuisance.

I grabbed his arm.

"Sit down and drink your drink," I said to him. "Be a nice man."

The man smiled at me. "That is David MacFarlane, isn't it?" He looked at my fingers around his arm and back at me. "What's it to you?"

"He's the owner of this dive. My boss. A nice man. He's here to hear the music. He's never played the piano in here, not once. Leave him alone. Sit down and drink your drink. Stop lookin' at him."

"Or what?"

"Or you're going to get a very fast personal escort to lower Broadway."

He didn't sit down. I knew he wouldn't. He did finish his drink. I knew he would.

He didn't leave a tip.

But he did leave David MacFarlane alone. He knew he'd better.

In a few minutes Owen Farber came in dressed uptown, you know, the color of his shirt collar not the same color as his shirt, and sat at the table with David MacFarlane.

Bar rag in hand I went over to the table because I love badgering and being ignored by Owen Farber. I drag it out as long as I can.

"'Afternoon, Mr. Farber. What can I get you this afternoon?"

Glancing at the musicians he said, "What do you think?"

"No energy," David said. "Also I haven't heard a good musical idea yet."

"Ugly," Farber said.

They also sound awful, too, I could have added.

"Would you like a drink, Mr. Farber?"

Not looking at me, he said, "Ummm."

David said, "Your grandfather's arriving tomorrow."

"Yeah. I'll drive him down to the farm."

"He'll want to look at the books. Hear any new tapes we have."

"Yeah," Owen Farber said, "I'll take care of all that. Milton wants to look at the books because he thinks you don't."

"He knows I listen to the tapes."

"You copy them and take them home with you."

David didn't say anything.

Lifting David's beer glass I wiped the table.

Besides this dive, The Spider Web, I knew MacFarlane owned Treble Clef Recording and Publishing Company, Incorporated, a recording studio in a beautiful glass building over on Music Row. Owen Farber ran it for him. I don't know how Treble Clef did as a business, but I hoped better than The Spider Web. A dive on lower Broadway was not much of an investment but it sure didn't give much of a return. MacFarlane owned it to be a spider web, exactly that, to attract musicians off the street, the people, not all of them young, dragging into Nashville, hoping for a break. Like the other joints here we would agree they could play for nothing, for the chance to be heard, but usually we'd give them something out of the till. They wouldn't go hungry or without a place to sleep if they played here. And David MacFarlane would hear them. He'd stop by at odd hours of the day or the night, sip a beer, give a listen. He found a few musicians that way, people he thought showed talent, and turned them over to Farber to see if he could start careers for them. I'm sure you've heard of Sarah Downey by now. I take some credit for her. She got up and sang here one night. After her third song, I was on the phone to Bass Clef Farm. *David, you gotta hear this girl sing!* He came the next night. I'd told her to be sure and come back. The rest is history, as they say. I'm a discoverer of talent in disguise. Sarah comes by once in a while, when she's in Nashville, and gives me a kiss. David gave me a big check, after a while. *Here, Lank. This is for what you did for Sarah, for all of us.* I'm not sure the point of all this Spider Web—Treble Clef thing is to make money. I suspect it does. David MacFarlane knows what he's doing. I know it keeps young Owen Farber in mighty expensive suits and trick shirts.

"What will it be, Mr. Farber? Name your poison."

Farber looked up at me as if I had just appeared. He loved to be thought considering the whole range of what he might have to drink.

David said, "Have a beer, Owen?"

"No. Not a beer. I've got two bands for the wedding, David. The Smashers, sort of funky, the younger crowd will like them, and Estrellas Nuevas, nice to dance to."

David laughed. "About six groups so far have notified me they intend to crash the party."

Farber looked as if he were trying to read David's eyes. "Will you play?"

"No way."

"Vodka and tonic, Mr. Farber?"

"Perrier," Farber admitted. "Fresh lime."

I love that. This young executive, wearing so much gold around his neck and wrists you'd put your life in danger just to walk down the street with him, who never discovered any talent I know of, who inherited David MacFarlane's business affairs from his grandfather, Milton Farber, if I have the story right, and he makes a big act of never really wanting a drink. A cokehead if I ever saw one.

Of course he'd gone to use the telephone in the back office before I ever got the drink of water to him. You dig?

"Just put it on the tab, Lank," David MacFarlane said.

"Another beer, David?"

"No, thanks. Got to get home."

"Are the wedding guests beginning to arrive?"

David nodded. "We have some bull calves arriving."

7

"David, how very nostalgic of you," Janet said.

When David entered the house Janet and Ellie were sitting in the small front living room sharing a bottle of champagne. Ellie wore tan slacks and Janet designer jeans.

"Nostalgic?"

"Buying a farm like this."

"Sentimental," David said.

He went across the hall into the study and poured himself a Scotch and soda.

When he had driven onto Bass Clef Farm in the dusk a few minutes before, the lights in the tenant house and the main house were on, but the light-sensitive spotlights had not turned on yet. There was light in one shed, where William and Frank were working on a tractor engine. The steers had come down from the hills, as they always did at dusk, and were nestling around the crick between the tenant house and the big barns.

Jester, hearing the truck, ran around the corner of one of the barns and across the pasture toward the road. The tall, slim boy, Josh, was chasing him, running really quite fast. In the pasture, Byron, the horse, began to canter in the same direction. The horse caught up to the boy and ran close behind him. The boy turned, to look, tripped and fell hard on the soft grass. The horse avoided stepping on him. Instantly, the boy stood, waving high at the truck as he saw it turn into the driveway of the main house.

Jester had given David his usual big greeting.

David had left the Whitbread ale in the truck for William to collect.

The shower in the bathroom off the study was running.

David took the small tape recorder from his desk and inserted a fresh tape and fresh batteries. Before slipping it into a manila envelope, leaving the flap open, he turned it on, the sound dial to high.

In the living room the women were going over what sounded like the wedding guest list. The Farbers, Milton and Owen, the Hollingsworths, Doug and Sorry, the Coswells, Bennets, Hartigans, Abraham probably without Sally, or Sally without Abraham, Haig Scott with whomever or whatever, the Kingleys, Websters, Greg, the Cantors, Harristons. . . .

David reentered the living room and sat quietly with his drink until the women stopped comparing notes and put them away. He had propped the open manila envelope against the leg of his chair.

Janet said, "Good thing I didn't drive home with you, David. At least my driver didn't get lost."

"I had a few things to do in Nashville," David said. "Thought I might as well stay and do them."

Janet said, "I badly needed a nap."

"Also to get myself sworn at."

Ellie said, "Did someone swear at you?"

"Five o'clock traffic, Nashville, intersection, everyone had had a green light and inched forward into gridlock. A man about thirty in a white shirt and tie jumped out of his BMW, took off his glasses and called me an old fart."

Ellie frowned. "What did you do?"

"I said, 'Watch the lights.' He said, 'What?' and I said, 'Watch the lights.' He put his glasses back on and got back into the car. Don't know why he chose me to yell at. We were all jammed up in traffic together. It's being called '*old*' first time in such circumstances that is a shock."

"I'm sure it would be," Janet said.

Ellie said, "You should have taken the time, David, to notify the man that he has only a few weeks before such a word will be used to describe him."

"That's it," David said. "He wasn't particularly young. Mid-thirties. In the old days we would have considered him a grownup." David heard someone moving quietly out of the study and up the stairs. "And then the first word hurled at me upon arrival home was *nostalgic*. 'David, how very nostalgic of you.' Didn't I hear that?"

Janet turned her body in her chair better to face him. "David, settling down on a family farm, at your time in life, at this time in history ... I'm sure it's a lot of hard work, and expense, and what sense does it make? I mean, really?"

David said, "You don't understand? This is the first generation that is not necessary for anything, that is not needed. They have been replaced by technology. And I'm afraid today's young people know it. There's not a thing left for them to do except serve each other fast food, which they don't even cook. And the more they realize this, the more they self-destruct, by chemical drugs, overpowered cars, or some other technological means. I really fear that if you make a loud noise at this generation—war, depression or natural disaster—they will swallow their young in terror like so many minks. Absolutely, the family farm has been replaced by technology, by the agricorp. Tell me what hasn't been replaced by technology, including pleasure, pain, responsibility and reality. People have been replaced by technology, and technology as well, television and other opiates, has insensitized us as to what is happening to us. Do you know what percentage of music recorded these days is actually played by live musicians? I mean, by human beings with their pianos and their horns and their strings and their drums, with their personalities, their histories, their experiences, their talents, their joys and griefs, playing out some composer's dreams while interacting with each other, making something fresh of a piece of music each time performed?"

"My, my," Janet said. "Someone has put you in a bad mood."

"I know there was a time in history before the piano existed," David MacFarlane said, "and I suspect there will be a time in history after the piano. There was a time before the family farm existed, and I suspect there will be a time after the family farm exists. But do I have to believe that mankind's ultimate state is to sit insensitized to reality in front of an electronic screen munching chemicals, his ability to interact as dormant as his tail-wagging muscles?"

Janet said, "Honestly, David. Will you ever forgive me for not riding in your damned truck?"

"Driving in just now I saw Dan's boy, Josh, run across a real pasture in real twilight chasing a real dog and being chased by a real horse. He fell down and hit the real ground and he really laughed and he waved at me to assure me he was all right. I'm sorry," David said. "But I'm not ready to have my life lived for me vicariously by stereotypes on television whose wages I pay by consuming coma-inducing chemicals. I use technology, too, but I do what I do consciously and deliberately in hopes I will not lose either my sense of reality or my ability to interact."

Janet said, "Oh, you interact very well, David. I can tell that."

Ellie said, "He calls life here reality therapy."

"I see. Definitely not nostalgia."

"Do you realize," David asked, "what percentage of conversation right now is comprised of the last things heard, seen on the electronic media? There is almost no other conversation. If something real happens to John or Jane Doe, they are in a real storm, for example, or a real accident, the first words out of his or her mouth are, 'It was just like being in a movie!' In fact, I do believe people now are creating problems for themselves, marrying, divorcing, committing crimes, motivated by the desire to enhance their reality by thinking themselves worthy of the attentions of film."

"David," Janet said, "you are preferring a less contemporary reality."

"I am preferring reality. Electronic reality is not reality. It is an illusion sponsored by illusions. It is the biggest drug of all sponsored by drug manufacturers. What you call my nostalgia is my consciously selecting, eclectically if you like, means at my disposal to interact with nature, other human beings, myself, and what-have-you."

Janet poured herself more champagne. "Nice you can afford it."

David grinned. "There is that."

Ellie said, "I'm afraid he's been attacked on this matter before. Milton, Owen, other people who work with him do not understand what David MacFarlane is doing on a farm."

"I know this aspect of David well," Janet said. "He was always an impostor. The man was writing the sexiest, most advanced music of his time, living the most glamorous life, and all he wanted was to go to some mythical home. I'm afraid there was a time when he thought I could show him the way home."

David heard someone coming down the back stairs.

"And what did you want?" Ellie asked Janet.

"I wanted to go days, weeks, months without ever seeing the same face twice . . ."

Janet's chin raised. Light came into her eyes.

Dan Prescott stood in the doorway to David's right.

"Let me see." Dan tipped his head at Janet in mock curiosity. "You're the mother of the bride? Lucille's mother? The lady who is to be Tony's mother-in-law? Am I right?"

"Speaking of faces seen twice." Janet put down her champagne glass and stood.

In the middle of the small parlor at Bass Clef Farm, Janet Twombley Nelson and Dan Prescott, childhood friends now middle aged, hugged each other, but only for the briefest moment.

Dan said to Ellie, "I'm afraid I fell asleep in a chair. Rude of me and inconvenient for you."

"Not a bit inconvenient. We vacuumed around you and you never batted an eyelash."

"In fact," David said, "Clara Reagan said she rubbed furniture polish on you and you took a shine nicely without ever waking up."

"Ummm." Dan held the back of his hand to his nose. "I thought I smelled of lemon."

Janet stood aside openly studying Dan, his face, his hair, what she could see of his body. He wore worn running shoes, loose trousers more than an inch too long for him, a drably colored shirt and necktie, and a shapeless old tweed jacket that again seemed two sizes too big for him.

"Anyone know where Josh is?" Dan asked.

Standing up, David said, "Outside playing with the critturs and the varmints. I saw him when I drove in. What can I get you to drink?"

"Nothing," Dan said. "Not anything. Thank you."

Janet smiled.

"Aren't you hot, Dan?" Ellie asked. "This is a June night in Tennessee. You're dressed warmly enough for a New England clambake."

Sitting down again, Janet said, "Now, Ellie. You're trying to tear the clothes off Dan Prescott the very first minute you see him."

David sat down when he saw Dan sit.

When the lamp light hit Dan's face, David saw he was blushing. David couldn't help laughing.

Dan Prescott blushing!

Dan's clear brown eyes glanced at David.

"Sorry," David said.

"Well, Dan," Janet began. "David's just been explaining to us, in great detail, why someone called him an old fart this afternoon. Of course, such is not news to me. I've always known David is an old fart. Haven't I, David?"

"You've always said so, anyway."

Dan said, "Is it time to beat up on our host? So soon? I should think we'd at least wait until after dinner."

"That's all right," Ellie said. "We're just having lasagna."

David looked from Janet to Dan, back to Janet. The similarity between them had always amazed him. Both, basically, were tall, neatly built, brown-eyed blondes. Dan's hair was graying nicely. Janet's hair probably was, too; it could not naturally be the coppery gold it appeared. Dan's eyes and skin were clearer than Janet's. Janet's face had wrinkles appropriate to her age; Dan's had none. Janet wore makeup, but well. Physically, Dan looked incredibly fit. Clearly, Janet did not have a weight problem she couldn't manage, but David doubted she could run a ten-kilometer race before dinner. David wondered how much the world missed the children they might have created together.

"Tell me, please," David said. "After everything . . . how did your kids meet and decide to marry each other?"

"It is odd, isn't it?" Janet said. "Luce marrying a boy from Columbia Falls, Maine."

"Dan's son!" David stressed.

"I'm not sure I know," Dan said. "I read in a newspaper Tony was going with a model named Cille. Next time I talked to him I asked him if he thought it was wise for a young politician, a White House speech writer, to be seen going out with a model."

Janet said lowly, "A half-black model, I suspect you said, Dan. A mulatto."

"I know I didn't say anything like that."

"No?"

"No."

"You did say, however, '*to be seen* going out with a model.'"

"Yes," Dan said. "I said that."

"But, Dan—" Ellie said.

"I know."

"The story I have," Janet said, "is very dull. They met at a party in New York, at the United Nations, or someplace. They shared a cab back to the airport. Exchanged phone numbers."

"Ah," David said. "Modern romance. Can't stand it. Starts with an electronic exchange."

"That was more than a year ago," Janet said. "Tony came to Paris, where I met him. Then I spent a few days in Antibes with them. I liked Tony immediately. It was only then that I realized he was Dan Prescott's son."

"Has John met him?" David asked.

Janet said, "No."

Dan cleared his throat. "I've yet to meet Cille. I mean, Lucy. I didn't realize Cille was Lucy until a few months ago. I mean, that she was Janet's and John's daughter. I met her when she was first born, of course, in Paris."

"You brought her a stuffed dog, Dan."

"I did?"

"Blue. Luce still has it. It's in her bedroom in the apartment in Paris."

"I've never seen her since. Except in the magazines, of course. A beautiful woman."

"And you're right to point out, Dan: she is older than Tony."

"Did I point that out?"

"By a year or two."

"How did I point that out? Why would I want to point that out?"

To Ellie, Dan was looking very hot.

"I don't think it means a great deal either to Luce or to Tony, David, that their parents knew each other," Janet said. "Of course, they don't listen."

David said, "I find it amazing. You two are in line to be grandparents of the same child, or children. It's as if your genes had been fated to get together, in one generation or another."

"Dan," Janet said, "Ellie and I were discussing something over lunch, and I think the best thing is for me just to come right out with it."

"With what?"

"Are you a minister?"

"Trained and ordained," Dan said.

"Do you have any thought to perform the wedding ceremony for Luce and Tony?"

"No. Good heavens, no. Absolutely not." Dan laughed. "I have given up marrying people, in every way."

"Are you sure?"

"Janet." Dan took a deep breath. "You know I was never assigned a church."

"I don't know anything at all," she said.

"When I applied I wasn't hired. I never received a letter saying I wasn't a minister . . ."

"You were put in coventry," David said.

"I've always had to do other things. I taught school for a while. Then, when there was the publicity, it was mentioned I was an ordained minister, as part of the story. I thought I'd hear from church officials then, defrocking me, but I didn't. Guess they figured any official action on their part would just generate more publicity. I have never served as a minister. And I'm certainly not licensed to perform a wedding in the State of Tennessee. I wouldn't ask."

"I see," Janet said.

David wondered what Janet was thinking.

"Anyway," Dan said. "I've been married twice myself. And divorced. Twice."

"You have?" David asked.

"Tony and Josh are by different mothers."

Ellie asked, "And may we expect Tony's mother to come to the wedding?"

"Tony's mother," Janet said, "was killed in a car crash some years ago. On the Pacific Coast Highway."

Dan said, "Yes. With her third husband."

David was too surprised to say anything. All this was not what David had envisioned as Dan Prescott's life. And there had been many times that David had tried to envision Dan Prescott's life.

Dan stood up. "Guess I'll go find Josh."

"Yes," Ellie said. "We should eat soon."

8

Halfway down the dining room table, more light from the chandelier on him than on anyone else, because of his height, because of his position at table, again Josh asked, "But you did live together?"

"Who?" Dan expostulated.

"Really, Josh," Janet said. "You keep asking that question!"

"All right, if you won't tell me ... I can't get what you're all hiding."

Over dinner, the older people, laughing, frequently hilariously, had been telling him, or not telling him, this sixteen-year-old boy; telling each other, or not telling each other, as much of what did not happen a long time ago as what did happen, making jokes that only two of them sometimes could get, sometimes more, sometimes only the person who made the joke, sometimes seriously informing one or more at table of some misunderstanding that still had not been cleared up, of some expectation denied, now seen humorously, maybe, of some resolution or understanding that had been gained only with perspective and after pain. Josh did not care very much. It had been good lasagna and Italian wine and now good cake and ice cream for dessert and all the grownups had laughed all the way through dinner and Josh was glad to have contributed to that. He didn't understand many of the jokes, or references. When his father had come out of the house to find him for dinner where Josh was sitting on a white fence patting a horse's head, Josh had seen how wet with sweat his father's face was in the moonlight, had heard how his voice shook, just slightly. He knew all this had deep meanings for them, but not for him; that they did or did not understand certain things about themselves but he never would. He liked their laughter.

"Mr. MacFarlane," Josh said with mock seriousness. "Let me get this straight. Who did you live with?"

"Bea."

Even Ellie wrinkled her eyebrows at that one.

"Bea who?"

" B.E.A.," David said. "No longer exists as such. British European Airways. It's the actual truth!" David exclaimed. "I slept aboard her damned near every night!"

"It is the truth!" Janet laughed. "That's what's so sad!"

Before dinner David had put on a linen jacket ostensibly to join Dan in wearing a coat to table. He had changed the tape in his small recorder and slipped it into a side pocket of the jacket.

"Those were different days, Josh," Dan said again. "We were brought up with a sense of permanence."

"What does that mean?" Josh asked.

"Well," Dan said, "that relationships would last a long time, for life, and therefore life was more interesting if we took it slowly with each other. Now, population has doubled, we have become more anonymous in our worlds, relationships more impermanent, and I guess we consume each other faster."

"We're all disposable goods now," David said. "Consume each other and throw each other away."

Josh asked his father, "So who did you live with?"

Dan shook his head.

"Now, wait a minute," Josh said shrewdly. "I've just discovered that you and Mrs. Nelson have known each other since you were younger than I am."

"A lot younger," Janet said.

"You were best friends?"

"Yes," Dan said. "I thought so."

"Best friends, boy, girl," Josh said. "And you didn't sleep together? What sense does that make?"

Dan seemed to be studying the water in his glass. "Somehow I never thought the question would embarrass me." He smiled at his son. "Somehow I never thought the question would come up."

Josh said, "And here you are sitting at the same table, lo, these many years later."

"'Lo'!" David exclaimed. "Apparently high school English hasn't changed."

"So you lived together. Right?"

"Josh," Ellie said.

"Just trying to figure out who I am."

"You know who you are," his father said.

"Yeah, I'm the son of Whistler's Mother," Josh said. "I'm just worried my half-brother is marrying my half-sister, that's all."

"Yes." David offered mock seriousness back to Josh. "Not to worry. That's what's happening."

"How can I be sure?" Josh asked.

"You can be sure," Janet said. "That's not happening."

"That's what should be happening," David said. "Except I got in the way."

"What did you do?"

David laughed. "I asked your mother, I mean, Ms. Tuesday, I mean, Janet, for a date."

"Now you've ripped it," Janet said.

"I thought everyone here agreed Mrs. Nelson isn't my mother," Josh said, grinning.

"Josh," Ellie said. "If I understand it correctly, many people expected your father, that is, Dan Prescott, to marry Mrs. Nelson, that is, Janet Twombly, who Mr. MacFarlane, that is, David, for some reason has always insisted upon calling Ms. Tuesday. Now, is all that clear?"

"By the way, David," Janet asked, "why have you always called me Ms. Tuesday? I never have known."

David shrugged. "To me, you never looked like a Wednesday."

Josh asked his father: "So who did you marry?"

Dan laughed. "I married Janet and David."

"Oh, come on!"

"I did," Dan said. "At least I thought I did."

David said, "I've got something to show anybody who's interested."

"What?" Josh asked.

"I'll give you a hint. It's in a garage."

"Ah," Josh said. "Family rubbish. You want to show us your family rubbish."

"A Mercedes Benz convertible," Janet said. "David, are you that sentimental?"

"Not a Mercedes Benz."

"I've already seen your farm truck," Janet said. "I've even ridden in it, a short way."

After dinner, only David and Dan and Josh went out to the garage.

9

"What is it?" Dan asked.

"It's a car, Dad." Josh was helping David remove the dust cover. "An automobile."

"Don't you recognize it?" David asked.

"Not really," Dan said.

David stood back and looked at the tall, proud machine, its polished metal and chrome gleaming in the fluorescent garage lights.

"You know what it is?" David asked Josh.

Josh read from the rear bumper. "Winslow."

"That's right," David said. "A Winslow car."

"Guess I've heard of them," Josh said.

"A Winslow," David said. "The last good model Winslow ever put out. The first model produced after the war."

"Which war?" Josh asked. "World War One, World War Two, the Korean War, the Vietnam War?"

"You're right, Josh," David said. "That's a different literature."

"That's history," Josh said.

David wasn't sure whether Josh meant wars were history or the car was history, or he and Dan Prescott were history.

The dog was trying to pull the car's dust cover across the garage floor with his teeth.

"Wars can't be important," Dan said. "There are so many of them."

David said, "It is better to measure history by the ideal objects of human aspirations."

Dan chuckled. "Like family cars."

Leaning over, Josh was looking through the car window at the walnut dashboard.

"After 1947 the Winslow people started fooling around with automatic transmissions, fluid drives, designing for better aerodynamics," David said. "The car lost its grace. The company collapsed in 1950, I think."

Dan said, "It must be hard getting parts for it."

"It takes time and money," David said. "But ain't she a beauty?"

"Just like you, Dad," Josh said. "On a pedestal in a museum. I suppose they put a dust cover over you, too, nights and holidays."

David watched Dan's face.

Josh said, "Come on, Jester."

The dog dropped the dust cover and ran after Josh through the garage door.

"I'd like to tell you about it," Dan said.

"About what?" David asked. "About how Dan Prescott became a thing of beauty, a joy to behold forever?"

"I can't blame my sons for never having gotten used to it, never fully accepting it. I haven't either."

"Do you feel you need to explain it to everybody you come across?"

"I did at first. Obviously I explained it to lawyers, but that never did me any good. After a while, after years, I stopped pulling at people's lapels trying to explain what happened, how it happened. Actually, I haven't tried to explain it to anybody in a long, long time, many years in fact. I've never tried to explain it to my sons. I've thought of trying to do so, often enough. It's just a fact of their existence, something they have to live with."

David smiled. "You know, Dan, in a way I suppose I've always thought of you as an icon."

Dan opened and closed his hands to say he did not particularly understand that. "By trying to explain to my sons what happened, how it happened, how I felt about it then and later, I've concluded, hundreds of times, that I'd only be trying to control what they thought, think, about it all, and I cannot control what they think. The impact upon them has been what kids in schoolyards, their mothers, teachers, coaches, dates, whoever else have had to say about their father, most of it, I suppose, neither polite nor understanding. David, you're different. You knew me way back when. I affected your life, for good or bad—"

"I exploited you," David said, "as much as anybody ever has, to get what I wanted. What I thought I wanted."

"Certainly the innocent, asinine way I behaved in Paris affected my life."

"Dan, you'll never believe how innocent I was. We were caught believing in things, you and I. You believed in more than I did, but I, too, believed. That permitted me to exploit you. The century has moved on. We have gotten older. What do we believe now, Dan?"

"Knowing me then, wrapped in a ministerial black suit and a collar, you have to be curious about what happened, about what I did, to turn into a public embarrassment."

"You were a withheld gift to the world, Dan. You were going to get unwrapped one way or another. We all knew that. But I admit to being surprised when I first saw, in Rome, that poster of you, naked as a stallion, promoting Summer in New York."

"What did you think?"

"I thought you were beautiful. The whole world thinks you're beautiful. Whatever else you may think, Dan, you've been a pleasure. I assume there's been some pain involved for you. There always is. I've gone to the New York Museum several times, and admired you. I've even caught myself talking to you, the sculpture of you. Mighty lifelike. Dan Prescott, it's not everyone in this life who becomes a genuine, immortal work of art."

"David, it's not a work of art. I'll explain that to you. It's also not a work of pornography."

"Has anyone ever said it is?"

"It is prurient . . ." As Dan stood in front of David in the lit garage, David saw the same urgent sincerity he had always seen in Dan's deep brown eyes, the plea to be heard more than to be seen. ". . . only in that I'm still alive . . . you see."

"My, my," David said. "Your celebrity is a burden to you."

"I am the obscenity. One of the things that has happened during our lifetimes, David, is that the male has become as much of a sexual object as the female. Have you noticed?"

David said, "I think it's called sexual equality."

"I could not have conceived of myself as a sexual object. Believe that."

"You do represent something, Dan. Or we flatter ourselves by thinking you do. I've thought about this. I suppose you couldn't have looked the way you do if you had been born two hundred years ago, one hundred years ago. You probably wouldn't look the way you do if you had been brought up any other way, in any other—"

"David, I never knew I was anything special, physically, mentally, or spiritually. My parents never told me. Janet never told me."

"I believe that."

"Sure, I noticed women looking at me. Men, too. I thought everybody got looked at that way. I was to be a minister of God, I was one, I am one, except I've never been allowed to carry on a ministry. I never took advantage. David, I was a virgin when you knew me, when I was oh-so-nobly trying to marry off the love of my life, Janet, to you, in Paris. It was after I knew you, later, in Yugoslavia, that I first knew woman, to use a biblical expression. How old was I then?"

"Oh, Dan. Come off it. People don't look like you without effort. I mean, look at you even now. You have to enjoy what you look like, because you sure have kept yourself up. And that takes conscious, deliberate work. Even when I knew you before, in Paris, everyone else your age was developing wine flushes and beer bellies and you always looked as if you'd just played three sets of tennis, napped and showered."

Quietly, Dan said, "I can explain that to you." David sat on the Winslow's running board. In his jacket pocket the reel of his tape recorder was turning slowly. "It's taken years for me to put together an understanding of me, of what happened to me, and why. For example: endorphin. You know what that is?"

David smiled. "I've made its acquaintance only in recent years."

"I just read about it a couple of years ago, in a newspaper. Strenuous exercise gives one an endorphin high. It makes you feel good. It is addictive. Okay, here's this kid who plays sports all through school, does hard farm labor, goes into the service, through boot camp, gets wounded to such an extent he has to spend eighteen months in hospital, having operations and taking therapy—exercising strenuously. David, I didn't realize it until I read that article about it a couple of years ago, but I've been an endorphin addict since I was a child."

"*Twentieth Century American—Male*," David said.

"At least they didn't call it *Preacher Boy*." Dan took off his oversized tweed jacket and hung it from a hook on the tool board. "If I don't get strenuous exercise, every day, I feel worse than someone who's never had any. I feel like an old shoe. I feel terrible right now, because I just spent all that time in a car."

"If you've got to have an addiction, that's the one to have," David said. "Okay, I get your point: you're not ninety-eight percent muscle or whatever for reasons of vanity or narcisism."

Dan nodded. "I came home from Europe, a year after the last wedding we all attended, the only wedding I ever performed—supposedly your wedding to Janet. I forgave myself my belated sexual indulgences in Yugoslavia and elsewhere and applied for a ministry, assignment to a church, anywhere. The hypocrites in charge of such things never said no, they just stalled me. In the meantime, I lived with my parents and got a job teaching high school. I taught math and basic science. I coached all three seasons, football, winter track and baseball. I ran and worked out with the kids. I also tried to keep up my Daddy's little farm. I was in great shape. I married another teacher. We bought a trailer and put it in a patch of wood on my Daddy's land. Tony was born. I guess I thought that was going to be my life. I wasn't serving as a minister, but I was serving as a teacher, and that was fine. My father, whom you remember was a minister, died. And that does affect a man, a son."

Standing on the garage floor in his overly long trousers hanging loosely from his waist, Dan began to fold up his shirt sleeves. His forearms were muscular, tanned; fine, blond hair on his forearms caught the light.

David shook his head. *It is prurient . . . only in that I am alive . . . you see . . . I am the obscenity. . . .*

Dan continued. "An older couple, in their late fifties, named Barkerslee, moved to Columbia Falls from somewhere in Connecticut. They bought one of the old summer houses out on the coast, winterized it, and built onto the house a big, glass-walled room overlooking the ocean. Barkerslee referred to it as his studio. So everyone understood he was an artist, or wanted to be thought so, but no one in town knew of his art. He said he painted and sculpted. A nice couple. The old-time town librarian was getting fired because she wouldn't shift to microfilm or something. The Barkerslees got up a petition to keep her employed until she got to collect her pension. The Barkerslees did that sort of nice thing. One day Jack Barkerslee came to the high school to work with the kids in the art classes. I met him in the teachers' room. After school he came out and watched football practice. The next Sunday afternoon, Mr. and Mrs. Barkerslee, Jack and Louise, showed up at the door of our trailer with a couple of bottles of good wine and better cheese than I'd had since I left Europe. We had a nice afternoon together, playing with the baby. Jack talked about his work, a little bit. I gathered he was no great success as an artist, not a recognized success. He wasn't making any money at it. He had inherited and run a furniture store they'd finally sold and they were living off what money they had. It was like having grandparents in the house, you know what I mean?

"He called me Monday or Tuesday night, and straight out asked me if I would do some modeling for him. I said, 'You mean, Georgette.'"

David asked, "Your wife?"

"Yes. I thought he wanted Georgette to model for him, that he was asking me if I'd mind if he asked Georgette. I mean, Georgette was a girl. A woman. Women modeled, not men. Not unless they had some compulsion, wanted to be an actor, or something.

"In a deep voice, Jack said, 'No, I mean you.'

"That really surprised me. Right away, I said, 'No.' I gave him my excuses. I was teaching full time, coaching, which means I didn't have the afternoons or Saturdays free. I was working the farm. He said all he needed was a full afternoon of taking pictures of me every which way. You know, I wouldn't have to sit for weeks or months having my picture painted, nothing like that. The suggestion rattled me. I didn't mind going over to a neighbor's and letting him take my picture so he could paint a portrait of me, if it would do him any good. Like anyone else, I was sort of curious as to what it would look like. Truth is—you know what was mainly in my mind?—I thought my wife would be jealous. She was the pretty one. How could I go even to a neighbor to have my picture painted when she hadn't been invited? So I said, 'No.'

"A couple of Saturdays later he showed up at a football game and said, 'Come over tomorrow so we can take those photos of you.' I was busy, so I don't think I answered. He met me on the street a week later, and said, 'When are you coming over?' I just laughed. On a beautiful fall Sunday morning, he called early and said, 'If you come over now, everything is set up. Louise and I were doing some photography yesterday. It's hard work setting this equipment up, taking it down, setting it up again. As long as it's all set up, we thought we'd give you a call. What else have you got to do today?' In fact, I hadn't anything much to do that day. Georgette had taken the baby, Tony, to spend the day at her parents' house. I was just going to laze around the trailer, correct some school papers. I wasn't even going to attend church. Maybe I was a little lonely, without my wife and baby. So I said, 'Okay. I'll be right over.' This is the funny part. I polished my loafers, put on clean white socks, clean jeans and a checkered red shirt Georgette had just given me for my birthday. I thought it would be nice if he photographed me dressed that way.

"I had never been in their house before. It was beautifully furnished. We sat in the living room and Louise gave Jack and me coffee and pastry. He sat in a soft chair playing with a camera. Every few minutes he'd aim it at me and take a real casual picture. We laughed about things going on in the town. After a while, Jack said, 'Ready?'

"'Haven't you got enough pictures of me already?'

"'I haven't started yet.'

"I followed him into the studio. The sunlight reflecting off the ocean through the windows was dazzling. I went to the window and looked down into the pine trees between the house and the sea.

"He said, 'Dan, what I want is to do a full sculpture of you, standing. What I need is a full anatomy.'

"'What do you mean?'

"'I need to make a full anatomical study of you. Everything about your body. How it works.' He laughed. 'In two words: strip, kid.'

"In the studio, a camera was set up on a tripod, lights were affixed here and there, reflectors, everything aiming at the space before a side wall. Otherwise the studio was a clutter of muddy abstract paintings and twisted steel sculptures. Clearly, his inventory was not moving.

"Louise yelled from the kitchen, 'Jack? Absolutely we must have his permission.'

"'Oh, yeah,' Jack said. 'I almost forgot.'

"On a dirty, small table were a telephone, a note pad, a pen, and a single piece of paper. He handed me the piece of paper. 'This says you give me permission.' He handed me the pen.

"In fact, I didn't read it too well. I, a school teacher. The word *likeness* was repeated over and over again. I saw that. I was thinking furiously, or, maybe, feeling. I don't know what was going through my brain, or my glands. All this isn't much of a story; I mean, who basically cares if a guy gets his picture taken in an isolated house in November on the coast of Maine? I mean, gets his picture taken naked? A difference to me was that my father had been a preacher and I had meant to be a preacher. This was happening to me. I saw my hand signing the piece of paper. And that brings up the question I'm sure you will ask, because I've been asking myself the same question for well over twenty years now, of what I wanted at that moment of my life, in that place, what I really wanted.

"At the moment I was in a bit of a cold sweat. I had just given Jack Barkerslee permission to do something he couldn't do unless I did something. I had to get naked. I had spent enough of my life in locker rooms so that being naked in public meant nothing to me. In fact, I remembered my father saying, 'One is not comfortable with oneself unless one is comfortable as naked as created by God. Naked we come into the world, and naked we leave it. Naked are we in the eyes of the Lord.' The old man had something to say about everything. It was the fact that someone deliberately was going to be looking at me, taking pictures of me, for whatever reason, that was unsettling. I had enjoyed running down a football field. I had never fantasized myself doing so naked. You know what I mean? I decided I was about to go for a swim in the river, or in the pond, think of it that way, or, I was in a locker room with Jack.

"I kicked off my shined loafers, pulled off my socks, pulled my shirt out of my pants, removed it, dropped my jeans, stepped out of my underpants, all very quickly. And stood there.

"Now, David, however odd it may seem to hear me say so, after all that has happened to me, I have to tell you that that was one of the nicest days I have ever spent in my life. There are few days I have enjoyed more. The room was warm, filled with sunlight sparkling through the windows off the sea, filled with the big, white photography lights Jack turned on. It was cold outside, November. Maybe I had been missing my body the way you do in November, as you bury yourself more and more under winter clothes. Jack seemed to work professionally, expressionlessly. When he stopped fiddling with the lights and looked at me, up and down, standing nude in the middle of the room, he said, 'That's right. Leave your wristwatch on. That's a great idea.' He called me to the side of the room, to the space in front of the wall, facing the cameras, and I was just bathed in this warm light. Truly, it felt just nice, as if by standing there nude in the lights having my picture taken I was saying, *Hey, I exist, I'm okay, I am ashamed of nothing. This is what I am.*"

David said, "It is your relaxed masculine pride that is so apparent in the work, your non-aggressive self-assurance that makes the work so magical yet so non-prurient. The way you stood, the expression on your face, which, give him credit, Barkerslee did catch, said exactly that: *This is what I am, and that's okay with me.*"

"That day in Barkerslee's studio I found myself thinking about the doctrine of original sin, and doubting it. Can you believe that?"

"I suppose so."

"I found myself thinking, *I was not born morally deficient, or deficient in any way. And I have never sinned.*"

"All that feeling about yourself is what Barkerslee caught."

"It was also slightly sexually stimulating."

"Also visible."

"After a while, Louise entered the room with a tray of cut sandwiches and a pitcher of cold cider. Jack opened a package of cigarettes and handed me one. 'Here, hold this in your hand.'

"'I don't smoke.'

"'I know, but I've got an idea.'

"Jack continued to use the camera on the tripod.

"Louise moved around me, taking pictures.

"After a while, Jack said, 'Okay. Let's take a break. You must be getting tired.'

"I did not reach for my jeans, or my underpants. I did not want them on. I was comfortable, maybe more comfortable than I had ever been in my life, or have been since. Thinking about that day all these years I realized there was something infantile about it all. Here I was, naked as a newborn, with an older couple who were feeding me and giving me all their attention. I sat on the paint-scarred hardwood floor and ate. Both Jack and Louise kept moving around me taking pictures of me.

"In fact, I was becoming a piece of meat hung up in a public market.

"'Why are you taking pictures of me now?' I asked. 'Why don't you eat?'

"'We need to see how your body works,' Jack said, 'record you in different positions. See what happens to your stomach when you sit.'

"I had never had such an experience, of course. I cannot calculate how much film they used that day. More film than I knew existed in the world. After I ate they had me move around the studio, their cameras chattering continuously, sit here, there, this way, that way, pretend to kick a football, run a few steps. They even had me roll around the floor while they took pictures. It was fun. What has amazed me since is how absolutely sure of myself I was that day. They even took close-ups of every part of my body, my ears, my neck, my collar bone, my biceps, nipples, thighs, calves, ankles, and everything else, penis. Jack, using a tape measure, measured every inch of my body, the circumference of my legs, arse, waist, chest every few centimeters, the length of absolutely everything, as Louise noted the measurements on a drawing she had made of a body on a pad of paper."

"You must have felt very much like an object."

"That, too. I realized that. I remember admitting to myself, with a lazy sort of indifference, *I am an object. Isn't that nice?* I met all kinds of reality that day."

David asked, "Is there any chance you were drugged? Are you sure this nice older couple didn't slip something into your coffee?"

"I've wondered. Talking to the lawyers, I wished I could say I thought so. But I have no reason for thinking so, except that I acted that day in a way I had never acted before. I've had no experience with drugs. But I had no sensation of being drugged, during the day or later. If anything, I was sort of drugged on myself, the attention I was getting. I have to be honest."

"I know. I wonder how much how we all treated you in Paris had to do with this."

"As the natural light was going they put me back at the side of the room under the photography lights, again with cigarette in hand. While I stood reasonably still, Jack moved the tripod around me, taking pictures of me more slowly, deliberately.

"During that day was put together the source material for the life-sized bronzed statue now in the New York Museum, *Twentieth Century American—Male*: me, nude, standing sort of on one hip, wearing a watch on my left wrist, cigarette in my right hand. Table-sized reproductions available in probably every museum gift shop in the world. Also every sex shop."

"Dan—"

"No, I want to continue telling you my feelings of that day. Finally, Jack said we were finished. He turned off the lights. He said, 'Let's have a drink, and then you can take a shower before heading home.' And that's what I did. I sat with them in their living room, naked, to use your expression, as a stallion, and drank two whiskeys with them. Again, we talked about my teaching school, coaching, my kid, people in the town. Nice none of the townfolk took that moment to drop in. I tell you again, I was perfectly comfortable."

"I understand that."

"Then I took a shower, got dressed, and went home to the trailer."

"Did you tell your wife?"

"No. I told her I'd walked over and had a drink with the Barkerslees. Great mistake. You see, David, I thought nothing would come of it. To me, Jack Barkerslee was just an old guy messing with his toys in a converted beach house. I thought, sooner or later, I'd see some unrecognizable, twisted steel version of me in their yard.

"About eighteen months later I read in the newspaper that the city of Portland had turned down the gift of a sculpture called *Twentieth Century American—Male,* offered by the sculptor, Jack Barkerslee. The city turned it down because it was a life-sized and unabashedly nude statue of a male. Portland wasn't the up-and-coming city then it is now. And in the newspaper was a photograph of what was quite clearly, at least to me, my head. No one else seemed to recognize it. I mean, Georgette, the other teachers didn't. So I said, 'Phew. That's that.'

"About three years later I saw a photograph of the sculpture in a magazine, from the belly button up, promoting the New York Museum. I called the museum from a pay phone outside a garage in Columbia Falls. Someone had bought the sculpture and given it to the museum."

"Wait a minute. You never saw the Barkerslees again?"

"Not really. On the street. You see, after the fact, I became a little embarrassed with them."

"They never invited you and your wife to their house again, to see the finished work?"

"No."

"They really had you, didn't they?"

"At some point, they moved to New York. I was still keeping quiet about all this. I dreaded someone recognizing that statue as me. But, you know, people are not prone to identify a statue in the New York Museum with the young teacher living in a trailer in a patch of woods not far from the church."

"I suppose not."

"Then the damned book came out. A huge, beautifully printed coffee table book, with the sculpture of me on the cover, and, inside, nothing but hundreds of pictures of me, bare-assed, in color, in every kind of position, including close-ups of my skin, my ears, my nipples, the calves of my legs. Called *Studies for Twentieth Century American—Male.*"

"I know," David said. "We have a copy."

"Everybody has a copy. I'll try to make the rest of this story short. I wasn't rehired, to teach the next semester. I wrote the Barkerslees, congratulating them on their success and telling them I had lost my job. No answer. I went to a local lawyer. He treated me like the town disgrace. I had signed a release. No part of the profits of the book, etc., could be mine. I had given my rights away to the Barkerslees. There was no point in suing. Also, the local school board had the right to hire and not hire whomever they pleased. He said, 'In fact, they have the obligation not to hire anyone they feel would be detrimental to the morals of the town young.' I went to a lawyer in Portland. He said the same thing. Georgette and I literally were down to a few dollars."

"How did she take all this?"

"'Mortified' was the word she used. She said she was mortified. She said every time she was with other women, she could just feel them thinking about her husband's privates. Most of the people in Columbia Falls couldn't afford much, but they all seemed to be able to afford that book. I was staying on the farm as much as I could."

"Nice."

"A Hollywood producer appeared at my woodpile one morning. Invited me to Los Angeles for a screen test. We were so broke, we went. At least we got fed free for a week. I tried acting in front of the cameras; I was terrible. I tried not acting in front of the cameras; I was terrible. I was so disappointing, I don't think they wanted to pay our hotel bill.

"Georgette was with me, but sometime during the trip, she turned quiet. Ten days after we arrived home, one of the cameramen who had worked with me in California showed up at the trailer in Maine. Georgette was real glad to see him. Well, six weeks later she started divorce proceedings against me. I had caused her mental anguish, she claimed. 'Mortification.'"

"You've done a lot of modeling over the years, Dan."

"Yes. I've modeled shirts and suits and shorts and socks and sneakers, trousers and towels, bathrobes, slippers, eyeglasses, you name it, you've seen it all, I expect. What else could I do? It was my only way of making a living. Preacher-teacher becomes male model."

"That was profitable, wasn't it?"

"Not as much as people think. Also, there have been times in my life, most times, when I've been paying two alimonies and child support for two children who needed airfares to transport them among as many as seven different residences. Boarding school tuitions and camp fees. Tony's college expenses. Georgette's second marriage didn't last long. I married a woman in New York, Josh's mother, who, I guess, wanted to be married to a sculpture. She wanted to parade me through New York cocktail parties, pet me possessively in public. She was oh, so surprised to discover I really wasn't a statue. My mother died and I inherited the farm in Columbia Falls. My second wife divorced me, charging me with abandonment, while I was spending a few weeks on the farm, trying to recover some sense of myself as a subject rather than as an object. Off and on I've worked in Mr. Twombly's hardware store. Do you understand me? The hardware store of Janet's father, in Columbia Falls. I had helped him out in the store as a teenager, so I knew where everything was."

"I daresay you attracted an uncommon number of women customers."

"Not funny, really. The joke was that women would come into the hardware store wanting a screw. Mr. Twombly was nice to let me work there. No, David, I have the farm, which is virtually worthless, and whatever I can make as an aging, over-exposed male model."

"'Over-exposed,'" David said.

"Exactly." Dan let out a big breath. "Is this what you expected from that virgin minister you once knew named Dan Prescott?"

"No." Sitting on the running board of the Winslow car, David folded his arms. "I've always enjoyed thinking about you, Dan."

"Why?"

"I guess I regretted my own background. Brought up in a city apartment. Being an entertainer of the night. In airports I've thought of you, up in Maine, making babies, preaching the good news to the folks, chopping wood. For some reason it never dawned on me that a preacher can't be a male model, for ... towels. Why can't he? It was that wonderful pride you had in yourself, as a man, that was your preachment to me. I heard it loud and clear, without your having to say a word. Could you look at it this way? That statue of you in New York in a way is your preachment. It says more about Man, and Nature, and God, God's creation, than probably you could have said in a lifetime preaching from some pulpit in Maine."

"It's not a work of art, David."

"Why not? It's in a museum, of which you are painfully aware."

"Isn't a work of art supposed to have some exaggeration, some lie that reveals the truth, some expression of the artist to be art? That sculpture is no expression of Jack Barkerslee. It is an exact, measured, centimeter-by-centimeter reproduction of me."

"You're the work of art, what you are, what other people and yourself made of you," David said. "Barkerslee was an artist, in that he perceived in you the statement of what you are, that we all are, sort of, that we all saw but didn't quite catch."

"Bullshit. I was a preacher's boy, half-educated war veteran as naive as life is long. Maybe with some good genes, which I didn't realize I had, that made my shoulders exactly twice as wide as my hips. Isn't that the Dan Prescott you knew in Paris?"

"Yes."

"Why didn't you tell me? I think Jack Nelson tried to tell me."

David said, "Isn't it a cliché that life is the process of self-discovery? Not all of us discover, reveal, if you will, so much about ourselves in one day, I will admit, as apparently you did. Who were we to tell you anything?"

"Why haven't you asked me that question?"

"What question?"

"As to why I really took off my clothes for those people, posed naked? What was I trying to show, as far as I was concerned?"

"I think you were trying to show pride in what a man could be, with innocence."

"Try bullet holes."

"I was wondering when you were going to mention that."

"David, I think I wanted people to see the holes around my waist of where the bullets entered and where they exited."

"They're there, visible," David said. "The wrist watch, the cigarette, the bullet holes. It's the bullet holes around your waist while you're standing there glowing with health, pride, innocence, that makes *Twentieth Century American—Male* so damned powerful a statement, at least to me."

"If anything, that was what was important to me. I don't really know why. I wasn't trying to say, *Look what happened to me, poor me.* I don't think so."

"That's just the point," David said. "The sculpture, the photographs are completely devoid of self-pity. Anything but."

"Maybe I wanted to say, *Look at what and how well you, I, we, Man can survive.*"

"How did you survive, Dan?"

Dan paced the garage floor. "It was snowing when I was shot. The wounds froze. Otherwise I would have bled to death. Or so the medics told me."

David said, "I was talking to Nonnie the other day. She's the daughter of our tenants. Fifteen years old. She had never heard the name of the particular war you were in."

"So it goes," Dan said, "when you are a citizen of a big nation, with worldwide interests. Important things happen to individual citizens that are not particularly important to the nation."

"I've drawn a parallel," David said. "Forgive me. I've always had trouble with religion. I suppose I commit heresy or sacrilege or something. Between *Twentieth Century American—Male* and Christ on the cross. Perfection, yet suffering. And you can't tell me they hung Jesus dressed in any kind of a diaper. After all, the purpose was to mortify Him."

Outside, Jester was barking loud and long.

In the lit garage, David MacFarlane, sitting on the running board of the Winslow, and Dan Prescott, standing in baggy clothes on the painted cement floor, looked at each other.

10

Josh came rushing into the garage. "Jester has found something, the other side of the fence."

The dog was barking hard enough to alert the moon.

"Probably just a wounded animal." Clicking off the tape recorder in his pocket, David stood up.

Josh said, "I think it's a person. Lying on the ground. I didn't go over the fence."

David and Dan followed Josh across the back yard to the upper fence. In the pasture a few meters the other side of the fence a person in the hay was struggling to get up. The dog danced around the person in the moonlight barking at him as if warning him not to move.

David said to the person, "Wait a minute. Take it easy."

All three climbed over the fence.

Head down, his face in shadow, a heavy young man was sitting in the hayfield as if dropped there. Nearby a few steers chewed indifferently.

David said, "Rupert? Is that you?"

"I'm all right."

"What happened to you?"

"I'm all right."

The young man spat on the ground.

David said to Dan, "A neighbor's boy."

Crouching in front of him, Josh touched Rupert's face. "Bloody."

Rupert turned his head away. "He's very bloody." Josh wiped his fingers on his own legs.

Dan asked, "Were you in an accident?"

"Can you move?" David asked. "Can you get up?"

Josh and Dan helped Rupert to his feet.

Scanning the white fence in the moonlight, Dan asked, "Where's a gate?"

"Too far," David answered. "Let's see if we can get him over the fence. Can you make it over the fence, Rupert?"

Once they had surmounted the fence, David went ahead to the house.

David propped open the kitchen screen door.

Ellie said to him, "David, *The New York Times* just called. Asked if we are expecting John Bart Nelson. I said we haven't heard from him. Also, Dr. MacBride called. I didn't know where to find you. What are you doing?"

"We have a bit of an emergency here."

Through the door Ellie saw Dan and Josh walking bloodied Rupert between them. "Oh, my," she said. "Do we need a doctor?"

"Yes," David said.

"No," Rupert said.

"We'll see," Ellie said. "Sit him here." She placed a solid wooden chair on the brick kitchen floor under the fluorescent light.

Rupert's head lolled back. His left eye had been hit hard. Both cheekbones were turning blue. His nose was broken and bleeding both from its bridge and nostrils. His lips were bleeding from several cuts. A blue welt was rising under the boy's left jaw.

Even with his head back Rupert's arms embraced his ribs.

Dan said, "He's been pretty badly beaten."

David asked Rupert, "Did you lose consciousness? Were you unconscious? Were you knocked out?"

Filling a pan with warm water at the kitchen sink, Ellie said, "He can't talk, David. His mouth is full of blood."

Josh picked up Jester's empty food bowl from the kitchen floor and held it in front of Rupert's face. His right hand urged Rupert's head forward.

Rupert spat blood into the bowl. Clutching his ribs, he vomited into it.

Dan closed the screen door. "Mosquitoes."

David said, "There are no mosquitoes."

Josh dumped the contents of the food bowl into the sink and

sprayed it down with the hose. Ellie was finding rags in a cupboard.

Then, while Ellie gently cleaned Rupert's face with warm water, to see the cuts, Josh stood by with the empty dog bowl.

David had never noticed the numerous slight scars on Rupert's face before.

Head down, Jester padded around the kitchen like a regretful hero.

Josh said, "He's wearing a medical alert tag."

"What does that mean?" David asked. "Diabetes?"

"Probably," Dan said.

"Are you diabetic?" David asked.

"Yes."

"Are you carrying insulin?" Josh asked.

Rupert spat more blood into the bowl. "At the house."

David asked, "Did your Dad do this to you?"

In svelte black negligee and wrap Janet floated into the kitchen. At the door, her eyes widened.

"Rupert," David repeated. "Did your Dad beat you up?"

After a moment, Josh said, "I think he's got some cracked ribs, too."

"Because if you think you lost consciousness, even for a moment, Rupert, we have to call a doctor or get you to the hospital."

Through blood and fat lips Rupert said, "They'd report it."

"Yes," David said angrily. "They'd report it."

What made David most angry were the streaks of tears through the blood on the boy's face.

"He could use some stitches on his face," Ellie said. "Over his eye. The nose probably needs setting."

"Got some Q-tips?" Josh asked.

"More trouble," Rupert said.

Ellie said, "Having it reported would just make more trouble for him, David. Some day, Rupert has to go home. That's life."

"That bastard," David said.

"It's okay," Rupert said. "I had it coming."

"I can probably do it with butterfly bandages," Josh said.

Still in the doorway, Janet said, "Is this real life, David? A half-conscious boy bleeding all over your kitchen at ten-thirty at night?"

"His father beat him up. Neighbors. Halburton. Bastard," David said.

Looking at the heavy young man, Janet said, "At least he's got enough blood in him."

"He'll need his insulin," Josh said.

David said, "Same bastard who shot our peacock."

Ellie dumped the bloodied water from the pan into the sink and quickly rinsed the pan and the sink. She went to the bathroom off the kitchen.

Rupert vomited again. Josh was ready with the water bowl.

"Oh, joy," Janet said. "What I really came down for was some warm milk."

Rupert was wriggling a front tooth with his finger. Printed on his bloody T-shirt was: TELL SOMEBODY YOU SAW ME.

Ellie took the vomit-filled bowl from Josh and handed him the medical kit from the bathroom.

Watching Josh, Dan leaned against the kitchen sink, hands in his trouser pockets.

David went to the wall phone and dialed Halburton's number.

"Mr. Halburton? David MacFarlane. I thought I ought to call you to tell you your son is here, in case you were worried."

"No," Rupert said. "It's okay. I had it comin'."

Halburton said, "I thought he'd go crawling to a neighbor."

"The dog found him," David said. "Your son is beat up pretty bad. Black eye, with a bad cut over it, broken nose, lose tooth, other cuts and abrasions, and, we suspect, cracked ribs."

"Yeah," Halburton said. "That would be about right."

"I suspect he's been unconscious."

"So? He's gone whining to a neighbor."

"He needs medical attention," David said.

Halburton said nothing.

"Is he diabetic?" David asked.

Halburton hung up the phone.

"Goddamn it!" David hung up.

Ellie said, "I'm afraid somebody has to go get Rupert's insulin."

"Not I," said David.

Dan said, "I'll go. Is it just up the road?"

"The only house up there," Ellie said.

"Not unless you want murder done in this valley tonight," David concluded. "I could not see that bastard right now without ripping his head off."

Dan grinned. "I'd be delighted to whack somebody tonight."

"Maybe Edith Halburton will bring it down," Ellie said. "If she's not locked in the basement."

"Ah!" Janet opened the refrigerator door and took out a bottle of milk. "Is there anything more soothing than the sight of a well-stocked refrigerator?"

Josh laughed. "Rupert probably will need something to eat. For his diabetes."

"I'd better go," Dan said.

"Maybe I ought to go with you," David said.

Dan laughed. "No, no, no, no. I'm not afraid to face one mad, ugly guy, but I don't want to have to deal with two of you at the same time."

"Take the dog with you," David said.

"Sure," Dan said. "Here, Spot."

11

In bed, David was reading Olive Ann Burns' *Cold Sassy Tree.*

When Ellie entered the bedroom, David said, "All that remind you of anything?"

Ellie grinned. "This beat-up boy wasn't carrying a saxophone."

He said, "I guess by the time you're our age not much can happen that doesn't remind you of something."

After she showered and got into bed, she said, "I put Rupert to bed in the common room, near the kitchen refrigerator and bathroom. I covered the couch with two sheets and left a vomit bucket on the floor. That boy, Josh, was a great help."

"Was Dan's mission successful?"

"Edith Halburton handed him the insulin through the door, opened just a crack. There was no trouble. I'll call her in the morning."

"Are you reading?"

"No. Let's get some sleep while we can."

David put his book on the bedside table and turned off the light.

"David," Ellie said. "With your friends here, I mean Dan and Janet . . . how do you feel about our . . . I mean, being together this way?"

In the dark bedroom, David blinked.

Ellie chuckled. "Janet said this afternoon, about me, about my having known you even longer than she has, that she hadn't realized you knew anybody *respectable* in the old days."

"I don't get it," David said.

"Well . . ."

"You haven't done anything all these other women, and men, haven't done. Except you did it professionally. And that means deliberately, consciously, for money, and, I expect, a hell of a lot more safely."

"It's the *for money* that matters, David."

"We all spend our lives selling ourselves one way or another," David said. "You just did it basically, consciously, and profitably." He said, "Maybe Dan has spent his life climbing a cross." David took Ellie in his arms. "Hey, I'm not the first guy who considers himself damned lucky to be in bed with a courtesan."

"An older courtesan."

"An old friend," David said.

"I like that word. 'Courtesan.'"

"We were both entertainers." David kissed her. "Nightly entertainers."

In bed:

I'm going to ride that horse tomorrow. A Tennessee walking horse. I asked William and he said, "Why not? Just ask the boss."

Mr. MacFarlane is the boss, I guess. I'll ask him first thing in the morning.

William said, "He's a Tennessee walking horse. That's why you probably think he walks funny. You've probably never seen a real Tennessee walking horse before. His name is Lord Byron or something like that, something funny. We just call him Byron. Nearly everything around here is named peculiar. Bass Clef Farm. Ain't no deep cliffs around here."

I told William I know how to saddle a horse, that I've ridden sometimes, at least when I've been up on the farm in Maine with Dad, although there are no real horses up there near where he lives. There ought to be. I never have saddled a horse before, but I'm sure I can figure it out. I found all the saddle stuff, bit and bridle, in a room in the barn. I can figure it. In actual fact, I've never really ridden a horse before, a real horse, but I absolutely know I can figure it out. Once I get on it I'll be all right, and I know how to get on a horse. From the left. You mount a horse from the left. You sit straight. You hang on with your knees. I know how to use reins. I know how to ride a horse.

William said, "Okay, but do me this favor, will you? Let me check after you get done saddling Byron. That horse knows enough to fill his chest with wind when someone he doesn't know saddles him. He puffs himself up so that no matter how you tighten things, as soon as you get on, the saddle is apt to slip right off. Did you know a smart horse is apt to do that?" I admitted I didn't. "Sure," William said. I like the way William talks, so careful. "A horse has just enough of a brain to be a right nuisance."

I want to ride up that big hill way behind the barns and see how the hill is kept so clean and look around from up there, down on the farm houses and barns, the whole valley, maybe figure out where Halburton lives. As I ride up the hill, maybe Jester will run along with me and the horse. Let's see. I mustn't ride the horse straight down the hill. If he got goin' faster and faster down the hill I wouldn't be able to stop him. I can figure out that much. I ought to come down the hill in a zig-zag. Up the hill, maybe, too. That would be easier on the horse. I can figure all that out.

Sure, I know how to ride.

I'll show Nonnie I know how to ride.

I wonder if she knows how to ride. Sure. She's brought up here.

Maybe after I ride a little bit by myself, the other side of the hill, Nonnie will come riding with me. We could ride on the same horse, the same saddle.

Think of bein' beat up so bad by your Daddy. That kid was really hurtin'. He'd been cryin', too. I figure him for about eighteen. He'd been unconscious. Jesus. What had he done to deserve that? Stole a car, maybe . . .

Mrs. Nelson might have been my mother. Think of that. That's what Mrs. MacFarlane sort of said. That would have been all right. Instead of going to New York City all these years to see my mother I would have had to go to Paris, France. I wonder what the airport in Paris, France, is like. I guess she's rich. She arrived in a limousine. I bet her apartment in Paris is bigger than my mother's apartment in New York. Maybe I wouldn't have had to sleep on the couch when I was visiting her. Maybe in her apartment I could have had a room of my own. Not be such a nuisance. Maybe I could have stayed with her longer periods of time because she had the room for me. I could have even had friends come over, meet my mother. Maybe if Dad had married Mrs. Nelson they might have stayed married and I wouldn't have to visit anybody. I could just be at home all my life, not away at school or summer camp, visiting people as a nuisance. I mean, they knew each other so young and all. They could have gotten married and had me as a kid and stayed put.

That would have been all right.

I wonder why Dad didn't marry Mrs. Nelson.

Maybe they had a fight.

I wonder if they remember what the fight was about, what it was all about. At least I know it wasn't about me. It couldn't have been . . .

In bed:

Jesus, he's beautiful. I'll never get to sleep. Oh, God, he is just gorgeous.

Kids growing up together in Maine, we did everything to each other, in the Jeep, on the grass by the pond, in the den at my house, when we could, with our fingers, with our lips, with our mouths. We fingered each other ecstatic and licked and kissed each other sore. It's a wonder we left each other any skin. Never, never have I held Dan Prescott inside me. Oh, God, to do so; to ever have done so. The first, when you're kids, is the most thrilling, whatever it is. It was thrilling. Those incredible legs of his wrapped around me. His long, strong back. Those eyes filled with lust a nose length from mine. There never has been anything so thrilling. Why didn't I know it? Why didn't I wait for him to do his minister thing, to do life together? Why didn't I accept that he did not want to commit what he considered sin, get absolutely naked together, fuck fully, and just wait, wait, wait for him, and have our lives together, a life of making love to Dan Prescott, his skin, his muscle mine, his eyes always in mine? We had a life of time, then.

Dan Prescott, Columbia Falls, Maine, just wasn't big enough for me. I had the real need to breathe, to explore, to rush out into the world, to find me. I had my independence. Why not? If I hadn't, I wouldn't speak French now. I wouldn't have had John. I wouldn't be married to somebody vaguely famous. I wouldn't have run my own business. I wouldn't be rich. And I am rich.

I found me, sort of.

Jesus. Do I love Dan Prescott more than the me I found?

There is still time.

He is some kind of a physical miracle. He hugged me, a little. What's the word? Perfunctorily. He hugged me perfunctorily. He still has a hard chest, hard arms. His back is still as hard as wood. The clearest eyes, the clearest skin I've seen all these years in France. How has he done it? He's some kind of a miracle. After being so badly wounded . . . during those eighteen months we knew he was wounded but didn't see him because he was in the hospital the other side of the world . . . I wonder if Dan Prescott died for me at that time, somehow, died a little. I realized he could die, and that frightened me. Maybe I loved him so much I could never take the possibility, the terror of his death again. Maybe knowing he was so near death released me somehow, unbound me from him. I came unglued. I ran from him. I did not spend my life with him, loving him, being loved by him, going to bed with him, being touched and hugged and fucked by him. His body seems the same, the body of the same teenager, young man I once knew, the same, by some miracle. He's been married, twice. All that sense of sin must have been beaten out of him by now. It's been beaten out of everybody. Now I can get into bed with him, between cool sheets, lie with him naked, feel his whole body, the length of it, tight against me, around me, take him inside me . . .

He is in the next room. He is in a bed just the other side of this wall, so close . . .

Oh, Jesus, oh, God, he is so beautiful . . .

Merde. That damned boy, his son, what's his name? Josh? Is sleeping in the room with him . . .

12

.22 rifle in hand, towel around his waist, barefooted, quietly and slowly David MacFarlane opened the door onto the upper balcony of the house. Holding the door open with his left elbow, he sighted along the rifle barrel in the early dawn light. They never gave him much time. Sharp-eyed and sharp-eared, excellent at communicating with each other, at the slightest sight or sound of him they would be gone.

He fired quickly.

This morning, midst the great crying and fluttering, one hesitated, then dropped down through the branches of the big tree onto the ground.

David did not raise the rifle again. The rest were in the air now, flying away.

There was never time for more than one quick shot.

"Who's shooting?"

In underpants, Josh came through the door onto the balcony.

"Good morning," David said. "Starlings."

"Why are you shooting starlings?"

"Hate to," David said. "They're noisy. They get in the house, the attics, make a mess and a smell. The real reason is they can give us a disease. A lung disease."

"Really?" Josh's sleepy eyes examined the rifle.

David clicked the safety on and handed the rifle to the boy. "It's only a .22."

"I know." Josh took it and after checking for himself that the safety was on began aiming it here and there around the barnyard across the street. "I've been hunting with my Dad. In Maine."

"Where is he now?"

"Who?"

"Your Dad. Is he up yet?"

"Yes. I guess he's gone running. He's not in bed."

"Then who's that?" David asked.

"Who?"

"That man at the corner of the nearer barn."

Josh lowered the rifle and looked.

To their left there was a slight fog over the meadows the half mile down to the river. The barnyard was perfectly clear.

A powerfully built young man dressed in white slacks and a dark blue shirt was standing at the corner of the barn looking up at the house. He wore glasses. A late model car was parked near the tractor shed.

"It's not William," David said.

Josh said, "It's not William."

"It's not Jock."

"It's not Jock."

"It's not Frank."

There was a wonderful grin on Josh's face in the light of the rising sun.

"It's not Frank."

David said, "It's not Josh."

Josh said, "It's not Josh."

"Who is it?" David asked.

"How would I know?"

David waved.

The young man by the barn waved back. He turned and disappeared from view.

"Guess he's a friendly," David said.

Josh said, "That's why I didn't shoot him."

Looking to the road down to his left, David said, "Here comes William."

Josh squinted into the sunrise at the small blue pickup truck coming up the road. "He's being followed."

"The new bull calves," David said. "Come watch them unload. They're funny when they arrive. They have jet lag."

"Have they been on a jet?"

"Travel fever. They've spent the night on that truck coming from Florida. They'll stagger around just like people getting off an all-night flight. Only don't laugh too loud in front of William. Sometimes critturs die of travel fever."

"Do humans die of jet lag?" Josh asked.

"I have," David answered. "Several times."

In the kitchen, while David was pouring himself a mug of coffee, Ellie said, "He was gone when I came down."

"Who?"

"Rupert. He cleaned up after himself pretty well."

In the common room, sheets were neatly folded at the end of the couch. A rinsed bucket was in the sink.

David asked, "Do you still intend to call Mrs. Halburton?"

"Oh, yes. Without delay."

Ellie picked up the phone and dialed.

"Edith? Good morning. This is Ellie MacFarlane. Have you seen Rupert this morning?"

"He showered and went to work. Couldn't eat the breakfast I made him with those loose teeth of his. Went right off to work."

"Naturally, we're concerned about him." Across the kitchen, Ellie made an exasperated face at David.

"Don't you be concerned about him. He should be concerned about himself."

"Edith, he had a concussion, a broken nose, broken ribs, cuts that needed stitches."

"He sassed his father, you know."

"Is that what happened? I mean, is that all that happened?"

"That's enough, isn't it? Rupert needed setting down. Can't live in his father's house and sass his father, can he?"

"He was severely beaten, Edith."

"Rules are rules. They never change. Now, if you'll excuse me I've got to fix his father's breakfast."

Ellie hung up the dead phone. "Oh, my."

David asked, "Did she thank you for your help and concern?"

"I didn't call for thanks."

"I know."

"Or to be a nosy neighbor. I called to make sure someone had seen Rupert this morning."

"Has she?"

"Yes. He's gone to work. David, apparently she feels it's all right for a man to beat the hell out of his son for giving him back-talk."

David rinsed his empty orange juice glass in the sink and picked his coffee mug up from the counter.

"Probably isn't the first time it's happened," he said.

Ellie said, "Or the last."

The long trailer had been backed into the area between the two barns. The trailer's ramp had been lowered. About half the calves had been off-loaded.

"How do they look, William?" David asked.

"I'm not sure." William was never sure about how calves looked when they first arrived. He knew many of the things that could be wrong with them that one could not see at first. He was particularly nervous about these calves because he had bought them sight unseen from Florida. They were inexpensive, as there was a drought running in Florida; they could prove to be very expensive indeed, if they were diseased.

"They'll be isolated a week or two?" David asked.

"Oh, yes."

The bull calves were staggering off the cattle trailer, swaying and blinking, heads lolling, just like people looking for passport control. From where they were let off the trailer they could have gone into the fresh pasture; they could have gone into the back barn, where William had set out hay and fresh water for them; every one of the dumb beasts headed for the nearest fence and tried to stick its head through the rails to get at the grass in the next pasture.

Josh was noticing this, and smiled at David.

Looking around, David sipped his coffee.

The powerfully built young man wearing wire-rimmed glasses was helping the driver off-load the cattle. He was working hard at it. He seemed in charge.

More than anything, Josh was noticing Nonnie, the tenants' daughter.

Nonnie was fifteen, dressed this morning in a sleeveless body shirt, braless, David was sure, cut-off shorts, thigh-high boots. She had fed the hens, her morning chore. A red bucket of eggs was on the ground near her feet. She had blond curly hair, very blue eyes, freckles, and was as cute as a field of wild flowers.

"Good morning, Nonnie."

"Morning."

Josh, in T-shirt, cut-off shorts and sneakers was standing a meter behind her in the sunlight sopping her up like a sponge.

"You met Josh?"

Not turning to look at Josh, Nonnie giggled. "Yeah." She knew he was there. She was enjoying being absorbed.

My, my, David thought to himself. *Sexual tension in the barnyard. And they are equals, somehow. Josh's being in shorts, too, makes them sexual equals: equally vulnerable, to each other, in a way. Dan is correct in what he says: Josh is as much a sexual object to her as she is to him. There is an equal sexual awareness of each other. Either could be the aggressor.*

Standing beside David, William said, quietly, "I found that right good beer in the truck last night."

David said, "I thought you might."

"Thanks for remembering it."

"Should be grateful I didn't drink it myself, on the way down from Nashville." The two men slid the ramp into the truck and were slamming the tailgate closed. "That's a long road."

"Help yourself," William said. "Anytime."

David waved at the driver pulling the trailer truck out of the yard. The other man did not seem to be leaving. He had gone after a strayed calf.

"Who's he?" David asked William.

"I don't know. He was here when I got here. Helpful enough."

"I want to look at their eyes," David said. "Are you going to give them shots now?"

"Yeah," William said. "Need to run 'em through the back barn. Where's Jock?"

"I expect Ellie's got him shaggin' around the house. I mean to help. Plus we've got the help of whoever he is, I guess."

The big young man was walking the stray back toward the herd.

Josh and Nonnie and David stood here and there in the barnyard guiding the calves into the back barn. Josh and Nonnie were not much help as they seemed concentrated on staying exactly one meter away from each other, just out of each other's reach, but it was not that big a job. At some point Josh tried to juggle three eggs from the bucket and succeeded in breaking all three, which made Nonnie giggle and look at David. Jester made a second breakfast of the eggs.

In the barn William and the young man put the calves through the run and gave them their shots.

It was not that unusual in Jameson County for a neighbor to stop by and help out when he saw help was needed. In this case, help was not really needed. Sometimes neighbors stopped by and helped out just for the sociability of it. David could not figure out who the young man was. Sometimes, when he didn't know who a person in the county was exactly, he could figure out which family he belonged to from the looks of him. David ran through all the family names of his neighbors. He could not put this young man's face, his big, powerful, square body, his steel-rimmed eyeglasses together with any family name. Also, the car parked by the shed looked to David like a rental car. He ran through the names of people expected for the wedding.

After a while, David went into the cool darkness of the barn.

The young man was shoving a reluctant, bellowing calf into the run. His white trousers were dusty and soiled.

David asked, "Have a nice trip, Paul?"

The young man smiled. "Arrived pretty late. Or early, depending upon how one looks at it. Thought I wouldn't disturb you."

"You slept in the car?"

"Yes."

David realized no one could have succeeded in arriving on the farm in the middle of the night, opening a gate, pulling into the barnyard, closing the gate and settling down to sleep without their knowing it if the peacock had been there, had been alive. "Good thing you found the right barnyard."

"I saw the sign. I doubt there's another Bass Clef Farm."

"I guess not. How are things at Princeton?"

"Fine."

David continued to scan his brain for facts about Paul from bits of letters, snatches of conversations, from or with his parents, Doug or Sorry, over the years. Paul was always wonderful. Always he had just won the grandest prep school award for skiing, the collegiate boxing championship, the most prestigious fellowship. "You have your Masters, now, in Chemistry?"

"Ph.D. Biological electronics."

"What's that?"

Pushing another calf into the run, Paul said, "I agree. The words don't mean much."

Sorry's son. Doug's son. Born on a plantation in the West Indies, resident, for a while, of the French Riviera, graduate of an exclusive Swiss boarding school, then Princeton, a B.S, an M.S., a Ph.D., Paul Hollingsworth had arrived on the farm in the middle of the night without letting anybody know, made his own accommodations, gotten up in the morning and without breakfast, as far as David knew, or a word of greeting to anyone, helped unload bull calves and wrestle them around a barn.

"Been a while since I've seen you, Paul."

"Years. I attended a concert of yours, in New York, Carnegie Hall, when I was an undergraduate. You and Mr. Hardy. You played 'Sorry.'"

"Ah. That is your mother, isn't it?"

Paul said, happily enough, "Yes."

"Why didn't you come backstage to see us? Could have gone for pastrami together."

"Figured you probably had enough people pressing in on you. Had to catch the train back to Princeton. Do you remember that concert?"

David shrugged. "Not particularly."

"You always play 'Sorry'?"

"People seem to like it. Do you?"

"Yes. A lot."

Paul had also survived the radical diminution of his parents' wealth.

"Aren't you hungry?"

"I've got some food in the car," Paul said. "Picked it up at one of those all-night stores in Nashville driving from the airport. I'll have something when we're through here."

"I can do this," David said. "Go eat."

"That's okay." Paul rounded up another calf and walked it to the run.

"When are your parents arriving?"

"Tomorrow. I'll pick them up at the airport."

"You think they're happy in Los Angeles?"

Paul nodded. "They're in good shape."

"Oh, I know that. Perish the thought."

Paul laughed. He put his shoulder to the rump of a calf. Bellowing, the calf found itself moving very fast indeed into the run.

A meter apart, Nonnie and Josh came into the barn with the last calf.

"This is Nonnie Simpson," David said.

Paul said, "Hi, Nonnie."

"Josh Prescott," David said.

"Hi, Josh."

"Dr. Paul Hollingsworth," David said.

Josh cocked an eyebrow. “Doctor?”
“Yeah,” Paul said. “Are you impressed?”
“Yeah,” Josh said.
“I thought you would be,” Paul said, “seeing you don’t even know you’re standing in bullshit.”

13

"How do you keep in such wonderful physical condition?" Janet asked. "You're still built like a twenty-year-old champion swimmer."

"Never forsake childish for adult activities." Resting in the long chair in the morning sunlight by the pool, Dan did not open his eyes, at first. Beginning just before dawn he had run what he figured was about twenty kilometers on the roads around the farm. Then he had swum fifty laps in the pool. "Never give up running, jumping, playing, for sitting at a table drinking too much coffee and gin, eating Danish pastry and crabcakes, talking anxiously about your next medical checkup."

He opened his eyes and sat up a little in the chair.

Janet, a filmy wrap over her two-piece bathing suit, was placing a tray of coffee and cake on the little poolside table.

She said, "I take it you don't want coffee."

"I don't drink it. Never did, really. You know that."

Removing her wrap, Janet sat on the edge of another long chair. "I don't know what I know about you."

"I haven't changed."

"Oh, no, not much." Janet poured herself a cup of coffee. "Two divorces."

"That's true. I wouldn't have predicted that."

"Male model. A statue of you naked in the New York Museum."

"Also unpredictable," Dan said. "Like life, it just happened."

"My shy Dan Prescott who wouldn't have removed his pants in public if they had been on fire."

"Did anything predictable happen to you?"

"What do you mean?"

"I don't know what I would have predicted for you. The way things were going for a while there in Paris, I think I might have predicted you ending up as a bag lady."

"Thanks a heap. That was your perception, Dan."

"Yes. It was. Which was crazier, my perception, or your behavior?"

Janet put her cup and saucer on the table.

"We were both crazy," Dan said, more easily. "As if our growing up together in Columbia Falls, Maine, had been some kind of a disease we had to get over."

"All of us," Janet said. "Look at how much has changed. How much has happened. David was talking last night about the onslaught of technology. It's true, what he says, feels. It's wrought more change than could any major war or mass migration."

"There's change in every life," Dan said. "We grow up."

"You just said it's better not to."

"Did I?"

"Something about never forsaking the childish for the adult."

"I was speaking physically," Dan said. "But I guess you're right. I've fought the good fight. I guess I've matured as slowly as possible."

Janet smiled. "I think you've set some kind of a record that way."

"And you?" Dan asked. "When did you grow up?"

"Really?" Janet took the question seriously. "I guess when John left Paris for the London School of Economics." She poured herself more coffee. "Luce was about four years old. Three of John's plays had been produced, in Paris, Geneva, Scandinavia, London, not New York, of course. He mentioned applying to L.S.E. A few months later he mentioned being accepted. Then he began packing up books and clothes to go."

"Was it understood you weren't going with him?"

"Nothing was understood. John had always mumbled about his unique position in the world, a black North American, born and brought up in Maine, well-educated, multi-lingual, a recognized poet and playwright."

"Jack never mumbled in his life."

"I forgot you're a fan of his."

"Could it be you weren't listening?"

"I'm prone not to listen when people get on a save-the-world kick. Aren't you?"

Dan hesitated. "No."

"He had money, you remember, from his uncle, which he had invested well. John had not been obliged to teach, or anything, to work on his poetry and plays. We had Luce, still a baby, really, the apartment in Paris. I felt our home was there."

"You were brought up to believe your home was with your husband."

"Dan, if you intend to insinuate yourself back into the role of my moral mentor, I'm not going to talk to you. You and I will just go through this wedding with a nod and a shrug."

"Sorry." Sweating in the sun, Dan looked around the brilliant pool area. "That's the trouble with old friends. We feel we have rights to each other, having known each other when, and we don't. Makes us ruder to each other than we would be as strangers. Carry on. I'll listen like a stranger on a plane."

"The hobbyhorse John always rode, call it mumbling or not, was the ever-widening gap between the Industrial World and the Third World, the haves and the have-nots, the rich and the poor. His thesis was that the Industrial World harmed the Third World profoundly by exploiting it and, just as much, through its various do-good, supposedly internal development schemes." In the shade of the umbrella, Janet finished her second cup of coffee and sat back, knees up, on the long chair. "You're right: one hears that sort of thing, but perhaps does not listen with the understanding that the speaker, particularly if the speaker is one's husband, the father of one's child, intends to use such a thesis as a personal life motivation."

"You didn't understand him."

"I didn't understand he intended to go play John the Baptist crying in the wilderness, a prophet heralding a new era."

Dan said, "The Comforter."

"I didn't respond. He talked about going to the London School of Economics. I didn't. Why would a poet and playwright want a degree in Economics? He talked about moving to London. I didn't. My home was in Paris. He packed up and left. I didn't."

"Was it a rift, a separation?"

"No. He flew to Paris for weekends, holidays, vacations, if he didn't have research to do or a paper to write. He's always doted on Luce, and, I think, has always loved me. He made jokes about how much more work he was able to get done without his wife and daughter underfoot."

"Jack always was gracious."

"Dan . . ."

"Sorry."

"Well, to go from the sublime to the pedestrian, from economics to mercantilism: my American clothes had worn out, my jeans and shorts and T-shirts and sneakers. I had replaced them, of course, with casual clothes available in France, from Galeries Lafayette and wherever, but such clothes never seemed comfortable on me, and they did not wear well. France has always been very big on *haute couture* but had never paid much attention to clothes for playing about in."

Dan smiled. "With the French, it's all or nothing."

"Exactly. So I sent my sizes to my parents in Maine and they went shopping for me. My friends in Paris noticed I was wearing new jeans and asked if I could order some for them. My mother dragged around the stores several times with shopping lists. Of course this was also the era when things American had great currency in Europe. People would see Hollywood movies and want the clothes. Finally, I made a shopping trip to America myself, mostly to Chicago, and bought the most simple, cheap American casual clothes in popular sizes, and in large quantities."

"That was when you came to Columbia Falls."

"For a few days, yes. To see my parents. You were in New York. Being a statue, or something."

"Yes."

"I made contacts in the clothing business then that have lasted me all these years. I rented a big, ugly store in Paris, did nothing to it, and opened. I had no idea what I was doing, really. Occasionally, I was buying at retail prices, shipping by air, paying outrageous import duties; I did nothing to make the store look good, did not advertise. Almost immediately the bookkeeping became a nearly irretrievable mess. All that didn't matter. People came in droves and paid utterly ridiculous prices for American casual clothes."

"Where did you get the money to try this?"

"John."

"Do you own the business together?"

"No. I paid him back. He didn't want to be in the clothing business. That's not exactly true. John is a nasty purist. He's not keen on the unbridled profluence of American culture."

"You own the whole business yourself?"

"Yes. On one of his weekends in Paris John looked at the bookkeeping and nearly turned apoplectic. He set me up with a good accountant. My cash flow was such that we not only were able to, we needed to open several more stores in Paris, in Lyon, Marseille; then Italy, Germany, Scandinavia. . . . The amazing discovery was that the more business we did, the lower our costs became . . . oh, yes, I grew up. Nothing ages a person faster than having to hire and fire people."

"And John? And Lucy?"

"John got his degree. Dragged his books back to Paris. There was another play, his fourth, produced. Then he began taking trips, to both Africa and South America, once or twice to India, Pakistan, the Middle East, longer and longer trips."

"Did you ever go with him?"

"No."

"Not once?"

"Never. I had a business to run."

"I see."

"At some point there, John began writing his column, "How Things Are." I don't know exactly when, or how it all happened. Suddenly it began appearing in newspapers around the world. My husband was accused of being politically left, politically right, radical, conservative, extremist. From day to day I never knew how to defend myself."

Dan said, "He's given voice to the people of the Third World. He's tried to get us to understand that the people of the Third World are not just slower versions of ourselves; that they come from worlds completely different: so different that our political and religious ideologies are virtually irrelevant to them. I appreciate what he's done, what he's doing."

"How nice. I'll be sure and tell him."

"You don't appreciate him?"

"Dan, it's a little hard to appreciate your husband's vocation or avocation when strange people in robes of one hue or another follow you and your daughter around Paris. Twice I've been rather too near bombs that have gone off."

"Really. Were you the target?"

"Once, definitely. My car blew up a doorman."

"I didn't know that."

"Then his books began appearing, compiled of his newspaper columns, expanded, *How Things Are in South Africa, How Things Are in Peru, Libya, Angola, so forth.* I call them his This-Is-John-Bart-Nelson-Inside-a-Swiss-Watch books."

"How encouraging of you."

"Dan, this is not a career one would pick for one's husband."

"It's a wonder he's survived."

"I don't think about that. I can't. I guess John has done what he's felt he's had to do. I thought I had discouraged and rid myself of all you idealists during those early days in Paris. I couldn't have been more wrong. In the garden of love I plucked the biggest idealist of all. But John's going off to London and then to the world's dark spots forced me to be independent."

Dan laughed. "Come off it, Janet! Jack forced you to be independent! Nobody ever got to hold your hand for long. You always had some place to itch."

Janet's jaw was tight. "John left me in Paris with a baby."

"Tell it to the press. Jack moved on with his life, and you didn't go with him."

"Dan, can you see me dragging over the sands of Africa wrapped in robes and veils, eating goat and rice?"

"Why not?"

"Would you?"

Dan said, "I doubt I'd have the courage. I suppose I could have become a missionary."

"Why didn't you?"

Dan was silent a long moment, while Janet waited, studying his face.

Finally, he said, "It seemed patronizing."

Janet nodded. "You have read a lot of John."

"I've read all his books. I'm enormously proud of him. Proud to have known him, had him as a friend during a weird time of my life. Proud to have been nailed by him on the football field when we were in high school."

Silently, Janet continued studying Dan.

Dan said, "And Lucy. Tell me about my daughter-in-law to be. She was sent away to boarding school anyway, wasn't she?"

Janet shrugged. "What else could I do? John was God-knew-where. I was running the business day and night, spending time in each of the stores. As you know, I built the clothing factory in Provence, hired designers for more fashionable yet still comfortable clothes—"

"I'm asking about Lucy."

Janet swallowed. "Luce turned into a first-class model. Her looks, tall, skinny body, half black, half white, with fairly straight red hair, were, and are, absolutely striking."

"I know."

Janet swallowed dryly again. "She was ideal to model the kinds of clothes I was selling in my stores, and, later, manufacturing. Yes, she went to boarding school in Switzerland. With John making friends and enemies around the world beyond human understanding, it was safer for her. As John is, she's multi-lingual. She's been designing some of the clothes I manufacture since she was about eight. She's the best public relations and salesperson I have. Quite simply, at a very early age, Luce became Cille, an internationally famous model. You know all that."

"Whose idea was it to call her 'Cille' professionally?"

"Her's."

"Is she a nice person?"

"So nice sometimes I can't stand her." Janet appeared to be serious. "All of which brings up the reason I sought you out this morning."

Dan looked at her warily.

Janet asked, "What's your excuse?"

"For what?"

"Always refusing me."

"Have I?"

"Don't play dumb with me, buster. For years and years I've been offering you jobs, through your New York agent."

"Oh, was that you?"

"Through my parents."

"Your Dad mentioned it once or twice."

"Written you personal letters. You never answered them, not once."

"Never could afford the postage back to Paris."

"You could have afforded plenty, if you had taken some of the jobs I offered you."

Dan said, "Why don't you drop it?"

"Drop what?"

"This, as a topic. Clearly, if I had wanted to do modeling for you, model clothes for the Janet Twombly Clothing Empire, or whatever it's called, I would have responded, at some point. You've been trying to contract me every three or four months for damned near a quarter of a century. Can't you take a hint?"

Janet sat up in her long chair and put her feet on the pool deck. "Persistence is a characteristic of a good business person." She poured coffee into her cup. "And the business is called N. Sue Sance, S.A., by the way. And don't pretend you don't know it. One is apt to make that kind of mistake early in business, before one really grasps what the business is. What originally strikes one as cute later appears as embarrassingly puerile." She sipped her coffee, made a face, and put the cup back on its saucer. "Cold."

Dan said, "Of course it's cold."

"Did you think I was trying to do you a favor?" Janet asked.

"I didn't care. I never thought about it."

"You were working in my father's hardware store, damn it!"

"Are you telling me you were trying to do me a favor?"

"Christ's sake, Prescott! You're *Twentieth-Century American—Male*, recognized, accepted as such. You've pushed that in our faces enough."

"I never pushed that at anybody."

"Do you think I, or anybody in my position, selling distinctly American casual clothes in Europe, wouldn't have wanted you? Why wouldn't you work for me?"

Dan did not answer.

"You could have come to Europe. You could have made several times the money you've made here. Why didn't you?"

Dan said, "I should think the answer would be obvious."

"It's not."

"You can't understand?"

"No. You've never given me the honor, the courtesy, of an explanation."

"Janet . . ." Dan sighed. "Okay. Can't you understand my unwillingness to sell my body to the girl I grew up with, to the woman I once thought I was going to marry?"

"No. Models don't sell their bodies. They sell pictures of their bodies. You've done enough of that. What's our having known each other have to do with it? Anyone in my position would have tried to hire you to model American casual clothes in Europe. Anyone would have paid you a fortune for that. You wouldn't do business with me simply because you knew me?"

Dan shook his head. "My doing modeling . . . all that was a mistake . . . something I slipped into. Janet, you were the first girl I kissed, and, I'm pretty sure, I was the first boy you ever kissed—"

"Because you used to get on top of me in a Jeep, with your jeans on, I might add, you wouldn't become an underling of mine?"

Dan said, "We had images of ourselves, at one time. I had an image of myself. Of you. Some things are better left alone."

Sneering, Janet said, "'A man's a man, for all that.'"

"A man has his pride . . . I do . . . for all that." Dan slapped the arms of his chair with the palms of his hands. "What the hell are you and I doing sitting here this June morning by a swimming pool on a farm in Tennessee?"

Janet said, "Life is unpredictable. Isn't that the cliché we're working over this morning?" Watching Dan, she tapped her thumbnail against her lower teeth. "Would you have prevented Luce and Tony ever meeting, if you could have?"

Dan blinked at her. "It surprised me."

"Luce's marrying a boy from Columbia Falls, Maine, I don't know, seems like a backward move to me."

Dan said, "I guess they recognized something in each other, something probably quite deep in each other, maybe the drinking water, something from my father's Sunday sermons, the way the doctor made his rounds, the mailman walked his route. I don't know. It's too much to be a coincidence."

"I so wanted to leave all that behind."

"Do you still?"

"Oh, yes. My parents come to Europe to see me. Except that once, I've never been back."

"They're pretty old."

"Sure." Reaching over with a towel, Janet dried the sweat off Dan's chest and stomach.

"The center of town, where your father's hardware store is, has been replaced almost completely by a big shopping mall near the highway."

"I suppose so."

"The guy who's running your father's store isn't making much money out of it."

"I suppose not." Leaving the towel on his chest, Janet kneaded Dan's stomach muscles with her fingers.

He brushed her hands off and started to get up. "'To every thing there is a season.'"

Her fingers grasped the elastic waistband of his light running shorts. She said, "You know, I've never seen your wounds. The bullet holes."

Holding onto his shorts, one leg each side of the long chair, he stood up fully. "Everybody has."

"Not I. Not really."

He swung one leg over the long chair. "Give it up, Janet. We're not kids anymore. In maturity we trade charm for dignity."

Dan dove into the pool and swam another twenty laps.

For a long time, Janet sat in the shade watching him, just as she had sat in the stadium watching him during high school football practice, watched him go off to war in an ill-fitting uniform and clean boots, watched him do pull-ups from tree branches on his father's farm the summer he returned from the war, after his long hospitalization. Now she was thinking different thoughts. Once she thought of the future; now she thought of the past: there is no moment, no time in life without every other moment and time buried within it.

After a while, Janet stood, put on her filmy wrap, picked up her coffee tray, and walked back to the house.

14

Essentially, Ellie made three phone calls that morning.

The first was to her stockbroker in New York.

"Gerald? Ellie Adams. Please punch up on your computer the name of and a quotation for the parent company of Kleen Ride Windshield Wiper Manufacturing Company here in Jameson. Spelled with a *K*, I regret to say, and two *e*'s. No wonder no one in this country can spell."

"Hello, Ellie. How are things on the farm?" Over the telephone line, Ellie could hear Gerald's computer keyboard rattling. "Wilmot-Farina Industries, Inc. Headquartered in Chicago. Low of eight and a quarter, high of eight and three-quarters."

"Per usual, it is beautiful here. Do I have any cash around?"

"Credit of seventy-two hundred from last quarter. I should have called you anyway. How's David?"

"He's fit as a fiddle. Buying at eight and a half would give me about eight hundred shares, right?"

"Eight hundred and forty six, actually."

"Doing without your commission today, Gerald?"

"Right. About eight hundred. Ellie, we do not recommend this stock."

"Oh?"

"Management considered old, stuffy, too conservative, no new blood whatsoever. Not much cash. Scraping along. It's been at this price level for years and its P/E is among the worst. When are you coming to New York? We need to go over your portfolio."

"Maybe I'll come up in August. That's okay, Gerald. Please spend this cash on Wilmot-Farina, at whatever it comes out to."

"Whatever you say."

"And Gerald? Register my name as owner immediately."

"Okay."

"I mean within minutes, Gerald. You're a dear. How's your racquetball game?"

"Slipping."

"Poor dear. I'll send you some fresh vegetables."

For her second call, Ellie used her best Tennessee twang, which she knew was far from perfect but was acceptable as the accent of someone who had spent time in Tennessee. She also spoke slow and low.

She telephoned headquarters of the International Brotherhood and Sisterhood Union in Memphis, Tennessee.

"How do. I'm calling from Kleen Ride in Jameson, Tennessee? I'm wondering if there is an organizer, I think you name them, who's available to talk with me?"

"Sure thing. I'll give you Mr. Mann."

"'preciate it."

The line buzzed. Instantly, the phone was answered.

"Mann."

Ellie smiled. "Is this the man?"

"Yes. This is Sawyer Mann. What can I do for you?"

"Mr. Mann, I'm a worker at Kleen Ride Windshield Wiper Company in Jameson, Tennessee?"

"Yes."

"I can't give you my name, of course."

"I understand."

"If it ever got out I made this call, I'd be fired quick enough."

"That's right."

"The reason I'm callin' is that several of us have gotten together here—"

"How many of you?"

"Twenty-two, the first time. Sixteen last night."

"Okay."

"Things are pretty bad here."

"Things are terrible there."

"There's not much we can do about it by ourselves."

"We tried to organize Kleen Ride about three years ago."

"Things are worse now. We have a new manager."

"Give me specific complaints."

"Sexual harassment."

"Specific incidents?"

"Sure."

"Good."

"Late paychecks. Sometimes the amounts are wrong, you know? They try to keep overtime pay until the next week. They always say it's an accountin' problem."

"A usual trick."

"We work overtime 'cause we need the money now and not next week."

"Of course."

"Rough stuff," Ellie said.

"What kind of rough stuff?"

"Abusive. Mr. Halburton, who runs this place? is abusive."

"You mean, he yells at the workers?"

"He yells at the workers. He also bumps them."

"What does that mean?"

"He walks right into people when he's mad at them. Shoulders them. Bumps them hard." Or so Clara Reagan's niece had told Clara and Clara had told David and David had told Ellie. "It humiliates the men, if you know what I mean."

"You mean, he physically touches workers?"

"He sure does. Mr. Mann, there's goin' to be trouble here."

"There sure is. You still doin' without an employees' lounge over there?"

Ellie thought hard. She had never been in the Kleen Ride factory. "Well, there's the ladies' room. And the men's room." Mann chuckled. "There are the soda machines."

"Great. You'd think you were livin' in the last century over there. Workin' twelve hours a day at minimum wage . . ."

"Well, we decided we can't organize by ourselves, no way, so I was elected to call you up."

"Is tomorrow a good time for me to come?"

"Sure. But, Mr. Mann, we can't greet you at the gate, wavin' banners."

"I understand."

"If it ever got out we had gotten together and decided to call you—"

"As long as there is a hard core of sixteen of you somewhere in the plant who will sort of work with me, quietly, you know, see the pamphlets get distributed, talk up what I'm doing and sayin'—"

"They'll never let you in the plant."

"I'll be in the nearest beer joint between shifts. Can you get people to come to the beer joint after work?"

"Sure. That's not hard."

"That's all I ask. You don't have to identify yourselves to me. You just be there. Have people there. You-all just talk and I'll listen. I'll make a few suggestions as to what we might do, together."

"Mr. Mann, we don't want to lose what jobs we got. We don't want them to close the plant, or get other workers, just 'cause we're actin' ugly."

"Don't you worry, sugar, they're not goin' to put themselves out of business while they're makin' a profit. Organizin' a plant, 'specially that one, ain't goin' to be easy. But if we can show strength, show the managers we're together on this and we mean business, why in no time at all we'll start gettin' concessions and before you know it, you-all will be workin' in the style of this century."

"I mean, we can't afford to strike, ever."

"Sugar, you need a union. And the union you need is the I.B.S.U. Now I'm not makin' you any promises, but you get the I.B.S.U. behind you, and that's what's called support for your movement. Real support."

"Well, I hope so."

"I'll drive over tomorrow. You'll find me in the beer joint. Don't you worry your little head. Everything will be just fine."

"'preciate it."

Ellie hung up. She walked out to the kitchen, where Clara Reagan was shifting food from the freezer to the refrigerator. "Clara, what's the name of the beer joint closest to where your niece works? You know, Halburton's factory?"

"Ask Jock."

"Where is he?"

"Upstairs trying to fix that crooked window."

"Jock?" Ellie called up the stairs.

"Yes, Ma'm?"

"What's the name of the beer joint nearest Halburton's factory?"

"Shag's."

Clara said, "I was pretty sure he'd know."

Walking back to the study, Ellie muttered to herself, "'Don't you worry your little head, sugar.' My God. Anyone who had the bravery to make that call shouldn't be called 'sugar.'"

Ellie's third call was to Wilmot-Farina Industries, Incorporated, in Chicago, Illinois.

For this call, Ellie used her most brisk New York City manner.

"Wilmot-Farina, good morning."

"Good morning," Ellie said. "Your vice president in charge of stockholder relations, please. This is Ms. Adams."

"Yes, Ma'm."

A secretary answered, but did not hesitate to put Ellie through to a Mr. Tompkins.

"What can I do for you, Ms. Adams?"

"You can ease my mind. I'm calling from Jameson, Tennessee. After I bought eight hundred shares in your company, Mr. Tompkins, I learned that a major effort is to be made by the I.B.S.U. to organize your plant down here, the Kleen Ride Windshield Wiper factory."

"You're kidding."

"I kid you not."

"I'm pretty sure that's news to us. May I ask how you know about it?"

"Everybody who matters in Jameson County knows about it. In fact, a Mr. Sawyer Mann of the I.B.S.U. is driving over from Memphis tomorrow to begin meeting with the Kleen Ride workers in Shag's beer joint after each work shift."

Ellie could tell Tompkins was making notes.

"I.B.S.U. Them again."

"Shag's Tavern, or whatever it's called."

"I seem to remember the I.B.S.U. tried to organize Kleen Ride a few years ago."

"This is a more serious matter, Mr. Tompkins. This isn't just worker unrest, from what I hear. You have a new manager here, what's-his-name?"

"Halburton."

"Halburton, yes. I understand the workers are talking about sexual harassment, verbal and physical abuse."

There was a long silence from the other end of the phone line. "Sexual harassment? Physical abuse?"

"So I understand. Now, Mr. Tompkins, I don't have all the money in the world. I bought my eight hundred shares in your company as a means of supporting local industry, but really, I can't pour my savings down a sewer. If the workers under this what's-his-name, Halburton, start organizing . . ."

Over the phone line, Ellie heard Tompkins' computer keyboard rattling. Obviously he was confirming that she was a stockholder.

"I understand, Ms. Adams. Halburton's new to the job down there—"

"Exactly. If a few months after he arrives the workers are up in arms and calling in the I.B.S.U. to unionize them—"

"This company has always taken excellent care of its employees, Ms. Adams."

Ellie smiled. Apparently there wasn't even an employees' lounge at Kleen Ride. "Perhaps you should send someone down . . ."

Tompkins said, "Someone will be there tomorrow."

"It seems to me if someone from the I.B.S.U. will be listening to the workers in Shag's Tavern, someone from top management ought to be there listening, too."

"Not to worry. There will be. I guarantee it. Ms. Adams, we're very grateful to you for letting us know all this. We can't know something is going wrong in one of our factories unless somebody tells us."

Ellie said to herself, *That's the problem with you, buster.* To Tompkins she said, "You'll take whatever steps necessary to correct whatever's wrong down here?"

Tompkins said, "Whatever is necessary . . ."

Essentially, Ellie received one telephone call that day.

"Ellie? Gerald. I've put through your order on Wilmot-Farina."

"Thanks."

"I can't help wondering, though, what you're doing buying such a stupid stock."

"What am I doing?"

"Yes. What are you doing?"

"You may not understand this, Gerald . . ."

"Try me."

"I'm squashing a bug."

"You're right. I don't understand."

"I'm buying a house."

"Clear as mud."

"I'm exterminating a carpetbagger."

Gerald sighed. "Okay. See me next time you're in New York, please."

15

"Guess I'd better go up," David said to William. From where he stood in the barnyard David saw Owen's BMW parked on the driveway near the main house. Around it stood Ellie, Jock, Josh and Owen. Rourke was lifting the wheelchair out of the trunk. "More guests."

"Okay," William said. "Before you go . . ."

"Sure. What?"

"Just a matter of draggin' that bush hog out of the way."

"Sure."

"Into the shed. So I can let the steers in here."

"Right."

Ellie spoke through the opened rear window of the car. "Milton! Good to see you. Have a good trip down from New York?"

"I'm fine, Ellie," the old man in the back seat said. "Just have to relieve myself in the worst way."

"You'll be in the upper guesthouse, Milton, where we always put you."

Without saying a word to her, Rourke took Ellie too firmly by the elbow and put her out of the way. He lifted Milton Farber out of the back seat and dropped him in the wheelchair.

Jock and Josh watched Rourke silently.

Rourke was dressed in white. In his fifties, he had a big chest and shoulders, with a stomach just as big. His nose was squashed, one ear was cauliflowered, and he had the scars over his eyebrows and the lace scars back of his neck typical of an ex-boxer.

Jock was less than half his size.

Milton Farber was old and skinny and his clothes looked nearly as old as he. He did not protest being dropped in the wheelchair.

Coolly, Ellie asked, "Remember where you're going, Rourke?"

"Yeah." Avoiding the gravel path, Rourke pushed Milton jiggling over the lawn around the back of the house. Limping, Jock followed with the luggage.

Ellie said to Josh, "That's Milton Farber, the man who's been David's manager forever."

Josh seemed to struggle with what a manager is, but he said, "Oh."

"And Rourke," Ellie sighed. "Mr. Farber has had two strokes. He needs Rourke."

Josh nodded. He had a book in his hand.

"What's the book?" Ellie asked.

Josh held it out to read the title himself. "*Run With the Horsemen.* Ferrol Sams. Found it in that little library, where the desk is. Okay if I read it?"

"Sure. Good book. You'll learn mischief from that."

"Okay if I go for a swim?"

"You bet," Ellie said. "Only don't get wet."

A few minutes later, after he had changed to swimming trunks, book still in hand, Josh entered the pool area.

In his wheelchair, Milton Farber sat in the sun.

Josh said, "Hi, Mr. Farber."

The old man was sweating profusely.

Quietly, he said, "I have to pee in the worst way."

Josh looked around for Rourke.

"Don't bother with him," Milton Farber said. "He's being cruel."

Josh said, "He left you sweating in the sun when you have to pee to be cruel?"

"Yes," Milton said. "Oh, my God. Will you help me?"

"Sure."

As Josh began to push the wheelchair, Milton pointed to the upper guesthouse.

"This wheelchair is motorized," Josh said. "You could move around yourself."

"Rourke keeps the battery."

Josh helped the old man in the bathroom.

"Don't mind my clothes, boy," Milton said. "At my point in life, there's no point in buying new ones."

Josh had Milton back in the wheelchair and half out of the bathroom when Rourke appeared in the guesthouse's front door. With bright sunlight behind him, he looked enormous.

"What're you doin', kid?"

"Helpin' Mr. Farber."

"That's my job."

"Well, if that's your job, you weren't doin' it."

"Get away from there." Rourke pushed Josh aside and wheeled Milton to the side of the room, facing the wall. "Mr. Farber is my job and he pees when I say he can pee, and not a moment sooner."

"What's the point of that?"

Josh had placed himself near the front door, his back to it.

"None of your business, kid. When I need help, I'll ask for it."

"You left him broiling in the sun."

"How I do my job is my business." Rourke spoke to Milton Farber's back. "Did you ask for help?"

Josh said, "You big jerk."

Rourke turned and started toward Josh.

The boy darted through the screen door.

After the screen door slammed, Josh said, "Come on, Lardball. I can outrun you any day. Let's see you sweat a little!"

Rourke did not pursue him.

In the kitchen, David was making a pitcher of martinis.

Entering, Ellie said, "Now C.B.S. has called asking if John Bart Nelson is expected here."

"Still haven't heard from John?"

"No." Ellie noticed the martini pitcher. "I guess you've noticed Milton has arrived. Rourke is his usual sweet self. Owen is in the study bathroom."

David said, "The new steers look just fine. One looks a little lopsided. They should be okay, once they settle down."

"That's good. For lunch Clara is just going to leave plates of cut sandwiches and pitchers of iced tea around."

"Fine." David let vermouth fumes escape into the martini pitcher. Broken sprigs of fresh mint were already in the pitcher. "Two steers seem to have slightly infected eyes, but William's medicine should cure that quick enough."

"David? I think your Ms. Tuesday and Dan Prescott had a hell of a row by the swimming pool this morning."

David said, "Probably." He put two martini glasses and the pitcher on a tray.

"At least she came back looking like a thunderhead. She took one of her bottles of champagne with her to shower. I don't know where Dan is."

David picked up the tray. "Send Owen out, will you? If he ever comes out of the bathroom."

16

David felt like a butler, walking so carefully through the pool area with a martini pitcher and two glasses on a tray.

From the pool, Josh made a not very serious attempt to splash him.

"Cut that out!" David shouted. "These are supposed to be dry martinis!"

Laughing, the boy swallowed water, choked, and stood up in the pool.

Stopping a moment, David said, "Josh?"

Still laughing, still trying to clear pool water from his throat and nose, the boy tried to answer.

David said, "There's a horse down there that hasn't had any exercise today. His name is Byron. Would you mind riding him when you get a chance? Jock or William will help you find his bridle and saddle. Even Nonnie might help, if you can find her."

David thought the sight of Josh's eyes, brilliant sunlight reflecting from the surface of the pool into them, reflecting again from the water in the boy's eyes, looking up at him over a happy smile, had to be one of the best sights he had ever seen. *That's why I bought this place, why I live here*, David said to himself: *to see that absolutely real joy over something really simple in any human's eyes.*

"Okay," Josh said. Then he said, "Thanks."

"Thank you," David said. "You just paid the cover charge."

In the guesthouse, Milton Farber sat in his wheelchair at the side of the room facing the front door.

Entering, David said, "How are you?"

Running his hand over his face, Milton said, "Fine."

"Brought you your heart medicine."

"I need it," Milton said. "With crushed mint?"

"With crushed mint. I picked it ten minutes ago on the way up from the barns."

"Can't get fresh, crushed mint in New York City."

"Not this fresh," said David, pouring. "This mint is so fresh Ellie had to slap its face."

Milton took his drink. "The farm looks alright. Still operating at a loss?"

"Depends what you consider profits." David remembered Josh's shining eyes in the swimming pool a few minutes before and smiled.

Milton nodded to the window. "That's a nice boy out there."

David looked. He had not realized Milton had been watching Josh through the window.

"Yes, he is. His father is *Twentieth-Century American—Male.*"

"'Twentieth-Century American Male': what's that, a rock group?"

Martini in hand, David sat in an easy chair. Old and supposedly retired as he was, Milton still had his ear out for anything that sounded like a new musical group. "No."

Milton sipped his drink. "So how goes it, David?"

"Milton, I've never had a conversation with you that didn't begin with your asking, 'So how goes it, David?'" In the big pocket of his baggy trousers, David snapped on his small tape recorder. "Always the same inflection. 'How goes it, David?'"

Milton tried to shift his position in his chair. "So: how goes it?"

David laughed. "Fine. *El mismo.* What could be wrong?"

"Suddenly you're in the business of giving weddings?"

"Milton, over my lifetime I've saved a lot of money on weddings."

"I've noticed. No children of your own. But who are these people. Who are they to you?"

"I'm not sure. Just people whose lives I butt into every quarter of a century."

"This Janet Twombly Nelson is the same Ms. Tuesday you were married to once, but weren't; having a child by, but weren't?"

"Well put, Milton. Couldn't have put it better myself. We had a relationship back in the days when social forms, such as marriage and paternity, were becoming increasingly illusory."

"I remember. It made a mess on paper I had to clean up."

"Yes," David said. "Social forms as unhousebroken puppies."

"And the groom, the presidential speechwriter?"

"Tony Prescott. Son of another old friend, Dan Prescott, I haven't seen in person in over twenty years. The above-mentioned *Twentieth-Century American—Male.*"

Milton nodded at the window. "So the groom and that boy out there are brothers?"

"Half brothers. Different mothers."

Milton shook his head. "I don't like it, David. Today everyone is a condominium on the twentieth floor. Very expensive, but a generation from now when the building must come down to be replaced, no one will know who owns what, what is what, who is who. Everyone is just a rectangle of air in the sky."

"I own real estate."

"People still read the stories in the Bible but for too long now they've been skipping over the long lists of 'begats.'"

"The bride, Lucille Nelson, better known as Cille, is the daughter, you remember, of Ms. Tuesday and John Bart Nelson."

"Oh, I see. She must be brilliant."

"And beautiful. Famous model."

"Does she sing?"

"No, Milton."

"John Bart Nelson. I read his column, sometimes. What's it called?"

"*How Things Are.*"

"That's right. "*How Things Are.*" Inconceivable to us, how other people around the world think. His columns are real news to us."

"Yes. They are."

"Will he be here?"

"No one knows. An effort has been made to contact him about the wedding but, as usual, he's someplace we haven't heard of yet."

"His newspaper syndicate must be in almost daily contact with him. Has anyone tried reaching him through the syndicate?"

"I don't know, Milton. Left all that to Ms. Tuesday. One never knows how things are in a family."

"'Family.'" Milton spat the word. "Such words have no meaning any more. 'Marriage,' 'family,' 'father,' 'mother,' 'son': all so much mess on a piece of paper. Mrs. Farber and I had one son who married and had one son. Begat, begat."

"And begorrah," said David.

Milton's wife had died of cancer in her fifties; his son, Owen's father, of a heart attack, at fifty-two.

"A generation from now half the population will have to be lawyers and accountants to straighten out the paper mess this generation has made. They'll have plenty of work."

"And the other half?" David asked.

"Some kind of psychotherapists specializing in identity loss."

David said, "Everyone will live in numbered electronic boxes in the sky."

"Don't we already?"

"I guess."

Milton said, "Maybe everyone will end up like that poor boy." Milton always had referred to Chump Hardy as a *boy.* David turned off the recorder in his pocket. "Comatose. Inert. Having an electric machine doing his breathing for him."

"Did you see Chump this morning?" David asked.

"Yes. Owen stopped at the hospital for me to see Chump on the way from the airport. Needless to say, Rourke resented the side trip, the extra work it meant for him lifting me in and out."

David said, "Everyone here, Dan Prescott, Ms. Tuesday, seems to think Chump is dead."

"Isn't he?"

"Obviously not. I believe Chump can still hear. Chump could always hear."

"You still play your tapes for him?"

"Yes."

"Believe what you like. Never so many times have I had the grief of attending the wake of the same person." David said nothing. "It's the way we handled the publicity," Milton said. "Only in response to curiosity have I issued a small paragraph, again and again, saying 'Chump Hardy is resting comfortably in a Nashville hospital.' Like hanging a DO NOT DISTURB sign on a door. People have just enough decency to respect it. Never have I said resting comfortably from what. From what? Life. From genius. From hearing and making sounds no one had ever heard before." David saw that Milton's eyes were watering and continued to say nothing. "Also from living crazy. That boy lived like life was so much counterfeit money he had to get rid of fast under the counter."

"Chump cared almost nothing about himself."

"He cared nothing about life," Milton said. "Only sound. David, when did you see him last?"

"Yesterday."

Milton said, "Maybe it's these old eyes."

"What do you mean?"

Milton wiped his eyes with his hands. "You didn't notice a lump behind his right ear?"

"No."

"My eyes play tricks on me. Maybe what I saw is from a bad haircut, or a lump on the head from being in bed three and a half years." David knew Estelle Manning cut Chump's hair, and she cut it short, without much regard for fashion. What Milton had seen, if anything, was not a hair knot. "Being in the wheelchair, I see things from a different angle, you know, lower. So maybe I saw something you haven't noticed yet. I don't mean to worry you. Of course I couldn't reach to feel it."

"Did you speak to Ms. Manning, the nurse?"

"She wasn't there. Some woman was there I'd never seen before, making goo-goo eyes at Rourke, so I knew she was a fool. Owen, of course, stayed in the car."

David said, "I'll find out about it."

"There has to be a special place in hell," Milton said, "for these doctors who have just enough technology to cure little but prolong the symptoms, the suffering, the dying, so-called 'life,' and their own incomes."

"Chump isn't suffering."

Milton said, "I'm suffering. I've been to fifty wakes for that boy, and not one funeral." After a moment, Milton held out his glass. "I have two cavities in my teeth, and we've only filled one already."

Standing, David filled Milton's glass from the martini pitcher. "To fill your second cavity."

"Don't take it personally, David, but you'd be surprised the number of calls the office gets asking if David MacFarlane is still alive." Milton tasted his drink. "I changed my mind, now that I have my drink in hand: take it personally."

"What do you say?"

"Everyone is instructed to say you're fooling around on a farm in Tennessee, non-productive: both you and the farm."

David said, "That's about right." He sat in a chair different from the chair he'd sat in first.

Milton had to turn his wheelchair to face him.

"That's not at all right," Milton said, "and I know it."

"Why isn't it?"

"What about all this musical equipment I keep paying bills for, synthesizers, speakers, what is it, sixteen, thirty-two, sixty-four track tapes, always the latest thing, ordered sent to Bass Clef Farm, Jameson, Tennessee? I write so many checks to that store on 47th Street you'd think I'd married into the family."

"They're just toys."

"They're not toys, David. Other people use them to compose music."

"They are toys, Milton. Nothing electronic they've invented yet is like a piano. None of these things has any personality, any character of its own. After years of making love to women, using these instruments feels like making love to a life-sized, air-filled plastic doll."

"Interesting," Milton said. "So that's why so much of the music sounds like you're liable to slip off it?"

"And very few are composing on these instruments, if I may correct you. Mostly so far, people are playing *with* these instruments instead of playing these instruments. Tell me the last time you heard a kid walking down the street humming a melody he'd heard."

"Since before my first cavity. Kids walking down the street wear earphones and glazed expressions. They look like they're in Stalingrad during the siege. They can't even hum along."

David said, "They'll be all right, as long as they look both ways at the corners."

"David, all the times I've been to this house, I never have seen all this equipment I've been writing checks for. You say you don't like this electronic equipment. What are you doing with it, giving it all to the local high school mummers?"

"I didn't say I don't like it, Milton. I use it. I have fun with it."

"You refer to the piano as something real. Didn't I pay for a piano, a Steinway yet, for this house, had it shipped down special from Nashville in some kind of a leather-padded ambulance or something? Where is it? I've never seen it in the house. In all the years you've lived here, I've never heard you play it. Are my ears failing me, too? Of course, I've never been able to talk the wheelchair up the stairs. Is the piano such a woman to you you keep it locked and silent in your bedroom?"

Milton always had talked as if the checks he wrote for David, and for Chump, had been on his own bank accounts, spending his own money. All the money, of course, David MacFarlane and Chump Hardy had earned. It was theirs, to do with as they pleased. Milton Farber collected it and managed it for them. He paid himself a percentage of the income to do so. His attitude, that it pained him to write checks for other people's money as much as if the money were his own, and that each check must be considered as if it were the last, over the years clearly had kept David's and Chump's expenditures down. Neither David nor Chump ever had known how much money was there, their total worth. Whenever they had asked, Milton's answer was some variation of *You'll be all right as long as you keep working,* which had always been true, regarding their general health and productivity, regardless of financial matters.

Then the moment came, well after David MacFarlane and Chump Hardy had stopped producing, that David had had to hire a doctor, a lawyer, a pilot and a jet airplane for a night, fly to Mexico, take Chump, comatose, out of a hospital there, fly him back to Nashville, breaking rules, regulations and laws all the way, put him in a private room in the coma unit of the private Savior Hospital in Brentwood, Tennessee, where, so far, Chump had remained three and a half years. Never had Milton mentioned writing a check, the expense of anything regarding Chump's condition, no more than Milton would mention what dinner at his apartment would cost. Imagining what the expenses must be, David had worried. He had not asked; Milton had not said.

"Where is this studio of yours on the farm we keep informing the Internal Revenue Service about?" Milton asked. "I've never seen it, heard a note out of it. Is it a fiction to give the tax auditors pleasure to contemplate every three months?"

David gestured with his thumb toward the building along the long side of the swimming pool. "It's sound-proofed."

"Is that where all this musical equipment is?"

"Yes."

"And the piano?"

"Yes." David smiled. "And a Universal exercise machine, a rowing machine, a one-wheeled bicycle, a Jacuzzi, a sauna, a bookcase, some reading chairs, fireplace, wet bar, a huge television screen, videotape and cassette recorders—"

"And Saint Peter tends the bar?"

David laughed. "Yes. If Saint Peter used to ride bulls in rodeos."

"David, you've never not worked. Never since you used to come home from school as a little kid, a latchkey kid, every day, every night to an empty apartment, no one, nothing ever there to respond to you except the piano. No wonder you think of piano as woman, mother, wife, mistress, whatever."

"True."

"Never could you leave piano, music alone, even to take a vacation, rest up from traveling, playing every day, every night. When

I'd insist you had to be at contract meetings, you'd sit in my office fingering chords on the side of my desk."

"We've given you a hard life, Milton. How could you ever stand us?"

"I've enjoyed. But, David, look me in the eye and tell me you've been doing nothing these years."

David looked Milton in the eye. "I've been doing a few things."

"You have tapes for me to hear?"

"They're not much good."

"With the expense of all the equipment you have, your tapes are not good? I should ask for the money back?"

"Radical," David said. "They're radical."

"You've been experimenting?"

"Yes."

"So how much longer am I going to live?"

"Forever, Milton."

"Maybe not till lunch. Even if forever, I'd need time to get used to, understand such radical music."

"You want to hear what I've been doing."

"Thank you for the invitation to a wedding, I always enjoy a party, it's always nice spending time with you and Ellie on the farm, but better caterers I know in New York, they're not new to the business."

David laughed. "I'm not sure what you're asking, Milton."

"I want to hear the music."

"Are we in financial trouble?"

"David, you write music. So, for you, either you're composing, or you're decomposing."

"Are you trying to tell me something about Chump's expenses? I mean, Treble Clef is making money, isn't it? Look at the people we've discovered, Johnny Lee Rich, Sarah Downey—"

"Did I say this is a business discussion?"

"If the question is, can I put together a popular recording of my own this year, yes, I suppose so. If money is needed for Chump's expenses. But I don't want to. It would mean going back on tour—"

"Is that what you're afraid of? Going on tour without Chump? Is that why you won't let even me hear the new music? You're afraid you'll find yourself at Atlanta International Airport again, but without Chump?"

"Being on tour with Chump was exactly like being on tour with a particular piece of luggage that just kept getting lost. You know that." David frowned. "Except when we played."

"So you're afraid to walk onto a big concert stage without Chump. I understand that. We'll start small, again. There are still some small clubs."

"Yuck. Milton. Listen. Understand. If I have to issue a recording of David MacFarlane, on piano, reinterpreting standards, to meet expenses, I can do so. I'll tour if I have to. But that's not the kind of music we're talking about. Nowadays, you don't compose on an instrument, even a synthesizer. Believe it or not, you do your composing on a tape recorder. The sound only comes together on tape."

"I understand. I'm not as new to this business as you are at giving weddings."

"What I'm composing, I can't perform in public. You want to book me into Carnegie Hall and have me stand onstage and play a tape?"

Milton stared long at David. "I see."

"So," David said.

"So."

David said, "I am right where I am supposed to be, doing exactly what I am supposed to be doing."

"You can make a recording, but how to sell it if you can't tour it, performing?"

"I knew you'd understand this business, Milton, if you stayed in it long enough."

"Put together a band. Jesus Christ, what am I saying?: *personalize the instruments.*"

"Fine. When you can sell seats in Carnegie Hall for the price of five fancy dinners each, instead of one, call me. There are plenty of first-rate, unemployed musicians around."

"That big a band?"

"That big. If you're going to use a synthesizer it's natural to use all of it." More quietly, David said, "Just like a piano."

"So who will ever hear this new music of yours?" Milton asked. David looked into the sunlight coming through the window. Milton said, "Chump Hardy." Milton said, "You poor sod."

"'Sod'? I didn't think that word was a part of your vocabulary, Milton."

Milton continued contemplating David.

"Sure, you can hear the music," David said. "Maybe next time you're here. There's a wedding supposedly going on here. I'm picking the bride and groom up at the airport this afternoon." He put down his empty martini glass. "Ellie has lunch set out here and there around the place like bird feeders. I think I just saw Jock drop some by the pool."

At that moment, Owen could be seen through the window coming through the pool area.

"Your relationship with Chump has always been very special," Milton said. "Musical sodomy."

"Ah! I knew *that* word was part of your vocabulary."

Owen stood inside the doorway of the guesthouse looking at his grandfather, to David, then back to his grandfather. To David, Owen always looked distinctly self-conscious after one of his long sojourns in a back office or a bathroom.

"Come in," Milton said. "There's about one more mint martini in the pitcher."

Milton held his second in his hand. He had sipped little of it.

"No, thanks," Owen said. "David, I've been meaning to tell you. Maxie called from Philly the other afternoon. Said if you were giving a bash, he was coming to it."

"Max Brown?"

"Yeah."

"Wow. Was he serious?"

Milton said, "Was he invited?"

David popped his eyes at Milton. "Max knows he doesn't need an invitation—anywhere in the world."

"I doubt he's well enough to make it," Owen said. "He said if this wedding is important to you, it's important to him."

"Did he call himself?" David asked.

"Ol' mud voice himself," Owen said.

"Another one," Milton Farber said, "many people think has to be dead by now."

"Ol' Mister Music Maxie Brown," David said. "I never thought of inviting him."

"Doubtlessly he'll insist on performing," Milton said. "He's as blind as a cop in Times Square."

"What does that matter?" David asked. "He's one of the finest blues singers who has lived—ever."

"He's the only blues singer," Milton said, "who has lived forever. You'll have to be careful he doesn't fall off the stage."

"Well," David said. "It's a nice thought. I appreciate it. I'll have to call him, once this wedding is over. Make sure I do, Owen."

"Sure. He still lives with his wife, in Philadelphia. Together, they have to be one hundred and seventy years old."

Milton said, "I don't see how anyone can be singin' the blues all his life and yet live to be almost one hundred. Something not honest about that."

David laughed. "I guess he's been happy enough bein' blue."

Rourke entered the guesthouse. Acknowledging no one, he took the nearly full martini glass out of Milton Farber's hand. He placed it on a side table just out of Milton's reach.

"Hallo, Rourke!" David said cheerily. "How are ya doin'? Nice to see you again!"

Rourke responded by going into the bathroom and closing the door.

"Same ol' Rourke." Getting up, David handed the glass back to Milton. "Better chug-a-lug, Milton, or you'll be kept after school." Milton finished off his martini in two big swallows. "Haven't been able to find anyone to replace Rourke, uh?"

"Wish to God I could."

David put the empty glass back on the table where Rourke had placed it.

To Owen, David said, "I've got to shower and change before driving into the airport. Was playin' around in the barnyard this morning. See that your grandfather gets lunch before you go, will you, Owen?"

"Sure thing."

"If it were up to Rourke," David said, "Milton would get the crust and Rourke the sandwich."

17

PERSPECTIVE: *Estelle Manning*

"Good afternoon, Ms. Manning."

"Good afternoon, Mr. MacFarlane."

When you get to watch a person over a long period of time, especially a person under stress, as I have David MacFarlane, you come to love him, if you know what I mean, not because you perceive how wonderful he is but because you come to perceive how human he is; not by appreciating his greatness but by appreciating, silently, his little mistakes.

That afternoon, for example, David MacFarlane entered Chump Hardy's room and closed the door. Now, why did he close the door, I wondered. He never did that before. Later, I discovered tapes of a kind he had never brought in before. Tapes of people talking. One tape sounded like it was of a lot of people laughing and talking, maybe around a dinner table, because I could hear references to food, and the sounds cutlery makes against plates. A boy's voice kept asking things like, "So who did you live with?" and everyone would laugh. The voices answering him were sometimes serious, sometimes not. Another voice was that of a woman with an accent that didn't sound exactly French, but had some French inflection and pronunciation. Everything she said sounded like some kind of a put-down, like, on another tape, "Oh, you interact very well, David. I can tell that." And a man's voice that sounded more serious than the rest, sadder somehow, a virile voice but not, I think, the voice of a very young man. On the dinner tape he said, "We were brought up with a sense of permanence." Although the woman sounded interesting, listening to the tapes I really wanted to meet that man (although on a different tape I am sure it was his voice that said he had been twice married, twice divorced, which is pretty hot for someone who was a minister, "trained and ordained"). He did most of the talking on another tape I didn't listen to much, something about people taking photographs of him in the buff years ago. Work in a coma unit as many years as I have and the human body pretty much becomes a sausage. Why should anyone, particularly a male, care if people take pictures of him naked? We are what we are. The way he described it the whole thing sounded like some kind of a big deal for him, though, some kind of a personal crisis. Maybe until that point in his life he had thought of himself mostly as a spiritual rather than a physical being. Maybe he was concerned whether his soul showed up in the photographs. In a coma unit, you don't find yourself thinking about the spiritual being much, if you know what I mean. The beings I deal with are fed intravenously, respirated mechanically and evacuated via a catheter. In the final moments, in the darkest nights, I've never seen that spiritual glow of song and story. But that man sounded like he took things seriously, really cared about things, is still doing the spiritual double-think, and I don't often meet people like that. Another woman on two of the tapes was Ellie, I think, Mrs. David MacFarlane, who visits Chump with David once in a while, and has come in more than once by herself. She keeps flowers in Chump's room, although I'm not sure Mr. MacFarlane notices; he's never mentioned them; I know Chump has never noticed. That's one real cool lady. Even from the few things she says on the tapes you can tell there isn't *anything* she can't handle. Every time I see her I sure wish she was running this hospital. And there was a short tape of Mr. MacFarlane and Mr. Farber talking. I know that old man's voice well enough. He had been in earlier that same day, I was told, but I had missed him. (That morning, I had been trying to buy new drapes for my living room. I'm so sick of those pink ones I've had since I moved into that apartment. Same patients, year after year; same drapes.) I was glad I had missed old Mr. Farber's inevitable tears. And that dopey male "nurse" that goes everywhere with him, who is about as much of a nurse as I am a ballerina and who would as rather take a knife to your throat as ask how you're feeling, I'm sure.

Anyway, David MacFarlane went into Chump's room and closed the door I guess to play these tapes which he probably thought were private, they being of people talking, forgot about the tapes, left them there, opened the door and came to find me.

You see, besides being the chief custodian of David MacFarlane's grief, I am the case nurse, and that gives me a difficult role to play. I do the work of caring for Chump Hardy, yet must remain passive, if you know what I mean.

If I said what I really felt sometimes . . .

Mr. MacFarlane said, "Ms. Manning, there's a bandage behind Chump's right ear, just above the neck . . . a lump. What does it mean?"

"Has Dr. MacBride talked with you?"

"No." Mr. MacFarlane's eyes searched around the corridor. "Not lately."

"You should talk to Dr. MacBride."

"I didn't notice it yesterday. The lump, I mean."

"You were only here a minute."

"Yes."

"I had called Dr. MacBride about it the day before, and—"

"You didn't mention it to me. Yesterday."

"No. Dr. MacBride hadn't been in yet." How could I say to Mr. MacFarlane, *for once you were acting happy around here, you said you had some plan. Was I to stop that?* He was planning the tapes, I guessed later, of people talking. "He came in yesterday afternoon. A biopsy has been taken."

"A biopsy?"

"Yes. To determine if the growth is a malignancy." Now this is the thing I will never understand about the families and friends of my patients: seldom, if ever, do they take "bad news" with hope, relief. The dismay that registers on their faces is the same as if the "bad news" concerned a healthy, vibrant human being. Mr. MacFarlane's face had all the fright in it of someone facing a great loss.

"And is it? Malignant?"

"I haven't seen the report yet. You'll have to ask the doctor."

Mr. MacFarlane swallowed hard. "What do you think?"

I gave him what I consider the "bad news": "The lump grew to its present size very rapidly, and then stopped. That might be a good sign." One has to say something.

"That it's not malignant?"

"Yes."

"Could he have gotten a bump on the head some way? Chump was always getting bumps on the head."

"Not likely, Mr. MacFarlane." I tried to share a smile with him. "He hasn't been out much lately."

Mr. MacFarlane sort of smiled. "MacBride did call me last night. I forgot. Something else was going on. It was late."

"Whatever." I had to say this much: "I hope this isn't going to be treated as an emergency, in any case."

"What do you mean?"

I am very fond of Mr. MacFarlane, and of Ellie and, of course, of Chump. I said, "Necessarily you may be faced with certain medical, surgical options." And I stopped myself right there, and said no more.

His eyes continued to search the hospital corridor. I hoped he was thinking about what I had just not said.

He said, "Today the expression on his face has changed. Don't you think so?"

Oh, yes. I knew so. That heavy-set, baby-faced, middle-aged man they had brought in here three and a half years ago over time had become a gaunt, sunken, shapeless near-skeleton covered with dry skin. And the expression on his face had changed over the last three days, had become more pinched. I said, "I expect some pain is involved."

"Pain? He feels pain?"

I shook my head. "Who can tell? Maybe it's just some kind of contraction of the facial muscles, nerves . . ." Because I wanted Mr. MacFarlane to be sensible when confronted with the options Dr. MacBride was obliged to present to him. But what is sensible to one person . . .

"Guess I'd better go call the Doc."

"Yes."

Forgetting the tapes, leaving them in Chump's room, forgetting what he had come there to do, Mr. MacFarlane, his heavy chest and head always seeming forward of his body, started down the corridor toward the elevators.

I walked to the elevator with him.

"Mr. MacFarlane, you know we'll do the best we can. I mean, to keep Chump comfortable."

"I know you will, Ms. Manning."

"All right."

I had said, hinted enough. Still, I was not sure he had heard.

And I thought he had never yet read the advice from my eyes.

I found the tapes, and knowing Mr. MacFarlane had meant to play them for Chump, I did so, softly, only hearing sections of them when I was in and out of the room. When I realized they were tapes of people talking I understood why Mr. MacFarlane had closed the door. For a moment I wondered if I was violating privacy. For only a moment. Mr. MacFarlane had left them there by mistake. So what. I was the only person hearing them, and what did I care? Besides, working in a coma unit if you don't keep some sense that there are people out there, conscious, alive, you might get comatose yourself. You might lose all sight of what all this is for, if you know what I mean. Anyway, I wasn't really listening.

At some point on one of the tapes, a man's voice, I think the interesting, spiritually concerned man, says, "I was not born morally deficient, or deficient in any way. And I have never sinned."

That's a ripe one.

What a luxury, a self-indulgence, it is to consider things spiritual.

There are those, you know, who insist that the spiritual lives of my comatose patients, these sausages in a freezer, continue despite all, and therefore must be allowed to continue, by whatever means.

Such thinking is a luxury, if you know what I mean, not for the patients, but for their families and friends, and, if not for them, for the courts.

"Is it malignant?"

"Where are you, David?"

"At the airport."

"Perhaps we should talk later, when you are at home. Or stop by the office on your way home. Are you on your way home?"

"I'm all right. I'm in the V.I.P. lounge, seated in a comfortable chair, facing a pacifying seascape on the wall."

"Okay. As you know, a lump has appeared—"

"Is it malignant, or not?"

"Yes."

"What happens next?"

"We should discuss that."

"We are discussing that."

"Well, we do have certain, fixed options. I do not yet know the size or shape of the malignancy."

"What are the options?"

"The usual. Medical, then surgical. First we try to treat it medically, that is, with medicines, suppuration, if appropriate, to see if we can simply contain it for a while, or, for good. In fact, the way it grew quickly at first and then stopped indicates it might already be in some kind of remission. If it resumes growth, surgical removal will be indicated."

"Pain?" David asked.

Dr. MacBride sighed. "Who knows, David, who knows? We believe the patient hasn't felt anything in years. Why should he feel this?"

"The expression on his face," David said.

"What about it?"

"It's changed."

"David, you're very close to this situation, to Chump. You're in a position where you see one thing, in this case, a lump on the head, and believe you see something else, a pained expression on his face. It may not be there." David said nothing. "I wish you'd come by the office. Or meet me for a drink, or something."

"No. I've got to meet some people and drive them down to the farm."

"We are going to take pictures of the growth this afternoon, David. We'll know more after we see them."

"What more will we know?"

"I don't know. More about what it is, its size and shape, whereall it is, which way it may grow, what it is up against."

"It is fact that it is there, it is malignant, and it won't go away by itself."

"Oh, no," Dr. MacBride said. "It won't go away by itself. That's too much to hope for."

Walking down the stairs in the airport terminal building, David had no trouble spotting Lucille Nelson.

She stood alone in the baggage claim area, nowhere near the middle of it, but absolutely the center of it. Other people waiting for luggage in the cavernous room stood in loose, knotted concentric circles around her, each man, woman and child positioned to see her, watch her, with surprise, recognition, pleasure, amazement, wonderment on his or her face.

Her own expression was of patience and live curiosity as to when her luggage was coming. To David she appeared completely oblivious to the attention she was attracting just standing there.

Lucille Nelson was much taller than David had expected from her pictures, much leaner, with a long slim neck carrying her perfectly formed head with all the dignity due a most precious object. Her posture, despite wide shoulders, full breasts, a very slim waist, was ramrod straight. As her head turned slowly her brilliant dark brown eyes were so enormous and wide-set they appeared to absorb everything in the world. Her skin was the perfect tan to which many pure white people aspire and seldom achieve, yet had the internal glow, sheen, of skin seldom, if ever, touched by sun. Her hair was auburn, slightly wavy, tied in a bun at the back of her head by a simple white ribbon in a bow. Her dress was brown and white silk of simple, straight design that looked as if it would slip off her at a shrug of her shoulders.

Seeing David stopped on the bottom step of the stairs, staring at her, she smiled widely and waved at him like a schoolgirl spotting a boy she liked.

"My God," David said, after walking up to her. "You're magnificent!"

"Oh, now, Mr. MacFarlane," Lucy drawled. "You're not going to compliment me, are you?"

"Isn't one supposed to compliment the bride?"

"Oh, yeah," she said happily. "I guess so."

Arms around his neck, she kissed him.

David looked around at the other people waiting, watching. David MacFarlane said, "I've never felt like such a celebrity before!"

Laughing, she said, "Oh, come now, Mr. MacFarlane. You were a celebrity before I was born."

"Thanks, kid. I was hoping you didn't know that."

"I mean, you're the real celebrity. You create things."

"Call me David."

"Not 'Uncle David'?"

"God, no."

"Mother has taken to referring to you as 'Uncle David' lately."

"Maybe she thinks I'm her uncle."

"Maybe! Anyway, it is truly wonderful for you and Ellie to lay on this wedding for Tony and me. Whatever made you think we deserve it?"

David choked. "Wow! I just decided you do. Where is the groom, anyway? Did you lose him en route?" A chute began to vomit baggage which then spilled down a rotating cone. "Ship him freight?"

"No. He's getting the car."

"Car! What car?"

"The rental car."

David flopped his forearms in exasperation. "What rental car? I'm here to pick you up."

"Tony thought we'd want a car of our own. Aren't we supposed to drive away into the sunset after the wedding, alone?"

"Well, I sort of had that arranged, too."

"Here's Tony," Lucy said.

Turning, David saw a face resembling Dan Prescott's coming through the glass door. Beneath it was a well-filled Palm Beach suit, brown-striped shirt, brown and white tie, polished brown loafers.

"Tony, this is David MacFarlane. You said you'd never met."

Tony was not quite stout but he was not the disciplined-looking physical wonder his father was. His physique already showed too many hours over a luncheon table, a desk, a dinner table. Clearly, Tony was not aiming for the politician pin-up look.

Also, he was a centimeter or two shorter than Lucille.

Tony's hand shot out from his side, to shake. "It's a pleasure and an honor, sir."

David said, "And that's enough of that shit."

"May I say, thank you, thank you, thank you?" Tony's eyes were filled with smile.

"Better wait on that, too," David said. "I'm new at giving weddings, but I suspect it's a damned dangerous enterprise."

Tony laughed. He raised both arms, put them around David's shoulders, and hugged him.

"That," said Tony, standing back with high seriousness, "is my way of expressing the belief that you are doing the right thing!"

"You're your father's son, all right," David said. To himself, he said, *But you're not. You're much looser than Dan, less serious, more relaxed about yourself, the world, more accepting of the world as it is. And as a result, you'll get much more from the world.* "Well, you're Josh's brother, anyway." *But are you? No. Josh's humor comes out of himself; his appeal from some quirky loneliness. Maybe you're just older, but you study up the right responses. Your informality is really a broken formality.* "Your parents have arrived. Well, Ms. Tuesday and Dan have. Josh."

"No word from my father?" Lucy asked.

"Not yet."

"Who's Ms. Tuesday?" Tony asked.

"Just about to ask the same question," Lucy said. "Who's Ms. Tuesday? Oh, there's our luggage. Quick, Tony! Before it gets away!"

Bride and groom darted for the revolving luggage while David watched. At Baggage Retrieval: Bride 4, Groom 2.

Aloud to himself, David said, "Damned if I know."

Putting two suitcases down to take a third from Lucy, Tony asked, "Is 'Ms. Tuesday' what you call Lucy's mother?"

David nodded.

Lucy asked, "Why?"

David shrugged.

Lucy said, "About the only personal thing I know about you is that you hate taxi drivers."

"I do? I do not."

"Every time I've ever complained in a cab Mother has always said, 'Now, Luce, don't do a David MacFarlane on me. We want to get where we're going.'"

"Utter rubbish," David said. "I've always gotten where I was going."

"I guess you have," Tony said. "I expect we're going to find out a lot during the next few days we never knew before."

"The first thing you're going to find out is that the farm is eighty miles from here. I didn't expect you to arrange a car of your own."

"I'll drive down with you," Lucy said to David. "Keep you company."

"Oh, no," David said. "Early days yet to abandon your groom. You two ride together. See if you can keep a conversation going. If you can't entertain each other for eighty miles, there's slim chance you'll be able to entertain each other for the next eighty years."

"Eighty years?" Lucy asked. "Do we have eighty years?"

"Easily," David answered. "If you eat your bran."

On the sidewalk outside the terminal David gave the same directions that he had given Janet's driver the day before, to wait for him outside the short-term parking lot.

Except this time David was driving a dark blue Town Car rather than a yellow pickup truck.

18

"When I saw him on the stairs to the baggage claim area, suddenly I recognized him, knew I had seen him before." Lucy steered the rented LeBaron convertible onto the soft shoulder to await the appearance of David's blue Town Car. "Isn't that funny?"

On the seat beside her, Tony Prescott, jacket removed, was rolling up his sleeves. "You said you'd seen him onstage, in London, or someplace."

"No. More intimately than that."

"You've seen David MacFarlane on television. Everybody has. Didn't he appear in a movie once, with what's-his-name, Mister Music Mad Max Brown, or whatever?"

"Mister Music Maxie Brown. 'Mad' is not a part of his appellation, as far as I know."

"Ummm. Lucille Nelson knows from classical music names as well as the appellations of jazz constellations."

"I'm educated," she said.

"So am I. I looked up 'Bizet' in a book."

"But have you listened to his music?"

"Not yet. My secretary has."

"So to this point, your secretary is educated, not you. Here he comes." Lucy waved as David passed them. He beeped his horn. She pulled out behind him. "Really odd. I saw him and suddenly felt very close to him, as if he were an old friend."

"He is an old friend. Of your parents."

"No, I mean, someone I once knew very well. Knew the smell of. I remembered I knew how his hair feels. I saw him at a distance and immediately saw close up, in my mind's eye, his huge, powerful wrists and hands. Did you feel the same way?"

"No."

"He must have come to visit when I was small, a baby. I don't know. It just feels odd to find someone like that in Nashville, Tennessee, where I've never been before."

"He's signaling. We're taking, let's see, Route 65 South."

"The past," Lucy said. "How much is in it we think we've forgotten but we bring to every moment?"

"Is that a question for the floor?"

"Every single second is swelled by accumulating thousands of other moments. Thus we all get richer as we get older."

"Resolved," Tony said. "He didn't waste any time getting into the speed lane, did he?"

"Anyway, I'm awfully glad he refused my offer and let me drive down with you."

"He just didn't want to have to entertain you for eighty miles. Without a piano."

"Because," Lucy said, "I have something to tell you."

"The marriage is off? Couldn't you have said that on the phone?"

"Before you see your father, because he might know about it, and, I, uh, don't want it to pop out of his mouth, you hear it first from him, because, uh, I mean it as a surprise, I mean it as my surprise."

"Lucy Nelson: incomprehensible in seven languages."

"You haven't asked about the wedding present."

"What wedding present?"

"Exactly."

"You have your distinguished engagement ring."

"Yes, I do, and it's lovely." She moved her hand on the steering wheel so that the ring's stone was visible.

"Distinguished by being the smallest diamond you ever wore."

"I shall wear it forever," Lucy said, "and none other."

"It's damned near being an industrial diamond."

"Well, that's to prove you're industrious."

"And I have our two wedding rings packed away very carefully in my wallet. I think." Wriggling under his seat belt, Tony took out his wallet. "What other present do you want?"

"I want to give us a wedding present."

"We're giving ourselves to each other in marriage. Isn't that the idea? Ooops!" One of the wedding rings dropped out of the wallet. "Damn. Where'd it go?"

"Would it seem to you that in my giving us a wedding present, I would be giving the wedding present to you?"

"Yes." Tony removed his seat belt.

"Because that's not the way I mean it. I bought this wedding present for me as much as for you. I bought it for us."

Free of his seat belt, Tony, bent over, was looking around the floor of the car for the dropped wedding ring. "I hope it was my wedding ring I dropped." He checked the one in his hand. "It wasn't."

"Aren't you curious?"

"Yes. Where is it, damn it?" Tony, on his knees on the floor of the car, facing backwards, was feeling along the rug under the seat and between the seat and the door. "I don't like the idea of your putting a ring on my finger and my not putting one on yours. Bad for my image."

"Tony, I bought a house."

"A house?" Kneeling, facing backward in the car, he frowned at her. The wedding ring was in his hand, between thumb and forefinger. "Where? Where have you declared our home to be? Washington? New York? Paris?"

"Columbia Falls, Maine."

After looking at her a long time, he looked at the ring between his fingers. "Columbia Falls, Maine."

"Oh, do get up, Tony. You look like some sort of a berserk choir boy kneeling that way with Tennessee streaming by your head at sixty-seven miles an hour."

"The lady said, 'Columbia Falls, Maine.'"

"Isn't that where we're from? Isn't that where our roots are?"

"Your roots?"

"My Nelson grandparents, long dead, I admit I never knew them, are from near there, thirty miles away. My father was brought up there. My Twombly grandparents still live there. I've visited them."

"I know you have."

"Will you get up, Tony? You look cherubic enough, you know, without being on your knees."

Tony put the ring back in his wallet, the wallet back in his trousers, and twisted himself back onto the car seat.

"You're from there, Tony. That's the district that will elect you to Congress. And I know how you would hate running for office from your father's farm, having to keep that as your legal address."

Tony muttered, "My grandfather's farm."

"Tony, your grandfather has been dead almost since you were born."

"My grandmother's farm."

"You barely knew her. It's your father's farm, Tony. Or you wouldn't so resent having to use that as your legal address."

"True."

"So now we have our own address, our own home in Columbia Falls."

Tony replaced his seat belt. "Lucy. The reason I haven't bought my own place in Columbia Falls is because I can't afford it. I had to buy the stupid condominium to live in Washington—"

"I bought the place in Maine. It's my wedding present. To us. You knew I flew up to see my Twombly grandparents Sunday night. I passed papers on the house Monday morning."

"I thought you were playing thoughtful granddaughter, seeing your grandparents just before the wedding. You really bought a house? It's a *fait accompli*?"

"You have to sign the papers, too. As co-owner. Mr. and Mrs. Anthony and Lucille Nelson Prescott. The papers are in one of my suitcases."

"You have a deed to a house in a suitcase?"

"Yes."

"You sent a house deed through with your luggage?"

Lucy shrugged. "It's not that expensive a house."

"A deed that is incompletely signed?"

"Oh, Tony, you hang out with too many lawyers in your job."

"That I do. Why didn't you tell me you were doing this?"

"I wanted it as a surprise. It worked, didn't it? You are surprised?"

"I'll say."

"See?"

"What bank did you use for the mortgage?"

"No bank. No mortgage. Couldn't be bothered. Didn't have time."

"My God." For a moment, Tony watched the grassy, rolling hills of middle Tennessee through his side window. "I wonder how I keep forgetting I'm marrying a rich woman."

"Famous, too," Lucy said. "Don't forget gorgeous. 'Magnificent,' was Mr. MacFarlane's word."

"Phew. Maybe you're too much for me."

"You can cope."

"What house did you buy? Do I know the house?"

"It's away from town, on the coast, overlooking the ocean. Off Lapstrake Road. An old place. Clearly at one time it was just a summer house. Whoever originally turned it into a year-round house, twenty years ago or so, must have been an artist of some sort. Visually, it's beautiful, well-proportioned, comfortable, everything goes together, flows nicely. One room must have been built as an artist's studio. It's cantilevered half over the edge of the cliff, windows three sides. You've never seen a room that so fills with light. Track lighting for night, as if maybe the artist was a photographer, but there are still gouges and oil paint stains on the floor. There's something terribly familiar about that room. I felt I knew that room, somehow, the minute I walked into it."

"I think I know which house. I've seen it from the sea side, sailing by it."

"Sure. You can't see it from the road. It's well set back, with a long driveway through the pine trees. The name of the most recent owners was Carlyle. Did you know them?"

"I think he was a retired professor from Orono."

"Yeah. He died. She doesn't want to live out there by herself. I first saw the house about six weeks ago."

"You went up there looking for it?"

"Yes."

"'Thoughtful granddaughter,' indeed."

"The grandparents were sworn to secrecy. They've been very helpful, really. Then I visited it again early Monday morning, before I signed the papers. Of course, it needs some work. Not much. The inspector's report was very good. Don't you think your father must have heard about my doing this? I mean, such a small town and all."

"The townspeople don't have much to do with him. He embarrasses them. When he's there, he stays on the farm, except for trips to the grocery store, for his fruits and greens. He doesn't even attend his father's old church; I think by popular demand."

"I've so wanted to meet him. He was never there when I was. Last weekend, of course, Granddad said your father and Josh were there, in Columbia Falls, but I wanted to avoid them, to keep the secret."

"If he knows, he hasn't mentioned it to me. Not that we talk much. We say what we need to say to each other, little more."

"Are you going to feel this way about your father forever?"

"Lord Godiva?"

"I wish you'd stop calling him that."

"What should I call him, *Twentieth-Century American—Male*?"

"Tony. Everybody has parents. Being older, parents have had more opportunity to make mistakes."

"My father is a victim," Tony said. "He didn't need to be."

"Tony, your father was brought up in a different world, with entirely different standards. Almost everything he believed in has been reversed, within his lifetime. Have mercy."

"Your father came from the same world, Lucy. Growing up in that world he was an isolated black. Look what he's done. If your father hasn't actually wrought many of the changes in this last generation himself, at least he's helped interpret them."

"No argument. But obviously my father had things to prove. He's also brilliant, don't forget. Your father belonged to the world into which he was born, the apple of everybody's eye, I expect. Which is a different kind of burden, but a burden nonetheless. He had nothing to prove."

"Yeah: he proved he had nothing to hide."

"Oh, Tony!"

"Lucy, the son of a bitch became world-famous for being a male nude, and then has spent the rest of his life keeping up his stomach muscles while saying, *Shame on me!* He didn't even do it for economic reasons, to support a family, or anything. He's worked at his profession of modeling, of being a brainless mannequin, just barely enough to keep the wolf from the door."

"'Brainless mannequin.' Thanks a heap."

"You're not brainless. What you do makes sense. It goes along with your mother's clothing business, which you own."

"Which she owns."

"My father has used his energies all his life just doing physical exercises, running, swimming miles a day, just doing pull-ups, push-ups, sit-ups, up, up, up. He is a vain, useless man."

"Oh, Tony. Don't be so harsh."

"My father is a self-made victim. Your mother is a self-made, international tycoon."

Lucy checked the rear view mirror. "Don't be so sure."

"What do you mean?"

Lucy said, "Maybe my mother was never woman enough to give herself fully to a man."

Tony said, "I thought women weren't expected to give themselves 'fully to a man' anymore."

A passing truck driver tooted his horn in friendly greeting.

Lucy waved at him gaily.

She said, "I expect to give myself fully to you. I expect doing so will enhance my being a woman, and whatever else I am, whatever else I choose to do, not diminish it." She swung the LeBaron convertible back into the speed lane to close the gap behind the Town Car. "There is a less-than-positive perspective on my mother, you know. She started her business with my father's inherited money, then bought him out. When he came back to Paris after getting his degree from the London School of Economics, yes, he stayed long enough to have one more play produced, but it was painfully obvious, to him, and to me, that he wasn't *at home.* All the activity in the apartment swirled around my mother and her stores. Could you see John Bart Nelson becoming an adjunct to a mercantile wife?"

"I don't know him."

"You read him. Obviously it was not his purpose in life to cover people's asses in blue denim or tan corduroy, nor could it be."

"I suppose not."

"And there is a perspective that sees my mother keeping her daughter out from underfoot by bouncing me from one boarding school in France or Switzerland to another, only letting me out on holidays to exploit me."

"You feel exploited?"

"Tony, I don't know how much you know about little girls. Indeed, they do have an instinct to vamp, show off, be the center of attention, at least, more so than little boys, I expect—"

"I thought we'd stopped talking about my father."

"—but not as the only living alternative to studying Maths and German. I dreaded holidays. There was always a full line of clothes for me to model, ten, twelve hours a day. School food is apt to be starchy. My report card would have all A's, but if I had one inch of fat on me, anywhere, which I usually did, my mother would spot it at the airport, and I would be harangued worse than if I had dunked the headmaster's cat in acid. I used to make friends with other children I thought had a mother and a father in place, a home somewhere, just in hopes of wrangling an invitation to their house for the holidays. Needless to say, being featured in magazines constantly, whatever popularity I had with other girls was hard won and easily lost. If it weren't for Paul, that boy I knew at boarding school in Switzerland—I've told you about him; son of some friends of my parents—this lassie might have withdrawn right down the rabbit hole into the mirror world. I was never allowed to accept such invitations, when I received them. I had to go back to Paris and work. All the time I was growing up."

"I've guessed as much."

"I am not saying, *Poor me.* No way. I like what I am, and who I am. I'm just pointing out that any parent can be criticized. Some people say my father abandoned me. You know? He certainly has placed his work ahead of me, of watching me, helping me, being with me much as I grew up. Parents can always be judged harshly. What I'm saying is *how* harshly you judge them is a decision you have to make."

"You recommend mercy."

"For your own emotional well-being. You can't accept very well what you are until you accept pretty much what your parents' influence upon you has been."

Tony said, "Points well taken."

"I'm only rattling on this way because we're about to walk into a situation completely surrounded by parents and their friends, all of whom have a past together that you and I know was rocky to say the least. Guaranteed a bloody awful time if you enter looking like a cherub thinking of your father only as 'Lord Godiva.'"

"You've bought a house in Columbia Falls, Maine."

"I have bought a home in Columbia Falls, Maine, for us."

"Your mother will never go there. She told me in Antibes she hates Columbia Falls worse than a public *pissoir.* Her words, exactly."

"Fine."

"Is it a daddy-trap?"

"What do you mean?"

"Do you see your father, *the* John Bart Nelson, ever returning to that area?"

Lucy smiled. "Maybe."

Tony said, "Better get over. MacFarlane's signaling for a right-hand turn."

19

Lying on his back on a long chair by the swimming pool, sunning himself, Josh knew he was exhilarated from riding the horse and he knew he was wondering about Nonnie's breasts, but he was not particularly aware that his penis, confined under the nylon of his tank trunks, was engorged, swollen, stiffened, arched like a rainbow, or at least he did not particularly *care* because it seemed to him it *was* erecting more these days and nights more than it *was not*; he had been told such was the pleasure and pain of being sixteen, healthy and male; he was alone in the pool area, he would hear anybody coming; there was no shame to it anyway (hadn't his father been photographed pretty much that way?); he was doing nothing, at least manually, to encourage it, because, after all, he was visible to others, if others were around; he never needed to encourage it; he couldn't help it if there was a fifteen-year-old girl on the place who looked like Nonnie, and he couldn't help thinking about her.

Besides, he was half asleep, feeling real nice after riding the horse, cooling off in the pool, lying there in the sun, and everyone knows the sleeping or nearly sleeping have no responsibility for how they appear to other people.

Suddenly a fist grabbed his penis as if it were a handle and lifted him off the chair.

"Jesus!" yelled Josh.

The sun-filled sky swooped sickeningly as he opened his eyes.

Rourke had lifted Josh's waist more than a foot off the long chair by his penis.

Trying to raise his shoulders off the mat and sit up in midair, Josh swung at Rourke's wrist, then at the inside of Rourke's elbow.

"You little son of a bitch," Rourke hissed.

"Let me go!" Taking his shoulders off the mat had only increased the weight suspended from Josh's penis. "Goddamn you!"

Rourke dropped the boy's waist back onto the mat.

Josh sprang off the chair. He stood two meters from Rourke, facing him, with his fists up. "You cocksucker!"

"You goin' to come for me, boy?" Rourke moved into a relaxed boxing stance. He beckoned Josh forward with the fingers of both hands. "Come on."

Blinking through the sunlight, Josh saw the enormity of the heavy old boxer, the smooth way he moved his feet.

"You crying, boy?"

"Shithead!" Josh backed a little farther away. "You think I'm not going to tell my Dad about this?"

Rourke snorted. He dropped his hands. "Your Dad is a tulip."

He walked over to the flower border. Rourke raised one foot off the ground and lowered it on top of a crocus, crushing it. "That's what I do to tulips."

"Jesus."

Josh's body relaxed as he watched Rourke turn and saunter into the guesthouse.

Then Josh jumped into and quickly out of the pool. He grabbed his towel and left the pool area.

20

David called to one of the Shoup brothers, the nearer one: "You sure the circuits can stand all that?" Mainly electricians, the Shoup brothers were also carpenters, plumbers, general contractors; like many others in Jameson County, jacks of all trades. David had never been able to tell the brothers apart.

"We're running extra wires from the house."

"Okay." David guessed that was an adequate answer.

David had pulled into the driveway of Bass Clef Farm a half a mile ahead of the bride and groom, whose car had slowed as they came through the valleys leading to the farm.

Workmen were setting up a bandstand under the roof of the double carport. Others were putting a dance floor together on the wide, flat area at the top of the driveway outside the carport. On the lawn off the east porch of the house, a striped serving tent was being set up. A big truck in the middle of everything was loaded with collapsible wooden tables and chairs.

To no one in particular, David said, "It looks like there's going to be a wedding here."

The other Shoup brother said, "Will people never learn?"

The nearer Shoup said, "David, you want us to put your piano on the bandstand? Ellie told me to ask."

"Naw. I'm sure the bands will just use electronic ... instruments."

"How about you?"

"No. Don't bother moving it for me."

Ellie and Janet were coming through the back door of the house. "Dan?" Ellie called back into the house. "Josh?"

Watching the LeBaron convertible turn into the driveway, David said, "Here come the bride and groom!"

As Lucille Nelson stopped the car in the driveway, turned off the engine, released her seat belt, opened her door and unfolded herself from behind the steering wheel, heavy silence fell in the yard. Workmen stopped talking; hammers stopped hammering, a drill stopped its whine, the wooden tables and chairs being unloaded from the truck stopped their rattle and bang. Not a footstep could be heard.

David chuckled. *I can't even hear their necks turning.*

The groom was unlocking the trunk at the rear of the car. No one was noticing him.

Coming out of the house behind his father, Josh slammed the screen door.

Lucy looked three hundred and sixty degrees around her, seeing all the people. She waved at the greatest collection of workmen, at the top of the driveway. "Hi, guys!" she called. "Workin' hard? Sure hope you-all come by and have a glass of champagne with me at my wedding!"

"Yeah!" said one of the shirtless young men.

"Shoot," said another. "I knew I'd get to use that necktie my wife bought me, someday!"

Lucy laughed and turned toward the house. "Hey, Mom! Heard anything from Dad yet?"

Mid-path there were general greetings. Lucy and Janet kissed Parisian feminine style: left cheek to right cheek while kissing the air outside each other's ears, to not muss the hair, the cosmetics. Lucy gave Ellie a happy little hug, thanking her immediately and simply for providing the wedding. At first Lucy shook hands with Dan, standing back, looking at him with great interest; then she kissed him, lightly on the cheek. Josh was agog. He stood to one side, folding and unfolding his arms across his chest, stepping a little to the right or the left as the group moved, not to lose view of Lucy. She found him through the crowd and extended a hand to him, not to shake, but to hold. "Ah, I see," she said. "This is the *good*-looking brother!"

Josh took Lucy's hand as if it were a ten-pound emerald and, David was sure, took all of Lucy into his heart, forever.

Tony put down one suitcase and met Ellie.

Lucy asked Janet, "You haven't heard from Dad?"

"Not a rumble. Don't even know if he got any of the messages."

Jock came up from helping unload the truck, ambling on his crooked legs below his crooked hips in his skinny jeans. For a moment, Clara Reagan had watched the arrival through the screen door.

"Jock," Ellie said. "Here are the b. and g.. Jock Reagan."

A bag in each hand, Tony nodded at Jock.

Lucy said, "'Stop your ticklin', Jock.' You know that old song?"

"No, Ma'am."

"It's a good one," Lucy said. "Seein' you're here, maybe we'll play it instead of *The Wedding March.* "

And Jock was beaming.

David said, "We'll play *The February March.*"

Ellie said, "Jock, we're putting the bride and groom in the lower guesthouse."

"Right." He went to the car to get more luggage.

The matter had been discussed, lightly. David thought Ellie ought at least ask the bride and groom if they wished to sleep together at Bass Clef Farm before the wedding, but Ellie had said, "Nonsense. Good form went West with Davy Crockett."

The bride and groom did not protest the decision.

Janet asked, "David, is that your Town Car in the driveway?"

"It is."

"You have a Town Car, and you picked me up at the airport in a farm truck?"

"I did. But, that's okay. You had your own limousine anyway."

"Let me help with the luggage," Dan said. He moved toward the car. To that point, he had been staring at Lucy with a kindly but amazed expression on his face.

David went into the kitchen, took a Sun Drop from the refrigerator and retreated to his study. He closed the door and turned on the small air conditioner.

Ellie found him there almost immediately.

"That," Ellie said, "is a woman."

David said, "She is magnificent."

Ellie closed the door behind her. "David, what's wrong?"

"Chump has a knob on his head." She watched his eyes. "A malignancy. Top of his neck, behind his right ear."

"Oh, dear. They know it's a malignancy?"

"Yes."

"What did MacBride say?"

"Foolish stuff, as if to a child. Wanted me to envision magical medicine, drains, whistling clean surgery." David took a deep breath. "He said it won't go away."

"Oh, David." Ellie put her hand on David's forearm.

"The expression on his face has changed."

"Yes?"

"More pinched somehow."

"What did Ms. Manning say?"

David shrugged. "You know how she is."

Ellie said, "I think you have to read her eyes."

David let out another deep breath. "So it goes."

Ellie held out both hands. "We seem to have a wedding going on."

"Yes."

"By the way, without a minister scheduled."

"Oh. Right. Dan won't change his mind?"

"He did nothing about getting the state's permission to perform a wedding in Tennessee."

"Yeah. I'll talk to Chuck. Maybe he can help out."

Ellie said, "The bride and groom are here. Ms. Tuesday and Dan. Josh. Milton. Paul has gone in to get Sorry and Doug off the Los Angeles flight."

David said, "Guess I'll go talk to William. See how the critturs are doin'."

Ellie said, "You go talk to William."

Carrying his unfinished Sun Drop, David left through the front door of the house.

"Do we need more rain?" David asked.

"Could use it." William lit a cigarette. "We're all right. Ponds have enough in them this time of year."

Walking down to the barnyard, David wondered how he had failed to notice the fresh paint on the barn doors before. Surely the Simpson family had not had the time to scrape and paint those doors that day, or even that week.

"Maybe next week."

"I'd sooner it held off, next week," William said. "Grass has pretty much stopped."

"Yeah." David had learned that when grass grows tall enough to fall into its own shade it stops growing and it is time to cut it. It is necessary to harvest the grass between rains. One cannot store wet hay in a barn.

"Thought you wouldn't appreciate the traffic of hayin' through here this week."

David looked at the late afternoon sky. "Hope we're not missin' the weather."

"Should be all right."

"Still some hay in the barn from last year," David said. "The front barn."

"A little. In the loft. It's good hay."

"Also, you hayed one field last week."

"Yeah. The lower field, where the pond is. Figured I'd get that down before there was too much traffic around here."

Hay to a cattle farmer is capital, security, comfort. In the years David had watched, worked with William, learned from him, he had never seen William, even during the drought year of '86, come close to spending his last bale of hay.

"Appreciated," David said. He loved to watch the haying operation, help out as much as he could, without being in the way of someone else earning a paycheck. The mathematical precision with which William cut the big fields and his old father tossed the hay up for the bailer; the way the hay was bailed, then left in the fields in no particular order to cast shadows in the neatly gleaned fields in the setting and rising sun; the athletic, frenetic speed with which a gang of white and black men danced around the fields following the big, old flatbed truck, tossing the bales of hay up onto it, stacking the hay so neatly on the truck you'd think that was its permanent place; rush it to the barn, always with the threat of rain coming, no matter how clear the sky (of course it would rain before the long process of haying was over), tossing it onto the hay elevator, men in the lofts stacking the hay again to take advantage of every cubic centimeter of space. To David, haying had the mathematical precision, the rhythm, pacing, form, structure, dimensions of a good piece of music or of a good novel.

Once, at dusk, when the sky in the west was heavy and dark with rain clouds, David had seen William out in the fields running alongside the flatbed truck throwing bales of hay onto the truck by himself. No one was on the back of the truck. It took David a moment to realize, watching from the upper balcony of the house, that no one was driving the truck, either. As the truck approached the fence, William ran around it, jumped into the cab, released the steering wheel somehow, turned the truck around, headed it back across the pasture, reset the wheel, jumped out of the cab and continued to load the moving truck by himself.

"Your house is getting pretty full, David."

"Yes." David crushed the Sun Drop can in one hand, folded it, and crushed it tight. "That was the bride and groom who just arrived."

William asked, "David, who is Paul?"

"Paul? Oh. Paul Hollingsworth. Son of some friends. He's gone into the airport to collect his parents now, I guess. Why do you ask?"

"He spends all his time down here."

"That kid's got more education than all of Jameson County put together, I expect," David said. "He's got his doctors degree in something I don't even know what the words mean."

"He sure is helpful."

"Does he know what he's doin'?" David asked. "I mean, around the barns?"

"Not particularly."

"Guess he's glad to be outdoors," David said. "He works at a university, in New Jersey."

"He's as strong as a bull," William said.

"He was a champion boxer, in school."

David suspected William was telling him something, but David didn't know what.

William said, "After he helped me with the steers this morning, he ate something in his car, then scraped three of the barn doors down damned near to their natural wood, and painted them twice."

David looked across at the barn doors. "I was wondering how they got painted."

"You tell him to do that?"

"No."

"Mention anything about barn doors?"

"No. He's here for the wedding."

"He set about it just as if it was his plan for Thursday."

"You didn't say anything to him?"

"I ran the weed eater around that door we hardly ever open when I saw what he was doin'."

"Didn't he talk to you?"

"Yeah. He got out of me every single thing we do, buying bull calves at one price per pound, turnin' 'em into steers, feedin' 'em up over a year, then sellin' 'em at pretty near the same price per pound, heavier. He had me recite the medicines I give 'em."

"Make any recommendations?"

"Nope. Just drank it all in."

"What are you saying, William?"

"Well, he's no spoiled kid."

David thought of Paul's parents, Sorry and Doug. "No. He wouldn't be."

"He slept out here last night?"

"Yeah. Said he didn't want to disturb us."

"Slept in the car," William said.

"Yes."

"I don't recollect him ever bein' here before."

"He never has been."

"Well," William said. "He sure is helpful."

Also, David thought, *what you are saying, William, is that that is a very odd way to behave.*

David asked, "Did he go up to the big house at all? Did he see Ellie?"

"Yeah. He went up, got all showered and shaved, came back down here to his car and changed clothes to go to the airport. I guess he saw Ellie."

"He changed clothes down here?"

"Yup."

"Sounds like he intends to stay down here."

"Yes, it does."

David saw Paul's rental car come along the road and slow to make the turn into the driveway leading to the main house.

"Ever hear a tune of mine called *'Sorry'*?" William didn't answer. "Anyway, I wrote a song once I called *'Sorry,'* after his mother."

"What kind of a name is that?"

"Her name is Sarah. I guess her stepfather, Jack, took to callin' her 'Sorry.'"

William nodded toward the house. "They're here."

"Yeah. Guess I'd better go make my manners."

21

"All my life," Lucy was saying, "I have been hearing about women's rights. Never once have I heard the phrase, 'women's responsibilities.'"

The dining room table had been extended by two leaves. Lucy sat to David's right; Josh to his left. At the other end of the table, Tony, the groom, sat to Ellie's right; Milton, in his wheelchair, to her left. At the middle of the table to David's left sat Janet; across from her, Dan. To Dan's right sat Sorry Hollingsworth; across from her, her husband, Doug. Their son, Paul, looking cramped, sat between his father and Janet.

For some reason unknown to David, but to Tony's grinning amusement, Lucy had chosen that moment to infuriate her mother.

"My father raised me to believe," Lucy continued in her slightly accented diction, "that there are no rights without responsibilities."

David was pleased he had a tape recorder working in his pocket.

"Your father," Janet said, "did not raise you. When next you see him, review the question of responsibilities and rights with him, will you?"

"By the way, David," Milton interjected kindly. "That music you wrote for John Bart Nelson's long poem, that *Pentecost* thing, has been performed lately, in Australia."

"Is that so?" David asked.

"Two or three months ago. We got a check."

"That's nice," David said. "Maybe we can afford this roast beef."

Josh snickered.

Lucy said, "One accumulates rights only by exercising responsibilities."

"Then your father has few, if any, rights," Janet said. She had been quaffing her French champagne since her reported altercation with Dan Prescott beside the pool that morning.

Mildly, Lucy said, "There is no one in the world more responsible than my father."

Ellie said to Milton, "Is Rourke helping you to be comfortable in the guesthouse?"

Janet said, "If I hadn't assumed all the responsibilities early on, baby, you'd have been an abandoned urchin on the streets of Paris with me, at best, trying to sell flowers at the corner."

"'Abandoned'?" Lucy asked rhetorically. "You had the choice of going to London with my father when he enrolled at the London School of Economics. Why didn't we go with him? He didn't 'abandon' us. He went off to do something eminently reasonable. You just didn't choose to accompany your husband, with your daughter."

"Can anyone present see me dragging through Africa in a burnoose?" Janet asked.

"You wouldn't have needed tropical dress in London, Mother," Lucy said, "and that was the initial, significant move Father made in his career, wasn't it? Furthermore, for the owner of clothing establishments and the employer of clothing designers, your education regarding African *couture* seems unenlightened at best and indifferent at worst."

David found himself tossing a quick grin down the table at Ellie.

"More string beans, anyone?" Ellie asked. "Sorry? Do you prefer the salad?"

Sorry Hollingsworth had taken very little food and eaten, so far, one leaf of lettuce. The food on her plate she was stirring around like a child, as if by separating its elements she could make it disappear.

Before dinner, back and forth getting drinks for people in the living room, David had noticed Sorry's arms and legs were as thin as blades of grass. What was visible of her deeply tanned skin was marred by many evidences of skin cancer, most of which had been surgically removed. The short moment he had spent with her he had inquired politely about the health spa she and Doug operated in Beverly Hills, California.

"I would like to ask you, young lady," Janet said to Lucy, "exactly how much time your father has spent with you while you were growing up, or, for that matter, since?"

"True." Lucy's sniff was executed perfectly. "He seldom, if ever, met me at airports."

"Airports," Doug Hollingsworth said. "What's the line? 'Airports are the places where, when you have to go there, / They have to take you in.'"

"Airports," David MacFarlane said, "are something somehow I haven't deserved."

Doug Hollingsworth's skin, although lightly tanned and freckled, apparently had not been as often and as badly sun-poisoned as his wife's; nor was he as sickly thin. He looked your standard middle-aged, southern California businessman, in good physical condition, with good color, and he was a cheerful twenty pounds overweight.

"Let me ask you, Mother," Lucy said, "especially seeing we're all such very old friends here ..." Visibly, Janet was bracing herself. "... when my father went to L.S.E., to London, why didn't we go with him?"

Janet said, "Our home was in Paris."

Dan Prescott said, "Your home was in Columbia Falls, Maine." Janet's eyes threw knives at him. "I'm sorry," Dan said. "I just meant that seeing you had made the adjustment from Columbia Falls, Maine, to Paris, France, surely you could have adapted to London, England?"

"Or to Botswana, or to Peru," Lucy said.

"Luce," Janet said, "seeing we're all such old friends here, let me ask you if being dragged over deserts and through jungles is a life you would have preferred to the one you have?"

"It would have been interesting," Lucy said. "More interesting, I expect, than being sent to Switzerland and told not to eat the chocolate."

Dan said, "It's an old belief that New Englanders are the most adaptable people on earth."

"An old belief among New Englanders, I expect," Sorry said.

"If I'm not permitted, by the presence of my daughter," Janet said, "to say that I had my rights, as a woman, as an independent, self-determining person, to remain in Paris and make my own life, for myself and my child, then perhaps I can say I had the responsibility to do so."

Lucy said, "Responsibility is what you assume."

"What does that mean?" Janet asked.

"You assume the responsibility for a husband," Lucy replied, "and all that implies, regarding home and family."

"And a husband assumes the responsibility of a wife, home and family," Janet said.

"But of course," Lucy said. "But there is a difference between men and women, yes?"

"Long live the difference!" Doug said.

Lucy said, "Men and women have different basic instincts. They act differently."

"Can't go into my barnyard without seeing that," David said. "When chicks are born the only way you can tell the male from the female is by the way they act. A bull acts differently from a cow; a dog from a bitch. They are born that way. Most of us are born that way, with either distinctly male or female instincts. How can such a simple, basic fact of existence be so obfuscated by today's media?"

Ellie said, "Their only remaining view of nature is at the supermarket's meat counter, wrapped in plastic."

Lucy asked, "Am I going to start a riot by stating such an obvious truth, that nurturing is more in a woman's nature than a man's, and that aggression is more in a man's nature than a woman's?"

David said, "We had some new bull calves arrive on the place this morning. Paul and Josh helped out with them. I'd be pleased to show them to the rest of you tomorrow."

Janet said to Ellie, "Apparently my daughter does not believe in the equality of the sexes."

"Oh, but I do," Lucy said. "The equality, but not the similarity."

"Good point," Milton said. "Any society that confuses male and female instincts and roles is just causing itself a lot of sickness. We can't get away from the basic facts of our natures even if we all do live in plastic, electronic boxes in the sky."

To Paul Hollingsworth, David said, "I hadn't realized you and Lucy are such old friends." He had seen the warm hug and kiss Paul and Lucy had shared at first sight of each other in the living room. Clearly Lucy had been greatly surprised and delighted to see Paul.

Paul nodded. "Lucy and I were at school together, in Switzerland. A long time ago. As teenagers."

"Except Paul was a great deal older than I," Lucy said.

"Three years."

"And a great deal wiser."

Paul said, "Just more cynical, probably."

"He may have even saved my life," Lucy said. "Or sanity, or something."

In lieu of further explanation, Paul said, "At one point we found ourselves in East Germany together."

Janet said, "Luce has never been in East Germany."

"Ah, but Mother, I have," Lucy said.

"When? Doing what?"

"When I was fourteen. Eating chocolate."

"Isn't it amazing how our young people get about?" Sorry asked. "We were so pleased, and surprised, to find Paul waiting for us at the airport in Nashville this afternoon."

Doug said, "No more surprised than I am to hear he's been in East Germany. Were you really?" he asked Paul.

"Yes."

Doug said, "Glad I didn't know about it at the time."

Lucy said, "We were talking about the vacuum cleaner."

"We were?" Tony asked.

"The electrical household appliance in general," Lucy said.

"Not the first time you've talked about something of which you have no personal knowledge," Janet said.

"It's my theory," Lucy said, "that with the advent of electrical home appliances the modern woman slipped her moorings and has been increasingly adrift ever since."

"Oh, my God," Janet said. "This is the generation of retrogression."

"I believe you could do a mathematical graph showing that as woman's homemaking labor has diminished, so she has felt her nurturing responsibilities have diminished. Totally incorrectly, the modern woman has equated the two. The electrical home appliance, instead of just making things easier for all of us, mistakenly has separated woman from her nature. Not needing to wash baby's diapers by hand, I expect she spends less, not more, time just sitting quietly, with baby cradled in her arms. Does anyone here agree with me?"

After a moment, Paul said, "The same can be said of men. By doing business by telephone or computer—"

"—he's become as soft as a grape," his father finished for him. "He comes to our health spa in California to row a machine, but would never think of testing himself against white water rapids."

David MacFarlane sighed. "The white water rapids are polluted."

Dan said, "Technology drives a wedge between ourselves and our basic instincts. Is that all bad?"

"No," said Doug. "I'm really looking forward to the irresponsibility of our next, computer-operated nuclear war."

"Woman has abandoned the home, and the family, to the appliance," Lucy said. "She has abandoned her nurturing instincts to something she can plug in."

Josh laughed. "What do you mean? Television is a fine babysitter, I can tell you. How many other babysitters can teach you how to get through a locked door with just a credit card?"

"I am presenting a feminist argument," Lucy said. "That is, one in behalf of women."

"Not to my ears," Janet said. "I hear you advocating washing diapers by hand, when you've never done so."

"I don't see the logic of women having to deny their basic instincts, particularly that of nurturing husbands and children, and fleeing the home, destroying the concept of family, just because someone has invented the vacuum cleaner!" Lucy said. "That doesn't make sense!"

David asked, "Do you think a woman needs to sit home all day in a house or an apartment that runs itself?"

"I think she should take the freedom granted her by the home appliance to be more involved in her husband's and children's lives, not less; to enhance her nurturing function, not diminish or deny it; to fulfill, not frustrate herself; to foster family, not destroy it."

Into the silence, Dan Prescott said, "Well, what I think we're hearing is the bride, two nights before her wedding, telling us she has thought out what she believes pretty well."

"Oh, no. That's not what we're hearing," Janet said. "What we're hearing is Luce's little tirade against me. What I'm hearing is Luce's contention that her father, John Bart Nelson, has acted appropriately to his role as aggressive male and gone off to explore the world, while her mother, Janet Twombly Nelson, has not acted appropriately to her role as nurturing female by attending to either one of them. Therefore, that her father is somehow more responsible than I."

Dan again spoke into a silence, to Sorry. "Do I understand you and your husband run a health spa in California?"

"Yes. In Beverly Hills."

"Oh, wow!" Josh said. "Do movie stars use your place?"

"Yes," Doug answered. "Several of them."

"Like who?" Josh asked.

Doug and Sorry remembered several names that pleased and excited Josh.

"What are they really like?" Josh asked.

Doug laughed. "What they're really like is that they're really slow to pay their bills!"

Apparently continuing their argument, Janet said something to her daughter in rapid French.

Lucy continued to answer smoothly, also in French.

"Beverly Hills is a very odd world," Sorry said, ignoring the French. "Everyone there seems to be exactly thirty-four years old. You seldom see children and almost never really old people."

"Rather like the world Lucy was just complaining about," Doug said. "Everyone has rights without responsibilities."

David recited: "'Conception without her due birth; / Bells ringing heedless of the time; / Man without his fulsome labor; / A song without its rhyme: / So mantled, Olympus enthroned/ With ambrosia and honey.'"

"What's that from, David?" Milton asked. "I sort of recognize it."

Janet answered over-loudly: "That *Pentecost* thing!"

22

"My, my."

As the studio was reasonably well sound-proofed, David had not known until he slid open the glass door to what music all his house guests were listening.

After dinner, David had retreated to his study. Using his telephone for an hour, he had made a dent in his correspondence by dictating letters to a machine at Treble Clef in Nashville. He then had been unable to find anybody (except Ellie, who was in the back of the house, managing dishwasher, clotheswasher and clothesdrier machines, all of which she had running simultaneously) and had wandered around the place until he spotted all his house guests through the glass door, in diverse postures, on the divans and floor of the studio.

The music to which they were listening was a piece of David's new music, composed on his synthesizer, called *Symphony #**.

He slid the door closed behind him and sat down cross-legged on the hardwood floor. He figured as long as his friends had found the tape, and were listening to it, he might as well, too, and develop some sense, if he could, of their understanding of it and reaction to it.

When he entered, the tape was at the beginning of the second movement of the symphony.

In composing *Symphony #**, first David was trying to use the music synthesizer as fully as his state-of-the-art equipment and, of course, his music education and background permitted. (During these same years, David had been working on, and had not yet completed, a great variety of shorter compositions, the primary purpose of which was simply to show what the synthesizer could do as a musical instrument itself, given its range and indefinite diversity. He thought of these pieces as ultimately a single work, or collection, somewhat as a *Well-Tempered Synthesizer.* As seemingly limitless as the sound the synthesizer can duplicate, vary, fragment, enhance, combine—not only of musical instruments but of human voices and all sounds in the universe, natural, mechanical, other electronic—so also was his task seemingly limitless. Knowing his continuing to eat regularly did not depend on his next paycheck at this point in his life, and that he could expect many years of productivity still ahead of him, he had not tried to narrow or limit his task. For example, some of the raw tapes of country, city, human, mechanical, electronic sounds he first played for Chump Hardy he later incorporated through his synthesizer into this new music; therefore, including every sound perceptible to the human ear in his definition of *music,* David's task was limited only by his own human ability to restructure sound. He thought, if he ever finished, or more likely, when he was at the point when he was no longer able to continue, for one reason or another [most likely because he would have exhausted his own ability to create form] that he would dedicate this work to Bach and Copeland.) In *Symphony #**, there was a disciplined, refined, light, implicit, even restrained, but full, use of the electronic music synthesizer.

Beyond interesting use of the instrument itself, David tried, in *Symphony #**, to perceive and to cause people to hear in a new way the eclectic nature of contemporary sound. Of constant amazement to David maturing was the rapid increase in numbers and varieties of sounds the modern human ear not only could but had to distinguish. Not only could modern man identify the sound of a horse approaching, but that of a car, a bus, a motorcycle, a truck, a train, an airplane, a helicopter; not only the voices of people around him, family, friends, fellow workers, but an even greater number of electronic voices, even the difference between the voice of a friend and the taped voice of a friend; not only the sound of the rain but that of a dripping faucet, a natural shower and a shower bath, a babbling brook and an exploded hydrant; not only the sound a stick makes drawing on the ground, but that of a pencil on paper, the hum of a word processor. Human senses had been increased immeasurably by exposure to accelerating technology, more than anyone probably would have predicted possible. In music such as *Symphony #**, David thought it worthwhile, amusing, useful, artful to observe and indicate ironies that exist between varieties of sounds, for example, the sound of a bullet hitting wood, and the sound of a kiss.

If rhythm once had been limited to the human pulse, the sound of the rain, the work song, Lord Byron's horse, the basic industrial noise, most modern rhythm, from the speaking human voice to the popular song to the monitored pulse, is underlaid by the electronic hum, that has a continuing rhythm of its own, that sets its own pace for human activity and, although it has many eclectic, usually conflicting rhythms imposed on it, needs its own identification as a bass line. And in *Symphony #** David used that hum, in varying pitches, as his basic rhythm.

Admittedly, David's concepts for *Symphony #** at that time were novel, but he felt they fell within the definition of *simple* in that they were obvious, existent for anyone to hear, in fact so clearly perceptible that he expected people generally had perceived them, grabbed them into their working knowledge without ever having been specifically conscious of them. He saw his job as a creative artist to make this working knowledge conscious by indicating the ironies that exist within contemporary sound.

What he did not realize himself, of course, was that what is simple, obvious, conscious to a person who has spent his life focusing on a single element of existence, such as sound, or time, refining his own perceptions in a single area, requires a generation or more of simple repetition to make conscious in less- or otherwise-focused sensibilities.

So David MacFarlane sat after dinner cross-legged on the hardwood floor of his studio listening with his friends to the second movement of his *Symphony #**, thinking, hoping they were hearing something similar to what he was hearing, to what he had composed, thinking they might be.

After ten minutes of David's being there, Josh rose from where he had been sitting on the floor beneath the tape machine. He snapped his fingers a few times at Jester to invite the dog to follow him as he crossed the floor and slid through the door.

Shortly, Janet rose from where she had been sitting on a divan and, respectfully *sotto voce*, asked if anyone wanted to join her in enjoying a bottle of French champagne she was about to open. And she left.

Lucy followed her. David thought, hoped, possibly to make amends with her mother.

The groom followed the bride. David thought, hoped, possibly to guarantee peace between the two women.

Having the courtesy to grin sheepishly, but saying nothing, Paul Hollingsworth put his eyeglasses back on, and left.

At the sound of Jester's barking from outside, Dan Prescott rose, stretched a little, muttered something about *going to see what Josh has gotten himself into now*, and left, sliding the glass door closed behind him.

Before the general egress, Milton Farber's head had tipped over in sleep.

For a moment, David remained where he was, listening to the music by himself, again.

Then he got up.

He turned the tape player off.

At the sound of silence, Milton Farber's head straightened. He blinked around the room, now empty of people except for David and himself.

David said, "Well, that separated the wheat from the chaff."

"No, David." Milton Farber put the palms of his hands on the arms of his wheelchair. "It separated from those who can't move."

David rewound the tape.

Milton said, "Of course, I'm not a music critic."

"You've always said that, when you've hated a piece of music."

"David, I hate this piece of music."

"You don't understand it."

"Maybe if I understood it, I'd hate it properly. Maybe I'd admire it. As it is, however improper of me, I hate it."

"Milton, I don't expect this music to be on the Top Forty Most Popular Tunes list this week."

"Not even this year. Maybe not even this lifetime."

David agreed. "Maybe not even this lifetime." He turned the tape player off, took the tape reel off the player, placed it back in its box, and reached to replace it on its shelf. "How did you find the tape, anyway?"

"I had help. I conspired with that teenaged boy. Josh. I remembered boys are very good at getting into where they don't belong, like trouble. I was sick of listening to pretty women hissing at each other in French. I wanted to hear some good music."

David sat on a divan. "What attracted the others out here? Did you sell tickets?"

"After a dinner conversation like that I could have sold tickets to mud wrestling. Maybe they thought you were giving one of your new tape concerts."

"There will be no tape concerts, Milton."

Milton looked around the studio with sleepy eyes. "All this expensive equipment."

"I'm not wasting it, Milton. I'm using it."

"Tell me. What do you call this piece, 'Ungodly Hums, Rumbles and Squeaks'?"

"I can't say the title. It works visually."

"Can't say the title. Can't perform the music." Milton shrugged. "Can't listen to it, either."

"I can listen to it."

"You and Chump, and he's comatose."

David said, "Chump has a malignancy, Milton. In his head."

Milton rubbed the liver spots on his hand. "I know." Then he looked at David. "And you're spending years out here in this studio-gymnasium recording hums, rumbles and squeaks. How could you, David MacFarlane, after all you've done, after all your talent has given you, express such contempt for piano?"

"I'm not expressing contempt for piano."

"Soon he'll be hissing at me in French."

"I use the piano in this symphony."

"You play a note, a chord on the piano, exactly when you think the listener is about to commit suicide. Are you making a joke of the piano?"

"I'm using the piano to clarify the sound, when I feel it is needed."

"'Clarify'! Nothing is clear. It's as clear as ice. And just as cold. Is that what all this farm life has done for you? I don't believe it. I'm an old man, David, confined to a wheelchair, but I'm still alive, I still have blood trying to course around my veins. When I was a young man I needed warmth, vibrancy in my music, and now that I am old, I need it even more. I need to be told I'm a human living with humans, not some vibrating tuning fork living in a plastic box with microchips for company!"

"But that's what you are, Milton. That's what we all are."

"No!" Milton pointed toward the house with a fully extended arm. "Listen to that wonderful young woman at your own dining room table. Humans have not changed because someone invented the vacuum cleaner!"

"Wrong," David said. "That 'wonderful young woman' is today's young idealist. She's trying to tell us she can go from New York to

Nashville between lunch and dinner and that shouldn't affect how members of her family talk to each other. Technology profoundly has affected human nature. The bicycle, the car, the airplane, the television deeply have changed our sense of time and space, of how we relate to nature. Chemicals—pills, Milton, pills—radically have changed how we relate to ourselves, each other, sexually and every other way. I'd like to believe her. Whether technology enhances or diminishes our lives, technology is a fact."

"So who shot the piano?"

"I'm not to move beyond the piano?"

"I remember when you were young, David, the first time you worked in a big nightclub, and they stuck a microphone under the lid of your piano. You called me in New York and swore at someone's turning your piano into 'an electronic box.' Your words. You asked me if you had to put up with such a thing. It frightened you."

"I got used to it."

"David, David, I'm too old to argue about human nature with you. And it's true: without the pills, I wouldn't be alive. You could progress into making hums, rumbles and squeaks without me around to remind you of anything."

"I didn't want you to hear these tapes." David's eyes scanned the shelves of tapes along the inside wall of the studio, including a whole different set Josh and Milton, the other intruders could have found. "I said they're radical."

"David, it's you I'm talking about."

"I am doing necessary, exploratory work in music. I know what I'm doing."

Milton grinned. "All the melodies are written?"

David's eyebrows wrinkled. "You don't hear melodies in this?"

"What I'm trying to say, David, is that over a lifetime you've come to be able to do something special with a piano, not only because you've played piano hours a day, but also because you've lived; as a person you've experienced Chump Hardy, Ms. Tuesday, Ellie, me; you've put together a personality which, as far as I know, has no transplanted parts, no microchips, and when you compose it is that David MacFarlane, that personality, that I need and want to hear. You've lived; you've got your talent; you've got your skill: there should be no one better at expressing, through music, what it is to be alive in this time and this place." David started to say something but Milton put his index finger to his own lips. "That music I just heard, David, is the music an airplane might write, or a vacuum cleaner, or a computer itself. That I can die without hearing."

David said, "You're wrong. If we followed your thinking, we never would have gone from the drum to the violin to the harpsichord to the piano. This work, this *radical exploration,* needs to be done. Who can do it better than I?"

Milton sighed. "Maybe you're right. Everybody's a specialist. Maybe a music needs to be written just for musicians. As your manager, however, I must tell you, your new music won't hold an audience any more than my sandals will hold water. As your friend, I must tell you I'd rather hear you telling me, through a piano, who and what you are now."

"Milton, don't you see? It is exactly because we have become overwhelmed with all sorts of new things this century that we must come to grips with them, take them into ourselves, know them, use them, or we shall perish."

"If I don't get to bed soon, I shall perish. Will you wheel me out and help me find the gorilla?"

"Sure." Behind Milton's chair, pushing it, David said, "Where are the batteries? Don't you like your wheelchair motorized?"

Bouncing over the low threshold of the door, Milton said, "Neither would I have believed I'd live to see the day the gorilla gets to keep the key to the cage."

23

"Oh." Tony Prescott said to his father: "I was sort of looking for you."

Dan Prescott said, "You sort of found me."

Tony had taken a glass of champagne out onto the east porch of the main house and stood in the dark looking at the moon. After a moment he had sensed someone behind him.

His father was sitting quietly, alone, in a dark corner of the porch, also positioned to watch the moon.

"Want some champagne?" Tony asked.

"No, thanks. I'm full of about everything at this point."

With one hand Tony skidded one of the wrought iron chairs nearer his father in the corner and sat in it.

Dan said, "One thing I'm full of is admiration for that young lady you're marrying."

"Thanks. Glad to hear it."

"She's amazing enough as a person. That she is the daughter of Janet Twombly and Jack Nelson, and to be your bride, absolutely astounds me."

"I suspect there are all kinds of things going on under the surface here that would astound me."

"Not really."

"Lucy and I don't even understand how all you people are related to each other, or even how you know each other."

"Very simple. Jack and I played football against each other in high school, met later in Paris. Janet and I, as you know, grew up together."

"And David MacFarlane? How did you meet him?"

"In a bar, a music joint, in Boston. Before he was very famous. Dave MacFarlane took Janet away from me. Jack Nelson took Janet away from Dave. Such is life. It's not so much a story of how we all relate to each other as much as it is a story of how we all never really related to each other. Not much of a story."

"I don't think anyone ever *took* Mrs. Nelson."

"I think you're right."

Tony said, "Lucy sure gave her mother a hard time at dinner."

"I'm surprised Janet expects to be admired by her own child. One seldom is."

"At least she answered her daughter back."

"Yes," Dan said, "She did."

Tony sipped his champagne. "Well, I've had my music appreciation lesson for tonight."

"Right." Dan said, "I sure was relieved when Lucy got up and walked away from that awful music. Made me feel less crass and cruel in doing so myself." Dan scratched his forearm. "Made me itchy. Can noise make you itchy?"

"Lucy sure is astounding, all right," Tony said. "In fact, she astounded me on the drive down from Nashville."

"Oh?"

"She has bought us a wedding present—a house in Columbia Falls."

For a moment, Dan was silent. Then he said, "That's nice."

"Perhaps you know the house," Tony said. "On the seaside, off Lapstrake Road. Originally just a summer cottage, remodeled some years ago. Has a big, glass-walled, studio-type room jutting out over the cliff. Recently belonged to a retired Orono professor and his wife, name of Carlyle. I've noticed the house from a sailboat."

Dan asked, "Has Lucy already bought this house?"

"As a surprise to me. Quite a surprise. She signed the papers Monday morning. I signed my name to the deed just before dinner."

"You mean, before dinner tonight?"

"Yes."

Dan said, "I was very comfortable in that house, the once I was in it."

"You've been in that house?"

"Yes," Dan said. "I think that's the same house."

"Well. Anyway. Guess I'll have to get used to the idea that Lucy has more money than I have."

"May that be the worst of your problems."

Tony took another swallow of his champagne. "How do you feel about it?"

"Lucy's buying that house? Delighted. It means that when you come home you won't be staying with me at the farm, of course, but I know you never really liked that. Now that you have a house of your own in Columbia Falls, maybe you'll want to come home more often. There will be grandchildren, won't there?"

"Certainly hope so."

"It would be nice to have grandchildren nearby."

"I meant: how do you feel about money?"

"I never expected to have any," Dan said, "so I guess I've never really missed it. I was brought up the son of an honest minister, expecting to be an honest minister. My father believed a minister should try to earn the same sort of living as his neighbors earn; hence, the little farm. The idea of making money for the sake of making money was just never given me, as a kid. Probably the truth also is I had no talent for making money. We've gotten along all right, haven't we?"

"Have you minded terribly not being able to serve as a minister?"

"In truth? Yes. Terribly. I think I could have been useful. It's been like having the football firmly in hand, a clear shot at the goal, and tripping over my own feet, falling in the mud. I guess, despite what I thought, I didn't have the calling."

"But you weren't serving as a minister when you posed for *Twentieth-Century American—Male.* You were teaching school."

"That's right."

"You've never talked much about all that."

Dan said, "'When you excuse yourself, you accuse yourself.' I figured you and Josh didn't need to be brought up by a father who spent all his time with you rationalizing himself, what he had done."

"It was the biggest thing in your life, wasn't it? I mean, posing for that statue?"

"No." Dan took a great breath. "I guess the most mind-boggling thing I ever did was spend a few days in a confused, far-off, historically unimportant war. All my life to that point I had lived under and respected authority. My mother, my father, my school, my community had observed and judged, usually favorably, always specifically, everything I had ever said or done. The biggest shock of my life was in discovering that a total stranger, without knowing me or judging me at all, was willing to give me the ultimate insult: was willing to kill me."

"Did you ever kill anyone?"

"Yes." For a quiet moment, father and son looked at the moon. "The idea that war is a glorious test of a man's metal is too romantic. War teaches you that we are all basically garbage getting rid of each other as fast as we can; all maggots in the same bucket of slime. I guess a father can say that to a son who is a speechwriter for the President of the United States." Tony said nothing. "War does affect one's idea of oneself. I was brought up aspiring as a child of God; then, running around with a rifle, perspiring in the Kins Forest, I discovered that as far as authority, the world, was concerned, I was as disposable as a used tissue."

"All the years I spent getting my degree in history, I never once saw or heard reference to the Kins Forest."

"Someone must have thought at the time that that patch of woods was important. I expect all the trees are grown back, now, too."

"Being in a war knocked the stuffing out of you."

"No. In fact, if you'll permit me to rationalize for a moment before my son and the moon, I think my experience at war was one strong motive for my subsequently asserting myself by appearing naked before the whole damned world."

"I guess I understand that."

"It took me years to understand that."

"But having so asserted yourself once, so blatantly asserted yourself, why have you never really asserted yourself again? Forgive me. I guess that question sounds insulting."

"Twice in my life I have asserted myself; once, spiritually, in insisting Janet Twombly marry David MacFarlane, which she took as a dare and he took as a dream; once, physically, spending a day as naked as a newborn with a comfortable older couple, the Barkerslees. Each time the result was a disaster. It was the sculpture of me, but even more, the popular, expensive book of photographs of me that set your mother on a short course that ended in her death in a drunken accident on a highway in California."

"You don't blame yourself for that."

"Don't I? I publicly mortified a little lady who, up to that point, had been busy being a schoolteacher's housewife and your mother. Nothing had prepared her for my doing such a thing. I wasn't really ashamed when I did it, of course, or I wouldn't have done it. Your mother's reaction made me ashamed. I've read enough of both Kierkegaard and Feuerbach to fix my guilt precisely."

"There are more modern ideas."

"Sure: accept guilt for nothing. My problem with that philosophy is that if you deny guilt, don't you also abandon prudence? My imprudence contributed to your mother's sad and untimely death. Tell me otherwise."

"The whole world feasts its eyes upon you, and you feel badly about yourself. If only they knew."

"Life has its ironies. And I feel no worse about myself than do most people my age, I'm sure. If we all get what we expect out of life, there'd be little reason for playing it out, would there? I feel very happy about you and Josh, that you are who and what you are, and I feel happy about the extent to which I have contributed to your existence and to your being who and what you are."

"Mrs. Nelson and Mr. MacFarlane were married to each other?"

Dan hesitated. "Yes. No. As a minister, I married them, the only wedding service I've ever performed. The wedding was rather public, in Paris. It got a lot of press attention. Soon thereafter, Janet left David for Jack Nelson. I've always understood the wedding was annulled. What Dan Prescott put together, Milton Farber put asunder."

"Were they legally married, or not?"

"I don't know. I don't think so. I guess it was all a nightclub act, between band sets, featuring, besides the bride and groom, and other widely assorted characters, a very young and innocent minister. If the legal facts are important to you, I'm sure Mr. Farber can fill you in. I can assure you that Lucy is the daughter of Janet and Jack Nelson."

"I don't question that."

"Absolutely. She has to be."

"But why do you feel guilty about that? I mean, about marrying Mrs. Nelson and Mr. MacFarlane? They were grownups. Didn't they know what they were doing?"

"No. In fact, I don't think they did. I don't think Janet ever loved David. She had no more of an accurate idea of him than he had of her. They were both leading a crazy night life. I insisted they get married."

"Why?"

Dan cleared his throat. "Because they were *living in sin.* Have you ever heard that expression?"

"Oh, wow."

"Oh, wow, exactly. The world has changed that much. I was a young minister studying in Paris. I took myself and my duties seriously. Janet was, or had been, a member of my father's congregation. I pushed her into marrying Dave."

"But you loved her, didn't you?"

"Yes."

"Do you think she ever loved John Bart Nelson?"

"No. I never thought so. I always thought her marrying Jack was another rebellion, a further dare. She was like that as a kid. Dare her to climb out on a skinny limb of a tree, or attempt an impossible jump from rock to rock, and she always would. She would usually get hurt, too. I learned early on not to dare Janet Twombly into anything. I wearied of helping her home, where she never wanted to go."

"Who did Mrs. Nelson love?"

Dan didn't answer. Instead he said, "Sons can't lead their father's lives, nor fathers their son's. We can't even know everything about each other. If certain things didn't happen a long time ago we didn't understand then and probably understand only a little better now, Anthony Prescott would not be marrying Lucille Nelson the day after tomorrow. Just think of that."

Tony chuckled. "Do we ever really understand anything? Do I really understand why I'm marrying Lucy?"

And Dan laughed. "No. And you never will. But you sure will keep thinking about it."

Lucille Nelson and Paul Hollingsworth watched the moon from wooden rocking chairs on the front porch of the main house.

"Paul, I had no idea you were going to be here."

"I wasn't invited. Mother mentioned your wedding to me on the phone. I got the particulars out of her. I wouldn't miss your wedding, Cille."

"I didn't know where in the world you were. We wrote each other, for a while, but that was years ago. I didn't even know where your parents were. David must have invited them."

"I think that's what happened. My parents would do anything David MacFarlane asked."

"No one knew about our illicit time in East Germany."

"Illicit and illegal," Paul said. "I was seventeen. You were fourteen."

"How did you know enough to get on that train in Switzerland? You had money, a passport. Was it a coincidence?"

"Partly. I had gone to the Crédit Suisse branch in the village to cash my allowance check. So I had my passport on me, and some money. On the way back, I saw you climbing on that train with a suitcase. Cille, it didn't take an especially large brain to realize you were running away from school. I didn't know you very well. I knew you were the daughter of friends of my parents."

"You had always ignored me at the school."

"You were a tall, skinny brat."

"I was not a brat."

"You were. Everyone thought so. You were always trying to be so nice to everybody you were as sweet as Swiss pastry."

"Probably true."

"Absolutely true."

"I was sitting on the train, scared to death, and you walked down the aisle. I hid my face in my hands, because you were also from the school. I was afraid you had been sent to run after me. Were you?"

"No."

"You sat on the seat beside me. And never said a word."

"You were going to East Germany."

"Yes. I was."

"Where you thought there were no models, no pictures of models in magazines, no pictures of you in a red, plastic miniskirt riding by on the side of a bus."

"You remember that picture? Disgusting."

"Someone had told you that because people in Communist countries have few material goods, they have a much greater sense of family, closeness."

"I could cry right now."

"That was what you told me that weekend."

"Why weren't we expelled?"

"I'd already been accepted at Princeton. Early acceptance. They weren't about to expel me. I don't know why you weren't expelled. You should have been. Maybe old Herr Doktor Rogou had some understanding of why you did what you did."

"Herr Doktor Rogou. What a sweet man."

"To girls maybe he was sweet. To boys he was a royal bastard."

"Oh, no."

"Oh, yes. I've got the whip lashes to prove it."

"He never whipped anyone."

"No. He'd just make us ski-tour all night with a wind-chill factor of forty degrees below zero."

"He never made girls do that."

"I'd rather have been whipped. The pain would have been shorter and warmer."

"Made a man out of you."

"Damned near made a frozen eunuch out of me."

"I should have invited Herr Doktor Rogou to my wedding."

"Wouldn't you rather have me?"

"Much. You didn't say a word to me all the way to the East German border. Just sat and read your book, as if you hadn't even noticed me. The train was cold. As we approached the border, I got about as scared as I've ever been. I was shaking."

"There was no way off the train, at that point, except to jump off into an ice and snow bank."

"I grabbed your arm."

"You put your Goddamned arm through mine, as if to say to all the world, including border guards, that I was responsible for you."

"I was just a little girl."

"You were as tall as I was."

"But I looked young."

"And stupid."

"You gave me this crazy look, Paul: *Oh, hello. How are you? What are you doing?*"

"As if I really cared, I bet."

"Were you scared, too?"

"Very. I remember that train as being very, very hot. I was sweating."

"What would have happened to me, if you hadn't come along, taken the risk . . ."

"You would have done as well without me."

"I needed someone to talk to, cry to, be with."

"It was pure impulse that made me jump on that train after you. Like diving in an icy river after a puppy."

"Without you I would have just cried. With you, I cried, and laughed, and talked. And got back to school."

"The East German border guard inspected our passports and asked why we wanted to enter East Germany."

"And you didn't say a damned thing!"

"I didn't want to enter East Germany! Besides, your German was better than mine."

"You didn't know that."

"After a minute of staring bug-eyed at him you said, 'For the chocolate. Ice cream. Cake. Cookies. Pie. Pastry. Candy. . . .' You recited the whole sweets menu! Frederick Mooney never recited Hamlet's soliloquy with greater meaning, expression, feeling! The border guard—remember his big mustache?—watched and listened to you as if you were Frederick Mooney on the stage. Then he threw his head back and roared with laughter!"

"He patted my head."

"He let us through. I had been pretty sure he wouldn't."

"You had been hoping he wouldn't."

"Right. I didn't know where you were going or why."

"Remember the man who opened the door to the boarding house in East Berlin? Here on his doorstep was a tall, skinny mulatto girl and a pebble-faced white boy—"

"And you said, with the greatest aplomb I had ever seen, that we were brother and sister, our name was Moreno, we were from Cuba, and we wanted a room. *A* room!"

"—and one suitcase. And that book you were reading."

Paul said in a low voice, "*Still Waters Don't Run At All.* By Abraham Baxter. That was the time I read that book."

"A giant book. Weighed almost as much as my suitcase. He believed me!"

"I doubt it."

"He said, 'Ah, Americans!'"

"He caught the odor of foreign currency. Hard currency."

"What a nice time."

"What a nice time."

"We ate all the pastry in East Berlin. I think they had to work their sweets factories around the clock to keep up with us."

"We walked a lot."

"And talked a lot."

"You talked a lot."

"And you listened. Paul, that was probably the most important time of my life."

"You see, Cille, at dinner tonight, I expect I was the only one there who understood what you were saying: how you really feel about your mother, and your father, and yourself. I'd heard all that before, in East Germany. Not as well said, of course."

"Did I put on that show at dinner because you were there?"

"Did you?"

"Maybe. Probably. I remember part of your advice was for me to tell my parents how I felt about them—as if I ever had a chance. I did so tonight, didn't I? At least my mother."

"You sure did."

"I hope I didn't hurt her too much."

"She's a tough nut. I doubt she's in a corner somewhere, crying herself to sleep."

"If it hadn't been for that few days with you, Paul, I never could have come back and faced myself in a red plastic miniskirt on the side of every bus, faced those so-called holidays in Paris that used to exhaust me more than a full term at school; faced, accepted the life, career of Cille Nelson. I had a few screws that needed adjusting and you adjusted them, by listening, caring."

"Hell, I enjoyed the pastry orgy, too."

"What would have become of me, if you hadn't jumped on that train?"

"Later, as an undergraduate, later still, many, many times, I have remembered that I slept three nights in a double bed in a cold room in East Berlin with Cille Nelson—when you were fourteen."

"I've remembered, too."

"I didn't even have a night shirt."

"I helped you, every night, so you could sleep."

"Yeah."

"You taught me how."

"You never really got the hang of it."

"Poor, suffering Paul. Full of all that sugar energy. Ever tell anybody?"

"No. Who'd believe me?"

"You talked me back to school, back to my life."

"Who's this guy you're marrying?"

"Tony Prescott. Nifty guy. I love him. He's a straight arrow. He has a goodness, a desire to be useful to the world, to his fellow earthlings that I really admire. I don't say this to him too loudly, but I think he has that instinct from his father. Tony's still a bit of a child about his father."

"I recognize his father."

"Yes. He's a model, too."

Lucy sighed and looked to the moon. "Where's my damned father?"

Paul said, "Maybe we should have sat through that terrible music. Be kind to our host."

"No," Lucy said. "I know enough to suspect the music we heard tonight is brilliant. I just couldn't sit through it, concentrate on it, two nights before my wedding, when I wanted to talk to you."

24

Lying in the hay, Josh Prescott sneezed.

He knew Paul Hollingsworth, lying in the hay near him, was not asleep.

Josh could not understand why Paul said nothing.

"Hey," Josh said.

"More likely the dust in the hay."

Josh said, "Yuck, yuck," then asked, "What are you thinking about?"

Josh had found David MacFarlane having a glass of milk in the kitchen. Janet Nelson was stacking bottles of champagne in the refrigerator.

Josh came into the strong light of the kitchen from the darkness outside blinking like an owl.

"Okay if I sleep in the barn with Paul?" Josh asked.

Squinting in the strong light, Paul followed Josh into the kitchen from the front porch.

David looked at Paul. "There's no reason for you to sleep in a barn."

Paul smiled. "I'd rather. Princeton, New Jersey, is rather urban. I like to smell and hear natural things."

"You won't sleep."

"I slept in the car."

David said, "I guess our peacock doesn't disturb anybody anymore."

"You have a peacock?" Josh asked. "I haven't seen a peacock."

"Used to have a peacock," David said. "Josh, why do you want to sleep in a barn, when you've got a perfectly good bed upstairs?"

Josh shrugged. "I want to sleep with Paul. I figure he can teach me everything he knows before I go to sleep. I want to wake up in the barn."

"Fine by me," David said. "No matches. Don't bring any matches into the barn."

Josh turned out the front pockets of his shorts. "No matches. No cigarettes. No maryjane. I'm as innocent as a baby lamb. *Baa-aa.*"

After the front screen door of the house banged shut behind them, Ellie dropped thin, gray blankets on their heads from the balcony.

Lying in the hay in the barn, Paul returned the question to Josh: "What are you thinking about?"

"I asked first."

"So you should answer first."

"If I tell you, will you tell me?"

"Definitely maybe."

"I have this trick, see," Josh said. "I know I can really only think about one of two things: girls and money. At night, in bed, if I think about girls, I won't get to sleep. So I think about money. Except sometimes I can't help thinking about girls. I try to think about money, so I can go to sleep."

"Must require great discipline."

"It does."

"I can guess what you think about girls. What do you think about money?"

"I have a problem there."

"Let Doctor Hollingsworth help you with your problem, young man."

"Mostly I think about how to spend money. You know the Jaguar XKE?"

"Not personally."

"I don't think enough about how to get money."

"You mean, earn money?"

"Make money."

"Acquire it."

"Earn it, make it, acquire it. That's the problem. I only think about how to spend it."

"Most philosophies of life require an axiom."

"Do you think these lotteries work?"

"Sure," Paul Hollingsworth said. "The state never loses."

"How do you make a lot of money?"

"I don't."

"Yeah, but you're a real bright guy, a doctor of somethin' or other. I bet you could, if you set your mind to it."

"Why do you want a lot of money?"

"To spend it, of course."

"Then you wouldn't have it anymore."

"Yeah." Josh was silent a moment. "What's the meaning of life?"

"Life has no meaning."

"It hasn't?"

"You have to create your own meaning."

"It doesn't come packaged?"

"You wouldn't want it to come packaged."

"No. I suppose not." Josh sneezed again. "So what are you thinking about?"

"About going to sleep."

"What are you thinking about while you're going to sleep?"

After a long moment, Paul said, "Susie."

"A girl."

"A little girl. We knew each other when we were kids together in southern France."

"Did you love her?"

"I don't think kids think about love. They just love. Susie was younger than I. Six years old. I was about ten."

"When you were a ten-year-old boy you played with a six-year-old girl?"

"There wasn't anyone else. The French Riviera isn't really for little kids. Mostly rich old folks live there, and their younger parasites. You know, mistresses, gigolos."

"Wow. Many fancy cars?"

"Nearly every car you see there is worth the price of a house."

"That's for me. Mr. MacFarlane has a Winslow he keeps under a dust cover in a garage. Is that worth a lot?"

"I don't know. Anyway, most of the year I lived on a plantation in the West Indies where there were lots of things to do, lots of kids to play with. The three months every year my parents spent in France were pretty boring for me. Susie was about the only one there for me to play with."

"What about her?"

"One morning we spent at the beach with our parents. We did that often. Susie and I played together in the water and then put stones together to make a little castle. Our families separated for lunch. At three o'clock in the afternoon, after her naptime, I walked over to her house. That afternoon I was going to help her father put up a swing for her in their garden. The maid opened the kitchen door to me. She looked down at me from under her starched white cap and said, 'Susie's dead.' Then she closed the door."

"Was she crazy?"

"I couldn't understand why an adult would tell me such a terrible lie. I banged on the kitchen door with my fist. It didn't open again. I wanted to get that maid in trouble. I wanted to tell Susie's parents the terrible thing their maid had said. I ran around the house and rang the front doorbell. I banged on that thick, heavy door. No one answered. The house seemed to be sleeping quietly in the sunlight. I couldn't wake it up. I ran around the other side of the house. I stood on my tiptoes to look into Susie's bedroom through the window. She was lying on her back on her bed. A sheet was drawn up to her chin. The color in her face was all gone. She was sort of a bluish gray. Her eyes were closed and she was very still. Her mother was sitting on the other side of Susie's bed, crying into her hands. Susie's father came across the room and spoke to me through the window. 'Paul, go away, for now.' That was all he said. He closed the window. I stood back in the soft earth of the flower bed. I watched the drapes of Susie's bedroom close."

"Was she really dead?"

"Yes."

"What happened?"

"She spent the morning playing with me on the beach, went home to lunch, and died. A six-year-old girl."

"Of what? How?"

"I wasn't told, for a long time. Then it took me years to understand it. Apparently she had an epileptic seizure. She'd never had one before. I guess it whacked out her heart."

"Just like that? A perfectly healthy kid?"

"Just like that."

"Wow." Josh watched the owls dart back and forth in what moonlight there was under the barn's roof. "Why are you thinking of that now? Of her?"

"My mother just told me that either Susie's father or her mother is arriving here tomorrow. They're divorced now, I guess, so they both won't come. Their name is Baxter. Sally, Abraham Baxter. Parents of Susie Baxter. I haven't seen them since Susie's funeral."

"Oh."

"I never wanted to see them again."

25

In bed, asleep, when Dan Prescott felt someone kissing his face, automatically he put out his hand, put it behind her head. His mouth began seeking her lips.

Startled, he jumped awake.

"Get out of here," he said.

His penis was engorged.

He tossed back his sheet and jumped out of his bed. He turned on the bedside light.

Naked, he looked down at her on the bed. Except where her bathing suit had protected her, her skin was lightly sunburned.

The one eye of hers he could see continued to look along the pillow. Otherwise, her nude body was still.

Dan glanced at the other bed in the room to be sure Josh wasn't in it.

He said, "You're not going to take another chunk off my heart, lady. Not at this point."

She rolled onto her back and drew her shoulders up a little. That position made her body look better.

Her eyes scanned his taut body in the lamplight. She looked a long moment at his erect penis. She looked specifically at each bullet wound at his waist.

She smiled. "You look like a statue."

"Not funny."

She stretched a little. "Isn't this why you got rid of the brat? Weren't you expecting me?"

"I didn't get rid of him. And Josh isn't a brat." Dan took the black negligee from the end of the bed and tossed it at her stomach. "I was expecting you a long time ago."

"You mean, years ago."

"Years and years ago."

"There's still time," she said.

"'There is a time for every thing,'" Dan said carefully.

"Great," she said. "I crawl into bed finally with Dan Prescott, after a lifetime, and he recites Ecclesiastes at me. Same old Dan Prescott."

"Same old Janet Twombly," he said. "Expects everything her way."

"I never had my way with you."

He turned his back on her. "Just get out of here, will you?"

She said, "The bullet holes in back are worse than the ones in front. Were they the exit wounds?" He said nothing. "How did you ever walk straight again, let alone run, and swim?"

"Janet, please."

She said, "My only mistake in life was in not raping you at thirteen. I didn't know it was possible. Girls are more mature than boys—all their lives."

When Dan looked around, Janet was standing near the door in her negligee.

Her face was fixed, unsmiling, chin up, a little proud. Again her eyes slowly scanned his body. She could see the tip of his penis, in profile, beyond his hip.

She said, "At least I'm leaving you miserable."

After Janet floated through the door, slowly, closing it after her, quietly, Dan clutched his engorged penis.

He found a tissue in his bedside table.

In bed:

At least four times I asked that bastard to get me my glass of water, leave it on the bedside table. He never did. That bastard. Rourke. Edward B. Rourke. The office makes the checks out to Edward B. Rourke. For enough money, too. Enough money to support ten families in my day, with lox on the weekends. For each time his name is written on a check may his name also go in the Book of Retribution. Not the first time he's done this. He is so cruel. How can anyone be so cruel? Where's the pleasure in it? I shouldn't have had the whiskey before dinner, the wine . . . Oh, God, am I thirsty. My mouth feels like that sand pit that used to be at the end of my street in Albany, when I was a little boy. I could get my own water, then, too. Get up out of the bed, go to the bathroom, take down the glass, turn on the faucet, see the water pour into the glass, lift it to my lips, drink it, never break the glass. . . .

You are not aware of all that you can do when you are young. You do it all so easily.

That boy, Josh. When looking for a tape of David's new music, I remember now he noticed some of the reel boxes had red dots on their spines, some did not. That's what he said. I must ask him.

Thirsty . . . if I called Rourke, got that lump to get out of bed, sure, maybe he'd get me my water. Also he'd pinch me or pull my ear or tomorrow happen to drop me down a step in my wheelchair to make my head, my whole body hurt for hours. I have no choice. I can't stand this thirst.

"Rourke? . . .

"Rourke? . . ."

More sharply now, as if I had some authority: "Rourke! . . ."

Maybe he'll think it's an emergency and be curious about whether he has to go get a new job. "Rourke!"

Crawling into bed, Lucy said, "Mister presidential speechwriter, you cannot hide that big, fat, white belly of yours under computer printouts." She brushed some of the papers aside.

"I'm not hidin' my belly." Tony put aside the piece of paper he was reading. "I'm proud of that belly. I've been supportin' that belly all my life, puttin' food in it, to make it grow."

"You've succeeded," she said.

"Marry me; marry my belly."

"I like your belly." Under the sheet, Lucy patted Tony's belly. "Don't worry. I'll see it's kept filled up."

"In fact," Tony said, kissing the tip of Lucy's nose, "I suspect you envy that belly."

"In fact, I do."

"You've always wanted one of your own."

"In fact, I have."

"In fact, I suspect it's not me you're marryin', but my belly."

"That's the truth."

He pulled her closer and felt along his body the whole, cool, smooth, slim length of her. Immediately, he was excited. Moving up, he had more of the undersides of her breasts against his chest.

"What's the matter, kid. Don't you know how to get a belly of your own?"

"I have one planned," Lucy said. "A great, big one! You're going to give it to me. It's going to grow and grow and after nine months, guess what happens then?"

"What happens?"

"Out pops this beautiful baby, which will be yours, and mine."

"It will be a wonderful baby. And it will have a wonderful life. We'll see to it."

"Then, under your protection, I'm gonna grow to be the biggest, fattest mama you ever saw!"

"That's fine."

Under the sheet, their arms and legs were loving each other.

"'Under my protection'?" he asked. "You're a laugh riot."

"Who, me?"

"You give me this big lecture all the way down in the car from Nashville about being kind to my father, not even *thinking* of him as Lord Godiva, gracious no, perish the thought, about not making trouble for the older people here, and the first chance you got, you attacked your mother in front of me *and* her friends."

"I did, didn't I?"

"You sure did."

"I don't know what came over me."

"Couldn't believe my ears. Here this lady preaches peace and love and kindliness, in deed, word, and thought, and then turns into a butcher at dinner. You cut your mother into smaller pieces than you did your roast beef."

"She's more seasoned than the beef."

"Very good. Oh, very good!"

"I really went after her with my knife and fork, didn't I?"

"With cleavers. You don't see your mother right, you know."

"I don't?"

"She's your perfect modern woman. Legally married once, has kept her husband, who is a huge success himself, without sacrificing her independence, had a notably successful career as an owner-executive of a big, international business, which she started and built herself, made the long trip from a little jumping-off place in Maine to the big world of Paris, raised a delightful daughter who, at this moment, is stroking my donk."

"I knew the story would end somehow with you."

"Lucy, I don't need too much stroking, you know."

"I suppose that's all true, isn't it? I mean, about my mother."

"The feminine ideal."

"Oh, God."

"Don't you agree?"

"Would you rather be in bed with her?"

"I wouldn't throw her out."

"You don't know her."

"I hardly know you, come to think about it. What I know, what I feel, *gr-umph*, I like."

"Do you expect me to be like her?"

"At the moment, I do not entertain expectations beyond the next few moments. Hey! Stop that!" Lucy had grabbed handfuls of his belly. "Who's this Paul character, anyway, I see you huggin' and kissin' before dinner?"

"I've told you about him. Paul Hollingsworth. We were at school together, in Switzerland. I told you about that crazy trip I took to East Germany once, when I was fourteen. I know I did. He was the kid who came with me."

"Did you sleep together? In East Germany?"

"Yes. In a bed with a feather mattress."

"What do I say to that?"

"Say, 'How nice.'"

"No."

"We were children."

"You're making me speechless."

"Are you jealous?"

"Yes."

"Am I supposed to tell you nothing happened between us?"

"Am I supposed to believe you?"

"You can imagine pretty much what happened."

"I am."

"Well, you're right. It was a cold room, with a little iron stove glowing in the corner. Pot bellied, like you. A girl and boy in a bed together, on a feather mattress, under one of those nice German quilts that keep slipping off, you know? Paul didn't even have a nightshirt. I had to keep him warm, didn't I? Make it possible for him to go to sleep?"

"What did you do?"

"What did I do?"

"What did you do?"

"I guess I fell in love with the pot bellied stove."

"Rourke? . . ."

Bastard. I know he can hear me. Both doors are open. He didn't leave me the glass of water on purpose, to be cruel, and now he's lying there like a lump getting some kind of enjoyment hearing me calling him. Did I do anything special today to make him so angry at me? I stopped to see Chump Hardy at the hospital. That made extra work for Rourke who probably felt he'd worked hard enough already getting me on and off the airplane. As if he were some kind of a petunia, can only take so much. He doesn't much like coming to David's farm, either. He's more a prisoner here. Can't pretend he's going out for a videotape for me and spend three hours at the corner bar swilling beer. No corner bars around here. He's more a prisoner here, so he makes me even more a prisoner here.

"Rourke . . ."

I can't sleep, for the thirst. I wanted to be awake for tomorrow, so I can enjoy the company, David and Ellie, watch that boy, Josh, play with that funny dog of their's, get Josh to help me explore David's shelves of tapes more. That hum, rumble and squeak can't be all David has done all these years. Has he forgotten there are people out there with ears? I'll never sleep, I'm so thirsty.

"Rourke!"

God, now I have to go to the bathroom, suddenly, badly. How can that be? Thirsty and have to go to the bathroom at the same time. Everything's too much. Too much. If I have to wet this bed, I'll be so ashamed. Rourke will have to clean it up. That's some consolation. But he'll make sure everybody knows about it. That will be my punishment for that.

"Rourke? It's getting to be an emergency!"

No answer. Of course no answer. I hope at least I'm keeping that bastard awake.

I've telephoned every employment agency in New York. They don't even have a candidate for the job to send over for an interview. Everybody's on unemployment, they say, on welfare. Why should anybody mess with an old man when they can make money sitting in a corner bar talking to each other about how hard life is? There are no strong, male, private nurses available, not in a city of nine million people. Just Rourke. Everybody in my office has looked for someone to replace Rourke. They see what I have to put up with in Rourke. No one can find anybody for me to replace that cruel bastard.

Maybe I should check myself into a nursing home. Give up the office. Give up being Milton Farber. Give up my identity. Become number something or other: the old man in room 1429.

"Listen, Rourke! I have to go to the bathroom, Goddamn it! I'm so thirsty, and I have to go to the bathroom!"

I'm just letting him know I'm suffering. That's what the bastard wants.

I'm just giving him what he wants.

What am I to do? What to do?

The difference between being born and dying is that no one is cruel enough to tell you you're going to be born.

26

At dawn, Josh heard the single gunshot from the upper balcony of the main house and knew it was David MacFarlane trying for his daily starling.

Paul Hollingsworth sat up from the hay, looked at Josh, said, "'Mornin'."

Josh said, "Ralalum."

He closed his eyes. He heard Paul rustle through the hay, clump across the wooden floor of the loft and scrape down the ladder.

Half-awake in the early morning Josh had found he had no choice at all: his penis had always risen before him, and he had to think about girls.

It was warmer, brighter in the loft when he awoke again, sneezing. Sitting up, he sneezed several times. He pulled on his sneakers and did not lace them because unlaced sneakers were the style just then. Going down the loft ladder one of the laces tripped him and he nearly fell.

He went around the corner of the barn, checked to make sure no one was about and that he was not visible from the windows of either the tenant house or the main house. He pleasurably urinated a bladderful.

Zipping up the fly of his shorts, he came back around the corner of the barn and ran into Nonnie carrying her red, plastic bucket.

Josh sneezed.

With the fingers of one hand, Nonnie took some hay out of his hair. She brushed hay off his shirt.

Seeing only the freckles on her knees, he sneezed and sneezed.

"How are you otherwise this morning?" Nonnie asked.

"Just fine." Josh was still trying to zip his fly, but his hands kept springing to his nose.

"I brought breakfast." Nonnie held the bucket up for Josh to see into it.

"For me?" Josh looked in the bucket and sneezed.

Nonnie swung the bucket away. "You like egg salad sandwiches?"

"Sure." Josh sneezed. "For breakfast?"

"I made 'em last night, when I saw you were sleepin' in the barn."

"You knew I was sleeping in the barn?"

"I saw you and that older fellow, the doctor fellow, go down to the barn with blankets. Right late it was."

"Oh."

Looking in the bucket herself, Nonnie said, "Also got a couple cans of Sun Drop here."

"What's Sun Drop?"

"You don't know Sun Drop? It's a good drink for the mornin'. Got caffeine in it. A Sun Drop quick in the mornin' and you're ready to oscillate."

"We don't have that up north."

"It's my considerable opinion, Joshua, that you-all don't have all that much up north to brag on anyway. Why do you live there?"

Josh sneezed. "I dunno."

"The north is full of Yankees."

"Not now, it's not," Josh said. "I'm down here."

"Come on," Nonnie said. "We'll have this here breakfast I made up for us over by the crick."

Tripping on his laces, sneezing, zipping his fly, Josh followed Nonnie to the stream.

She sat on the bank.

Josh flipped off his sneakers, pulled off his socks and shirt and walked down into the stream. Bending over, he washed his face and his neck and his chest. Scooping with his hands, he sucked water up his nose, coughed and blew out.

Using the sides of his index finger, he rubbed his teeth and his gums.

"Never mind with that," Nonnie said. "I'm not going to let any old boy named Joshua kiss me."

"Yes, you are."

Toes squishing in the mud, Josh walked out of the stream and up the bank.

Watching him approach, Nonnie took a big bite of an egg salad sandwich.

Maybe he slipped. Anyway, Josh was on top of Nonnie. At first he looked her in her blue eyes and kissed some freckles on her face. She was chewing the sandwich. Then he kissed her on the lips. With her tongue Nonnie pushed egg salad sandwich into his mouth. Feeling her tight breasts against his chest and her bare thighs against his, he mixed the egg salad sandwich with his own saliva and sent it back into her mouth. Their tongues masticated the sandwich in each other's mouths. Beneath him, Nonnie did not move her hips.

Finally, they swallowed.

Something rough traveled up Josh's bare back and pushed the back of his head.

Startled, he rolled off Nonnie, and looked up into the morning sunlight.

A bull calf, its forelegs braced in the mud of the crick bank, was looking down at him with its round brown calf eyes.

Nonnie and Josh laughed.

Josh flicked some mud in the calf's face, made it move away.

Sitting up, Nonnie said, "You got my pretty shirt all wet. And I ironed it last night."

Josh said, "I pressed it this morning."

"You want a Sun Drop?"

"Sure."

Sitting together on the stream bank they munched their picnic breakfast while looking around the pasture and at each other in the bright morning.

She handed him another sandwich.

Josh asked, "Would you think of really making love with me?"

"You weren't too good on the horse yesterday," Nonnie said.

"I managed."

"I was watching you."

"They don't have horses where I come from. I go to sailing camp."

"They have girls where you come from?"

"They have girls."

"Well, Joshua, you sure have a Bible name."

"The best."

"How long you here for?"

"Just for the wedding. A day or two."

Nonnie said, "That's all right, then."

Josh counted the freckles across her nose. "That's all right?"

"Only you're going to have to have some protection, first," Nonnie said. "I'm not going to be left with any Yankee yard brat."

"I'll get some."

Paul Hollingsworth was climbing the back hill with an axe. Below the hill, William's truck bounced along a rutted track.

"All right, then."

"We'd better do it before the bomb goes off." Josh looked around the valley that was Bass Clef Farm. "Ka-bloom!"

"What bomb?"

"The thermonuclear bomb."

"The nuclear bomb's never going to be set off."

"Sure it is," Josh said. "Why do you suppose we have it?"

Nonnie began gathering up the wax papers in which she had wrapped the sandwiches. She put the wrinkled papers in her red plastic bucket.

"We've got to have a nice neat world," Nonnie said, "for when the bomb goes off."

Ellie settled Byron down as soon as she mounted. It was not her intention to run the horse hard, to give in to both their spirits this beautiful morning and gallop through the first long pasture as they normally did, in case Josh or someone else wanted to ride later in the day. Ellie was just taking time to herself away from the usual long routine house guests bring to the ritual of breakfast. Against the horse's wishes she walked him slowly along the driveway leading from the barns to the barnyard gate to the road.

Crossing the road, Ellie saw the Halburtons' car approaching. The car slowed, seemed to hesitate, then came up to her and stopped.

Ellie turned and stopped the horse.

"Good morning, Edith."

The car window was rolled down.

Edith Halburton wore over-sized sunglasses. Her face powder was thick. Nevertheless, in the morning sunlight Ellie saw the blue along Edith Halburton's left cheekbone and the welt on her right jaw.

"'Morning, Ellie. How are you today?"

"Just fine."

"Ellie, I sure am sorry about your peacock. You know how Joe is."

"No. I don't know how he is."

"He's never spared the rod."

"I don't want to know anything about a man who so beats up his kid. Or his wife."

Edith's hand moved to her face. Her fingers touched her cheekbone. On the back of her hand was a fresh scar.

Edith said, "You don't know how it is."

"How is it?" Ellie asked.

"I had it comin'," Edith said.

"Like hell you did."

Ellie turned the horse and opened the gate into the pasture beside the guesthouses and studio. She heard the Halburton car behind her accelerate. By the time she turned again, to close the gate, the car was far down the road.

In that pasture, Ellie let Lord Byron run.

27

"Chuck! Hallo, Chuck!" David had opened the door enough to lean into the little, sparse reception room. Like the church itself, it smelled of very old wood.

From the study beyond the reception room, Chuck yelled, "Come in, if you dare!"

In a Hawaiian shirt, slacks and leather slippers Chuck Hartigan sat behind the single-drawered desk in the study.

David said, "I dare."

"David! I don't suppose you're any better at figures than I am."

"Some figures."

"Sit down. Aren't musicians supposed to be good at math? I mean, isn't math what music is really all about?"

David MacFarlane said to the minister, "Every time the math works out in my music, I praise the Lord for intervention, because I know I'm not clever enough to have worked such a miracle myself."

"Which is every time you write something, right?"

"Just about every time."

"I could use a little divine intervention with the church budget," the minister said. "Don Kerry, president of the bank, tells me if I keep writing checks without funds I'd better learn the trick of turning water into wine right quick. Good thing he's a member of the congregation and I get to instruct him in patience every Sunday. What can I do you for this Friday morning?"

"I'm pretty sure you don't have anything to do tomorrow."

"Tomorrow? Not a thing."

"I mean, I know you don't have any plans."

"Me? Of course not. I'm a minister. You know ministers only work Sunday mornings. Tomorrow's Saturday." Chuck flipped the page of a diary on his desk. "Just thought I'd spend some time in the morning polishing my Sunday sermon, but I needn't bother, as you and Ellie won't drag yourselves in from the farm to hear it anyway. You never do. Frannie and I plan to take a Scout troop down to the river for a picnic. Then, let's see, beginning at four, I counsel two couples planning to get married and one couple planning to get divorced."

"Could the Scouts take a rain check?"

"It's not going to rain tomorrow, David."

"Ellie and I sure are hoping you can come out to the farm and perform a wedding about noon."

"Tomorrow?"

"Tomorrow. You and Fran were invited anyway. You forgot to put it in your book."

"David . . ."

"Patience. You see, the groom's father is a minister, from Maine. I had been thinking he would want to perform the ceremony. This is a man I haven't seen in years. He showed up having done nothing about getting a ticket to perform in Tennessee. It's too late now. He doesn't want to perform the ceremony himself anyway. It's all perfectly respectable."

"David, I haven't even had a chance to meet with the couple getting married, counsel them—"

"The bride is an internationally famous model and the groom is a speechwriter for the President of the United States. Cille Nelson and Anthony Prescott. Respectable enough."

"Hell, I don't even know people like that. Is this a young couple?"

"Reasonably young. Mature twenties. I'm sure it's the first marriage for each of them. Tony assures me they've done all the right things about blood tests, the license. All perfectly respectable."

"Has anyone counseled them?"

"Everyone. Even got in a few words of wisdom at the airport myself."

"What did you say?"

"Life is short, marriage is long. Something of the sort."

"I dunno," Chuck said. "A couple like that probably needs counseling more than anyone else. How do they know what to expect?"

"They don't. Who does? Life is a *piñata.*"

"You never heard that from my pulpit."

"Chuck, they are two grownups. They are going to get married. Tomorrow."

"You needn't remind me I have competitors in this business. You intend to have the wedding at the farm? What's wrong with having it in the church?"

"The farm is where I expected the Reverend Prescott would want to do his stuff. It's all set up there. I assure you, everything will be as respectable as tea at The Heritage."

"Why do you keep saying 'respectable'?"

"What?"

"You keep trying to assure me this wedding is respectable."

"Well, it is. Will be. Entirely."

"You've said 'respectable' three times if you've said it once. You're making me suspicious."

"We're expecting local people, old friends, family of the bride, family of the groom, a great gang of people coming down from Maine, Washington, New York, friends of the bride and groom, who will take over the motel tonight. I expect there will be a certain amount of celebrating."

"Of course there will be. What's the matter with you?"

"Nothing. I just want to assure you, you won't be walking into any kind of a wild and woolly . . . an embarrassment to you of any kind."

"I wouldn't expect that."

"Of course not. It won't happen. A quiet, fresh-air wedding."

"Respectable."

"That's what I said. I guarantee it."

Chuck shook his head. He looked at the page in the diary. "Guess we can disappoint the Scouts."

"Right. Teach the little bastards life's not all hot dogs and soda pop."

"On Sunday, will you come to worship?"

"The day after a wedding? Chuck, have mercy. Make a deal with you: Sunday I'll do a good deed."

Chuck said, "I know you will, David."

PERSPECTIVE: *Betty Conant*

Well, of course I recognized them. You can't spend your life behind a counter in a drugstore staring across the aisle at all those perfect faces on the magazine covers without recognizing two of them when they walk into the store on a quiet Friday morning. But, boy, was I shocked! Like every other plain folk, I guess, over the years spent getting to be forty I had spent time staring at the people on magazine covers saying to myself, *Wouldn't it be nice if everybody looked like that? Wouldn't it be nice if no one else in the world looked like that, but I did? Pshaw, no one in the whole world really looks like that!* And then a couple of them walked into the store, right in front of my eyes! And they really looked like that!

Followed by that boy and how he behaved!

I knew her name, of course: Cille Nelson. She's been a top model years now. She's been on the cover of just about everything but *Field and Stream,* and more than once. I can tell you she's even more beautiful seen with your naked eyes. She's taller than a flagpole and skinnier than a straw. I mean, I've heard these models aren't allowed to eat, maybe half a grapefruit on Sundays, no sugar, and it must be true. And she carried herself like a swan, her fantastic head moving so slowly on top of her long neck; when she took a step you could see her placing a foot, sort of sending her leg after it, however that's possible and, watching, I sort of felt like cheering her accomplishment every step. I mean, it was a pleasure watching her glide around: a swan on ice is what she made me think of. And her yellow dress, cut just so beautifully, all silk, I suppose, I almost wept. Never seen anything like that before in Jameson County, I tell you. She never even looked at her dress once, all the time she was in the store. She wore it just like she didn't know she had anything special on! She's a black lady, of course; you know that; with reddish wavy hair and skin so clear and transparent you don't look *at* it so much as you find yourself looking *into* it. All the cosmetics I've sold over this counter and here's this famous model come in and I couldn't detect she was wearing a speck of makeup anywhere! Her eyes in person look even wider apart than they do in the photographs, and are they ever enormous! When she laid them on me I felt like I'd been blessed.

I didn't know his name when I saw him, the older man, but I had seen plenty of photographs of him, too. After they left, I grabbed a copy of *GQ,* found a picture of him, of course, and figured out the credit. I wanted to be able to tell people who I saw. His name is Dan Prescott. Well, I mean, he was the handsomest man I ever saw. He was wearing just jeans and a white dress shirt, open at the collar, sleeves rolled up, but I doubt I had ever seen a body like that. Tall, his wide shoulders made a nearly perfect triangle with his sides going down to his waist, with sinewy forearms. I'm used to men in jeans around here, hardly ever see men dressed any other way, but jeans were different somehow on that Prescott fellow; I mean, you saw the shapes of his butt and legs through the denim and you knew, immediately, that that was what God intended when He started out makin' man. Everyone else I've ever seen is just a bargain. Let me tell you that in his face, first of all, he looked like a very nice person, I mean, like someone who would really listen to you, carefully, never make fun of you, or tease, or tell a tale on you, but would bring you along patiently, kindly, and let you be someone special to him, no matter what else he might have on his mind. Can someone who gets all the attention he must get really be like that? His coloring, too, was wonderful. I could tell from the way his skin had tanned he was basically a blonde, but now his hair was silver, and clearly he had had none of the trouble a lot of blond men have with their skin, acne, boils, that sort of thing; his skin was as smooth as a baby's arse, with wrinkles just in the right places to tell you he'd lived a little. And he had the darkest, brownest eyes I've ever seen in a white person. I looked into his eyes and wanted to say, *Lie to me! I'll believe anything you say!* I was just about to give up on him, sayin' to myself, *You're too much!* when he handed me the money (they were buying several rolls of film) and suddenly I saw he had a real man's hands, calluses, scars, everything, hands that worked, did real work, and I said to myself, *Oh, by golly, gee . . .*

After I collected myself, while I was waiting on them, when they were buying the film at the counter, I thought I'd try it out, so I actually called her by name. I said, "You want to make slides or prints, Ms. Nelson?" and she didn't even appear to notice I'd used her name, as if we saw each other every day, as if I'd ever really seen her before. She answered so easily I expected to hear her call me Betty!

I mean, how must it be to live that way? Everywhere you go, everyone who ever sees you knows who you are, knows your name, knows what you looked like as a kid with braces and a red braid? I can't even think how that must be.

"'Cherry Coke.'" Mr. Prescott was reading from the signs over the soda fountain. "Wouldn't you know David would live in probably the last town in America that has a drugstore with a real marble soda fountain, little marble-topped tables, wire-backed chairs, and where you can buy a fountain-made cherry Coke."

Then I figured out, of course, they weren't just passin' through town, they had to be stayin' out at Bass Clef Farm with Ellie and David MacFarlane. How else would these two extraordinary-lookin' people happen to be together, in Jameson?

"Want a real cherry Coke?" he asked.

Well, I expected Cille Nelson to say, *No, I drink a cherry Coke and I'll get fired, sure enough.* Instead, she said, "Sure. I'd love one."

They both thanked me as if they were in some kind of over-staffed boutique and walked across to the soda fountain.

I buzzed behind the counter and into the area where Ed Werk, the pharmacist, was rolling pills. "Look who's out there!" I whispered.

He looked up, straight at them over his half wall, and, would you believe it, said, "Who?"

"Cille Nelson!" I whispered. At his confused look, I said, "The model!"

"The model what?" he asked.

"He's a big model, too."

Ed said, "She's big, all right. Ask her if she can fix our sign before she leaves."

When I appeared behind the soda counter, he, Dan Prescott, recognized me. He smiled. Said, "Swear I just saw your sister, the other side of the store." He recognized me! "May we have two cherry Cokes, please?"

"You-all sit down," I said. "I'll bring 'em to you."

"'preciate it," he said, just as if he'd learned his manners here.

Frankly, I wanted to see what these two people looked like sittin' down. Like seein' two limousines foldin' into sports cars.

And what do you suppose these two sophisticated, glorious lookin' people were talkin' about when I brought them their Cokes? Some old dog named Blue! Would you believe it? I expected them to be talkin' about their friend, Paul McCartney, or partying with Mohammed Ali, one. But no, they were laughin' about some old dog named Blue, Cille Nelson had as a child. She was sayin' she still had that dog. Must be one pretty old dog, by now.

The story goes on.

I was just buzzing over to grab a copy of the latest edition of *GQ,* to discover the name of the man, hopin' I could call him by name, too, before he left, see if he noticed, when the door opens and in comes this boy about sixteen, in short pants, who I knew right away absolutely had to be the man's son. They looked just alike, had the same smile, same build, same coloring, only the boy was still blond, of course, and hadn't filled out all that much yet.

I mean, he saw his father. He smiled at his father and tossed this cool little wave at him. He knew his father saw him. The man smiled and waved back.

The boy went to the counter.

I buzzed behind the counter to wait on him.

"Hi. May I have some safes, please?" Well, I just stared into that boy's clear brown eyes. He had asked for prophylactics. Sexual prophylactics. With his father and Cille Nelson sitting right behind him! The boy didn't lower his eyes. He sure didn't lower his voice. I declare he didn't lower anything. I was expecting he had come in for a Mars Bar. In a clear voice, the boy said, as if I were deaf, or spoke a different language, "Condoms."

After showing him the price, I started to put the package into a sack. "Never mind," he said. "Save a tree."

He also bought two Lectric Pac batteries.

With the package of condoms in his hand as visible as dirt on a pig's snout he went over to his father and Ms. Nelson and said, "Hey, Dad. I couldn't find you. Figured you wouldn't mind my taking the car."

Both Cille Nelson and Dan Prescott were smiling at the boy.

Mr. Prescott said, "We came to town in style. A yellow convertible. Want a cherry Coke, Josh?"

"No, thanks. I don't like cherry Coke."

"Bet you never had a real one. A fountain-made cherry Coke."

"Naw. I want to get back."

Smiling, Ms. Nelson said, "I bet you do."

At even that, the boy didn't blush, or lower his eyes, or shuffle his sneakers, or anything. After saying something else to his father, I forget what, he came over to the counter, picked up the batteries, said, "Thanks" to me and left.

Pretty soon, Cille Nelson and Dan Prescott left, sayin' thank you again to me at the counter.

"You-all come back soon," I said. "You hear?"

Going through the door, that Mr. Dan Prescott turned and looked at me, really looked at me, as if he was really seeing me, and he smiled. I mean, at me.

28

David said, “Hello, old thing.”

Ellie was sitting quietly, alone, in a chair on the brick terrace under the tree at the back of the house.

After Jock took the bags of groceries from David’s arms, David kissed Ellie.

“This place is beginning to look like a Bedouin camp.” While David had been gone, red and white striped canvas roofs had been raised over the dance floor at the top of the driveway and over about half of the tables and chairs. The serving tents were fuller, with back and side canvas walls. Driving in, David had seen Janet Twombly on the lawn thick in discussion with someone in a white jacket. “Tired?”

David sat in a chair facing Ellie. “I did everything you asked. Bribed Chuck into officiating tomorrow by promising him an exemplary life in my name henceforth. Stopped at the motel. Checked to make sure said motel is ready for the onslaught of wedding revelers due to arrive from Washington, New York, Maine, Europe, other points north, east, west and south tonight. Staff of said motel declare themselves ready in both their buffet and their bar, in beds and baths. From the motel I telephoned the charter bus service in Nashville. Buses will be at the airport commencing at five p.m. to transport the above-mentioned revelers to the motel in Jameson. Said bus company staff declare they understand perfectly their orders to waft said revelers out here for the wedding tomorrow, and waft them away again later. Went next to the grocery store, where I went down and up your shopping list, down and up every aisle a minimum of six times, hunting, discovering, capturing, and buying every item you required. Oh, what a good boy am I."

Ellie smiled. "Oh, what a good boy are you."

"How did we get into this mess?"

"I left you alone a few days in April while I went to New York to see friends, do some shopping, attend theater and a concert, and you got attacked by a kind impulse."

"Oh."

"I think you got lonely."

"Without you. I did."

"You assured me no one would take you up on your crazy offer to give a wedding here."

"I'm seldom wrong."

"You said they wouldn't even answer your letters."

"Well, they did."

"You said all you really wanted was to be invited to the wedding yourself."

"Well, I was."

"We are surrounded by wedding." She waved a tired arm. "Everywhere you look: wedding. Here a wedding, there a wedding. It has pervaded nearly every nook and cranny, bedroom, closet and shelf. I'll never leave you alone again."

"Clearly you shouldn't."

"Next time, you might turn this nice old farm into a home for recovering concert hall stage managers."

"Not a bad idea. I'll think about it."

Ellie said, "Everyone has told me you don't want the piano moved out onto the bandstand."

"It might rain. Anyway, there'll be no use for it."

"A.B. has managed to arrive. Don't ask me how."

"Great. Where is he?"

"I sent him to your study to see if he can find himself a drink."

"I'm sure he'll succeed."

"I think he drove all the way down from the airport without one, poor dear. He must have forgotten how far it is. He arrived looking distinctly parched, and strained."

"Still keeping up his old habits?"

"Abraham is looking blotchy."

"He was the last time we saw him. The last several times."

"And I find I keep having an irresistible urge to encourage Sorry Hollingsworth to eat something. *Can I tempt you with a leaf of lettuce, Sorry? Sure you won't try a carrot?* It doesn't do any good, does it?"

"Not a bit."

"Oh, dear. Is there anything more ridiculous than self-flagellation?"

"Not when there are so many others around willing to do it for you."

"At the moment, the Hollingsworths, Sorry, Doug and Paul are taking a walk over the hills together."

"Hope they don't hesitate to check fences as they go."

"I'm sure Paul will give you a detailed report on every centimeter of fence that falls within his purview. Now there is someone I really worry about."

"Paul?"

"Yes."

"William worries about him, too, I guess."

"He spent the morning taking down that storm-damaged tree as if his life depended upon it."

"What tree?"

"You didn't ask him to?"

"Of course not."

"The one in the gully, over there." Ellie waved east. "I came across him while I was riding Byron. Shirt off, dripping with sweat, hair in his eyes, keeping up a frenetic pace. He chatted just long enough to be polite. He went back to work while I was still sitting there."

"Paul has always been that way."

"What way?"

"Too much. Bigger than life. Compulsively succeeding at everything."

"I fear he has inherited a false idea of the perfectibility of man from his mother." Ellie said, "At least he eats."

"Even carries food in the car with him."

"Milton spent the morning dozing in his chair, wherever put. Rourke, of course, just pads around snarling at everyone with his eyes. I've never known anyone who can snarl so well with his eyes. The Reagans, the Simpsons, even William, keep out of his way. Josh is in the studio looking at a movie on the big screen. *Once upon a Time in America,* I suspect."

"Was that the caterer I saw Ms. Tuesday chinning up and down?"

"Yes. She is over-ordering absolutely everything. She jolly well will get the bill."

"Never mind, old dear. Everyone will be gone by tomorrow night."

"David, the distressing news is that I saw Edith Halburton this morning. She stopped her car while I was crossing the road on Byron."

"Oh! I forgot the big news."

"What big news?"

"What did Edith have to say?"

"I think she tried to say she's sorry about Brummel."

"Anything about Rupert?"

"David. That Joe Halburton is beating up on her, too. She was trying to conceal a black eye behind big sunglasses, but I could see the welt on her cheekbone. She had another blue mark on her jaw. She had a fresh cut on her hand."

"Did you take notice?"

"I took notice. I let her know that I saw, that she wasn't fooling me."

"The big news is that Joe Halburton has been fired."

Ellie's smile was genuine. "Yes?"

"The town is agog. Apparently some big boys, executives from the home office in Illinois or Michigan or wherever, walked into the offices of Kleen Ride Windshield Wiper Manufacturing Company first thing this morning, and fired Halburton summarily."

"How nice."

"Rumor has it they were afraid of labor unrest. You know, that plant never has been unionized."

"Is that so?"

"Yes. In fact, there was a labor organizer reported seen in Shag's this morning. Over from Memphis. Same guy who caused all the fuss in that plant two or three years ago. The big boys don't wait long to duck and dodge when they spot a union organizer sniffing around, do they?"

Ellie said, "This time we will buy that house."

"I guess so."

Ellie said: "For sure."

"I was thinking I might take a nap. Can I tempt you to join me?"

Suddenly, Ellie was looking refreshed. "I could be tempted."

The LeBaron convertible appeared in the driveway. Lucy Nelson was driving. Dan Prescott sat beside her.

David said, "Why do I think I'm seeing a Chrysler commercial?"

"Too late," Ellie said. Carrying little packages, Lucy and Dan were shimmering up the sunlit path. "Must be polite to our house guests. Offer them bananas and protein extract."

"What am I hearing?" David asked.

"What are you hearing?"

David jumped up. "Milton calling for help. Jock!" David yelled at the back of the main house. "Come quick!"

As David ran toward the pool area, he shouted again, louder, "Jock!"

"Damned fool must have tripped putting on his pants," David said.

Milton had wheeled himself out of the way when he saw David running toward the screen door of the guesthouse. Milton had pointed toward the door of Rourke's bedroom.

Wearing shoes and socks, boxer shorts and a white, short-sleeved shirt, Rourke was sprawled on the floor of the bedroom, unconscious. He was bleeding profusely from the forehead.

Half under him were his white trousers.

Dan Prescott and Jock Reagan leaned over the crouched David.

From the studio next door came the sound of the videocassette Josh was watching.

"Hit his head on the edge of the bureau," David said. "Knocked himself out."

Dan said, "He's bleeding pretty badly."

"Got to get him to the hospital."

"Can we lift the bastard?" Jock asked.

David and Jock each took one of Rourke's arms; Dan, his legs. They lifted him like a sack as far as the front door of the guesthouse.

"He's out cold," Milton said, studying Rourke's lolling head. "He's never looked better."

William, of course, appeared instantly.

Together the four men carried the heavy ex-boxer across the back lawn. Rourke's head bobbed unceremoniously and dropped blood all the way.

Red in the face from the effort, Milton pushed himself along well behind them in his wheelchair.

"We'll put him in back of the pickup truck," David said. He called to Ellie, "Put some of those tarps from the shed on the back of the truck, will you?"

Lucy watched the four men carrying a fifth stagger by her. She still held her little packages. "Anything I can do?"

David said, "Picture this."

The four men dumped Rourke on the thick tarpaulins Ellie had laid in the back of the pickup truck.

"Dan, will you go to the hospital with him?" David asked.

"Sure."

"You ride back here." David jumped down from the back of the truck. "Jock, you drive."

"I don't like to drive."

"Jock, you know where the hospital is. Reverend Prescott does not."

"But—"

"No 'buts' about it." David slammed the tailgate closed. "If I drove, I'd leave the bastard in a ditch!"

"I'll be sure to." Jock climbed into the truck's cab.

The truck rolled down the driveway, narrowly avoiding the Shoup brothers and their electricians and carpenters, and Janet Twombly and the caterer and the caterer's helpers, and brightly colored party paraphernalia waiting to be placed decoratively. Holding his head and shoulders as high over the truck's steering wheel as he could, Jock navigated through this broken field uncertainly. Dan knelt in the back of the truck looking like a figurehead slipped sternwards by the speed.

As the truck went up the road in a darter snail's configuration, David whispered to Ellie: "See? I told you our guests would be leaving soon."

After Josh watched, through the studio window, David and Dan, Jock and William carry the inert and bleeding Rourke out of the guesthouse and through the pool area, followed by Milton straining in his wheelchair, he slipped out of the studio and into the guesthouse.

Josh went into Rourke's bedroom.

Being careful to get none of Rourke's blood on his knees, Josh knelt.

He removed the safety pin that clasped together the cuffs of Rourke's white trousers and threw it into the wastebasket.

A minute later he joined Ellie and David, Lucy and Milton on the back lawn watching the pickup truck weave down the road.

"Oh, Mr. Farber," Josh said. "I got some batteries for your wheelchair."

Leaning over, Josh slipped a battery into its compartment. He flipped the switch on the wheelchair's arm and heard the electric motor's hum.

"Oh, Josh." Ellie looked the boy as straight in the eye as the boy would permit. "How very nice of you!"

29

Josh stripped off Nonnie's shirt and sneezed.

"Bless you, Joshua."

"Oh, damn." Josh pawed the top of Nonnie's breasts where he could see some of his sneeze had landed. She took a step back. As his eyes cleared, he realized the beauty of what he was seeing. "Oh, wow." Nonnie's breasts were so full and firm, the skin so smooth they looked like they had grown just that morning. The rising nipples made them seem as if they were still emerging, visibly, before his eyes.

They stood in the hay loft, near where Josh had slept the night before.

"That's all right, Joshua." Nonnie stepped forward again. She watched the nearly cross-eyed wonder in his eyes. "Don't you feel badly about any old silly sneeze."

She tugged his shirt free of his shorts and pulled it over his head. Wrinkling his shirt into a ball she wiped his eyes and nose and upper lip with it.

Leaning forward, not touching her otherwise, he touched the tip of his tongue to a place on her cheek beside her nose, just that, and relaxed back on his heels.

Quizzically, she did the same thing to him.

He touched just the tip of his tongue to her left breast. He rolled his tongue, just once, around her nipple.

She did exactly the same to him.

Then he put the flat of his tongue against her stomach, just below her rib cage, to one side. He licked her skin, just once.

She whispered, "What's that?"

They both listened to a barn door scrape open.

Josh placed his right hand against her side. Slowly, his hand urged her body closer to his. Her breasts brushed against his chest. Gently, his hand encouraged her body to sway so that the nipples of her breasts traveled back and forth across his upper stomach muscles, his rib cage. Her eyes in his were wide and deep, staring, light-filled, receptive. He moved his feet forward a little, and bent his knees. Her breasts now traveled back and forth across his chest, just below his nipples. Below her shorts, her thighs were brushing his.

He put both arms around her shoulders. Swaying with her, he clasped her to him. Finally, removing his eyes from hers, he ran his tongue sideways across her lips. He kissed her lips. He kissed her lips again, this time sending his tongue through her lips to find her teeth, force them open, find her tongue. Her tongue met his with strength.

June sun beat down on the aluminum roof of the barn. In the hayloft, the skin of both Josh and Nonnie gleamed. They were slippery with sweat. They smelled themselves; they smelled each other. They also smelled the dry hay, of course, and the old wood of the barn, including the cedar posts. From below and from the barnyard outside they smelled the cattle and the cattle's waste.

Kissing, rocking, the calves of Josh's legs now against the calves of Nonnie's legs, behind hers, they fell over sideways into the hay. They broke apart like an eggshell. Josh, arms wide, was on his back. Under his shorts his penis again had risen to be a handle. Seeing it, Nonnie crawled perpendicular to him and through the cotton of his shorts bit firmly but carefully along the stem. His hand played with the hair at the back of her neck.

Her eyes spotted his stomach muscles tightening. She looked along to his face. His face wrinkled into an expected sneeze. Quickly, she placed a hand over his nose and mouth.

He sneezed into her hand.

She tried to dry her hand on his sweat-slick chest.

Then she pointed to the floor.

Wood knocked against wood.

Boots shuffled in the dry dust of the barn floor.

Nonnie put an index finger to her lips. She sprang up, first brushing some of the hay off her sweaty skin, then holding out a hand to Josh, for him to take, get up, go with her.

Quietly, they moved to the edge of the loft. Arms around each other's waists, hips against each other, moving slightly, each looked through a chink in the loft wall, down to the barn's central corridor.

One by one, William was taking three pitchforks off pegs on the wall, examining their tines, collecting them under his arm. Seeing William from above made Josh realize the thinness of William's hair.

Silently they watched William at his work. Josh raised the arm he had around Nonnie's waist. His hand cupped and moved her breast. His fingers played with her nipple. Still keeping her hand outside his shorts, she clutched his penis, just once, then petted it.

Both Josh's hands began to fly toward his nose.

Nonnie's hands got there first. She held his nose so tightly the sneeze shot into the back of his head.

Laughing silently, they looked at each other.

William tramped along the corridor in his boots, pitchforks under his arm.

He swung the barn door shut.

After looking into the sunlight of the opened barn door, the light in the loft seemed dim to Josh and Nonnie, speckled with nodes of light from holes in the barn roof, walls. Swallows stirred up by William's being in the barn began to settle down again.

Josh and Nonnie faced each other in that light. They put their hands on each other's hips. They studied each other's eyes.

The fingers of Josh's right hand found the button to Nonnie's shorts. Watching her eyes, his fingers released the button. Continuing to watch her eyes, his fingers found the tab to her zipper and lowered it. Losing sight of her eyes as he sank to his knees, seeing instead her chin, her breasts, her stomach, his hands lowered her shorts and her underpants at once. She stepped out of them. His hand felt that her underpants were damp. Kneeling before her, he used the backs of his hands gently to separate her legs above her knees. He kissed each thigh. He raised his nose into her pubic hair and nuzzled her. Her hands stroked his shoulders, his neck, his hair. Then he sat back on his heels and untied her sneakers. As she raised each foot, balancing herself with a hand on his head, he removed her sneakers and socks.

Nonnie crouched down with him. With one hand against his shoulder, she knocked him over, sideways. Sitting cross-legged beside him, she straightened his left leg, putting his calf onto her lap, and removed his sneaker and sock. While he lay propped on his elbows and watched, she brought his right leg onto her lap and removed his other sneaker and sock.

Then she looked along his legs to his shorts.

While he watched and waited, she stroked his shins with the palms of her hands. She felt around his knees with her fingers. She kneaded the muscles of his thighs with her knuckles. Crawling closer to him on her knees, she pressed her thumbs, then the heels of her hands into his stomach.

Finally, her fingers were around the waist band of his shorts. He raised his hips. Stretching the elastic, she pulled his shorts and underpants off his hips. His penis sprang from captivity into the air. Watching his penis, she pulled his pants down his legs, over his feet. She tossed his clothes onto a bale of hay behind her.

Sitting on her heels, crouched over, her arms folded under her breasts, Nonnie closed her eyes. Her lips found the tip of his penis. She kissed it. She ran her tongue all around it.

Josh fell back. Hands over his face, he sneezed.

Nonnie giggled. "Bless you, Joshua."

"Damn, damn." He struggled to his feet in the hay. "Double damn."

He went across the loft. Using fingers to close off one nostril, then the other, he blew his nose on the hay.

Naked, Nonnie stood a few meters from him, facing him. She didn't seem to know what to do with her arms, her hands: they fluttered around her body, apparently deciding again and again to form a bra, deciding again and again not to; wishing for pockets.

They were each well-tanned. Josh had been surprised to see even Nonnie's breasts had taken some sunlight. The small areas where their skin was not tanned were arrowed, indicating their genitalia, giving them each a small area of privacy they could share with the other.

Josh found his shirt and blew his nose into it. He wiped his face with it, threw it onto the hay bale near his shorts.

Sniffing, having to breathe somewhat through his mouth, arms at his side, Josh began to walk across the hay directly toward Nonnie. When he was near her, he began to raise his arms. She grinned and dodged to her left.

Nonnie ran across the loft and jumped onto a pile of loose hay.

Josh ran after her. Arms, legs extended he leaped through the air to land on top of her.

Giggling, she rolled away.

Josh landed face down, his head nearly buried in hay.

Barn swallows were darting back and forth in the air.

Standing, Nonnie put her heel in the crack between Josh's buttocks and pressed down.

He rolled over, tried to grab her foot.

Laughing, crouching a little, feet and legs apart, arms in position to wrestle, Nonnie stood in the middle of the loft.

As soon as he got up and began to go after her, she pirouetted, evading him, then ran to another corner of the loft and fell in the hay.

Again he leaped after her. Again she wriggled away.

Again he found himself spitting hay.

She was near him, lying on her back. She reached over and took his hair in her fingers, and played with it.

Josh crossed the loft to his shorts and picked them up. They were wet with sweat. He took the package of condoms out of his pocket and brought it to her.

They sat cross-legged in the hay together while Josh opened the package. Nonnie watched. Just as he was about to stretch the condom over his penis, she stopped him. She took his penis in both hands, felt the solidity of it, how little play was left in the stretched skin. She kissed the tip. Then she watched him as he fitted the condom to himself.

From then they kissed each other's mouths, and nipples and ears. Their hands loved every part of each other's bodies. Little by little, Josh's body came to cover hers.

He knew he had gotten blood on his fingers.

Watching her eyes widen, truly as if something real were entering her eyes; her throat muscles tighten, truly as if something real were entering her throat; feeling her back arch, as if something real were hoisting her to him; Josh penetrated Nonnie.

30

PERSPECTIVE: *William Fesdon*

One afternoon, some years ago now, I was standing beside Simpson's truck talking to Nell, Ms. Simpson, inside (she wanted me to run a fence behind the tenant house to keep the cattle off her new back porch), the radio in the truck playing, and suddenly, cocking an ear to the dashboard, she said, "You know who that is?"

"No, Ma'm. What are you talkin' about?"

"That music," she said.

I didn't let on I knew but the music playing on the radio was that silly old "Greasy Pig" I've loved about always. When I was in high school, "Greasy Pig" was about it. Soon as that played at a high school dance, Lord, we took off our boots and jumped around that gym floor like we had wasps in our socks and snakes slitherin' up our legs.

"Mr. MacFarlane wrote that," Nell said.

"Say what?"

"Mr. MacFarlane is the actual writer of that song. That there is one of the songs he wrote. I read that in that story on him in *The Tennessean.* You know that story they wrote on him a year or so ago?"

Now David MacFarlane had owned the farm 'bout two, three years, at that point. Just about everybody had told me he was supposed to be some kind of a music star. But you couldn't tell by me. I had been working with him, when he had a mind to do such work, all that time and I'd never heard him hum or whistle a note. I had been around his house enough, too, and had never heard a piano play.

Everybody said to me things like, "You work up there with David MacFarlane. That place must be rockin' all the time." I didn't know how to tell people I'd heard more music out of a squeaky gate hinge than I'd ever heard out of David MacFarlane. Sure, recorded music, all the time, radio music, classical music and country music and popular music, jazz and rock and roll all from that fancy hi-fi rig in the east room, you can hear that through the windows, all right, but never music a *person* makes, never music I could credit to David MacFarlane and say, "Yeah, I know his music." Out here in our own valley, no one around for miles, and I never had heard anything I could call the music of this man I saw every morning, noon and night, talked to and worked with the day long. I had begun to doubt he knew shit-all about music; to think that everybody had gotten together to feed me some kind of a story.

'Course, there were hours a day I couldn't account for him, at first.

It took a while for me to learn David MacFarlane spent hours, days and nights, in "the studio," which is in that big new section he and Ellie built beside the house, around the pool? Many nights when I was up late cruisin' the place I'd see the lights on in that section and sometimes when I'd be back on the place before dawn I'd see the lights would still be on over there. Sometimes the lights would be on over there all night three, four times a week. Those days, Ellie would say he was "sleeping late." She never did say he had been working all night. Those days he would appear on the place about noon, rubbing his hands together, and say, as if he had been away a million years, or had taken a trip to the moon and back, "What's goin' on?"

I saw the lights, but I never heard a note.

Once, when Ellie and David were both away (she was seeing friends in New York and he had flown to Italy or someplace to honor a friend who'd died), I found the studio door unlocked, when I was just checkin' around, and said to myself, "That's not supposed to be. . . ." Well, I decided that since it was open and I had never been in that room before I'd go in and check it out, just to make sure no one had gotten in to do damage, or take anything, before I locked it up. Looking into the room through the thick glass door, I had always thought it mostly some kind of a gymnasium, exercise equipment everywhere up front on the hardwood floor. There was also in the room, on its own carpet, the biggest piano I had ever seen, some kind of a limousine piano. That piano was so big I imagined that when someone played it he'd have to have someone in a uniform and cap sittin' up under the lid pluckin' the strings. When I went inside, I discovered the big room had thick, cork-lined walls. That place was as insulated as a banker's heart. I've often thought, hot days, cold days, I wouldn't mind bein' up there in that big room. Sound-proofed is what it was, except for the sliding glass door, and the glass of that was as thick as I am when it comes to keepin' Ezekial separate from Mordecai. I closed the sliding glass door and stood in the middle of the room and sang the Jameson High School song as loud as I could. Felt good, makin' so much noise when no one could hear me. I never had been able to sing it all the way through before without noticing the eyes of other people telling me they didn't much need to hear me finish. There were two other keyboards in that room, each hooked up to more neat-lookin' electronic equipment than I had ever seen before. There were at least three different huge tape recorders. There were eight big speakers in the room. Never saw so many dials and gauges and buttons, what all, in my whole live-long life. I couldn't begin to understand what they were all for, or what they did. Maybe they could make the studio fly. I didn't touch anything.

So I knew David MacFarlane worked, at his own thing. I mean, besides what he did around the farm. And I'm pretty sure he worked damned hard at it.

But don't you think it's strange that a man like that, a declared successful musician, way out in his own valley in the middle of almost nowhere, so insulated and sound-proofed himself no one could hear the music he made?

I expect it would have been a sheer pleasure walkin' around the place, doin' my work, listening to his music in the distance, if much of it is like "Greasy Pig." He could have had the steers buck-dancin'.

Nope. I never heard peep-all out of David MacFarlane.

None of that was for me to comment on, though; I never would.

Slow and easy. I was brought up hard workin' by parents whose farm, and me, and the Church of Christ are all that ever mattered. They did not look beyond Jameson County except to the Lord, and He surely is here, too. I was invited away by the United States Army and that history made me realize there is something outside Jameson County. By the time I went to the Army, I had never seen a stranger, you know. What I'm trying to say is that my parents relate to the world in a certain way and so do I relate to it in the same way, with exceptions and differences. They taught me that kindliness toward others, manners, is more apt to be in what you don't say than in what you do, and depends upon *when* you finally come to say what you've got to say. I'm in my forties now myself. What I've learned (and probably never will succeed at passing on to my daughters) is that when you have something to say usually there comes a time when you can say it kindly, when it means something good rather than bad, positive rather than negative. Leastways, I've always found it so. Manners, near as I can figure, is watchin' and waitin' and bein' helpful when you can.

Neither David nor Ellie is from Jameson County. I'm not precisely sure just where they are from, specifically; "nowhere"—north. Listen to David, you'd think he was born and raised in an airport. That man does not like airports.

When I heard these two strangers bought the old Maury Place, frankly, I was nervous. "He's a big time musician," everybody said, and that to me meant a lot of noise, fancy people comin' and goin', parties, drugs, one. Supportin' my parents by workin' their farm for them, supportin' my wife and daughters in the city of Jameson by working doubly hard runnin' the Maury place as well, you can see the people who took over the Maury place were important to me. What would any strangers want with an old farm in Tennessee? Why would they want such a thing? What were they going to do with it? Did he have some idea he was going to work it himself? Did he know farmin'? Why would they want to come here, be here, where everyone is so rich in land and rich in family, rich in the Lord, but damn-all cash poor? Most people, seems to me, have been tryin' to leave here since Reconstruction and many have succeeded. Why would anyone want to cast their lot with us?

Well, I learned there's more than one way to cast your lot. And that has taken a whole new, steady, say nothin', watch-and-wait, then talk, to-be-kindly, learnin'.

It takes a long time for a country boy like me to figure out someone can (and is willing to) put a whole lot of cash money into something, expectin' less than no cash money out of it, just 'cause they think they'll enjoy a way of life everyone else is tryin' to shirk and escape.

First all, David made no bones he knew nothing about farming. His honesty on that point made it easier on me. He even said, "I never will know enough about farming ever to call myself a farmer." Well, I guess he knows about other things. He divided everything on the farm into "critturs and varmints," and then would laugh at himself. The steers, the hens, the horse, even the dog are "critturs" to David; groundhogs, snakes, possums, starlings, weasels are all "varmints." It was interesting working with him, hearing some of the innocent things he'd say. To name you one, after being on the place a year or so, he said, "Farms are about fences, aren't they? Fences and gates are how everything is controlled." Sometimes, he'd scratch his head, laughing, and say, "No day on a farm is what you expect it's going to be." And that usually was when something had gone wrong to the point it was going to cost him money. Of course, David doesn't make money off this farm. He doesn't expect to, which is an idea it took me some gettin' used to. I suspect the money I give him just about pays taxes on the place, never mind mortgage money, insurance or any sort of a return on his investment. I make the money: buy the cattle, feed 'em up, medicine them, do everything that needs doing, the year 'round, sell the cattle, make the profit. It's almost as if they keep the place for me. Nevertheless, Ellie and David worry about "the critturs," care about them just as much as if they did own them. Sometimes, worrying a thing out, I've mentioned a problem to David, something he couldn't really know anything about, and, you know, I've found his advice real good. He doesn't know about farmin' but I guess he's had enough experience at other things to know how to think about things in general, how to make a decision.

Then there's the ongoing joke between him and me about the wrench. First time, we were working on the old cultivator and there was a nut rusted on so bad I never thought we'd get it off. "I'll go get the wrench," I said. When I came back, the nut was off. "How'd you do that?" I asked. He said, "It just came off." That was the first of many times. I'd need to go get a wrench, and by the time I got back, David would have whatever job needed doing done. At first, I was a little upset. If he had a wrench, why would he let me go get another one? I never could see he had a wrench. I'd say, "Where you hidin' that wrench, David?" and he'd just chuckle. Well, it took me a long time to figure out he wasn't using a wrench. His hands are that strong. He does not need a wrench, hardly ever. Can you believe that? Now, I'm no seventy pound weakling, but I did not know one man's wrist and hand could be as strong as another man's hand with a wrench in it. And I still don't know if just playin' piano is a proper way for a grown-up man to make a livin', but I sure can testify it makes for strong hands and wrists. So then I had to make a joke of it. Whenever I had a problem I couldn't figure out right away, I'd say, "I guess I need to go get a wrench, David," and he'd chuckle and say, "Where's the nut that needs loosin', William?"

So I got pretty used to Ellie and David. No noise. Not too many people comin' and goin' and the people who would come, besides the local folk, were more apt to be like old Mr. Farber and his creep grandson, Owen, (you know, people who look at the farm at a distance, like it's a park or something), than like that Chump character. No drugs, surely not as far as Ellie and David were concerned, just that right good beer David found in Nashville, a little Jack Daniels bourbon now and again. Ellie and David really care for the farm, help out as they can, never get in anybody's way. They really care about the people 'round here, worry about 'em, talk about 'em, laugh with them, love 'em.

Ellie, of course, she looks at a man as if she has personal knowledge of every sin that man ever committed or ever contemplated committing, and as if, somehow, she understands; she tolerates; it's all right with her that you are a man, do man things and think man thoughts.

After we all came to figure out Ellie and David really didn't want anything more than they have, anything more than they are, didn't want anything from us other than what we are, well, I guess we all came to appreciate 'em.

Then, little more than three years ago, I felt a change. What do you call it, atmospheric pressure? I felt the atmospheric pressure lowering. I felt a storm coming.

David took to going to Nashville almost every day. He'd walk around here not really noticing anything, unless I pointed it out to him, which was real unusual for him. It looked to me like he was talking to himself all the time, without saying a word, without moving his lips. He didn't even spend much time in his studio, for a while there. Ellie grew quieter, too. She kept everything running, all right. I was pretty sure there was no trouble between the two of them. Most evenings they'd sit on the porch together, not talking much. They took to going to bed real early, more as if they were discouraged real bad, tryin' to get rid of the day rather than begin the night.

All this was just after David disappeared unexpectedly for a couple of nights, and I heard some talk about Mexico.

It took me a while watchin' and waitin' to figure David had a problem he needed to bring home, and he didn't know how, 'cause he'd never had a home.

One night I could tell Ellie had gone to bed without David. Their bedroom light went on and off. The kitchen light was left on. I knew Ellie would never go to bed leavin' the kitchen light on without a reason. The studio lights were not on. You can tell a lot about what's goin' on in a house by watchin' how the lights work.

The atmospheric pressure had been very low that day. David had been acting even more tired and jittery. I had never known him to be jittery before. It looked to me like he needed to storm.

So, about ten-thirty that night, I parked my truck in the driveway of the main house, not even near the path to the back doors. I turned off the lights and the engine. I got out of the truck and just stood quietly in the driveway, wondering why the kitchen light was still on; where David was. I just watched and waited.

So I stood there in the dark.

"William?"

I hadn't seen him, or heard him.

David MacFarlane was sitting alone in a dark corner of the east porch.

I didn't answer. I didn't want to be the one to wake Ellie.

I heard the metal chair he had been sitting on skid on the brick.

In a moment he lurched out of the shadows of the porch. He had a drinking glass in his hand.

He staggered across the lawn toward me.

David said, "He's not drunk, you know."

"Okay."

He waited until he got up right close to me, so close I could smell the liquor on his breath.

"I mean, he's not dead, you know."

"Who's not?"

"Chump," he said. "Chump."

Saying "Chump" seemed to wear him out, for all time, as if that was the last word he'd ever say, ever wanted to say.

"Who said he is?"

"He died without dying. If you know what I mean."

"No. I don't."

"He's in a hospital."

"That why you been goin' in to Nashville every day?"

"Yes."

"What's the matter with him?"

"Coma. Drug-induced coma."

"Don't people ever come out of comas, David?"

"It's been three weeks."

"They wouldn't have him in a hospital, if there wasn't hope for him, would they?"

"Oh, yes," David said. "Oh, God, yes. These days."

"Drug-induced?"

"Yes. Something that didn't need to happen at all. Chump just screwed up on his chemicals, you see, made a slip somehow, a little mistake, I guess, mistook one thing for another, maybe forgot when he was taking something that he had already taken something else, or had more of the same. Did that damned woman he was with feed him drugs, William, maybe as some kind of a joke, or think she was doing him a favor; then see she had made a big mistake, dump him at the hospital in Mexico, and then disappear? Or did he kill himself, William? I ask him every day, 'What happened, Chump? What did you do? Where are you now, Chump?'"

"He can hear you, you think?"

David answered with such strength I was sure he'd wake up Ellie in the house. "Oh, yes!" The bedroom light did not go on. "Chump can always hear. Everything."

David leaned against the truck beside me. He drained his glass and bowled it across the lawn. It did not break. I had never seen him do anything that careless in all the time I had known him.

I figured he had had a lot of liquor by then.

"The trouble is, William, I am so mad at him. So goddamned mad at him. How can you have a friend in such a state and be so goddamned mad at him."

"You're talkin' about Chump Hardy."

"Yes."

We talked all the rest of that night, the two of us, standin' in the dark, leanin' against my truck.

"Let me tell you about . . . Chump, what he hears, how much he hears, how he hears things, if I can . . ."

I didn't understand all that David MacFarlane said that night, of course.

He started out saying something about Chump hearing something on the piano David called "grace notes," I remember that expression, wondering what on earth it could possibly mean, saying Chump could hear grace notes even when David hadn't played them; Chump could hear "the absence of sound," know what it meant, how to respond.

David talked about standing at the bottom of a stairwell in some rooming house in Chicago or somewhere a long, long time ago and hearing the sound of a saxophone coming down the stairs at him. It was the first time David had ever heard an instrument played so precisely, he said, every note shaded so interestingly, held so perfectly in relation to each other, with such tone, with such surety, self-confidence. He told me how hard it had been for him to bend his style to Chump's, because Chump was so sure of himself, so natural, so finished a musician, and David knew Chump could never change.

He told me about the hot, stinking nightclubs where they had spent their youths playing their instruments together, the countless freezing motels they had stayed in, the long nights they had spent on buses going through snowstorms, in airplanes, landing sometimes so tired they found themselves asking the customs people which country they were in; he told me some city names I'd never heard of, in Scandinavia, in India, in Africa; about always being too cold or too hot, too hungry, always something wrong with his belly, always too headachy. He told me about the women, here, there, everywhere, who were usually stupid and dirty and gross. Hear David tell it, he hardly ever saw a woman in his whole life who didn't have lipstick stuck to her teeth. He sure made stayin' put in Jameson County sound pretty good.

Apparently Chump would wander off, get lost, fairly frequently, and David would have to search through whatever city, to get him to the nightclub, concert hall, recording studio on time. At some point when I was getting confused, he referred to having to look "all over the world" for someone named Ms. Tuesday; I didn't understand any of that. He kept saying, "Where are you now, Chump? I can't come get you now." He talked and talked, through the setting of the moon.

I did not understand much of what he said about music, or having to travel that much; that being everywhere at once was like living in some continuous "nowhere," he said. Airports.

What I guess I understood was that because of their way of life, traveling so much, playing their instruments together that many years, neither one of them ever had a home, ever had anyone else ever to relate to, know, love, and therefore maybe they only related to each other, whether they wanted to, or not, because each other was all they ever had. They were sort of mixed up in each other like twins in a womb. I understood circumstances had made Chump Hardy David MacFarlane's best friend. And that David's best friend was in this not-dead, not-living state, and that David did not know what to do about it, how to feel about it.

In half his heart he felt guilty, he said, for having bought the farm, changed his way of life, "abandoned" Chump.

In the other half of his heart, he was furious Chump would "sneak off" and put himself, all of them, in this sad, useless state of living death, suspension.

Finally, I said, "David, I don't know if you'll ever be able to believe this. But I know Chump Hardy better than you do."

"You can't."

"I recognize him."

"Sure you do."

"That's not what I mean, David. I recognize him from all my life. I'm a country boy, born and bred. And I recognize a useless country boy when I see one."

"Yes," David said. "Chump came from somewhere down here, originally. You don't mean you knew each other when you were kids?"

"I knew him lots of times. I knew him in the barnyard. And I knew him in the schoolhouse. And I knew him in the army. I've known lots of Chump Hardys."

"You mean, you think you know his type."

"David, Chump Hardy is the type of boy a hard-workin', God-fearin' farm community like this takes up a collection for, to buy him a one-way bus ticket out of town."

David chuckled. "I suppose that's true."

"That's the only way he got to that roomin' house in Chicago, or wherever. He was recognized trouble."

"Chump Hardy was a genius," David said. "A natural genius."

"If you say so. You know about that. I know he was a sneak and a shirker, a lyin', lazy, useless, trouble-making, self-centered son of a bitch."

"Ow."

"Never cared for him much, myself."

"Guess not."

"To use your word, David, he's a varmint. It's just plain natural for him to be up to no good at all for himself, or for anybody else. Stories you tell me about his disappearin' in foreign places, makin' you go look for him, don't surprise me one bit. I know all about it. That he's stuck things that aren't a bit good for him down his throat and up his nose and in his ears, in his veins, whatever, knocked himself senseless with drugs and chemicals doesn't amaze me one bit either."

"William, he hasn't been out here at Bass Clef that much. Maybe a dozen times, a few days at a time."

"David, you and Ellie have said Chump Hardy seldom came out to the farm 'cause he was bored here. You said he was uncomfortable here."

"That's right."

"I'm here to tell you that's not true."

"It's not?"

"Chump Hardy was barnyard born and bred. He could move around a barnyard after a heavy rain and get neither shit nor straw on his boots. He could get through a gate he'd never seen before without even lookin' at the latches. He knew more ways to disappear, and more places to disappear to on a farm than you would if you spend your next one hundred years here."

"Okay. He was born country. He left. He didn't like it."

"David, he knew everybody in Jameson County recognized what he was at first sight. He was uncomfortable here 'cause he knew we were wise to him."

I then told David about some of the Chump Hardys I had known. No matter what job you give him, he'd find a way to shirk off. Offer to feed him, to pay him to work; offer to beat him if he didn't: always some excuse, didn't understand the job, machine broke, tools are lost, hit his head, needed help, too angry 'bout somethin' to work, sulkin', had a better idea, somebody told him to do somethin' different. Truth is, he'd just disappear.

Truth is, Chump Hardy was not the kind of boy you left alone in a hen house—if you know what I mean.

"You're not talking about Chump Hardy, William. The individual."

So I told David about Chump Hardy the individual.

Chump never did talk much. He'd just look at you gooney-eyed, listenin' to hear what you were going to say, force you to say something. So you'd say any pleasantry, and he'd never answer. He'd look away like a toad who'd just swallowed a bug. He had that way of embarrassing you.

David said, "He has his own way of listening."

"He has his own way makin' you feel like a bug."

"He hears different."

"You say he hears better. He knows what he's doin' around a farm, too. David, when he left a gate open, which he did more times than I can count, he did it on purpose."

I told David that once I watched Chump step this way and step that way as if he wasn't even aware of what he was doing, getting a whole herd of steers jammed up in a corner of the pasture against the barbed wire fences, sending them against the fences so they were cutting themselves, liable to knock the fence down and find themselves in the road.

I hailed him, shouted at him, asked him to come help me carry something. He came, slowly. After not trying hard at helpin' me pick something up, he said it was too heavy for him to lift. He said he'd go get David to help. He never came back.

"He wasn't bored around the farm, David. He knew I was wise to him. It was a community just like this that got rid of Chump Hardy in the first place."

Leaning against my truck, arms folded across his chest, David was silent a while.

"You hear what I'm sayin', David?"

"I'm not sure."

"I'm sayin' it's okay for you to be as mad as hell at your friend, Chump Hardy, no matter what state he's in."

"I see."

"Chump Hardy is your friend, and I respect that. Maybe he's the best horn player who ever lived, and I respect that. I don't know how it is wherever you come from, but around here, we allow people eccentricities. We even know that if someone is special good at somethin', he might be a little off-center some other way. But, 'round here, a crittur who tries to run cattle through a barbed wire fence into a road we recognize as a varmint, and we shoot it."

"Okay."

"I'm tellin' you I know that boy, David. I know he wouldn't have lived as long as he has, if you hadn't taken care of him every hour of every day. People tell me you're some kind of a musical genius. I know you're a genius 'cause somehow you got some work out of that son of a bitch. No one else could have."

After a good long time standin' there, seein' the driveway become black and the lawn become green, David looked up and said, "My God, William. Is that the sun?"

I turned around and looked east, smiling, as if I had to make sure.

"That's the sun," I said.

"What time is it?"

"Well, it's about sunrise."

"I've kept you up all night." David was dry-mouthed, talked-out sober by that time. "What will your wife say?"

"She'll know I was up to no harm."

David said, "I'll help you around the farm today."

"That's good." I figured he needed that. He needed to get the rhythms of his life goin' again. I never did know a better consolation than that provided by work.

David said, "Thanks, William. Guess I needed a nut loosened, and this time you had the wrench." And when he put it that way I knew he truly meant it.

"Shoot, David. Just don't you feel any worse than you have to, you hear?"

David said, "I hear."

So David MacFarlane and William Fesdon, from two different patches of this garden earth, somehow had become friends, without my ever having heard a musical note come out of him (and without his ever havin' heard me sing even the first few notes of the Jameson High School song).

Then, in that dawn light, David noticed the drinking glass on the lawn. He looked at it as if he didn't know what it was doin' there, or how it got there, as if he'd never seen it before.

"Coffee?" David asked.

"You know I don't drink stimulants."

"Guess I need some coffee. You want to come in and shower or something?"

"I'll go home." I stretched and yawned. "Then I'll come back."

31

"What now?"

David slid open the glass door to the studio.

Inside, alone, Milton Farber sat in his wheelchair listening to a tape of Richland Symphony Six.

David crossed the room and switched off the tape player.

Milton said, "I was enjoying that."

"Suddenly you're a music critic?"

Milton smiled. "I know what I like."

After napping, showering, and dressing in clean slacks and shirt for the evening, David had stepped out onto the upper balcony of the house to overlook his acres. William and Frank and Paul were shifting a herd of steers into a pasture farther from the house. Dressed only in shorts, Josh was ambling down the side of the road toward the river, trailed by Jester. From a distance, the boy looked like he had been run over by a hay rake.

Downstairs, in the kitchen, at the back of the house generally, inside and outside, David found Ellie and Clara and Nell moving like slightly overheated amoebas setting out the buffet that had arrived from the hotel. Jock was slicing limes at the bar.

"Where is everyone?" David asked.

"Retired to neutral corners," Ellie said.

"Good thing this place has lots of neutral corners."

"Napping," she said. "No telling when those buses will arrive."

"Isn't the hotel supposed to warn you when the buses leave there?"

"Supposed to. Haig called before taking off from San Antonio. Asked if he should use Jameson Airport or land in one of the pastures. I told him we have one mowed pasture he can land in. Right?"

"Yes. E.T.A.?"

"In about an hour, I should think. Some other news outfit called to ask if John Bart Nelson is expected."

"Who?"

"Clara took that call. David, why don't you get out from underfoot?"

"I'm underfoot?"

"Like fescue."

David had headed for the studio expecting a quiet moment by himself.

In the studio with Milton, David watched the big tape reel unwind. "When you don't like something, you're not a critic. When you do like something, you are a critic." David took the full reel off the machine. "Well, you're a lousy critic, Milton."

"Why? Because I like music with a tune to it? With warmth and power and intelligence and beauty and vibrancy?"

"Because you don't play fair. Either you're a music critic and you know music and you know what you're listening to, talking about, or you don't. How did you find this tape anyway?" David looked at the shelves. "How did you even reach it?"

"Josh. Nice boy. He noticed yesterday some of your tape boxes have red dots on them, some of them don't. The tape we listened to last night did not have a red dot on it. I thought about it overnight. I did not sleep well, David. When Josh came back to the guesthouse with me, to make sure my new wheelchair batteries worked, after Rourke departed so ingloriously, I said to Josh, 'Let's try a tape with a red dot.' He took one down and started it for me. He even listened a minute. Even he liked it, and what does a boy know? His exact words were: 'All *right*!' He might have listened more, except he had the sort of gleam in his eye you never ask a boy about, just wish him love. He showed me how to rewind and play again. This is the third time I've listened to this tape already this afternoon. Does listening to a tape three times in a row make me a music critic?"

"It makes you numb."

"It's wonderful, David."

"It's not."

"Who knows better?"

"I do. It's just a bunch of old tunes I've strung together to make a lot of noise."

"I recognize the old tunes, some of them. Old tunes of the American South. Many of them with Scottish or Irish antecedents. Some of the tunes that never made it to New Orleans or made their way into American jazz music. Some of the folk tunes that never made it into rock. How am I doing so far, as a critic?"

"Okay."

"From what I've heard this afternoon, you've put them together, beautifully, beautifully arranged, orchestrated, in six symphonies, playing the simple melodies with each other, harmonizing them somehow beyond me, against each other, creating musical ironies no one would ever think of, realizing each one, perfectly, making each one more than it has ever been before, without departing from its inherent simplicity." David said nothing. "Are there more than six? My old eyes see more reel boxes with red dots on them."

"Yes."

"And isn't this how symphonies sometimes are written, from the folk music? Forgive me my ignorance, for having to ask." David didn't answer. "David, you have created six gorgeous symphonies of American music, from what I've just heard. Curse at me if you want. To you, I say congratulations."

David sprawled in a couch and looked at Milton steadily.

Milton continued: "David, in the music I've been listening to this afternoon, I have heard this place, this Tennessee of yours. I've heard the sound of the wind I hear from my bed in there, the farm sounds, the twang of the people's talk, even the noise of the funny old trucks that go by. I've heard the sadness and the sense of story and the relief of laughter. Closing my eyes I've seen the rolling hills and the dirt roads and the tumbling-down barns; I've seen the lean people standing both sides of a fence, talking. I've heard their songs, David, put together in a way that I can feel all of their lives, their sorrows reconciled by their hard work, by their appreciation of the beauty of their land. I have heard it all, David, and I have felt it, sitting here in this air-conditioned, sound-proofed room in my wheel chair."

David's eyebrows were slightly wrinkled as he studied Milton, listened to him.

"And, David, may I say it is also good to hear your piano again? I never knew you would be this mature, as a pianist. You see, there is a point in staying alive. To me, who is not so knowledgeable in electronics, who couldn't understand all this fancy new equipment if God gave me two more lives, from my lips to His ears, it sounds to me you have every instrument ever invented at your command, right here in this room. You use these instruments well, better than you probably have any right to; I don't know how. But you use the piano as the driving force behind everything, wonderfully. The piano is your instrument, you've grown up with it, grown older with it, the extension of yourself, and now I hear the full, mature, well-balanced David MacFarlane speaking through your piano. I hear the terrible, terrible loneliness of your own life I have always known so well and regretted: the sorrow of your unique talent that has made you so terribly alone in your life. I hear the personality of David MacFarlane resolved, the sadness that has always been there, balanced before by your carefully measured, youthful energy, now balanced by serenity. And, if not as a music critic, then as a friend who has known you since you were fighting pimples, knowing David MacFarlane, hearing you, hearing what you have to say at this point in your life, hearing the wonderful way you say it, is maybe the greatest pleasure of my life." Still, David said nothing. "Now you can stop giving me the fish eye. Did I teach you that?"

David continued staring at Milton.

"And this music I just heard," Milton asked. "Does it have a name, a title?"

"Richland. Richland Symphonies."

"See? Not only can you listen to this music, you can refer to it."

David laughed. "I think I'll send Rourke a get well card." He sat up on the couch. "I've done a lot of work."

"I knew that. You've never not worked. We'd send you away on a vacation, just a long weekend, and always I'd have the second thought and phone again the hotel you would be staying at to make sure they had a piano available for you."

"You did?"

"Even for your honeymoon with Ms. Tuesday."

"I just thought every place had pianos."

"Every place you've ever been had pianos."

"Oh."

"Your isolation in your talent, David, has been so complete that the only real pain you've ever felt, the only real loneliness, has been when you have been separated from your work—even on your honeymoon. Am I right?"

"Chump . . ."

"Oh, my God, what's that?"

The sound of an airplane passing low overhead heard from inside the sound-proofed room was almost unrecognizable.

David said, "Haggus MacBagpipe."

"That's his airplane? My nice afternoon shouldn't end with such a shattering noise. Yee, gods, here it comes again."

"He's buzzing the house. Letting us know he's here."

"Postcards are quieter."

David stood. "I've got to drive down to the pasture to pick him up. You all right? I'll send Jock in to help you change your shirt, whatever you need to do."

"Jock is all right. He knows how it is to be thrown. Is that the right expression? Thrown off a bull? I've been thrown by two strokes, which is no bull."

"Milton, I don't want to leave you with the impression I agree with you."

"You never have."

"The music you heard last night is far more important, has much more meaning, will live much longer, than the music you heard this afternoon."

"That's all right, David. I believe you. While we're waiting one hundred years for last night's music to become recognized as important, just don't mind if I enjoy myself listening to this afternoon's music. At my age, I haven't time to wait for greatness to strike."

32

"Josh!" David yelled through the truck window. After his swim in the river, wet-haired and open-mouthed, the boy was standing at the side of the road watching the airplane land in the pasture. Jester seemed less surprised by the appearance of the airplane than did the boy. "Open that gate for me, will you?"

Watching the boy through the truck's windshield, David regretted having asked him. Barefooted and barelegged, Josh had not hesitated to plunge into the brambles and open the seldom-used gate. David saw blood streaking his legs.

David drove through the opened gate.

"Wait a minute!" Josh yelled. He closed the gate and climbed into the back of the truck.

David drove the truck slowly through the high hay. Jester zigzagged in front of the truck, barking, playing with it.

"Who's that?" Josh's face appeared at an odd angle near David's left shoulder. Hanging on, the boy was leaning from the truck's bed to talk to David in the cab.

"Mr. Haig Scott," David yelled back. "A friend."

"Oh." Josh's head bobbed outside David's window. "Why does he need an airplane?"

"He's a smuggler."

Josh said, "Oh."

Haig stood on the wing of the airplane with his walking stick and his overnight kit.

"Hello, old man," Haig said.

Standing between the truck and the wing, David said, "Nice of you to drop in. Need any help?"

"Just locking up. You've got good weather for a wedding."

David scanned the cloudless sky. "Yes, we have."

After looking at Haig from the back of the truck, Josh jumped down onto the field. He scooted into the middle of the cab's seat.

Haig tossed his kit to David. Hanging onto his cane, Haig slithered clumsily off the wing onto the ground. As he walked toward the truck, Josh saw how very crippled Haig was.

David threw Haig's kit into the back of the truck. He let down the tailgate and told Jester to jump into the truck's bed.

By the time David slammed the tailgate shut, Haig had climbed with difficulty into the seat beside Josh and slammed the door.

Getting into his own seat, David said, "Nice of you to come."

"Figured you'd have enough of the bright and beautiful here."

"You'll fit in real well," David said. "By the way, this is Josh. Found him around the place."

Haig nodded at the boy, then looked out the window as the truck proceeded through tall grass. "Place looks okay. Hope I didn't scare any of your pregnant cows."

"They're not cows," David said. "And they can't be pregnant."

Two big buses turned the corner into the main road leading to Bass Clef Farm.

Josh tried not to be rude in his scrutiny of the man sitting beside him. Josh had moved his feet to make room for the man's walking stick. Haig's left leg was bent cruelly inward, just above the ankle. The man had to walk on the left side of his left foot. The middle three fingers of his left hand were missing.

When the truck stopped at the closed gate, Josh made a move to get out, either one side or the other.

"I'll get it." David got out and opened the gate.

Alone in the truck's cab with the man, Josh said, "Mr. MacFarlane made the joke that you're a smuggler."

"No joke." A deeply rutted scar made a diagonal across Haig's face, from above his left eye, across a broken, twisted nose, to his right jaw. His left eyelid drooped, and the right side of his lips was pulled down from the scar. "I am."

"No foolin'."

"No foolin'." There was a whole different scar across the man's forehead, and a third across his right cheek, just below the cheekbone.

"Well, he sure was jokin' about having found me on the place."

Haig said, "I'm a smuggler, all right. That's what I am."

Leaving his door open, David drove the truck through the gate. He got out again to close the gate.

Josh asked, "What do you smuggle?"

"Drugs."

Josh didn't say any more to the man. Haig smelled of things, earth and plants and trees, foods, Josh supposed, that Josh had never smelled before.

Haig exhaled heavily. "I was in Honduras this morning."

"You know," David said. "I don't think I ever played in Honduras."

"Your music is there."

"Yeah?"

"I heard 'Mercy Me Oh My.' In a cantina."

David said, "So you don't have to tour, to sell records," and laughed.

The charter buses already were pulled into the main driveway and unloading. Wedding guests in party clothes were blinking around at the valley. Some already had little plastic drinking glasses in their hands.

"The bright and the beautiful," Haig said.

As David drove the truck through them in low gear, Josh heard a woman shriek, "Oh, God! I knew I should have worn my shit-kickers!"

33

"Paul, I suppose you know your mother is anorexic," Lucy said, her mouth nearly filled with potato salad.

"Oh, yes. I know it well."

For nearly three hours, the bride had moved around the lawns and rooms of Bass Clef Farm greeting the guests, her friends, Tony's friends, all the great lot from the buses, the MacFarlanes' friends, chatting with the minister who was to officiate at her wedding the next day, and his wife, trying to spend time with each and every one, to show appreciation for the trouble and expense each had gone to in coming to Tennessee for her wedding.

Hungry and tired of standing, finally Lucy had filled a plate with salads for herself, grabbed a fork and a glass of iced tea and headed for the front porch of the house, remembering the nice time, the peace and quiet she had shared with Paul Hollingsworth there the night before.

Tonight, the porch lights were on.

Paul Hollingsworth was there. "Here," he had said. "I've saved your chair for you."

Lucy wondered if she had ever eaten supper in a rocking chair before.

She said, "As a model, I've had lots of experience with *anorexia nervosa.* I guess it's not all that uncommon to be anorexic over the age of fifty."

"Ever suffer from it yourself?"

"God, no. I can't understand anyone who doesn't want to eat, and eat, and eat. That's all I've ever wanted to do, nearly every damned waking moment of my life. You know that. It's a wonder you and I didn't die of advanced gluttony, that time in East Germany."

"Well. We've tried everything. Psychiatry. Injections that supposedly make the urge to eat irresistible. She even attended one of those tough-love boot camps for anorexics in California."

"Is she bulimic?"

"I don't know. She has been." Paul said, "She still has her teeth."

"She certainly had a strapping big son."

"She insists on leading two or three aerobic sessions a day herself. Would you believe that? Not only for people her own age, but for people much younger. I don't see how she can have any cartilage left, anywhere in her body. She never complains. Maybe she doesn't feel the pain. Maybe she does, and that's the point: she's punishing herself for God knows what. We've been 'round and 'round in circles."

"Your folks run a health spa in Beverly Hills? I sort of missed that part of the dinner conversation the other night. I know Josh perked up at some point, about movie stars."

"That's the irony: a health spa run by a woman who is killing herself by refusing to eat."

"Care to tell me what happened? When I knew you at school in Switzerland, your parents were rich, living on a plantation in the West Indies, had a house on the French Riviera, Cap-Ferrat . . ."

"Never rich-rich. They owned a large, working plantation into which they had poured their assets, their lives. It was because it was so isolated that they sent me to school in Europe, and why they spent three months there a year. Their place on Cap-Ferrat originally had been just a little old fishing shack. Worth a fortune now, I suppose. They had to sell it."

"So how did they end up doing aerobics in Beverly Hills for a living?"

"Really? You care?"

"What happened to them, happened to you."

"Well, it is sort of interesting." Paul paused. He had finished eating. His empty plate was beside him on the porch floor. "Centuries ago, the colonizing navies of the world stripped those islands in the Caribbean of timber. Without timber, the islands lost their topsoil. Now, when it rains, the fresh water runs right down off the hills and into the sea."

"Ah. Why working models must limit their showers while on assignment in the West Indies." The chair rocked as Lucy shifted her feet. Alfalfa sprouts from her plate almost fell into her lap.

"There's plenty of water. Plenty of rain falls on those islands, but all the topsoil is washed away, so there's no real earth for the rain to sink into, be useful. Anyway, some years ago Dad devised a means of catching and holding the rain from tropical rainfalls. He built widening, spiral, cement gutters down one or two hills on his own plantation that caught the rainfall and poured it into big, underground water catchments. From the catchments he could draw water and sprinkle his fields any time he wanted. The system worked. He tried to sell the elected island legislature on the idea, described it to them, showed it to them, showed them it worked. He even had ideas on how the islands could create new topsoil over a few generations."

Smiling, Lucy said, "The officials were delirious over the idea and elected him Governor."

"They listened to him with glazed eyes and said nothing."

"Still, he could continue to use the idea on his own place. Once people got used to it, saw it really working, topsoil appearing—"

"That wasn't where their minds were. Our plantation had its own cove, a little harbor on the north side, fairly deep water. Originally a pretty place. One day, the island legislature voted to build a big wharf into that harbor. Dad's attitude was, what was good for the island was good for the plantation. Then they built a road through the plantation to the wharf. Then they built a massive tourist hotel on the hill overlooking the cove, on our land, not far from our house."

"Without compensating your parents?"

"Then they built an airstrip through what was left of the plantation. Without one penny in compensation, without any formal, legal process of condemnation or appropriation, without even a sham process."

"How could they?"

"We were not indigenous to the island."

Lucy said, "The people who did this were black people."

"Does it matter? They were people, the parents of people I was born with, grew up with, deeply loved, still do love."

"They noticed you were white folks."

"I think they also noticed we went back and forth to Europe. Can't blame them, in a way."

"But obviously your parents, you, really cared for the island."

"I've never cared for any place, any people so much. It's my home. I know my parents feel the same way. Our friends and neighbors pushed us off the island."

"I don't understand. It would seem to me your parents still must own a lot of real estate there, with a wharf, a road, a hotel, an airport . . ."

"When my parents tried to exert their legal rights, showed documentary evidence of their ownership of the place, the legislature said they had no records of such documentation and therefore whatever my parents had must be counterfeit. And they were the law. My parents spent years and all their savings on lawyers, before giving up. They ended up even without the house on Cap-Ferrat."

"Are you bitter?"

"Sad. We were sent east of Eden, as if we had introduced a snake to paradise instead of a water system. I miss it, terribly. So I live in two rooms near the laboratories in Princeton, New Jersey, a white man who plays his bongo drums quietly with his fingers alone some snowy nights, his heart aching for the sounds and smells of where he was born, brought up. And my parents lead aerobics classes in Beverly Hills, California."

"Your Dad doesn't lead many aerobics classes."

"No. He advises in the weights room."

"Oh, my."

"Incidentally, they wouldn't have the health spa without David MacFarlane. Especially under these circumstances, you and I sitting on his porch in Tennessee, you being married here tomorrow, I must tell you that."

"What did he have to do with anything?"

"You know, years ago he wrote a song he called 'Sorry,' after my mother?"

"Yes."

"When my parents were very nearly flat broke, living in an apartment in Washington, D.C., freezing with the cold, David MacFarlane appeared, took them out to dinner, asked them what they wanted to do. My mother was attending aerobics classes at the time. David suggested they buy a health spa in a climate they were more used to. He said he would invest the royalties he had had from "Sorry" over the years. Nonsense, of course. It was his graceful way of making an offer to them they could accept."

"He owns the health spa?"

"They're paying him back, as they can, interest free. I don't think

I'm supposed to know all this. Dad told me once, when he was in his cups. I think one of Mr. MacFarlane's conditions was that no one was to know, except the three of them."

"Interesting. Tony and I had hoped, in coming here, to figure out some of the connections, the relationships, among these people."

"Mr. Farber knows, of course. He spent considerable time with my parents, showing them how to set up a business in this country."

Lucy rotated the eating of the five salads on her plate. "Tony says David MacFarlane and my mother were sort-of married, at one time. Or so his father says. Occasionally, my mother has referred to being married to David, then denied it."

"Really? How can you be 'sort-of' married?"

"Some sort of savage rite, I guess, which was annulled; I don't know why."

"Wonderful, the things the kids of a family don't know."

"Is this a family? That time you chased after me in Switzerland, across the East German border, you acted as if we were related; as if you were my brother, or a cousin, or something. Because your parents knew my parents, you said."

"What's family?" Paul asked. "A biological unit? A social unit?"

"A limited liability," Lucy laughed. "A société anonyme."

"A corporate structure," Paul said, "with acquisitions, mergers, divestments, liquidations."

More seriously, Lucy said, "I think a family could be a permanent, inward-directed unit, a mutual company; all other relationships being outward-directed."

"You think, or you hope?"

"I hope."

"Guess you can't get married without hope. Josh told me that Dan Prescott said something about permanence the other night."

"What did he say?"

"There isn't any. He said he was brought up thinking there was, but there isn't."

"That generation has been through an earthquake. Everything has shifted around on them. I don't think they really related to each other at all, any more than people can, when buildings and mountains and monuments are falling all around them, the earth ripping open at their feet. They can only grab each other for a moment, help each other over a chasm, maybe, then dash on to continue saving themselves."

Lucy put her empty plate on the floor, next to Paul's.

"Don't be hurt when I say this, Cille, but I suspect David's providing you with his place for your wedding tomorrow is at least partly an excuse for his getting certain people together at this point in their lives. I mean, you hardly know my parents, and they were invited. You know me, and I wasn't. I don't know what Abraham Baxter is doing here."

Lucy sighed and looked to the moon. "Where's my damned father?"

"Hello?"

Clara Reagan had told David there was someone on the phone who insisted on talking to him. Milton had offered to take the call.

David escaped the hubbub of the party by taking the call in the study.

"David?"

"Who's this?"

"Nelson."

"John Nelson, the bard?"

"What's left of him."

"Where are you?"

"At the Jameson Hotel."

"Great! What are you doing there?"

"Wondering how to find Bass Clef Farm in the dark. Finding Jameson, Tennessee, was almost as hard as finding honesty in a politician."

"Stay right there. I'll come get you."

In some haste, David looked around the house for Lucy, but did not find her.

Crossing the lawn to the driveway, he spotted Abraham Baxter making a drink for himself at the outside bar.

"A.B.? Want to come?"

"Sure. Where you going?"

"To collect John."

"He's here?"

"Wonders never cease."

34

"They don't allow drinking liquor in the front seats of cars in many states now." Abraham, with a full glass of Scotch and water in one hand, managed to put on his seat belt.

"They probably don't in Tennessee, either." David piloted the Town Car down the driveway, avoiding other cars, the two buses, and a lady's shoe.

He turned left on the road through the farm. "What are you working on these days, A.B.?"

"'Working on'?"

"Unless I've missed something, you haven't published a novel in years."

"Years and years," Abraham said. "I gave it up." He sipped his drink. "Took up drinking full time."

"At least you know it."

"Sure I know it. Whatever happened to the pleasure principle? You and I were brought up on the pleasure principle."

"I've lived off it."

"Why work, when you can drink?" He looked at the liquid proving the car's movement in his glass. "My drug of choice."

"You and I were also brought up on the work ethic."

"Drinking is hard work. It's hard feeling lousy all the time. You should respect that."

"Do you? Do you feel lousy all the time?"

"Most of the time. If I didn't drink I'd feel lousy all the time.

Drinking makes me feel lousy just most of the time. Gives me something to blame for feeling lousy."

David turned right. "Drinking doesn't have a product. Except a rotted liver."

"That's another good thing about it. You never have to publish a book about all you've thought, and felt. You never have to hand other people toilet paper for them to wipe their asses on."

"Is that what writing is like?"

"It's what publishing is like. You must have some sense of that yourself, David."

"Yes. I listen to how people react to my work, usually with interest. But I always know a couple of things they can't know: pretty much where that work is coming from and pretty much where it is going."

"Writing, composing music, drinking, being a model, a physical fitness nut: it's all narcissism. Let's see: what do I think, today? How do I look, today? Mirror, mirror on the wall, assure me I am alive, and wonderful. All is vanity."

"How many novels did you publish?"

"Two. Two big, fat, commercial, hugely successful novels filled with every cliché and stereotype the people just love: nasty rich men, immoral women, the noble poor. Jealousy, rivalry, greed. At best, they were just doorstops, David."

"A.B., what's the truth?"

"The truth?" Abraham sucked an ice cube. "The truth is human relations changed to the point where I did not, do not understand them. The marital bed is no longer sacrosanct. Adultery has become a symptom of healthy, excess energy. That does away with jealousy. The family no longer exists. Everyone has two, three sets of parents. Think of all that has done away with: the Oedipal complex, sibling rivalries. Nearly everyone these days has enough to eat, central heat, a car and a television. That's done away with greed, except in the shade of your credit card. Shall I continue? Your contemporary character leaves his work place, sniffs coke, grabs someone to sleep with that night, sniffs coke, and goes back to the office, to keep up his credit cards. Where's the story? Nothing is connected. Nothing leads to anything. I can't write it."

"What's the truth?"

"The truth?" Abraham shrugged. "Susie died."

"I know that. Your daughter died at the age of six. That was twenty years ago, A.B. You've published one novel since then."

"That's not all that happened." Abraham drank from his glass. "Sally decided she never wanted another child. Okay. I had met Haig Scott, racing motorcycles. He had the charter boat, then, that he had inherited from his grandfather. As a novelist, I was sort of interested in Haig, this guy who had never completed a year of school, who was addicted to danger. He was real. Thinking it would help snap Sally out of mourning, I chartered Haig's boat. We cruised the eastern Mediterranean for a month, the Greek islands. Haig was wonderful. He knew everything, every place, everybody. There ought to be a word for that period just before a marriage ends, you know? The reverse of honeymoon. Soursun. Sally and I had our soursun. When we got home, she unpacked her play clothes and, not even removing her suitcases from our bed, immediately packed city clothes. Her father, the advertising genius, Phillip Asgood, was getting older, lazier, had this big, rich advertising firm in New York. He was wearying of administrative tasks, he told Sally several times during this period. Sally knew nothing about advertising, nothing about administration; hadn't even particularly liked or respected her father very much. When she left she said she was going to New York to help her father out for a couple of months. It would help take her mind off Susie, she said. She went home to her daddy. And she never came back. Two months became three months, six months, a year, a year and a half. She became Chief Executive Officer of one of the biggest advertising agencies in New York. Never, never had she mentioned to me wanting a career. I published the novel I had been working on when Sally left, *Still Waters Don't Run At All*, and then, I guess, I said, *So what?* Unlike what you just said, David, I couldn't figure out from what I was writing, or for what. I was supposed to mess up a lot of paper with mourning, whining introspection and call them novels? The stores are full of such books, all written during the longest period of relative peace and prosperity a major civilization has ever known. I did the world a favor. Every time I had the instinct to write, I drank until it passed. I also got involved with Haig, as you know."

Abraham swallowed more of his drink.

"So when did you and Sally actually get divorced?"

"We never actually got divorced."

"You didn't?"

"I guess we didn't care enough about each other, finally, to get divorced."

"It might have given you a kind of new beginning."

"I guess neither of us wanted a new beginning, that way. There was no point to it. Neither of us would ever want to center our lives and love on a lovely small human being who could die one spring day during lunch. Why go through divorce and remarriage, all that crap, with no objective in view?"

"No product."

"When did you and Ellie actually get married? I don't remember having been invited to that wedding."

"Ellie and I never actually got married."

"You and Ellie aren't married?"

"No. We were beyond the point of having children. She was. She had her property. I had mine."

"Sally and I aren't divorced. And you and Ellie aren't married. And you expect me to write a novel?"

"We just couldn't see the point of going through legal forms just to generate more legal forms; you know, if we ever decided to stop living together, or one or both of us died."

"That's it, David. That answers your every question. How can there be literary forms, when there are no social forms?"

"Interesting point."

"That big young man around the house is Paul Hollingsworth?"

"Yes. He's here."

"He seems to be avoiding me."

"I think he avoids nearly everyone. A very self-contained young man."

"I have the instinct to avoid him, too."

"Why?"

"I don't know. Something from the past. I don't think I've seen him since Susie's funeral. I sure loved that boy, when he was ten. He was just so strong. And then maybe I hated him. He was alive and Susie wasn't. I ignored him at the funeral. I couldn't stand the sight of him. Do you think a ten-year-old boy could have sensed all that?"

"Sensed it, yes. Understood it, no."

"Maybe I should try to talk with him now."

"I really don't understand the words, A.B.; I can't even remember them exactly. I understand Paul Hollingsworth's science specialty is some kind of electrical biology. He has his Ph.D."

"So?"

"Didn't Susie die of an epileptic seizure?"

"Jesus."

David said, "What is communicated from one generation to another, how it is communicated, what we can really know about each other, is beyond this human's comprehension. Time is the universal solvent."

David turned left onto the main road.

Abraham said, "This ride is further than I thought. Can we stop at the hotel for a drink?"

"We're almost there."

"Okay."

David said, "Haig looks good enough."

"Yeah," Abraham said. "He has at least one more plane crash left in him."

"Does it have to end that way for him?"

"You know Haig." Abraham put his empty glass on the floor of the car. "Our lives result in our deaths. Don't they?"

In the bright lobby of the hotel, David said to John Bart Nelson: "You look terrible." John's extraordinary height never ceased to amaze David. Terribly thinned out, John's height seemed even more overwhelming.

"I've been traveling hard and fast for days and nights to get here."

Abraham said, "John, you're a skeleton."

"I've been reducing. Doing my slimming exercises." John looked down at his dark blue suit. "No, it's this suit. I don't get to wear suits much anymore. It's way too big for me."

Abraham said, "You need a drink."

John folded some papers he had been working on and slipped them into his jacket pocket. "Lead me to it."

John walked out of the lobby to the sidewalk.

David said, "Where's your luggage?"

"My God," Abraham whispered. "His head is just a skull."

John got into the back seat of the Town Car. "Big party goin' on, uh?"

David started the car. "John, Lucy is magnificent."

"Oh, I know that. She's my child."

"She's no child," Abraham said. "Much woman."

"Seems sensible, too," David added.

"What I want to know about is this maniac she's marrying."

David said, "Tony seems wonderful."

"Does he?"

David drove with his head tilted back better to hear John's deep voice in the back seat. "Well, he's Dan's son."

"I know that."

"Bright. Could be good lookin', if he lost a few pounds. Ambitious. Speechwriter for the present incumbent of the White House; you know that."

"He have Dan's moral sense?" John's laugh was almost a growl.

"Somewhere. Underneath." David turned right, off the main road.

"You mean, behind him."

"Right," David said. "He doesn't walk around with it in front of him. He doesn't seem to worry things to death. But it's there."

"That's good. I wanted that. In his background. I always thought I'd really appreciate the next generation of Dan Prescott."

David said, "I must tell you, John. Dan isn't working as a minister. Never has. Married twice. Divorced twice. You know he's a male model?"

"I know all that. All these years, Dan and I have corresponded. I've kept up."

"You have?"

"About monthly."

"Didn't know that."

"Who do you think brought about this marriage?"

"What do you mean?"

"David, this is an arranged marriage, if there ever was one. Who do you think arranged for Lucy and Tony to meet?"

"What?"

"How do you suppose a French female model and a male presidential speechwriter got invited to the same party at the United Nations, on a *must appear* basis? I had about three friends at that party charged with introducing them, and making sure they stayed introduced. Each of the three followed up with a dinner party invitation to each of them, where they could and did meet again. You think life's all coincidence?"

"You old fox!"

On the seat beside David, Abraham was laughing, hard.

John asked, "You think I've been out of town, or something?"

Abraham said, "John, you have been out of town!"

"Yeah. Maybe. But I haven't been out of *it.* I know what's best for my daughter. This is an arranged marriage, all right. I arranged it."

Abraham said, "I can hardly wait to tell them!"

"Better wait until after the ceremony," John said. "Young folks love to believe, as long as they can, they're in charge of their own destinies."

David tried to watch John's face in the rear view mirror. All he could see was John's white shirt and red tie. "You know Lucy bought a house in Columbia Falls, Maine?"

"Who do you think suggested it to her?"

They all laughed.

"Space hasn't got anything to do with anything," John said. "Distance. I know I've been away a lot. If there's a God, He's not in space, He's in timing, pure and simple timing. I suggested to Lucy in a letter in April she think of buying them a home in Columbia Falls. I knew she would. These are poor, homeless children, you know. They need a home in their hearts probably even more than they need each other."

David said, "I'm glad you got here, John."

"I wouldn't miss Lucy's wedding for anything in the world. You got my cables saying I was coming, didn't you?"

"No."

"I sent you about a half-dozen. Let's see: from Agadem, Alexandria, Rome, and Atlanta. I sent you four."

"We'll get them tomorrow."

"How's your Ms. Tuesday?" John asked David about John's wife.

"Janet is fine. She seems proud of you."

"Why not?"

"She also seems proud of how she manages without you."

John said, "She needs that."

"I tried to bring Lucy in the car to come get you, but I couldn't find her."

"Maybe she's run away with someone," John said. "Looks like I got here in the nick of time."

For the rest of the ride back to the farm John asked who else was there, what the arrangements were, how things were timed.

David was surprised at how cognizant John was of the facts of everyone's life, including Haig's and the Hollingsworths'.

Pulling into the driveway, David said, "After the buses go, you're both invited to share a quiet champagne cognac with me in the study."

"All right," John said.

Abraham said, "I can't wait."

35

Josh was tired.

He had showered and dressed in his suit, brushed his hair for the party, stood around, met people politely. He ate with Nonnie and the minister and his wife. They talked about how surprised they all were there was no music at a party given by Ellie and David MacFarlane. Quietly, Nonnie kept pointing out to Josh the tall, skinny "funny-looking women," as she called them, friends of Lucy's, who were also models. Josh said they looked to him like whooping cranes. The minister and his wife left. Nonnie said she needed to go home to sleep.

When the Town Car arrived back (Josh had not known it had left), momentary excitement went through the party. A remarkably tall, remarkably thin black man got out of the back seat. When Josh was introduced to him and told he was the bride's, Lucy's, father, Josh expressed surprise the man wasn't wearing flowing robes. "I'm from the same place you are, Josh: the state of Maine." Almost immediately Josh was elbowed aside. All the people from Washington, D.C., wanted to talk to Mr. Nelson. Mrs. Nelson and Lucy gave him big greetings when he arrived, big hugs and kisses. Everyone exclaimed how thin the man was. "I've been reducing," Mr. Nelson kept saying. "I've been doing my slimming exercises. No, really, it's this suit. Too big for me." Lucy never left his side. The tall man stood with his arm around his tall daughter, no matter with whom he was talking. The person with whom he talked the longest, the most privately in the big crowd was Josh's step-brother, Tony, the groom. At first, they laughed together frequently. Then they talked seriously. Josh listened for a while. Mr. Nelson kept mentioning *the Third World within the United States* which Josh did not understand. He figured the man must have his terms confused. Mr. Nelson said, "You keep buying these people, at home and abroad, and thus you keep enslaving them. There will be a real revolution, moved by simplistic fundamentalism, without and within your borders." Josh could tell his step-brother and Mr. Nelson liked each other. But he thought their conversation, for the first between a father and a son-in-law, sure was odd and hard.

Even more interesting to Josh was Haig Scott. The no foolin' smuggler stumped around on the side of his shoe, resting on his walking stick, talking with people who clearly were repulsed by his ugly, smashed, scarred face. As he approached a group of people, women would look away, especially if they still held plates of food; men would look nervous. Haig Scott would charm them. In no time, Haig Scott would have them talking about travel: where they had been; where they would like to go. He sounded like he had been everywhere in the world. He made recommendations for hotels and restaurants, airlines; he even knew airline schedules. People took notes. When a man asked him what business he was in, Haig Scott said, simply, "Export." Again, listening, Josh thought the man must be confused: didn't he mean to say "import"?

Josh was not sure of what he saw. He thought he saw John Bart Nelson wink across the room at Haig Scott. Mr. Nelson's head was turning as he did so, or may have done so, his face expressionless. It was hard to tell, the way Haig Scott's eyelid drooped, if he returned the wink. It looked to Josh as if he tried.

Josh did not want to leave the party. He was sure Mr. MacFarlane would make music sometime. But he was falling asleep on his feet.

He wandered outside, to the back of the house, above the little brick terrace beneath the tree. He sat on the lawn and looked at the stars. He lay back, for a fuller view of the sky.

He awoke when he heard his own name.

". . . Josh, that I am a smuggler, and the kid asked me what I smuggled, and I said, 'Drugs.' The kid really froze up on me. I could feel the hatred coming off his skin at me in the truck. It made me feel good."

Josh decided to keep his head down, not move.

"In the car a while ago, David was asking about you."

Josh recognized the voice of Mr. Abraham Baxter. Slow and

slurry, the voice sounded as if it were coming through a cheese grater.

The two men were sitting on the little brick terrace under the tree.

"What did you say?"

"I said I felt you were good for about one more plane crash."

Scott chuckled. "Thanks."

"He asked if it has to end that way for you."

"What did you say?"

"I'm asking you."

"One more plane crash," Scott said softly. "Maybe two. Going down, you never know if this is the final one."

"We're not kids anymore, Haig, racing motorcycles along the cliffs of the French Riviera. We could treat life carelessly then because we had so much of it left we felt we could squander it. Our physical coordination proved to us again and again that we could risk life and win. You don't have that much life left to risk, Haig, and you haven't the coordination anymore to win. Isn't that so?"

"You trying to tell me you're fond of me, or something?"

"Fond of you. Appreciative." Baxter said, "Why don't you think of quitting? Lease a cottage on the Greek Isles. Buy a little boat. Do daily charters for the tourists. You love the Greek Isles."

"I do not love tourists. Anyway, I can't get around on a boat anymore." Josh heard what may have been the sound of a walking stick whacking a shoe.

"I know John feels the same way. He'll probably speak to you."

"And say what? Urge me out of the smuggling trade?"

"Yes."

"If I quit, A.B., what does that mean to you?" Abraham Baxter did not answer. "I quit, and you lose the meaning of your existence."

"It's time I tried another novel."

"Bullshit. You're so brain-rotted with booze you could never get yourself up for it. You're so out of date you couldn't even get yourself up to the soap opera level you wrote twenty years ago."

There was a long silence.

Finally, Abraham Baxter said, "I find, when trying to make a decision, it is well to review the facts, everything that has led to one's present position."

Scott said, "I'm familiar with navigation."

"Growing up, you worked with your grandfather on his charter yacht, up and down the east coast of the United States, north in summer, south in winter. You never really went to school."

"Maybe I should retire and take up surgery."

"You inherited the boat and continued the charter business, mostly in the Mediterranean and the Caribbean."

"And met more awful people."

"Thanks."

Haig Scott spoke rapidly. "Until those stupid people from New York, two couples, insisted I sail them along the coast of Colombia, offered double the charter price if I dared. They wanted to go where other tourists dared not. I took the dare. A moonless night. Suddenly one boat on my port stern, another on my starboard. Colombian smugglers who wanted my boat. They were aboard before I could get out of the cockpit. My sleeping tourists got their throats slit in their bunks for their brave curiosity. I got cut and beaten and thrown overboard to drown. I found myself on a Colombian beach in the sunlight, beaten, broken, cut, my boat nowhere in sight. Three corpses on the beach with me, three of the brave, curious tourists, with their heads half off. The fourth was never found."

"Okay, Haig. I admit that was a rough time—"

"After that, I joined the smugglers. I decided I was not going to be their victim. I was not going to be one more broken, penniless beach bum. If stupid New Yorkers wanted to shove shit up their noses, I'd smuggle the shit for them, at a profit. What's the principle? Caveat emptor?"

"The principle of free enterprise."

"Right. I had lost my boat, my means of making a living. I thought I had better try free enterprise for a while, at least until I got a boat back. While I was recuperating, I went to Texas and learned to fly. With the last of my savings, I bought an old plane in British Colombia. It has never been hard to meet people who want to become your financial smuggling partners, when you have a boat or a plane and know how to move it."

"You made one trip. Or did you make several?"

"One. I brought one load of cocaine back to the United States. Landed not far from here, in fact, in west Georgia. And never felt worse in my life." Haig Scott paused. "I felt physically sick. Disgusted with myself. When I was a kid, sailing in the Caribbean with my grandfather, we'd see these old boats appear from behind an island, come about and disappear back behind the island faster than you could blink an eye. We laughed at their fear. At their shame. I was ashamed. Deeply ashamed."

Baxter said, "So I came out of the drunk clinic in Marseille, much more sober than I wanted to be, thirstier than ever, and there you were standing on the sidewalk. You said, 'Want to drink? I want to talk.' We drank three days. Or was it five? Anyway, we hatched this scheme. It has worked well, for a long time, now."

"I couldn't believe my ears when you said John Bart Nelson. 'Let's get John Bart Nelson into this.'"

"He had the knowledge, the contacts. He spent seven weeks in Central America doing nothing but setting up the drops."

"He deserves a plaque. And David MacFarlane. I said to myself, 'Boy, this Abraham Baxter. Some drunk. He has ideas crazier than mine.'"

"We needed the contacts and we needed the money. David MacFarlane put up the seed money: one hundred thousand dollars. And he's been good for one hundred thousand dollars each and every year since the beginning. He deserves a plaque too."

"Does David know John had anything to do with us?"

"No. Only you and I know, in this country. David wouldn't want to know. John wouldn't want him to. It's always better to leave statues on their pedestals, especially for other statues."

"We've done well, A.B."

"Damned well. I've put people in bed together who would be shocked indeed if they ever woke up and realized with whom they'd slept. I've raised money from Baptist conventions and Anglican dioceses. From white supremacist groups and gay alliances. And that isn't half the story." Abraham Baxter chuckled. "Amazing, the people who will take a drink with you and end up writing a check."

"The federals in Texas don't care if I fly medicines, drugs illegally to Central America. But they inspect my empty plane every time I return. No fail. I'm the easy part of their work. They can inspect me, write their report, and go home."

"Trouble is, Haig, you keep getting shot down at the other end."

"No trouble, really."

"It's no trouble being shot down?"

"It doesn't happen all that often."

"Often enough."

"It's just that the *Jefes* in some districts want their *yapas*. They can't believe we're not making a profit, somehow. They only uphold the law to fill their own pockets. So they take an occasional cargo, or what's left of it after they shoot me down, and sell it. But I never fear the people. In every group of men with guns, there are always one or two whose old grandmother, or sister, or child has been saved by the medicines I have flown in, dropped on the Baptist, or Mormon, or Catholic, or medical missionaries. They always see I get splints, whatever, bandages, steak, a bottle of wine, and out of there, somehow, as soon as I'm able to move."

"Yeah, but Haig. You know, I think of you a lot. Thinking about you keeps me awake, most nights."

Haig Scott laughed. "No. I've never found anyone willing to join me in this crazy enterprise. There's no one I can pass this business onto."

"Rational people only take personal risk for personal profit."

"I'm not rational. You know that."

"You're enamored of fear."

"You get your kicks from the bottle."

"Unless I'm standing at the head of a flight of stairs, which I am careful never to do, I can only fall to the floor. You fall to earth, from the sky."

"I'm sorry, A.B. You get your kicks putting all these crazy people, groups together, raising money for the drugs, medicine I fly into Central America. You do a wonderful thing. *You* deserve a plaque. I don't mean to make little of what you do. I couldn't do what you do. But what would happen to you if I quit?"

"Take up drinking alone, I guess."

"What would happen to all those people in Central America who expect, need, are dependent upon my weekly flights? If they could afford medicine, if they could get it legally, at any price, without it disappearing at the airports, we wouldn't have needed to do what we've been doing all these years."

"There comes a time, Haig, when a man has the right to save his own life."

"Does there really? Do you really see me sitting on a beach on some Greek island drinking ouzo, thinking of the numbers of people in Central America sufferin' and dyin' because they can't get medicine plentiful in every North American pharmacy? Can you really see that? That would kill me more certainly than a plane crash."

"I can see the day or the night when, because of weather, engine failure, or because someone shot at your plane, you hit the trunk of a big tree, or the side of a mountain straight on."

"I try not to do that."

"That's what I think about when I think of you. And after that happens, those same people will be sufferin' and dyin'. Only you'll be dead."

"Well," Haig drawled. "I will have done my dead level best."

"There's no persuading you?"

"What do you want me to do, declare myself dead? Sit on a beach in Greece and drink formaldehyde?"

In the driveway of Bass Clef Farm, a bus engine ignited.

"Haig, I want you to understand this: when you want to quit, when the idea first enters your head, even slightly, maybe next time when you see the trees coming up too fast, and you're trying to wriggle the plane to take the impact at least a few centimeters away from your head, remember that we want you to quit. Not to worry. We'll find the money for you to live comfortably, where and how you want. You've done your bit, lad."

A second bus engine was running.

"You want to retire me? I don't see the difference between now and twenty years ago. The need is still there."

"Time has passed. That's right: nothing has gotten better. You've gotten older, Haig. You can't walk out of that jungle the way you used to. Your risk is greater now. The fun has to be over sometime."

After a long silence, Haig said, "Who gives a shit."

"Will you think about it?"

"I'll think about it."

Noisy people were coming out of the house to board the buses.

Still lying on the lawn, Josh Prescott said to himself, *That Mr. Haig Scott is a smuggler. No foolin'.*

"Haig," Abraham Baxter said, "With some occupations, you don't get a plaque at the end. Don't wait for it."

36

The study door opened. Dan Prescott's head appeared around its edge. He looked at the snifters in the hands of David MacFarlane and John Bart Nelson.

"What's in those glasses?" Dan asked.

David said, "Brandy."

"May I have some?"

"Of course." David jumped out of his leather chair. He poured champagne cognac into a third glass for Dan. "Trying to corrupt you has been one of the nobler ambitions of my life."

Dan closed the door behind him. "I'm not interrupting anything, am I?"

"Absolutely not," John said. "Save us from talking religion and politics."

Standing in the middle of the floor, Dan said, "Don't know what got into that boy: Josh. Couldn't wait to get to bed. He's even sleeping in his own bed tonight."

John yawned. "It's all this Tennessee air, I expect."

David handed Dan his brandy. "Sit down, Dan."

Dan sat behind the desk.

In the slightly opened desk drawer nearest the telephone, David had a tape recorder running.

John asked, "You're not officiating tomorrow, Dan?" Dan tasted his brandy and shook his head. "Thought you might dust off that old license of yours."

"I doubt there's a record of my being a minister anywhere in this world."

"You got defrocked." John laughed. "Literally, if not figuratively. Or, should I say, figuratively, if not literally."

"John," David growled from his own chair.

"That's all right, David," Dan said, half smiling. "John can say any damned fool thing he wants to say. As long as he thinks it's funny. Remember, he gets paid for being impertinent."

"I do," John said. "That's a fact." He tried to make his bones more comfortable in his chair. "I don't see that you fit into contemporary American religion anyway, Dan."

David asked, "Is there a contemporary American religion?"

"As I see it, there is." John yawned. "It's sort of a confused catch-as-catch-can reaction to science. It explains origin by Darwinian evolution. It interprets history as material progress. It relieves sin through psychiatry. It establishes community through television. Its Bible is the media. It provides ritual in physical exercise routines. It has a mythology and a pantheon of demigods and saints through its sports, political and movie celebrities. It tells us to expect the end of the world, in a thermonuclear holocaust. It provides a hope for an afterlife in its exploration of space. What more do you want?"

"And its ethics?" Dan asked.

John laughed. "What you do, either good or evil, do big enough to attract publicity, thus you get to join the demigods on television."

"Sounds backwards to me," David said.

"People are dazzled by the biggest things in their worlds," John said. "For many generations, it was the sun, and the moon and the stars. I know populations still like that. For others, it was the law necessary to make urban, mercantile centers function. People right now, in much of western civilization, are dazzled by the key hanging from Ben Franklin's kite. He caught the sun and brought it to earth. Thomas Edison put a wire around it. And that wire is our grace, our link to ourselves, our link to each other, our only salvation."

Wryly, David said to Dan, "He's quoting his daughter, you realize."

"Has Lucy been shooting off her mouth around here?" John asked.

"Something about household appliances," Dan said, "She's not among the dazzled."

"Just among the dazzling," David added.

John said, "That's my child."

"In fact, she sort of lit into Ms. Tuesday the other night," David said. "Something about her not having accompanied you to London, years ago, when you went to L.S.E."

"And on to your subsequent career," Dan added.

John Bart Nelson said, "Sure, they're hurt, but they're fine. Time after time I've stood on one street corner or another, and said to one person or another, I'm going this way, that way, for this reason, that; come with me. One by one, they've just stood there on the corner. You see, they think they've used up all my pink parts."

"'Pink parts'?" David asked. "What does that mean?"

"Dan understands."

"I remember."

"I'm glad I've done what I've done," John said. "If I've created one iota of understanding among the peoples of this earth, caught in this unprecedented technological time warp, this culture clash, I'm happy. One thing I didn't know, though, when I was young and starting on this course, was that you can't do anything extraordinary in this life, bad or good, without somehow offending the people closest to you." David and Dan looked at each other. "Janet, for example, whom I love, feels what I have done has hurt her. She's too close to me to see what I've tried to do. Lucy, too. I could have spent more time with her. I have felt that in order to justify my being alive, pay the rent for the space I've consumed, pay for the air I've breathed, I've had to make the most of myself by giving the most of myself. And I've always known that if Lucy hasn't understood, at times, she would come to understand. She's fine."

"She is fine," David said. "I gather Lucy means to stand by her husband, play 'whither thou goes, goest I' all the way."

John grinned. "This particular lady we're talking about, Jan, Ms. Tuesday, Janet Twombly, my wife, hasn't stayed by any man in this room, come to think of it, not Dan Prescott, not David MacFarlane, and not much by John Bart Nelson. We three can admit that to each other in a closed room, at this time in our lives. My only distinction with her is that we had a child."

"She's the world," Dan said. "You feel you understand her, have her for a while, then you discover you don't."

"Maybe we never understood," David said. "Maybe we just heaped on her what we wanted, needed her to be."

"Yes," Dan said. "That's the world."

"Well, then, none of us has had the world we wanted, expected to have." John Bart Nelson said, "I'm here to tell you that I was wrong, each of you was wrong, she was wrong. Knowing you were wrong is an honest man's reward for a long life. Women right now are full of what they have to do. Men are always full of what they have to do. That's all fine. Maybe technology provides more jobs that men and women can do equally well, or together. But while getting used to that possibility, we had a slim chance of being right. Traditionally, that is, before technology, before the supposedly 'post-modern' world, there haven't been that many jobs men and women could do together, besides makin' babies."

"You're not against technology then," Dan asked.

"Oh, no. I'm a technology lover. But however much I love technology, I love wisdom more."

"David," Dan asked, "didn't you tell me at one point, when we met in Spain, that you had become a Roman Catholic?"

"Yes. Guess I wanted to belong to something that went around the world more than I did."

"What happened?"

"I discovered it didn't." David got up and poured more brandy into each of their glasses. Dan had drunk little. David stated: "It is inevitable, isn't it, that there be a thermonuclear holocaust."

John said, "It seems so."

Dan took a genuine swallow of his drink. "Every generation has had an end-of-the-world myth."

David put the bottle back on the counter of the wet bar. "Here you have a weapon capable of destroying the world. The technology regarding it is proliferating faster than any virus. We all have death urges. Some people have profound, universal death urges. We all know that. Sooner or later, this capability is going to get into the hands of such an imbalanced person. It is mathematically inevitable."

Dan said, "John doesn't sound convinced."

John folded his hands in his lap. "I'm not. I don't see this as a post-modern world. I see this as a post-adolescent world. God isn't dead. He's just a good enough father to say, *You've had my discipline; you've had my love: now, in the Spirit of all I've given you, fulfill yourselves as humans.* And I doubt you can be fulfilled as a human without the certain realization that you have it within your power to destroy yourself."

"You're Hegelian," Dan said.

"Yes. Starting with Joachim of Fiore."

"Hey, guys," David said. "I'm still here. I spent my youth playin' piano in bars, where the readin' light wasn't so good. What are you talking about?"

"But I believe in both subjectivity and objectivity," John said to

Dan. "I believe in the spiritual evolution of a human, Descartes, me, subjectively. I believe in the spiritual evolution of humankind, logos, objectively. Projection, of course; there is a physical metaphor for spiritual recapitulation: I believe I perceive a correspondence."

At the desk, Dan smiled. "The other day I heard myself referring to you as The Comforter. I wondered later why I said that. I've read a lot of you. Nice to hear you being so explicit."

"Damn," David said. "It's my brandy. Stop talking over my head."

John Bart Nelson said, "What I mean, David, is that I think humankind is about twenty-three years old right now. In actual fact, humankind is only about one trillion seconds old. In the thermonuclear bomb, humankind has the ability to commit suicide. Don't you agree that one cannot be mature without the certain knowledge that one can destroy oneself?"

"I guess."

"That is when baptism ought to take place," John said. "And one's first confirmation. After one has passed into maturity by experiencing and accepting the chilling reality that one has it within one's power to commit suicide. Maybe that lonely, *a-Theos* despair is the original sin without which we cannot live, mature."

David said, "Somehow I doubt Dan Prescott ever had the urge, or the certain knowledge that he could commit suicide."

Dan answered. "After the sculpture was in the New York Museum, after the book was published, after Georgette left me, taking Tony with her: yes, I had the urge, and the urge brought me to the certain knowledge that I could commit suicide. I made the conscious choice not to commit suicide. Perhaps, like everyone else, I've had to make that choice again every day. Yes, I joined atheistic Jesus in the Garden of Gethsemane and cried out, *a-Theos*, 'Father, Father, why hast Thou abandoned me?' I suffered with him the despair that is the original sin, in that it makes all other sin thinkable, and proved his, and my, humanity. All that was years after I was ordained as a minister."

John said, "Now that humankind knows, for the first time in our existence, that we have the ability to self-destruct, we also see we have to make our own lives, in our own world. That's the real tragedy of existence: we have to be mature; responsibly bring into every moment an awareness of every other moment, past, present, and future. We haven't lived, experienced our essence, until we have realized we are absolutely responsible for our existence. Humankind has a long life left."

David asked, "What makes you think so?"

John Bart Nelson smiled. "One always has the choice between optimism and pessimism."

David MacFarlane said nothing.

Dan Prescott said nothing.

John said: "I believe a human fulfills his spirit by acting optimistically when his own nature dictates he act pessimistically."

"On that," Dan said, getting up from behind the desk, "I will exercise enough optimism to believe that there shall be a tomorrow, however much facts indicate there might not be, and go to bed."

Dan Prescott's brandy glass was empty.

"Do you know where you're sleeping?" David asked John.

After Dan left, they remained in their chairs in the study.

"At the hotel."

Dan had closed the study door behind him.

"Really?"

"Really."

"Oh."

John Bart Nelson said, "David, I have Acquired Immune Deficiency Syndrome. Acquired in Africa. Heterosexually."

"Oh."

"After the wedding tomorrow, I am flying to Texas, and checking myself into a hospital to be cared for. Please allow everyone here to think I am simply flying back to Africa, or South America, or the Far East, or wherever."

"Ms. Tuesday, I mean, Janet, Lucy, they do not know?"

"Why put them through months of grief? No matter how a man lives, David, he must die alone."

"Won't Janet think it odd, your not sleeping with her tonight?"

"No. Janet has had herpes for years."

David took a deep breath. "You know Chump is still alive?"

"No. I didn't."

"A drug-induced coma. Three and a half years. Now he has a lump on his head."

"A.B. is an advanced acute alcoholic."

"And Haig has 'one more plane crash left in him.'"

"At least one of your guests, Sorry Hollingsworth, is starving herself to death."

"She's anorexic," David said. "So useless. She had some kind of an idea that she must be perfect drilled into her by her step-father, Jack."

"You contributed to it, David. You named a song after her. Have you ever thought what that might have meant to her?"

David leaned forward in his chair. He put his face in his hands.

"David? Are you crying?"

"Jack, what happened to us?"

John Bart Nelson said, "Someone held out to this generation a big juicy apple disguised as a new world, a paradise with technology and chemistry as our servants, capable of fulfilling our every wish, tempted us with every kind of freedom: freedom from work; freedom from dependence on each other, even on ourselves; freedom from responsibility for each other, for ourselves; sexual freedom; freedom from reality."

"Jack, what did we do wrong?"

"We bit."

37

David was not asleep when he heard the gunshot.

He got out of bed and went out onto the balcony of the house. He looked to his right, at what he could see of the lower guesthouse and of the pastures beyond the pool area, from where he thought the sound had come. His watch read three-eighteen. No lights were on that were not usually on, and none came on. He heard no one stirring.

After a while he thought maybe he had been asleep and had dreamed the noise.

He lay in bed for a while, realizing how awake he was, how awake he had been.

Convinced he had heard gunfire and knowing he ought not be hearing gunfire on his place minutes after three o'clock in the morning, he got out of bed again. He pulled on the trousers he could find in the dark. He could not find any shirt. He did not want to awake Ellie by opening the closet or a drawer. He couldn't find his boots, either.

Without using lights, David went downstairs, through the kitchen, and outdoors.

Behind the house, behind the upper guesthouse, he saw Jock Reagan lamely but expertly climb over the rail fence and approach. Someone with a flashlight stood at the far side of that pasture.

Jock limped to him.

In a low voice, Jock said to David: "It's the Halburton boy. Rupert. He's blown his head off."

"Of course he has."

"With a shotgun."

"On our land?"

"Yes. Near the fence. Not far from the Halburtons' driveway."

"I see."

"I came back to call the sheriff."

"Who is that out in the pasture, Jock?"

"Mr. Haig Scott. I was sleeping in the guesthouse, taking care of Mr. Farber, when I heard the gunshot. By the time I got out here with the flashlight, Mr. Scott was already searching the pasture. He can see in the dark like a cat. He found the boy. Mr. Scott is staying out there with the light to keep the animals off."

"No one else is out there?"

"No."

"There are no lights showing from the Halburton house?"

"No."

When Jock returned from the house, David was standing as he had before, not having moved, looking at the distant light in the pasture.

Jock said, "I called the sheriff. He said it would take him about a half-hour to get here."

"Jock, I'm not going out there."

"Yes, sir."

"I'm not going to be the one to inform our neighbors, the Halburtons, their son has killed himself. Sheriff Tom Wims will have to do that."

"Yes, sir."

"And, Jock, remind Sheriff Tom we have a wedding going on here in the morning. Ask him to do his level best to have his equipment out of here by dawn. He'll understand."

"Yes, sir."

"Jock, I don't want the bride and groom, or the wedding guests, to know this has happened. You tell Clara. I'll tell Ellie. William will know by the time he arrives. Tell Mr. Scott I have asked that no one else knows."

"Okay."

David said, "The cry of a peacock can wake Joe Halburton, but apparently the sound of his son blowing his head off with a shotgun does not disturb the bastard's sleep any."

38

Lucille Nelson and Anthony Prescott were married at an outdoor ceremony, noon Saturday, June eleventh, at Ellie and David MacFarlane's Bass Clef Farm, Jameson, Tennessee, the Reverend Charles Hartigan, First Church, Jameson, officiating.

In attendance were the bride's parents, Janet Twombly and John Bart Nelson, who make their home in Paris, France. Mrs. Nelson is Chairperson, President, and Chief Executive Officer of N. Sue Sance, clothing fashions, of Paris. Mr. Nelson is a widely read newspaper columnist on Current Affairs.

Also in attendance was the groom's father, Daniel Prescott, an artist who works in New York. The groom's mother, Georgette Bancroft Prescott (Sokowitz) lost her life in a highway accident in California when the groom was seven years old.

David MacFarlane, retired jazz pianist, is a friend to the parents of both the bride and the groom.

A graduate of Esterhazy Collegiate in Switzerland, the bride is employed as a fashion model in New York and Paris. The groom, a graduate of Bowdoin College in Maine, is employed as a speechwriter for the President of the United States and works in the White House, Washington, D.C.

Ms. Carol Tamson, of New York, was maid of honor. Joshua Prescott served his brother as best man.

The bride wore a white linen bridal suit, a creation of N. Sue Sance, Paris.

A message of best wishes and congratulations from the President of the United States was read, along with similar messages.

At four o'clock, after a large reception with music and dancing, the couple were driven off in a decorated, antique Winslow car, to start their honeymoon trip to San Francisco.

The Prescotts intend to make their home in Columbia Falls, Maine.

During the wedding ceremony, Ellie whispered to David: "Amazing."

"Yes. What is?"

"People keep getting married."

"Mr. Bennet." Mrs. Bennet nudged her husband. "Look at that boy."

"What boy?" Mr. Bennet asked his wife.

"The groom's brother. The best man."

People were milling around the lawn after the ceremony. The bride and groom, who had spent the last evening with their friends, were making a genuine and gracious effort now to meet the local people of Jameson County, Ellie's and David's friends, to come to know them a little bit, and David appreciated that.

The bar was open. The sun was hot. It would be a while before food was served.

David said to Owen Farber, "Which group is set up to play first?"

"Estrellas Nuevas."

"Well, plug 'em in. Turn the switch. Whatever. Let's have some music around here."

David had seen William working in heat over one hundred degrees and had seen him sweating often enough but never as much as he was sweating in his coat and tie at the wedding.

Before the ceremony and during the ceremony and after the ceremony, the person who looked most at loose ends was Dan Prescott. He stood around with a pleasant enough expression on his face, looking available, willing to be helpful, but never actually did anything. He initiated a few conversations with a few local people, but kept them brief. Ellie was sure Dan was deliberately avoiding Chuck Hartigan and his wife. He also was deliberately avoiding the few members of the wire service press down from Nashville. Lucy talked with him immediately after the ceremony, briefly, and danced with him after dancing with Tony and her father. Tony did not seem to go near his father. Josh was buzzing around with Nonnie, talking with Milton Farber, Paul Hollingsworth, Chuck Hartigan, helping Jock, ogling Lucy's model friends, examining the equipment of the band, talking with Haig Scott, but ignored Dan. When food was being served, Dan sat at a table far from the bandstand and the dance floor and the wedding party table. Between courses, when his table mates went to dance, Dan sat alone at the table, looking around as if he were enjoying himself enough.

For the longest time, perspiring, appearing to concentrate exclusively on her task, Janet oversaw Jock and Frank transport her five cases of French champagne from wherever she had stashed them to the shaded table covered with champagne glasses. One by one she sank the bottles in the metal barrels nearly filled with ice chips. As the time for the wedding toasts approached, Janet removed the bottles from the barrels one by one, oversaw the waiters opening them, pouring their contents slowly, carefully into the little glasses.

Except for the short time he spent talking with David, Paul Hollingsworth danced nearly every dance. After first dancing with Lucy, then with Janet, then with Ellie, he danced with nearly every woman at the wedding reception, models and farm wives, the young, the old, the matronly, the single, the married, the dancers, the talkers. He was the only one to dance with several of the women there. He danced well, in every style. At first he danced formally. When Estrellas Nuevas tried a few Latin rhythms on the guests, Paul executed Latin steps perfectly. While The Smashers were playing, Paul danced modern quick steps wildly but well, even playfully inserting a few punk threatening gestures into his routine.

Paul also made the first toast after the formal toasts.

His seemed to be the toast the bride most appreciated. She beamed throughout and kissed him when he finished.

"Mr. Bennet," Mrs. Bennet repeated to her husband: "That boy."

"What boy now?"

"The same boy. Watch the way he dances, with the Simpson girl."

Mr. Bennet said: "Boy dancing."

"Watch the way he moves. The way he moves his eyes. His build. Look at the length and straightness of his legs, and the length and straightness of his back. Look at his skin, his coloring."

"Try the corn bread, dear. It's delicious."

"Mr. MacFarlane," Paul Hollingsworth said.

"Don't you call me David?" In his jacket pocket, David fingered the volume wheel on his tape recorder higher to pick up Paul's voice over the sound of the band.

"David." Paul smiled. "Uncle David."

"I'm nobody's uncle," David said. "And I trust I'm not avuncular. Perhaps I am. Am I?"

"Do you need help around here?"

"You mean, around the farm?"

"Yes."

"Not that I know of. I mean, yes, of course. Always. Don't need any help that William or the Simpsons or the Reagans or their friends and relatives can't provide."

Paul looked at the sign at the bottom of the driveway. "I suspect you don't make any money off Bass Clef Farm."

"I don't. Not even tax losses."

"You could, you know. I mean, make money."

"I could put condominiums down by the road," David said with mock surmise. "Fill up the floor of the valley with a shopping mall. We could probably put in one hundred stores with parking for, let's see, fifteen, twenty thousand cars. Is that what you're thinking?"

"Row crops," Paul said. "You could use the hay fields for specialty row crops."

"They have been used for row crops. What are specialty row crops?"

"The sort of foods that sell for high prices in gourmet and health food stores."

"Such as?"

"That would take some research, which I could do."

"What are you saying, Paul?"

"I'm saying I could take some time off, come here, figure out with you what would really be the best, most profitable uses of this farm."

"Take time off?"

"A year or two. Three."

"You really miss the plantation, don't you, Paul?"

"Yes. Very much. But that's not what I am saying."

"It would seem a poor use of your education, Paul." When Paul did not respond, David said: "I don't know how to answer you. Do you think this is a pretty place?"

Paul looked around in the sunlight. "Gorgeous."

"It is," David agreed. "I sort of like it the way it is. Nostalgic of me, as someone said, but I like the way of life. Even the way it is, the farming is more than I can understand, but not more than I've been able to handle, so far, with a lot of help from my friends. I don't want the trees moved."

"Maybe we wouldn't have to move the trees."

"Paul—"

"What's wrong with turning Bass Clef Farm into the best farm it can be?"

"Paul, not everything, everyone has to be perfect, functioning at full capacity all the time." David sighed. "Let me answer you this way: I went to work as a teenager; I made of myself everything I can be; I dreamed of this place; I found it; I love it; I love the people around here. Do you understand?"

"Sure. I guess so."

"No. You don't. This is my dream; the result of my life. You've got to go do your own work, live your own life, have your own dream."

Looking into David's eyes through the sunlight, Paul Hollingsworth said, "You're telling me to get out of your dream."

"Am I? I guess I am. My dream can't be your dream."

"Okay," Paul said.

"I appreciate what you've done around here the last day or two, painting the barn doors, chopping up that old tree into firewood, and all."

"Enjoyed it."

"Paul, whatever your life is, you've got to go live it. I had to go live my life. Living your life is hard, but really, you do not want to avoid doing so."

"I understand."

"Paul, have you talked with A.B. yet? With Mr. Baxter?"

Paul looked down to where Abraham Baxter was waiting for a drink at the portable bar. "No."

"Why don't you?"

Paul shrugged. "Don't really want to."

"Paul, it is hard for any adult to understand that a child also mourns." When Paul did not respond, David said, "Life is as much dispelling nightmares, Paul, as it is fulfilling dreams."

"I'm talking about breeding," Mrs. Bennet said.

"You're always talking about breeding," answered her husband. "It's what we do. We breed horses. Didn't I write an enormous check just this morning for a horse which you insist will complete our stables for the season?"

"Yes."

"Then what are you talking about? Having just written such a large check for the purpose, Mrs. Bennet, I do not think I need hear one more word on the subject of breeding today."

Quietly, Ellie said to David, "I feel badly that we are having a bright, happy, noisy party next door to a family who lost their son, in the most horrible way, this morning."

"Not much we can do about it," David said.

"There's nothing we can do about it." Ellie said, "David, will you dance with me?"

"You know I can't dance."

"I know you don't dance."

"Ellie, you've never bothered me about that. Don't start now."

"The bride and groom have expressed puzzlement why you are not playing the piano at their wedding." She looked toward the bandstand where The Smashers were wailing. "I don't think these groups will even play any of your music."

"I'm not working," David said. "I haven't had to work a wedding since I was a kid. Ask Milton."

Ellie smiled. "I don't think Milton will play, either."

Milton Farber sat at a table occupied otherwise by Sorry Hollingsworth and four models.

"Maybe he'll play a tape," David said. "He's learned how."

David was aware someone was standing quietly behind him, and turned around.

"Hello, Josh."

"Hi."

"Having any fun?"

"Lots."

"Where's Nonnie now?"

"She's gone home to put on sneakers so we can dance better. She'll be right back."

"Good."

"Mr. MacFarlane, after I drive my father back to Maine, I leave for summer camp."

"Is that all right?"

"Sure. I've gone to the same camp every year since I was six, but this year I get to be a junior counselor."

"Great. Get paid?"

"A little bit."

"Be sure and pay your taxes."

"That's what I wanted to talk to you about: how I spend my earnings."

"Don't spend 'em. Just give 'em to me. I won't mind."

"Camp's over mid-August. Boarding school doesn't start again for me until September tenth."

"I see," David said, although he really did not see.

"Well, you made the joke to Mr. Haig Scott that you found me on the place."

"Yes, I did. I'm sorry."

"That leaves three weeks, you see, between camp and school."

"I guess it does."

"How would you feel if you found me on the place during those three weeks? I figure I'll have enough earnings from working at camp to pay my own way down here and then on to school."

David looked into Josh's face as Josh looked somewhere east out of the corners of his eyes.

"What about your Dad, Josh? Your mother in New York?"

Slowly, Josh said, "I wouldn't want to be some kind of a nuisance."

David said, "You wouldn't be any kind of a nuisance."

Josh's eyes snapped onto David's. "I wouldn't?"

"Not around here. I'm sure Ellie feels the same way. You're welcome here, Josh, any time you can come."

"All *right*!"

"But your parents have first dibs on you. If they're really going to be away, or whatever, during that period, you make a bee-line for Bass Clef. You hear?"

"All *right*!"

In the middle of the party, then, no one going anywhere, Josh Prescott shook hands with David MacFarlane.

Sorry said, "I don't believe it."

"You don't, eh?" All the models laughed.

Listening, Milton Farber kept his eyes on his plate.

"Look!" The model sitting next to Sorry at table leaned toward Sorry and not only opened her own mouth wide, she forced it open wider, held it open with her fingers. "Wook!" she said.

Sorry peered into the back of the model's mouth. "My God."

"Sure," the model said, having removed her fingers from her mouth. "We've all had our back teeth removed."

"Actually, I haven't," said one, a redhead.

"It gives us that glamorous gaunt look," said another.

"No," said a third. "It truly does make the camera lights work better on our faces."

"That's utterly ridiculous," Sorry said. "The very idea makes me sick."

"Eat your peach ice cream," Milton said to Sorry. "It will make you feel better."

Sorry had not eaten her lunch, but she did eat her peach ice cream.

David noticed that John Bart Nelson had stood little during the reception. When he first sat in the shade, he was surrounded by Tony's friends from Washington. After a while he had excused himself, gone to the bar for a drink, then found a different place in the shade to sit. He had danced with his daughter, danced with Janet, danced with Ellie. He sat down between each dance. And he had sat at the head table to eat with the wedding party (minus only the father of the groom). As soon as the wedding cake had been cut, and he had been given a piece, he found a third shaded seat.

To David, John Bart Nelson in the shade looked like an old log on a riverbank.

David joined John away from the noise of the music.

"Anything I can do for you?" David asked. Away from the bandstand, he lowered the volume of the tape recorder in his pocket.

"No. I mean, no, thanks, David."

"I mean, now . . ." David tilted his head away. "Later."

"No. I'm fine."

"You're not fine."

"I've paid my rent. I'm glad I was able to do so. I've had a good time. Seen things and done things I never expected to see and do. I've seen Lucy married to a fine young man, Dan's son. I've seen you and Ellie again. I really appreciate that, David. When I got the news what you were doing, offering to throw the wedding party for the kids, get everyone together, I wondered if you could possibly know. . . . But, you couldn't."

"I didn't."

"You've done enough, David. Lucy, Janet and I really appreciate it."

"I hate the thought of your being alone, in Texas."

"Oh, I won't be. I never was one to take myself off in spite of any kind. I think you know that about me."

"I think I do."

"It's just that I'm in for a long, hard time, they tell me. Why put Lucy and Janet through it? Let the kids have their honeymoon and start their lives without thought of me being a drag on them. News will leak out, soon enough. I won't go to the end without them."

"Or me? Or Dan?"

"Maybe there'll be a child by then. I do want to see that child."

"Maybe."

"David, people keep having children. Isn't that amazing?"

"They keep getting married. They keep having children."

"In a while, I'm going to slip away. I've got my rented car here, down the road. If you don't mind, I'm going to say goodbye to you now, and, thank you. Just so I won't make any fuss in leaving."

David stood up. "Not goodbye." He shook John's hand. "I'll see you in Texas."

Mrs. Bennet said, "I'm talking about breeding *him*!"

"What, dear?"

"Mr. Bennet," Mrs. Bennet said reasonably, after everyone had left their table. "We have three daughters."

"All unmarried," said Mr. Bennet. "Each one uglier than her sister."

"Mr. Bennet," whispered Mrs. Bennet. "We need that boy."

"What boy is that?"

"That Josh Prescott boy."

"Need him for what?"

"Breeding, I said!" hissed Mrs. Bennet. "Has the music made you deaf? I mean to breed that boy!"

"Mrs. Bennet!"

"Look at his bloodlines! His father is right over there! Look at his brother! That boy Josh is a handsome, high-stepping one, all right, healthy, high-spirited, and bright! Just about the best boy I ever saw! What do you think I've been talking about? We need that blood in our family!"

"Mrs. Bennet, are you matchmaking? Our youngest daughter is twenty-three years old! That boy is no more than sixteen. And I can absolutely guarantee you, he would not be interested in even our youngest daughter, even if she came in a solid gold Ferrari."

"I know that, Mr. Bennet. But, I am talking about all three girls."

"My God! Are you talking about getting that boy to stud our daughters, Mrs. Bennet?"

Mrs. Bennet said from between firm lips, "Artificial insemination. I don't care about pleasuring our ugly daughters, Mr. Bennet. But I do care about providing us with handsome grandchildren. You just tell me why not."

"Mrs. Bennet, you have had enough to drink this day. I'm taking you home right now."

"No one is ever going to marry them," said Mrs. Bennet, "Not with blackmail or bribery. We get a little bit of what that boy has inside of him inside of our daughters, and we've got some handsome, healthy, high-spirited, bright-eyed grandchildren sittin' up and takin' notice!"

"Mrs. Bennet, I am takin' you home right this minute."

"You're not listening, Mr. Bennet. Do I know about breeding, or do I know about breeding?"

"For the life of me, I don't know what you've been drinking, but you sure have had enough of whatever it is."

"Don't you pull me, Mr. Bennet."

"If you don't leave gracefully with me right now, our neighbors, the MacFarlanes, never will invite us back. And don't let anyone hear you saying such a crazy thing."

"Now, you just tell me why not, Mr. Bennet. You and I both know that boy has got semen going to waste. That's a sin. It's a damned shame, when we've got three ugly daughters—"

Ellie said, "Are you leaving so soon?"

"I'm sorry, Ellie," said Mr. Bennet. "I just realized Mrs. Bennet has been on the farm too long. She can't take her mind off breeding problems, it seems."

Ellie said, "Well . . ."

"Never you mind, Ellie," said Mrs. Bennet. "I'll telephone you."

"Not very soon, you won't," said Mr. Bennet. "Thank you for having us, Ellie."

"Our pleasure."

"Our car's right down here," said Mr. Bennet.

Mrs. Bennet said, "Boy like that always needs money. For school. Think of his semen going down a toilet somewhere. It's a sin!"

Ellie said, "What?"

Mr. Bennet said, "'Bye, Ellie."

"You could talk to him, Mr. Bennet," persisted Mrs. Bennet.

"We're spending money on breeding stock all the time. Why can't we take care of our own selves sensibly? You just answer me that."

"My God," said Mr. Bennet, "three ugly, unmarried daughters at home, all pregnant at the same time, by the same sixteen-year-old boy! How you do go on, Mrs. Bennet!"

"Mr. Haig Scott?"

Josh waited until Haig turned from the group with whom he had been talking about Micronesia and had resettled his feet and his walking stick on the lawn.

"Your name is Josh, isn't it?" Haig asked.

"Yes, sir."

"You did a fine job as best man, Josh. Can I borrow you, if I ever decide to get married?"

"Sure."

"That's good. I've noticed several women here eyeing me. Have you noticed?"

"Mr. MacFarlane has invited me back to Bass Clef for late August, early September. Any chance you being here then, Mr. Scott?"

"I don't know, Josh. Why?"

"You ever teach anybody how to fly a plane?"

"No."

"Think you'd be any good at it?"

"I suppose I could give it a try, if I had a reason."

Josh looked somewhere west out of the corners of his eyes. "I'm thinking of taking up smuggling for a living."

Looking into Josh's face, Haig Scott breathed deeply three times. "You sure got big ears, boy."

Josh said, "But I hear no evil."

Finally, Haig said, "I'll think on it, boy. You'd better think more on it, too."

"Thank you, Mr. Scott. I'll sure appreciate it."

39

After one of the buses, half filled with wedding guests who had to be returned to the airport in Nashville that evening, had left; after the food had been cleaned up; after the two bands, The Smashers and Estrellas Nuevas had played themselves out; after the rest of the guests had begun to wander around the farm, take walks, play in the pool, sit in groups here and there, talk and laugh quietly, David MacFarlane retired to his room to shower and change from his party clothes to his khakis.

An hour before, the bride and groom had left the farm in the back seat of the Winslow, which David MacFarlane and Dan Prescott had decorated that morning. Frank Simpson drove. (Earlier, Frank and Josh Prescott had placed the LeBaron convertible in the driveway of a neighboring farm to be picked up by the bride and groom on their way to the airport.) The bride had tossed her bouquet from the back seat of the Winslow. One of the tall models caught it.

David knew that people would wander around Bass Clef Farm until after dark (a light, cold supper was scheduled) when the buses would return the out-of-state wedding guests to their hotel, but as far as he was concerned, the wedding, and the party, were over. The caterer was removing most of the tents from the lawns.

Buttoning his shirt, David looked out his bedroom window. In the nearest pasture, Dan and Josh Prescott and Nonnie Simpson were trying to corral Lord Byron. Josh and Nonnie had changed to shorts. Dan was wearing blue jeans. The three ran after the horse, trying to triangulate in on him and grab his red bridle. Byron, pleased by all the attention he was getting from well-dressed wedding guests along the fence rails, was acting up beautifully, not only outrunning his pursuers but outsmarting them as well. Lifting his forelegs smartly, almost as if they had been sored, Byron cantered and galloped around the pasture, showing all the beauty in gait and the brains of the Tennessee walking horse. Laughing, still in pursuit with the young people, Dan took off his T-shirt and dropped it near the stream.

David heard the front screen door of the house bang shut.

Having played enough, apparently, Byron permitted himself to be caught in the near corner of the pasture where the most onlookers were gathered.

Shirtless, his skin gleaming with sweat, in blue jeans, Dan Prescott jumped onto the barebacked horse.

Janet, dressed in jeans and a light shirt, crossed the road, climbed the fence and, with a remarkably deft movement, suddenly was astride the horse behind Dan. Her arms were around him, her hands on his stomach.

Leaning forward, Dan looked around to see who had joined him on the horse. He looked into Janet's face.

Apparently knowing the horse had been neck-trained, Dan put his left forearm against Byron's neck and dug the heels of his sneakers into Byron's ribs.

No! David opened the door of his room and went out onto the upper front balcony of the house.

The people along the fence rail watched Dan Prescott and Janet Twombly Nelson gallop down the pasture together on Lord Byron. Among them, Nonnie, but especially Josh, looked after them longest.

From the balcony, David watched Dan and Janet ride the full half-mile down to the river, and disappear into the shade of the trees.

If what I think is happening, is happening . . . herpes . . . and she ain't telling him. . . . That is the key to Ms. Tuesday: the purest kind of selfishness. Why did we ever think otherwise?

Driving down the road in his truck a few minutes later, on his way to Brentwood, David could not help looking among the trees along the river for Lord Byron. Yes, the horse was there, grazing the riverbank. There was no one astride him.

There was no one in sight at all.

Why did we ever think otherwise?

As he accelerated the truck along the road, a yellow van passed David going the other way. There was a quarter note painted in blue on its side panel.

40

PERSPECTIVE: *Estelle Manning*

"Good afternoon, Mr. MacFarlane."

"Good afternoon, Ms. Manning."

That Saturday afternoon David MacFarlane looked as if he hadn't slept the previous night and, clearly, he had been drinking, but not much, and I was glad he had had something to drink, if you know what I mean, to soften the blow of what he was about to see.

With five or six tape recording cassettes in his right hand, he entered Chump Hardy's room. Mr. MacFarlane did not close the door.

I did not follow.

Unsuccessfully, I tried to think of something to do that would make me appear busy in the corridor. In fact, I stood there wringing my hands as if all this nursing in the coma unit were new to me.

From the room, I heard a God-awful noise, a deep, breath-catching sob, almost an animal noise. Just one. Then, to my ears anyway, there was a long silence.

Yes, the growth behind Chump Hardy's ear was wide and it was deep. I don't know if Dr. MacBride and the specialists he had brought in the afternoon before had decided it was inoperable. I don't know if Dr. MacBride had spoken to Mr. MacFarlane since he had had the specialists' reports. I suspect the doctor had decided to let Mr. MacFarlane come in and confront the situation himself.

Well, the situation had gotten worse since even the previous afternoon.

Chump Hardy's face, which had been expressionless for three and a half years, now was twisted in an expression of the most terrible pain. Sallow and sunken anyway, jaw, nose and eye sockets prominent, now his face looked as wracked with agony as the face of a denizen of hell in a medieval painting.

Mr. MacFarlane came out of the room in a rush, as if he did not want to be stopped, or seen.

I said, "David!"

I stood by the elevator with him. He had already pushed the down button. His face looked as pain-wracked as Chump Hardy's. The elevator door opened, waited, closed. I said nothing more to him. I just looked into his eyes. He pushed the button again.

The door opened again. David MacFarlane stepped into the elevator.

Without looking back at me, he was gone.

David had parked the truck in the traffic of lower Broadway in Nashville, and crossed the sidewalk cluttered with derelicts and demi-mondes and tourists, before he realized The Spider Web bar was closed. The sign on the door said, GONE FISHIN'—LANK.

"On Saturday?" David looked through the glass of the door to the interior, dark except for the bar light. He looked up and down the twilit street. "Lank, what are you doing, closing on Saturday night?"

David MacFarlane got back into his truck. "If you close whenever you want to, Lank, we'd lose less money."

41

The sheriff put his massive fists on the windowsill of David MacFarlane's truck. "David, why the hell didn't you give us some warning?"

"'Warning'?" David looked in amazement through the windshield at Bass Clef Farm. Through the open windows he could hear the cacophony. "What the hell is going on, Tom?"

"You don't know? You gonna tell me all this is a surprise to you?"

"Sure is. I'm just getting home from Nashville."

Sheriff Tom Wims looked through the cars and vans and pickup trucks and people jamming the road in front of Bass Clef Farm, up to the main house, which was lit up and jumpin'. More mildly, he said, "Some kind of a music festival, I guess. There are eight, ten thousand people here, David."

"Jesus."

"No good prayin', now. I couldn't stop this party now with half the United States Marine Corps. I knew you had a wedding going on here, today."

"That was over, hours ago. By the way, thanks for your help this morning, Tom."

David got out of the truck.

"Not much help I can be right now. I've got the Rescue Squad, two ambulances on stand-by. You know who-all you got here?"

"Eight to ten thousand people?" David climbed into the bed of his truck and looked around in the dark. "My God, Tom!"

Cars and pickup trucks were everywhere, jamming the road,

tipped into the ditches, up against the fences. Fence gates were open. Cars and trucks were parked in the hay fields.

"Fires, Tom!" From the truck bed David had to shout over the noise of electronic bands to be heard by the sheriff standing on the road. "The hot undersides of the cars will set fire to the hay fields!"

"Oh, that's happened four or five times already, David. The hordes of people just rush right in and stamp them out. I reckon you've got most members of every volunteer fire department in three counties here anyway. It's fires other places I'm worrying about tonight!"

Electrical wires streamed down from the top of the telephone poles. Each wire led to a separate rig that provided electricity to an individual band. There were about a dozen bands playing here and there around the farm, on the lawns of the main house, in the pastures, and one partly on the road.

David pointed to the wires. "Is that safe?"

"Ain't safe," said Sheriff Tom Wims. "Ain't legal, either. I expect the electrical company is going to have words with you, David MacFarlane, about all the electricity you-all are stealing tonight."

"I'm not stealing it. I didn't invite these people. I have nothing to do with it."

In the dark in front of each band a dense crowd of listening people were pressed like flies on the mouth of a honey pot. Behind the half-circles of people, other people buzzed around, dancing. Couples and groups moved from crowd to crowd.

"I'm not giving this party," David said.

In the driveway and on the lawns of the main house there was a horde of people packed too densely to move. They were standing, all facing the bandstand that had been built under the big carport, apparently just listening.

"Eight to ten thousand people," David said. "Jesus!"

Standing on his truck, David could not discern what everyone or anyone was hearing. Each band had its own set of amplifiers, and they were all working at full volume. All David could hear was an earth-shaking noise, all the bands through all their amplifiers, together.

Climbing down from the truck, David said, "I'm sorry, Tom. I honestly had no idea this was going to happen."

"I believe it."

"We had a wedding here earlier today, a couple of bands, the whole thing was over by five o'clock. I don't know where these people came from, or why. They sure weren't invited."

"They all seem to be having a right good time."

"How did you know enough to come out?"

"Well, sir, it was reported to me that all these band trucks were everywhere in Jameson County at once, asking directions for your place. Phone lines were buzzin', passin' the rumors that Sally Dalton was in town, then The Cons."

"Is Sally Dalton here?"

"She left. The crowd was too big for her. But she did sing a couple songs."

"Are The Cons here? That's a right famous band."

"Oh, yes, sir. And they aren't all. So I thought I'd better come out, investigate. Time I got here, your party was well out of hand."

"Tom. It's not my party."

"I know that. Week from now, you'll be proud to have had such a party. The whole country will be talkin' about it."

"If the farm survives it."

"That's right. If the farm survives it. I doubt it will."

"Have you seen William? William Fesdon?"

"No, sir, I haven't." The sheriff laughed. "What instrument does ol' William play now?"

"I can't move my truck."

"Leave the keys in it. I'll look out for it as much as I can. Not to worry, David: you're goin' to lose more'n your truck tonight."

"Thanks."

People were still arriving, walking past them on the road.

"David?"

"Yeah."

"When that Ms. Sarah Downey gets up to sing, will you send someone down for me? I surely would like to hear her."

"Is Sarah Downey here?"

"She is. And if I miss hearin' her sing, I just might pinch Ellie for all this ruckus she's got goin' on out here tonight, without a word of warnin' to anybody. You know I've always wanted to pinch Ellie MacFarlane."

"Sorry, William."

Walking down the road with the other late arrivers, David figured out where William must be and what he must be doing.

Going through the barnyard, David noticed that most of the

newly arrived bull calves were missing. There was one calf bawling in all the noise, with no amplifier but his own. David walked him out of his corner and guided him through an open gate. The cattle was gone from the back pasture, too.

Zig-zagging as much as he could behind the excited calf while climbing the steep back hill, David found himself slipping and puffing and cursing in no time. As soon as the calf heard bellowing from the other cattle at the top of the hill, he ran ahead.

After catching his breath, David followed.

William Fesdon and Jock Reagan and Frank Simpson were herding loudly complaining cattle into a small, high, rocky area with sparse grass at the crown of the hill. William's truck was there, with its headlights on. One piece of barbed wire already had been run from a back fence post to the truck, where it was wrapped around the tailgate, to a post stuck at an angle into the ground.

"I did not know this was going to happen, William."

Even a mile away from the amplified music, David had to speak louder than usual.

"I know that."

Scampering around on his crooked legs, Jock was trying to keep the cattle from flowing back down the hill to better grass. No fence had been arranged that side, yet.

"Is this all the cattle?" David asked.

"No." William swung another fence post from the back of the truck onto his shoulder. "There's another dozen down near the east pond. In the pasture next to the airplane."

"I'll go get them."

David figured it would take at least the three of them and considerable skill and luck to build a fence in the dark around more than one hundred excited steers deprived of decent grass and water. He also figured they had had their run for the night, rounding up the steers they had.

The east pond was a mile away, downhill. In the moonlight, watching his step as carefully as he could, David jogged down the hill.

Rounding the steers up, getting them out of and away from the water, through the lush grass, urging them up the hill in the dark without losing any, was a job David would not have chosen over most others. He used a big stick he found near the pond. He ran from left to right applying the stick to their flanks to get them together, going in the right direction. He cajoled them and cursed them. When he got them against the fence that ran along the property to his left, it was simple to stay behind them, slightly to their right, and walk them up the hill. Getting ahead of them and opening a gate halfway up the hill (not having thought ahead when he climbed over the fence on his way down), getting them all through the gate, closing it behind them, was not at all simple.

By the time David got the steers to the crest of the hill something that didn't look much like a fence but did work as a fence was complete. William and Jock and Frank helped David put the steers through the space between two posts in the fence. Later William would close that space with three strands of barbed wire.

David sat on a rock and looked down the hill.

At the bottom of the valley a mile away around the main house of Bass Clef Farm were lights where there had never been lights before; thousands of people gathered in the dark, distinguishable from the hilltop only as a flowing, shouting dark mass; hundreds of temporarily discarded cars and trucks: a confused, chaotic, disorganized, unplanned, unwanted, competitive music festival in full swing.

William sat on the rock beside David and lit a cigarette.

"Fires," David said. "Shit, William. We're goin' to lose this place, tonight, for sure."

William pointed over the crest of the hill at the back fence. "We can burst the cattle through that fence, if we need to. There's still that dirt track over on MacPhearsons' place we can run them down. They should be all right, here."

"The barns, William. The house. Jesus Christ, how did this happen?"

From behind them, Frank said, "William, you want to put up posts so you can free your truck?"

"No," said William. "That truck's been everything else in its lifetime. It might as well be a fence post." He laughed. "I'm not goin' far tonight, anyway."

"Too much traffic," Jock said.

Behind them on the hill, the cattle were still making a lot of noise, upset by being herded at night, upset by the noise coming from the valley floor.

"William, I really am sorry," David MacFarlane said.

Grinning over his cigarette in the moonlight, William Fesdon said, "Shit, David. It's good to hear some music around the old place."

* * *

David said, "There seem to be a lot of naked people in our swimming pool."

"Things have gotten entirely out of hand, David," Ellie answered.

"You might say so."

David had circumnavigated the crowds, jogging down the side of the hill, over fences, passing the barns on his right, crossing the road, passing the lightless Halburton house on his left, over more fences, to the west side of the main house. In the pool area, he had checked the studio. Someone had had the good sense to lock the studio doors and windows. No one was inside. People with hands cupped around their eyes were peering into the dark studio through the glass doors. They did not recognize David.

He found Ellie standing among a snake den of electrical wires on the brick patio behind the house.

She looked down at his boots and trousers. "You're muddy enough."

As they were near but behind the bandstand set up in the carport they had to shout, but they could hear each other. David did not recognize the band playing.

"We've been shifting cattle. Ellie, I'm scared to death of fire. Cars and trucks with hot engines parked in the hay fields. People smoking cigarettes, pot, all over the place. Did you see the wires running from the telephone poles? All these vans, generators, amplifiers. All these Goddamned wires!" David kicked a rope of wires at his feet.

Ellie nodded. "I've got every garden hose out of the shed and plugged to a faucet."

"Great!" David hugged her. "Garden hoses! We're all right, then!"

"David," Ellie said against his chest. "This is a great big mess!"

Letting her go, David said, "What happened?"

"Just after you left, some band showed up from Nashville. They began setting up. The boys said, 'Oh, fine,' and started dragging your piano out of the studio."

"What boys?"

"Well, Josh, and Paul. Dan Prescott helped them. And Nonnie, and Frank, and Jock, and William—"

"*William*?"

"Just everybody, David. Really, they looked quite comical, carrying your nine-foot Steinway on their shoulders across the back yard. Very stately, except they were laughing. Did you know William calls your nine-foot Steinway a *limousine* piano? Milton, darting here and there in his motorized wheelchair, laughing as hard as anybody, insisting he was their supervisor, pretending to whip them on."

"*Milton*?"

"Yes, David. Even I didn't put a stop to it. It was even a funnier sight than seeing Rourke carried out like a bleeding pig, his head bobbing."

David craned to look. "My piano is on the bandstand?"

"By the time the piano was on the bandstand, Lank had showed up. Suddenly there were a half-dozen musical groups here. There were a thousand people here. People began running wires down from the telephone poles, and setting up their bands on the lawns, in the fields." David was rubbing his forehead with his right hand. "I was about to speak to Lank, when Owen showed up, with Sally Dalton, and her whole entourage. What could I do?"

"You lost the battle of the front porch."

"Then there were thousands of people here, running, to get up front, in my flower beds. Cars and trucks were pouring in as if we were giving away money. I got out every garden hose we own."

"Garden hoses . . ."

"By the way, Sally Dalton really is charming. She did three numbers. Leaving, she could hardly get through the crowds. I've always liked Sally."

"Why did she come?"

"Oh, by the way, the press are here. Network television people, from Nashville and Huntsville. Plus filmmakers. If you look around the corner of the house, they are everywhere. You've got bullshit up above your knees, David. Owen said Treble Clef is recording all this. Did you authorize that?"

David shouted, "I did not authorize anything! Where's Lank? Where's Owen?"

From the stage, someone was announcing that Sarah Downey would return onstage, live and in person, in a few minutes.

"That's nice of Sarah," Ellie said. "She's already done one set."

The announcer was recommending that people up front in the crowd give other people a chance to come close to the main bandstand. He said, "There are lots of bands here tonight, folks, some you haven't even heard of yet, but I'm sure you will. Give them a chance, too. Go wander around, give them a listen."

Ellie said, "How's Chump?" She watched David's face. "I am sorry, David."

"He'd love this."

Lank came up the slope. He looked like a boy who had skipped school, knew he was going to get a whuppin', but considered it all worthwhile.

"You son of a bitch!" David said to Lank. "'Gone fishin'! Well, you sure caught yourself a whale."

"David—"

"Lank, you've got about one minute flat to tell me how this happened."

Lank shrugged. "I mentioned to a few folks you were havin' a party—"

"It was a wedding! That was this morning! A quiet, private wedding ceremony, respectable and well-organized! It is over! What are all these people doing here?"

Lank put a hand on David's arm. "These people are grateful to you, David. Lots of people. All the people you've discovered. All the artists who record for Treble Clef." Lank smiled. "All the people who'd like to be discovered."

"Did you call the press?"

"No one called the press, David." Owen stood behind David. Coatless, Owen wore thick ropes of gold around his neck. When David turned to look at him, Owen said, "Maybe the performers themselves tipped off the press. We didn't call them."

David asked Owen, "Did you invite people here tonight, too?"

"David, you told me yourself, at The Spider Web, that several groups had told you they intended to crash the party. You said so yourself."

"I didn't think they were serious."

Ellie said, "They were serious."

"I didn't encourage them."

Ellie said, "They didn't need encouragement."

"You're David MacFarlane," Owen said. "If you want to live quietly, move to New York."

David said, "You're a son of a bitch, too."

"David . . ." Owen tugged at David's sleeve. "Maxie's here."

"Maxie who?"

"Mister Music Maxie Brown."

"Good God!" David shouted.

Lank Kraft's face opened in delight.

"Maxie's here?" David asked. "Now? With all this crowd?"

Owen nodded. "I put him in your study. His wife's with him, too. Plus their keepers. They came all the way from Philadelphia. He insists he's going to perform."

"In all this mess?" David asked, arms out wide. "Mister Music Maxie Brown in my house and we don't even have a doughnut left to offer him?"

"David," Ellie said. "We never have doughnuts."

"He likes doughnuts!" David started toward the back door of the house. "Lank? Go down to the road and find Sheriff Tom Wims, will you? Tell him Sarah Downey is about to sing. He's a fan of hers. A big guy, with a hat."

Going through the house from the back to the front, David was amazed and deeply pleased that none of the crowd pressing against the outside walls of the house had had the audacity, the discourtesy to enter. Except for the incredible noise of a dozen electronic bands playing disharmoniously beyond the walls of the house, the inside was as undisturbed as any house would be, the night it had hosted a wedding party for three hundred people.

Then David thought of portable toilets outside, and realized there weren't any. Ellie had insisted three outhouses in the barns area be torn down when he bought the place.

At the bottom of the stairs, David wondered if he should go upstairs, shower the sweat and the grime off him, change into clean clothes quickly. He heard soft talking from the study.

Mister Music Maxie Brown . . .

David entered the study.

"As I live and breathe."

"David? That you?" The nearly blind, skinny old man tried to get out of a deep leather chair but did not succeed. He was looking right at David through rheumy eyes covered with thick lenses. "You heard I was here, uh?"

"Don't you get up." Putting his hands on Maxie's ears, David kissed the top of his ancient head. "You great man!"

Maxie's huge, twin nephews had stood. In their fifties, their occupation continued to be taking care of Mister Music Maxie Brown and his wife, Lurlene. They lived with them, nursed them, fed them, went with them everywhere, carried them everywhere. They were full of laughs and smiles as if they had carried off the biggest surprise of the century.

David hugged Lurlene, and kissed her on both cheeks. She had half a Scotch and water in her hand. She touched her handkerchief to her lips.

"You come here, boy," she said. "You come back here. Give me a proper kiss to take home with me!"

David kissed the old lady long and hard.

"Um-um!" she said. "I can tell I'm goin' home soon!"

"I'll be damned!" David exclaimed.

Maxie said, "Probably."

David shook hands with the nephews. "Carl, Fritz . . . aren't you guys somethin' else?"

"Aren't we just?"

"Did we surprise you any?"

"You sure did."

"Tell me something, David," Maxie said from his chair. "How come you give such a big party without invitin' me?"

"Party? I'm not givin' any party, Mister Brown. All these people just showed up! They must have heard you were comin'."

Maxie said, "Probably."

David sat cross-legged on the study floor at Mister Music Maxie Brown's feet.

Fritz said, "There's a chair right here for you, Mr. MacFarlane."

"I'm goin' to sit right here." David put his forearm on Maxie's skinny thigh. "And pat this man."

Carl put a Scotch and water into David's left hand.

"Heart medicine." David took a big swallow.

"You're all dirty, David." Lurlene had some eyesight left. "Smell bad, too. You been playin' in the cow dirt again?"

"In fact, I have, Ms. Brown."

"I remember you when you used to dress up, look nice for the folks."

"That was when he was scramblin'," Fritz said.

Carl said, "Now he's amblin'."

Lurlene said, "You remember when we were all playin' in Copenhagen, and you had that big blonde woman, David?"

"Yeah," David said. "She couldn't take her eyes off your big nephews. I had to tell her they're gay gentlemen."

"Her eyes may have been on us, but her hands were on you, David," said Fritz.

"Her hands!" shouted Carl. "The way I remember, her arms were shorter than—what I mean is, she couldn't reach out in front—"

Lurlene said, "I used to tease you about that woman in Paris. Never did no good. Everywhere you went, you had women, but you'd always say to me, 'Ms. Brown, the woman I really love is in Paris,' lookin' so serious, tryin' to get me to believe all you was sayin'. How was she called? Ms. Tuesday? Whatever happened to that woman, David?"

David pointed through the house wall. "She's right outside."

Fritz and Carl laughed at the good joke.

Lurlene said, "You tell me a lie."

"Actually not," David took another swallow of his drink. "For the life of me, I don't know why we were ever serious about anything."

"We couldn't have survived those long, long years," Maxie said, "none of us, not even you kids, you and Chump, if it hadn't been for the folks of north Europe, who loved us, were always glad to have us back."

Lurlene asked, "How's Chump goin', David?"

David said, "Chump's goin' soon, Ms. Brown."

"God love him," said Lurlene. "Take him home."

Suddenly the whiskey swilled in David's brain. Suddenly he saw John Bart Nelson as he was leaving that afternoon, after the bride and groom had left, after John had told Janet he had an airplane to catch, that he would see her soon, hugged her goodbye, left the house quietly through the front door, and walked down the road between the rows of cars alone, looking for his own rented car, getting into it, and, after a long moment, driving away.

"That's all right, David," Lurlene said softly. "God loves a joyful noise, and those that make them."

"Yes, Ma'm."

"So I want to know," Maxie said, "did you think ol' Maxie too old and foolish to invite to your party?"

"I didn't mean for there to be such a party, Maxie."

"You put up a bandstand," Maxie said. "That means a party."

David put his hand on Maxie's skinny knee. "How did you know we put up a bandstand?"

"I must have read it somewhere." Everyone laughed. Besides being nearly blind for years, it was doubtful Maxie Brown had ever known how to read. "Let's see, where did I read it? I read somewhere," the blind old man continued the joke, "that David MacFarlane was puttin' up a bandstand. That meant he's givin' a party. You meant that bandstand for me, didn't you, David?"

"I sure didn't mean it for me."

"You been shovelin' shit on this here farm so long now," Carl said, "I 'spect you've forgotten how to play piano."

"I about have."

Maxie said, "Probably."

The door opened and Ellie stepped into the study. Over the years, the Browns had known Ellie in New York. The huge nephews rose from their chairs. Maxie Brown again made a futile attempt to rise. Lurlene was full of kind remarks about how nice Ellie looked and how much of a better job Ellie was doing looking after David than she had ever been able to manage.

David, too, stood.

"He used to lie to me a lot, you know," Lurlene said, "about women. Can't do much to help a man who lies about women."

David said to Ellie, "I thought you went out for doughnuts."

"David, I think you'd better get out there," Ellie said. "Sarah Downey's hoping you'll go play with her."

"There he goes again." Lurlene shook her yellow wig. "Nothin' to be done with that man, not ever."

Ellie looked at David up and down. "You haven't changed."

"No." David kissed Ellie. "And don't you hope I never will?"

After David accompanied Sarah Downey on three numbers he knew she liked and had made famous, not knowing if she had sung them before at Bass Clef Farm that night, she put the microphone back in its stand while the people were cheering, and came to the keyboard, and kissed him.

She said, "I've got to be in Seattle tonight."

"I remember how it was." David kept the noise of the piano going, a few chords, rhythm, while the crowd cheered. "Thanks for coming, Sarah."

"Thank you, David." She kissed him again. "Thanks for everything."

While Sarah was leaving the bandstand, David glanced at his watch. It was a little after two o'clock in the morning.

David felt exactly as tired as he had in the old days, doing exactly this, sitting at a piano, using his hands on the keyboard, at this hour of the night.

Sarah was a good performer, but he hoped never to accompany her again. She was too deferential, to him. She was the singer, he the accompanist, but clearly she expected him to lead. She had kept looking back at him, waiting for him to take over, run the show. Accompanying Sarah Downey had been like making love to someone who could not forget the prestige of her sexual partner.

He looked forward along the nine-foot grand piano at the microphone tilting out of the tall stand in the light of the empty stage . . . of the empty stage.

Other bands, down in the meadows, were still playing. Their heavy rhythms and repetitious twangs wafted up the slope to him.

The microphone was too high, on that tall stand, and tilted at the wrong angle to pick up the sound of a saxophone. Stage light seldom mattered to Chump. Now the light on the floor just made that space, that empty space between the standing mike and the piano seem awfully big.

David heard soprano C-sharp striking on the piano again and again, calling. He looked down and saw that it was the little finger on his right hand striking that note.

Then he could not see his hand, his finger, the note, the keyboard. It all turned blurry on him.

David MacFarlane closed his eyes and swung into "Umbrella"; then, not waiting for the audience to applaud, his eyes still closed, he did "Trainman's Dust." He slowed and played "Sorry" at half beat until he realized he was making of it almost a dirge. He played with the theme in double time, ended in an almost strident march.

Playing "Greasy Pig," David opened his eyes. So surprised was he, he dropped a beat and then another. He had to fiddle around, grab the theme off the harmony, near the end, and virtually back into the beginning.

At the edge of the stage, three models draped around him, Milton kept the beat by banging both his fists on the arms of his wheelchair. His eyes were gleaming.

On the little dance floor, Josh, in shorts and sneakers, was dancing with another model of *haute couture*, this one dressed in the tallest jeans David had ever seen on a woman.

For a moment anyway, Sarah Downey was dancing with Sheriff Tom Wims.

Clara Reagan was dancing with Frank Simpson.

Lank Kraft was dancing with Nell Simpson.

Ellie was dancing with Paul Hollingsworth.

Sorry was dancing with Chuck Hartigan.

Janet Twombly was dancing with Dan Prescott.

But what caused David to hit three clinkers in a row and lose the melody entirely was the sight, up front and in the middle of everything, of Nonnie Simpson dancing wildly and happily, with William Fesdon!

William, even sweatier and grimier and dirtier than David was at that moment, was stepping around the dance floor, neck and back straight, head up, smiling, laughing, twirling Nonnie, possibly even singing, his arms moving in graceful, seemingly practiced complement to his legs, his boots stepping and hitting the dance floor, perfectly double-timing the rhythm from David's left hand!

Um, David said to himself, trying to regain control of the limousine piano. *Never knew William likes music!*

At the front of the crowd stood Haig, smiling happily on his walking stick. Next to him, Abraham led the applause and the cheering, even whistling through his teeth.

Beyond all these people seemed as big a crowd as David had ever seen, anywhere in the world, thousands of shining faces, beaming eyes, smiling mouths, moving shoulders, bouncing hair, bopping to the music of his piano.

Closing his eyes again, David felt something wicked go out of his neck, his shoulders, his spine, something that had always been there, or had been there as long as he could remember. He felt some structure inside him collapse; a barrel fall to staves. A lump gathered in his stomach, a sodden mass collected from all his body, from his brain, the back of his throat, the middle of his chest, his elbows, and dispersed down his legs, oozed through his toes onto the pedals of the piano, and up the struts, into the piano itself.

You know, I play the piano pretty well.

It could not be so, he knew, but it seemed that he was doing things with the piano that night that David MacFarlane had never done before. He played through a repertory of his most popular songs, making thematic configurations that had never before entered his head. He played melody against melody, hinted reverse themes (did, in fact, see relationships among some of his themes he had never realized before); at one point, he sustained hints of six different melodies at once, beautifully, to make and maintain a harmonious, progressive, moving whole.

God does love a joyful noise.

"Ladies and gentlemen, Mister Music Maxie Brown!"

Maxie, jiggling in the chair formed by his nephews' strong arms, was rushed from the east door of the farmhouse, through the crowd, and onto the stage.

Still at the piano, David stood to applaud loudly.

With expertise, the nephews lowered Maxie's feet to the floor, while handing him the microphone to hang onto, which Maxie did, his knees wobbling.

Maxie growled into the microphone, "Am I at home here?"

And the crowd, clapping rhythmically, chanted, "Mister Music Maxie Brown's / At home in every town!"

"All right!" shouted Maxie. "David? You know a tune you can play for me?"

David sat and opened "No Mo' Money" for Maxie. He and Maxie had performed that song together in a popular movie called *Silk Stockings.*

And Maxie was just singing "for my honey . . ." when sparks began to fly, literally.

Sparks flew off the tops of the telephone poles.

Sparks sizzled in lightening display down the wires to the various vans, transmitters, lighting rigs, musical instruments and amplifiers, causing many flashes of light and puffs of white smoke. The lines themselves burned and sagged off the poles.

Sparks flew all around the stage where David was sitting. Amplifiers and musical instruments and microphones popped and puffed smoke.

A few people shouted and screamed in alarm. Most *ohhhed* and *ahhhed* at the pyrotechnic display.

Suddenly nearly ten thousand people found themselves in the dark, outdoors, in a crowd, in the middle of a farm, in the middle of Tennessee, at three o'clock on a Sunday morning.

The smell of burned-out electrical things assaulted David's nostrils.

There was enough light for him to see that Maxie Brown was still standing, clutching the dead microphone stand.

His nephews were at his side.

"You boys there?" Maxie asked.

"Yes, sir." Fritz began to reach for his uncle.

"Then stamp yo' feet!" Maxie told his nephews, "the way your momma taught you!"

Fritz and Carl began stamping their feet on the stage.

To the sound of the stamping feet, Mister Music Maxie Brown, hanging onto the dead microphone's stand, started right over again: "No mo' money/ Fo' my honey!"

And David's hands were playing the piano.

For a short while camera lights worked the stage and the crowd. Shouts of protest from the crowd had them extinguished.

For the first time in years, David had to play loudly and clearly enough to be heard over the hubbub of an excited, moving crowd, yet stay behind the voice of a non-amplified singer. This singer was well into his eighties. David sat forward and stretched his ears like a creature of the forest to hear the old man's singing, to accompany him, stay with him, complement him, key him, stay below him in sound level.

When David understood, each song, Maxie was turning the music over to him, David let his limousine piano rip, brought the biggest sound out of it, and out of his fingers and forearms, and biceps and shoulders he could.

People came closer to the stage. They sat on the dance floor in the dark, on the driveway and lawns beyond, on the fence rails. Maybe they sat on the vans and the cars and the trucks down along the road.

They sat and they listened and sometimes they sang along, sending a sound wave up out of the valley that David at his piano could hear and feel washing back over them from the hills, and sometimes they clapped along, and, at the end of each song, they applauded hard and whistled and cheered.

Mister Music Maxie Brown and David MacFarlane sang and played for the people for another hour, until four o'clock, Sunday morning.

Continuously, David's eyes roamed what sections of the meadows and hills he could see from behind his piano on the stage, looking for fires.

There were none that he saw; there were no fires, from any source, that got out of control.

At some point, between tunes, David MacFarlane heard the voice of Nonnie Simpson in the dark:

"Hey, Mr. MacFarlane. How can you see what you're playin'?"

42

The sun coming over the horizon gradually warmed the face of David MacFarlane. He sat on a ledge on the west hill overlooking Bass Clef Farm.

In the hour or so before dawn David had sat alone on the hill watching for fires, witnessing the noisy but fairly orderly departure of thousands of people who had come to his home for a party he had not given, a music festival he had not planned, a memorable celebration of nothing more than a point in time.

Everyone had enjoyed the nameless celebration, and except for a little waste paper, many dropped beer cans, trampled lawns and flower beds, a few broken fence rails, burned-out electrical wires, Bass Clef Farm had survived it, and was almost as beautiful this dawn as ever.

Laughing, calling, shouting to each other happily, people in the valley below David still were collecting each other, extricating their cars and trucks wherever they had been ditched, piling into them, pulling out. Many of the departing vehicles had to maneuver around David's truck, which was still parked in the middle of the road. The vans of a few bands were still being loaded with burned-out wires, instruments, amplifiers. In the home pasture and two hayfields nearest the house David could see people still asleep, some wrapped in bedrolls, some wrapped in each other, others just singly collapsed there as if blown over by some wind, or sound. Haig Scott's airplane still sat in its own majesty in a distant hayfield. Here and there in the home pasture and in a few hayfields were round burn spots in the grass, evidence of fires that had been started one way or another, but not allowed to spread, and David appreciated that. At the crest of the hill to David's right, over a hundred steers still voiced their complaint at being confined in a small, grass-sparse, dry place. None had gained weight during the night, but they would catch up on their munching as soon as they were released.

In the dawn light, Bass Clef Farm was still there.

More than a mile away, down the valley, William walked along a fence, checking it, closing gates.

David wondered how Beau Brummel, the peacock, would have survived the night, the overwhelming competition in noise, in plumage, in strutting. Would he have been in the middle of things, competing, or, traumatized, would he have headed for the hills to contemplate the human/creature metaphor?

Ellie and the nephews had put Maxie and Lurlene to bed in Ellie's and David's own bedroom. Fritz and Carl slept in chairs in the common room. David did not know if Ellie had yet nested or, if she had, where. David still had not showered or changed.

The heat of the full sun on David made him realize how dirty and smelly and tired he was.

It was all right. There were no fires. No damage had been done that could not be repaired, in time. People had come, friends, strangers, from near and fairly far, blacks, whites, Hispanic-Americans, Asian-Americans, music lovers all, and they had been welcomed as much as a very surprised household could welcome them. They came to celebrate some moment. Maybe some of them came because David MacFarlane had been silent too long, and they wanted to hear, *one mo' time*, to assure themselves, and him, of something, of what? that he lived, and he played; whatever: it was all right.

Stiff and tired, the fresh morning sun causing fresh sweat on the dried sweat of his skin, David stood up. The dirt on his skin and his clothes cracked as he walked.

David stumbled down the hill. He climbed over two fences to get to his truck.

Once in his truck, he started it, put it in low gear, u-turned in the road.

And drove toward Nashville.

43

"Was it the hardest thing you ever had to do?" Milton asked.

David looked at the palm of his right hand. He turned the hand over, and looked at its back.

"It was the easiest thing this hand has ever done."

Milton looked at the transparent plastic sack David held in his left hand, at the dozens of tape cassettes in the sack.

Entering the pool area, exhausted, full of his own thoughts and feelings, intending just to put the sack of tapes in the studio, David had been surprised to find Milton apparently waiting for him, in the shade of an umbrella.

With a hose and brush, Jock was cleaning the other side of the empty swimming pool.

It was a cloudless, windless Sunday morning in June. Driving back through Jameson, David had waved through the truck's windshield at the people going to church.

"Tell me, David," Milton asked. "What were your last words to him?"

Standing in the sun near Milton's wheelchair, swaying a little, in exhaustion, David closed his eyes and thought. "'You're not listening.'"

After a moment, Milton said, "All your guests are gone. All your other guests."

David opened his eyes.

Milton said, "I'll stay for the funeral, of course."

"And then?"

Milton looked around the pool area, at the trampled flowers in their borders, a few beer cans, someone's abandoned bra, Jock scrubbing the side of the pool.

David said, "Ellie tells me we're buying the house next door. It's a little, shady, brick house. Probably needs work. I've never been in it. It's all on one floor. I'm sure it can be easily modified for a wheelchair. Around here, Milton, as you've seen, the people are still real. They understand being old, and being sick. I know we can find people here who will treat you just fine, really take care of you. There's no need for you to go back to New York, and to Rourke. You can have an office at Treble Clef, in Nashville, and keep up with things there. It would mean a lot to Ellie, and to me, to have you as a neighbor."

Milton said, "I'll think about it." Then he smiled.

White-faced, Ellie entered the pool area. She put her hand on David's arm.

She said, "Chump is dead."

In his wheelchair, Milton burst into sobs.

Ellie said, "I've been waiting for you to get back. Ms. Manning from the hospital called Mary Hartigan. Our telephone isn't working. Mary drove out to notify us. Ms. Manning said Chump apparently just stopped breathing. Some kind of natural suffocation. She said she believes it was easy for him."

Ellie saw the tears on David's cheeks.

Then she saw the transparent plastic sack of cassette tapes David was carrying.

She said, "Oh."

For a while, David stood under the umbrella with his hand on Milton's shoulder, while Milton sobbed. Ellie had her arm around David's waist, her head against his chest.

Jock climbed out of the pool, and left the area.

After a while, David unlocked the studio and dropped the plastic sack on the floor inside.

"You need anything, Milton?" David had taken Ellie's hand.

"Yes," Milton said. "David, would you do something for me?"

"Anything."

"Help me into the studio. Play me that tape I heard two days ago. The music you call Richland." David hesitated. "I need it, David."

"I can't, Milton," David said. "There's no electricity. Later. Okay?"

44

"Not too much damage," David said.

"Not too much," Ellie agreed.

David MacFarlane said, "It won't be music lovers who destroy this ol' world."

Arms around each other, they stood in the shade of the east porch of the main house at Bass Clef Farm. They looked at trampled flower beds and lawns, waste paper and beer cans, torn, drooping party decorations, burst balloons, a few crumpled wooden caterers' chairs, two broken fence rails, and, down to their right, dangling, scorched wires from the telephone poles.

"It was a nice wedding," Ellie said.

"I guess I still must have had a romantic idea of weddings," David said. "Will I never learn?"

"Everyone had a fine time. I suspect many little matters were resolved. I saw Paul Hollingsworth and Abraham Baxter, arms around each other's shoulders, last night, singing along with Mister Music Maxie Brown. They were both as drunk as bedbugs."

"That's nice." Sleepily, David blinked at the mess.

In the pasture beyond the broken fence rails, Jester was sniffing around, trying to discover traces of the groundhog he loved to chase.

"Everyone's gone, you know. Nobody knew where you were, to say goodbye. They all left notes, on your desk."

"That's nice."

To David, the piano on the bandstand under the big carport looked like a beached yacht.

Ellie said, "You sounded good, last night, on the piano."

"It felt good."

"I found myself thinking of that skinny teenager who used to come to Chicago to play piano in any awful bar that would let you, and used to come to me, to make love. You were just as nervous about one thing as the other."

"I was never nervous, that way. Either way."

"You wanted people to like you, you know, to like what you did. Wanting me to like you made me absolutely love you."

"I play piano better now."

"Yes. You do."

"Want to hear something weird?"

"Yes. Sure."

"Last night, playing piano for the folks, I swear, two or three times I heard the sound of a saxophone, Chump's saxophone, coming out of those hills, stuttering a little, waiting for me to get done with my riff, so he could burst in, full-sounded, soar across the sky. Crazy," David said. "Sentimental."

Ellie's fingers dug into his waist. "It's okay to be sentimental."

"You don't suppose he left tape cassettes for me, do you? Up in one of those caves somewhere?"

"Maybe." Ellie craned her neck away and looked at David's face. "You haven't slept in two nights."

"I think I know that."

"Why don't you go take a nice, soapy bath in the river—"

"Why in the river?"

"Because there's no hot water. No electricity. The water pumps aren't working. I'll make up a tray of sandwiches and milk, bring it up to the bedroom to you. We'll both go to bed. Sleep this day away."

David thought a moment, of sleeping the day away, of having sandwiches and milk in the darkened bedroom at mid-day, of a soapy immersion in the river.

"I think I'll go see William first."

Ellie said, "You go see William."

William had brought the new, young bull calves back into the barnyard. Clearly he had not bathed or slept or changed clothes since the night before, either.

Approaching him, David said, "What do you think, William? Are we going to get some rain?"

"Tomorrow." William scanned the sky, and the hills, and then the meadows. "Maybe."